SECRET VOWS

Catherine gazed round one last time, every object, each shadow seeming to burn itself with aching clarity into her mind. 'Twas here that Gray first came to her after their wedding, here where he'd soothed and cared for her. Here where he'd simply held her, safe and warm, until dawn.

These and so many other memories throbbed with a life of their own, but she must consign her memories to the dust now. Those and all her secret dreams of a future with Gray. Dashing her hand across her eyes, Catherine moved toward the door. It was over. She was leaving.

But as she reached the portal, she heard a loud noise in the corridor. Startled, she stepped back; at that moment the door crashed open and slammed against the wall. Gray stood framed in the opening, rain-soaked, his chest heaving, his expression feral.

He went still and gazed at her for what seemed like an eternity. His shadowed eyes burned, dark and vulnerable, his muscled frame outlined in stark relief by his wet shirt and breeches. Finally, he just shook his head.

"Damn you, lady," he growled softly, "but I want to know who the hell you really are, and what kind of game it is that you've been playing with me."

───────

"Mary Reed McCall makes a dazzling debut with *Secret Vows*. This lush and lyrical story captivated me from the very first page!"

Teresa Medeiros, author of *A Kiss to Remember*

Other AVON ROMANCES

Coming Soon

And Don't Miss These
ROMANTIC TREASURES
from Avon Books

ATTENTION: ORGANIZATIONS AND CORPORATIONS
Most Avon Books paperbacks are available at special quantity discounts for bulk purchases for sales promotions, premiums, or fund-raising. For information, please call or write:

Special Markets Department, HarperCollins Publishers, Inc., 10 East 53rd Street, New York, N.Y. 10022–5299. Telephone: (212) 207–7528. Fax: (212) 207-7222.

MARY REED McCALL

SECRET VOWS

AVON BOOKS

An Imprint of HarperCollinsPublishers

AVON BOOKS
An Imprint of HarperCollins*Publishers*
10 East 53rd Street
New York, New York 10022-5299

Copyright © 2001 by Mary Reed McCall
ISBN: 0-380-81785-3
www.avonromance.com

First Avon Books paperback printing: September 2001

Avon Trademark Reg. U.S. Pat. Off. and in Other Countries, Marca Registrada, Hecho en U.S.A.
HarperCollins ® is a trademark of HarperCollins Publishers Inc.

Printed in the U.S.A.

10 9 8 7 6 5 4 3 2 1

For my girls, who give me endless joy and inspiration—sweethearts, you are the greatest gifts and loves of my life . . .

For my husband John, my own valiant knight. From our very first date "to be better friends," I knew that we were meant to be together. I love you with all of my heart, always . . .

And for my parents, David and Marion Reed, who cherished a little girl and her dreams. You've read every word I've written, encouraging me each step of the way to achieving my goals. I love you both and thank you for everything—most of all for just being you.

Acknowledgments

My sincere gratitude:

To the members of Central New York Romance Writers, for always listening, lending support, offering critique, and just being great friends—particularly Kathleen Simmons and Theresa Kovian, whose help in brainstorming during one long car ride back home resulted in the ending to this book.

To Lyssa Keusch, who took a chance on an unknown writer's work and helped to turn a dream into reality.

And to the exquisite Ruth Kagle, my agent, whose expertise and guidance have been invaluable. Thanks for believing in me.

Prologue

The Year of Our Lord, 1233

I am Catherine of Somerset. A woman without place or time. A woman, God help me, without hope.

Even as a small child my first awareness of myself mingled inextricably with a keen sense of disappointment. I knew that somehow I'd failed, and that I was doomed to be corrected for my inadequacies. You see, I fail to fit the delicate, pale ideal of beauty for women in my world, and I was never allowed to forget it. My comforts were few, yet though 'twas difficult to keep my spirits up, I strove to remain cheerful.

When I was sixteen, Father managed to rid himself of me. He was lucky enough to find a man willing to take me as a wife, if only for the offering of a sizable dower. Father begrudged me that allotment, claiming he'd have been the one receiving payment and goods, if only I was beautiful.

'Twas naught but exchanging one brutal man for another, though the burden increased in that my new husband demanded the right to use my body for his pleasures. Still I considered myself fortunate to have escaped my father's household. To have made a fresh start, even if 'twas with a man who showed little care of me.

Life passed tolerably for me. Within a year of my union with Geoffrey, God blessed me with the birth of two fine children. Twins, as fair and bright as the sun itself. I named them Ian and Isabel, and lived the next years waking and breathing each day only for them. My darlings grew strong and healthy, with none of the coarse traits for which I'd been condemned all my life.

The year they turned seven was the most difficult of my life. 'Twas as if I'd lost my reason for living. As was customary, Geoffrey had begun to search for a proper family with which to foster the twins, to help Ian learn the skills of a page and for Isabel to study needlework, writing, and household management. But to hurt me, since he knew the love I bore them, Geoffrey chose to foster my babes far from us. 'Twas three days' ride to reach them, and since he rarely allowed me free movement off of our estate, I saw but little of my children that first year.

I thought my heart would break from grief. I pined

for the sight of their little faces and the smiles that would light them when they saw me. I longed to feel the sweet caress of their breath on my neck as I carried them to their beds of an evening. Now all was vacant and barren. Their tiny beds were cold, and I'd huddle in their chamber, sobbing my loss into the empty blankets.

But God showed me his mercy yet again in a way I'd never have dared to pray for. Geoffrey returned from one of his jaunts to London shivering with a fever. In less than a week he died of the ague, and I felt a sense of freedom I'd never known. I was readying to send for the twins, to bring them home at least for a while, when my brother by marriage, Baron Eduard de Montford, arrived, bringing with him his gentle sister Elise, and an entire garrison of men to witness Geoffrey's funeral.

Within two days, I was glad I'd waited to bring my babes home. If those innocent children had found Elise, as I did . . . I shudder when I think of the possibility. I walked into her chamber early one morning, intending to wake her, to accompany me to vespers. Instead of seeing the delicate young woman sleeping in her bed, I found a corpse, dangling from a sash tied to the bedpost.

'Twas not long I'd need wait to learn why Elise had chosen so desperate a path. Eduard heard my scream and rushed in. He helped me to cut the sash and together we lowered the body. Then he sent me to my chambers with a sleeping powder to calm me. When I awoke, my chamber door was bolted, and none would answer my calls.

Eduard came in later and told me of his diabolical plan. He had already primed Elise with beatings and threats to make her do his deadly bidding, but she'd escaped his plots with her desperate act. That left him with no other option but to find a replacement for her.

To my everlasting misery, he chose to use me.

I cannot describe the sickness and shock that flooded me upon hearing his scheme. I tried to tell myself that he played a perverse jest: that as Geoffrey's brother, he too enjoyed tormenting women. And he showed himself his brother's equal in one respect; when I refused to take part in his plans, he beat me savagely.

It took two days for me to rise from my bed after that first time, and yet he came again and again, trying to coerce me to take part in his evil. Each time I refused, the beating was repeated, until I began to tremble every time the door opened.

He never would have gained my consent, no matter what the physical cost to me, had he not used the one weapon he knew I could not bear. He gave me a choice—either I would help him, or he would kill my children, his own niece and nephew.

I begged him, pleaded on my knees . . . but he only laughed. I hated him even more for that, though I knew then that I had no real choice. I didn't possess the luxury of escaping as Elise had. My children's safety depended upon my cooperation.

And so I said yes. Yes, I would help Eduard to achieve his unholy ambitions. Heaven help me, but

I would do what he commanded in order to save my innocent children from destruction.

May God have mercy on my eternal soul and the soul of the one who must die because of me.

Amen.

Chapter 1

Ravenslock Castle, Wiltshire

'Twas but the first step toward damnation.
Catherine swallowed the nausea that rose in her throat and forced herself to stand stiff in the entrance to the chapel. She shut her eyes against the sun's glare, murmuring a prayer that the veil she wore would continue to hide her feelings from any that looked on her. But though the silken gauze might mask her guilt from the world, she knew that nothing could stop the horrible truth from piercing deep into her own soul.

In a few moments she was going to pledge herself in holy wedlock to the man she'd promised to help murder.

Revulsion washed over her again, and she swayed

into a cool stone pillar. Reaching out, she tried to regain her balance, squirming at the trickle of sweat that made its way down her spine. Her amethyst kirtle clung to her in sticky folds, worsened by the day's heat. 'Twas stifling for September, and undoubtedly a sign from God—a taste of the hellfire she was sure to suffer for the mortal sin she was about to commit.

"Damn you, Catherine," Eduard hissed into her ear. "If you faint on me now, I vow to make you sincerely regret it." He grasped her elbow and hauled her to a standing position.

The movement made her wince. Every inch of her body ached from the constant abuse he'd lavished on her in the past two weeks, compounded by the wrenching pain she felt in knowing that she'd never see her children again, never look into their sweet faces or hold them close. Thanks to Eduard, the twins thought her dead, and that truth had cut her even more fiercely than any of his beatings; she'd wanted to die from it alone. But she couldn't. He'd made certain she knew the deadly consequences of changing her mind. If she refused to go through with his plan, her children would suffer what she did, only worse, before he killed them.

The message hadn't been lost on her.

"I'm not going to faint, Eduard. Just get me some water."

He grunted in response, but soon a cup of metallic tasting liquid was pressed into her hand. When she finished, she handed the empty vessel back to him from beneath her veil.

"Are you ready now?" he demanded.

Catherine nodded, feeling too sick to hazard an answer. She had to save all her strength for her vows; she knew it would take every ounce of reserve she possessed to utter their blasphemy without choking.

Vaguely, she felt the pressure of Eduard's hand on her arm as they walked into the main portion of the chapel. Though heavy, the layers of fine gauze covering her face allowed her to see what was before her. The priest stood in his accustomed place below the altar steps, his hands folded in solemn piety as he awaited her arrival to the ceremony.

Almost against her will, Catherine swept her gaze over the other occupants. Four score guests whispered and craned their necks for a better view. Apart from them, all that remained were two men who waited high on the altar behind the priest. The first was older and dressed in servant's garb, the second a man who appeared to be about a score and ten, outfitted as a knight of the realm.

He, then, must be her groom, she thought. Bewilderment clouded her already weary mind. He hardly seemed foreboding. Eduard had warned her of her future husband's vicious reputation, wanting to prepare her for what she would face so that she wouldn't be distracted by undue fear when it came time to bed with him and ultimately clear the way for Eduard's hireling to kill him. If she hadn't dreaded another beating, she would have laughed at such skewed reasoning. It had seemed ridiculous that helping to murder someone could ever be made easier, regardless of what one knew about the victim beforehand. But she'd remained silent in her opinion.

Now she wondered why Eduard had bothered to tell her aught about her betrothed. It was clear that he'd exaggerated his description of Baron Grayson de Camville's powerful stature and warlike demeanor. This man looked sturdy, with fair skin and hair the color of wheat. But he was no musclebound monster. She wondered if Eduard's hatred of his rival was so great that it had made him see attributes that weren't there.

Until a third man strode out onto the altar.

Catherine gasped audibly before stumbling into Eduard. He let out a curse and managed to right both of them before they could fall onto the marble aisle of the chapel.

"By all that's holy, Eduard," she whispered frantically, "with all else that you told me about this man, why did you fail to mention this?"

"Silence," he hissed back, "I'll not have you botching our plans now."

She moved without thinking as he pulled her the remaining few paces to the altar, unable to drag her gaze from Baron Grayson de Camville. He was all that Eduard had said—a fierce warrior knight, taller by a head than any man she'd ever known, and carved from what appeared to be perfectly sculpted muscle and bone. But what Eduard had neglected to tell her was that her future husband possessed the face of an angel, so stunning that were it not for his utterly masculine presence and the way his mouth tightened into a grim line, she might have thought him one of heaven's messengers, sent by God to save her from Eduard's plotting.

The buzzing in her ears slowly gave way to an annoying sound. Gradually, the noise needled and poked at her, until she turned her attention to the nasal voice. It bleated a name, over and over, and her stunned mind suddenly realized its error in failing to respond.

"Elise de Montford?"

Worried that her silence might have exposed her falsity, Catherine quickly looked to the priest who'd been repeating her newly assumed name. He seemed to be waiting for an answer, and he was beginning to appear impatient. She hesitated to affirm the lie, but then her hand was gripped none too gently by a warm, immovable grasp. Another gasp passed her lips, and her gaze snapped to the man who'd touched her so possessively.

Grayson de Camville's smoky green eyes stared down into her own; he blinked, and she noticed how the sooty fringe of lashes accentuated their unusual hue. Looking into their depths made her feel hot and cold at the same time. His eyes were the color of a misty forest at twilight, his bronzed complexion and ebony hair only adding to his startling beauty. She would have continued to stare at him, but at that moment a corner of his mouth edged upward, in perfect time with one dark, arching brow. "My lady?" he murmured in French that was as flawless as his face.

Catherine found it very difficult, suddenly, to breathe.

"Yes?" she managed to croak.

"The Holy Father attends your answer."

A shiver progressed up her back. *Calm yourself. He's naught but a man—a man who will be murdered, thanks to you.* That thought sent a fist of nausea into her belly, and it was all she could do to breathe the appropriate words when the priest asked them of her.

When her betrothed faced the assembly and made the traditional vow granting a third of his estate to her, Eduard caught her gaze. For the first time in a week, her loathsome brother-in-law smiled.

Stealing a glance back at her groom, Catherine saw that he looked calm and expressionless. How did he feel about this union with her? Was he anticipating a long life of happiness and peace with a loyal wife?

The evil of what she was doing settled home in her soul with renewed vengeance. She clasped her hands so tightly together that the crescents of her nails began to bite into her flesh. She stopped when she realized that her reaction had drawn Grayson's attention. He'd shifted his gaze to stare at her, and she saw that his reserved expression changed to a look of concern that sent daggers of guilt into her heart.

By the Holy Virgin, how could she ever bring herself to aid in his murder?

And yet with her children's lives at stake, how could she not?

That terrible choice reverberated through her soul during the remainder of the interminably long mass.

Somehow, she kept her wits and her feet until the end of the ceremony. She'd almost breathed a sigh of relief, knowing that she'd soon be allowed to sit in relative peace, when her new husband grasped both of her shoulders and turned her to face him.

She froze. Panic spread through her as he began to lift her veil, and she realized that she'd forgotten about the kiss to seal their union. A whisper of breeze caressed her face as the gauze was pulled away. Blinking, Catherine looked up. For the first time, she stared directly into the angelic eyes of the man who was now her lord husband. Then her knees lost their substance as he fixed her with a stormy glare.

"Sweet Christ," he growled softly, "what the hell have I gotten myself into now?"

Grayson willed himself not to crush the goblet he held. He stood in his solar off of the great hall, staring at the water in his cup and fervently wishing he'd not taken the vow years ago to forsake strong drink.

He still didn't know how he'd made it to the finish of his wedding ceremony. Somehow he'd even managed to walk from the chapel to the castle's main chamber, where happy feasting was already under way. But from the moment he'd lifted his new wife's veil, he'd lost any desire he might have had to celebrate.

"I don't know what else to say, but that I'm sorry," Alban murmured, taking a step further into the chamber. Gray met his friend's gaze. Their shared history, the blood they'd shed for each other's sake in the Crusade, was the only thing making this turn of events a little more bearable.

"I did my best when you sent me ahead to seek information about her. But Montford kept her so secluded within the keep, 'twas impossible for me to gain an audience with her. I told you the only information I could gather from the people of the village. They described Elise de Montford as small and fair-haired. One of the villeins even likened her to a tiny sparrow."

Gray choked back a laugh. "Was the poor wretch blind as well as addled?"

"After having seen her myself, I would have to say he was, though he appeared as sound of mind and body as either of us."

Gray's mouth stiffened, and he felt a muscle in his jaw twitch. "Aye, well my *wife* is more akin to an warrior queen than a sparrow. She barely needed to lift her eyes to meet my gaze. And that face . . ."

His fist clenched as the image of her came to him again, lush and vibrant. Her unusual appearance had struck him like a blow to the chest. She was tall and solemn, her midnight blue eyes staring up at him, her face framed in rich brown waves that spilled from the circlet on her brow to fall below her waist.

"Damn Montford. The bastard played another farce, allowing me to think her a delicate Court beauty."

"He's more the fool then," Alban said. "You've never cared for the fashions of Court, especially when it comes to women."

"Aye, and yet I still lose. You of all people know why. God help me, but Elise de Montford is all that I vowed never to touch. Never again."

Alban shook his head. "Let it go, Gray. You've served penance long enough. Accept your lady wife for the boon she is and move forward."

Swallowing his retort, Gray reminded himself that his friend saw the world through clear eyes. Sir Alban Warton had no sin to hide, no rage churning relentlessly in his breast.

He clenched his jaw and looked away, glancing around the richly appointed solar of Ravenslock Castle—his castle—the most grand of the many strongholds he'd won through bludgeoning opponents in countless battles and tournaments for King Henry. He'd worked hard for all he'd gained. Spilling his blood was but a small part of what he'd suffered in the past seventeen years. He'd gone through hell and back before managing to earn this measure of success and prosperity.

And yet for all his efforts, for all his sacrifice, it had all almost slipped through his fingers only a few months ago. He'd almost lost everything, thanks to his new bastard of a brother-in-law.

As another of King Henry's champions, Montford had envied Gray's success. He'd wanted the same rewards, the same honors as Gray, whether he deserved them or not. And so to bring him down, Montford had ferreted out and exposed Gray's darkest secret. He'd told everyone at Court that Gray had killed his own twin sister nearly two decades ago—that he'd murdered his own sweet Gillian.

Gray breathed in sharply, the pain of Gillian's death still fresh even now. Montford's accusation had merely piled shame atop his misery, because he couldn't deny it. Not in essence, anyway. 'Twas true. He, Baron Grayson de Camville, King Henry's High Champion on the field of honor, justice and truth, had been culpable in his own sister's death.

Eduard's public accusation had disgraced him. It had pushed him to the brink of personal disaster. But it had also sparked volatile disputes at Court. Sides had been chosen and alliances made, lighting the wick to political unrest that had threatened to lead England's barons into Civil War.

Peace had finally been restored by the king, but not without a price . . . and Gray had paid it today in his marriage to Elise de Montford—the all too tempting sister of the wretch who'd tried to destroy him.

He cursed aloud. "I can't do it, Alban. I can't stay bound to her. I was a fool to think I could." Gray walked to the end of the heavy table, searching beneath its edge to retrieve the silken pouch with its iron key. Pushing aside the tapestry on the wall, he exposed the door that would lead him into the tilting yard and away from the rage and the agonizing memories that haunted him. "I'll seek an annulment."

"No you won't. There's too much at stake,"

Alban said. "King Henry commanded this union, and if you deny it now, you'll only awaken his wrath anew, which at the very least will mean losing your chance to be appointed Sheriff of Cheltenham come Christmastide."

That undeniable fact sank into Gray's bones with the swiftness of an executioner's blade. Alban seemed not to notice. Looking away, he added, "Of course, if you no longer wish to gain the position, or any others that might come along—"

"You know I do." Gray leaned against the door. His head ached, and his shoulders tightened until it seemed as if his muscles must shred from his bones. Christ, why couldn't he quench this constant need? Why couldn't he be satisfied with what he'd already gained? But he couldn't rest. He craved more power, more influence, more security, like his body thirsted for water or air. And he knew that when it came down to it, he'd do anything necessary to achieve his purpose.

Right now that meant being married to Elise de Montford.

Gray cursed softly again. "You know what this will mean, Alban. I'm not made of stone."

His friend didn't reply at first, but his quiet expression told him more than words ever could. "It might not be so bad," Alban offered. "'Tis not as if you need to fall in love with her to enjoy her. I know of many men who see their wives seldom at best. They needs only be alone with them when they wish to, ah . . ." Alban's face reddened, and he coughed. "Well, what I mean to say is that you need only forsake your privacy when you wish to get heirs on her."

Get heirs on her? Gray fisted his hands as tight as the knots in his stomach. God's bones, he'd never allowed himself to think that far ahead. He'd always taken precautions to ensure that his seed never took hold in any of the women he'd bedded. There had been many of them, but he'd never made a mistake.

After Gillian died, he'd known that he wasn't worthy to bear the responsibility of being any child's sire. He didn't want to be a husband, either, especially not to the bewitching creature who was his rival's sister, but it appeared that he'd have no choice in the matter. Not unless he wanted to risk losing all he'd worked so hard to gain.

"Bloody hell," he muttered, running his hands through his hair. When his arms fell to his sides, it was with a sense of defeat greater than any he'd ever known on the battlefield. 'Twas no one's fault but his own. He'd gotten into this mess by himself. He and his damned ambition. If he'd done as instinct had prompted, if he'd stood firm and refused the king's outrageous plan for peace from the start, he wouldn't be in this chamber, drinking water like a parched sea sponge and avoiding a woman.

A woman who now shared his name and his life.

With a growl of frustration, Gray picked up his empty goblet and hurled it against the wall, not caring that the emerald-encrusted vessel would be ruined from the impact. It was inescapable. With or without his liking, his marriage to Elise de Montford was achieved, and he needed to accept it.

Bitterness gripped his innards. Striding to the door that connected to the great hall, Gray swung it open and scattered several revelers who'd been drifting past. Then he gestured to the opening with a flourish, even as he mustered a sardonic smile. "Come, my friend, and accompany me. It can be postponed no longer. 'Tis time for me to join my lady wife and celebrate the joy of our marriage."

Catherine watched Grayson emerge from the far end of the enormous hall, grim purpose etched in every sculpted line of his face. Without wanting to, she tensed, her hand tightening around her tiny silver cutting knife so that it gouged into the bread trencher in front of her. "Sweet Jesu, Eduard," she murmured. "What if he's discovered our deceit?"

Eduard leaned in, his whisper a sinister reminder of all that she stood to lose if she failed in the task he'd given her. "Control, Catherine. Don't let your weak-minded tendencies get the best of you. He knows nothing. 'Tis impossible for him even to suspect."

Despite that reassurance, Catherine couldn't suppress the shudder that rippled through her. Eduard rolled his eyes. "Really, Catherine, your constant quivering begins to wear on me. 'Tis not as if you're an untouched maid about to be deflowered." Grasping her hand, he pushed it and the knife she held to the table. "Just don't fail to act that part when you join Camville in his bedchamber, or complications will arise that might be less than pleasant for you and your children."

Catherine hid her reaction to his threat behind her wine goblet, swallowing some of the tart liquid before attempting to answer. "If you'd have bothered to fully warn me about my husband beforehand, I might feel more prepared."

But even as she spoke, she knew that nothing he could have said would have readied her for the impressive sight of Grayson de Camville. Still, she'd touch hot coals before she'd admit that or any other truth to Eduard.

He shrugged. "I didn't tell you, because I didn't expect you to react like all of the other wenches who go aflutter with lust upon seeing him." Pausing, he glanced across the hall. "But alas, poor Catherine. Your husband is quick approaching, and he doesn't seem likewise affected by *your* charms."

Catherine pretended to ignore the jab. After almost eight years of marriage to Eduard's brother, such remarks were to be expected. Every time Geoffrey de Montford had insulted her excessive height and peasant build, every time he'd cursed her. like her father before him because she wasn't dainty and pale like a true beauty, she'd told herself that it didn't matter. But it had. The constant debasement had hurt in a way that went as deep as the bruises he'd periodically inflicted on her flesh; it had lodged an ache in her heart that refused to go away.

Taking a breath, she raised her gaze just in time to see her new husband halt directly in front of her;

she struggled to adjust her expression, to appear pleased, as befit the bride of a successful man. It was an effort made possible only by thoughts of Isabel and Ian's safety.

"My lord," she managed to murmur, tilting her head with what she hoped was polite grace.

"Lady," Gray responded, gazing at her for a brief moment. A shadow darkened his sea-mist eyes, and it sent a renewed stab into her heart. Eduard was right. Her lack of beauty disappointed her husband, and that meant she would be beaten for it later. She shuddered as she imagined the damage that this man's hands could inflict on her.

"I trust that the feast meets your favor, lady?"

His solicitous question startled her. Geoffrey had never cared if she enjoyed a meal. He'd usually been too drunk to notice. Twisting her fingers in her lap, Catherine murmured, "It looks superb, my lord. But I—I haven't tasted of it yet."

Gray scowled. "Why not?"

Catherine felt herself flush. "I thought it only fitting to wait for you, my lord." She decided not to add that she possessed absolutely no appetite. Not with Eduard sitting at her elbow like one of hell's gargoyles.

Her husband's face revealed no change, though the shadow deepened in his eyes. He looked away. Finally he said, "'Tis not my custom to dine with women, and I cannot be expected to remember the niceties of such occasions."

Waving his hand almost angrily, he gestured for someone to fill his goblet. A page darted forward with a cider pitcher, his young face stiff. The boy filled his master's cup with a trembling hand, and Catherine felt a prick of sympathy. It seemed she wasn't the only person who feared the presence of Ravenslock's Lord.

And so when her husband quaffed the contents of his cup and reached out to affectionately ruffle the boy's hair, it sent a thrill of shock through her. The feeling intensified when the boy grinned, his chest puffing out with pride and his grip steady as he refilled his lord's cup again. Then he bowed and retreated to his place along the wall.

Without comment, Grayson stalked around the end of the banquet table, making his way to the dais. It was all she could do not to stare. How strange that the man who seemed every inch the hardened warrior had just treated a boy with kindness.

She allowed herself to study Grayson as he strode nearer to his place next to her at the table. She hadn't allowed herself to dwell on much more than his face during their wedding, but now she could see that his form matched his visage. He was clad all in black, though his cloak and the sleeves of his tunic bore an intricate design embroidered in emerald silk.

When he sat beside her, Catherine caught a faint scent of spice mixed with smoky leather; it tickled her senses, and she dared to turn and stare openly at him. She'd rarely known men to smell good. Geoffrey, Eduard, Father—all had carried with them a scent that at its mildest couldn't be termed pleasant.

"Is something amiss, lady?" Grayson swung his

gaze to her after she'd been looking at him for what must have been a full minute without blinking.

Her breath stuck in her throat. "Nay." She felt her cheeks heat, her tongue tripping like a three-years' child. "Nay, 'tis just—" The force of his attention unnerved her, though not in the same way that her father or other men she'd known frighted her. Of course they had usually followed their intimidation of her with a slap or blow, and that possibility seemed unlikely right now, considering that she and Grayson were newly married and in the presence of scores of wedding guests.

Glancing down at the table again, Catherine willed the shaking in her hands to cease. "'Tis just that you're—you're quite different from what I envisioned."

"As are you, lady. Very unlike what I was led to expect." He paused, and she felt his gaze bore more deeply into her before flicking to Eduard. "I cannot help but wonder why I was so misled."

Catherine's stomach clenched, and Eduard coughed. She didn't dare look at her husband to determine what he might have meant, or even if he was in earnest.

"Elise experiences many changeable moods, Camville. 'Tis part of her nature. Hence no two descriptions of her are completely like, even among those who know her best." Eduard delivered his answer with smooth skill, leaning forward to pat her fingers as he spoke. It took all of her will not to snatch her hand from beneath his vile touch.

"I'd prefer to hear your sister speak for herself,"

Gray said coldly. Catherine's shoulders hunched, and she slouched forward as she tried to make herself less noticeable.

"My lady, would you care to venture an opinion?" Gray continued to gaze at her, his soft tone belying the granite-hard demand behind his question.

"I—I don't know what it is that you wish me to say," Catherine whispered, shrinking away from him as the knot in her stomach turned to nausea. It seemed she'd been wrong to assume that the presence of wedding guests would shield her from a beating so soon. Eduard had said that Grayson was a monster, and judging from the leashed anger in her husband's voice, it seemed increasingly certain that he was about to lash out at her now. She only hoped that he wouldn't kill her with the power sure to be contained in a blow from his massive fist.

"All that I require is the truth as you see it," Grayson answered evenly. "Nothing more or less."

Catherine felt her stomach unknot a little; she hazarded a glance at her husband. He looked calm, his green eyes directed at her with a warm, penetrating expression.

Uncertainty assailed her; she felt as if she danced on the edge of a dangerous precipice, where a wrong answer might spell immediate, painful retribution. Grasping the only position of safety she could see, Catherine murmured, "My opinion matters not, my lord. 'Tis trivial, while your knowledge is what—"

"And yet I will have it," Grayson insisted. "I am not accustomed to making requests more than once, lady, however, I'll ask you again. What is your view on why your own people gave descriptions of you that were so conflicting with your true appearance?"

Catherine flinched and looked to Eduard in desperation, more confused than ever about how to answer. Eduard's gaze was flat, and the thought flashed through Catherine's mind, then, of telling her husband the whole truth, so that Eduard could be detained and prevented from harming her children once the lie was revealed. But at that moment, Eduard lifted a tiny roasted starling from a platter on the table and snapped the delicate bird's head from its neck. Then he blinked at her and licked his fingers.

Catherine's idea fizzled to nothingness, doused by waves of fear. Eduard was not stupid. Even if Gray believed her tale of plots to kill him, her children would be doomed. Eduard always protected himself, down to the smallest detail, and he would have foreseen this possibility and prepared for it.

Her only salvation rested in concocting an answer that would sound plausible to her husband. What she had in mind meant humiliating herself, but considering the alternative, it was a small price to pay. Clearing her throat, Catherine shifted her gaze to Gray. "I'm flattered that you wish my thoughts on the matter, my lord. In truth I believe that the contrary description you received of me arose from my peoples' loyalty to me."

Gray's ebony brow arched in the same wicked way she remembered from the chapel. "Explain."

Though the word sounded conversational, nothing softened the severity of his command.

"As you wish." Catherine flushed but met his gaze straight on, for once confident that the core of what she spoke, at least, would be the truth.

"My lack of attributes has long been acknowledged, my lord. My own father revealed that from infancy, 'twas clear to all that I'd never achieve a state of feminine delicacy. 'Tis a fact that I have learned to accept, though, apparently many of my people do not. In their desire to aid me in gaining a husband, it seems that they painted me in a much fairer light than I deserve."

The heat burned so in her cheeks that she felt her face must ignite to flames. She looked away, finally, unable to bear Gray's searching gaze longer, but glad that her humiliating speech was done. She'd simply made use of the truth. Her unfeminine stature had been a source of shame for as long as she could remember. No man could be blamed for being disappointed when he looked upon her, and that was part of the reason, Father had assured her, that he, Geoffrey, or any other who held responsibility over her, found frequent occasion to beat her. She sighed and stared down at her hands folded in her lap.

Grayson studied his wife's profile, uncertainty making him scowl. He'd felt something soften in him at the resignation he'd heard in her voice, and it warred with the hard shell of reserve he'd erected around himself concerning this marriage. She'd sounded so sincere. To his mind, no sane person could call her plain, and yet she had just bluntly declared it so. 'Twas true she'd never be a Court beauty, not with her impressive stature and vibrant coloring. But those same attributes also attracted Gray like no pale and delicate noblewoman ever would.

Why, then, did she belittle herself? So caught up was he in thoughts of her strange response, that he hardly noticed when Eduard stood up and excused himself from the table.

Narrowing his eyes, Gray twirled the stem of his goblet and gazed at his wife. A tiny bell went off in his mind, reminding him that he wasn't considering all that he knew of the fairer sex. By the time he'd won his first tournament, he'd been wise to women's more subtle methods of entrapment, emotional or otherwise.

And his answer rested there, he decided. Like her brother, Elise toyed with him, only her game was in seeking compliments. Such banter was a form of intimacy, he knew, and of the kind that would lead to just the sort of emotional closeness he wanted to avoid establishing with his wife.

Gesturing for the serving boys to bring fresh platters of meats and delicacies to their table, Gray forced himself to turn his attention back to the feast. He'd not fall for such a snare. Nay, he'd do better spending his time in making the rest of the evening tolerable. Besides, he was surprised to discover that he was beginning to feel hungry.

He occupied himself with serving slices of

capon in a succulent gravy onto the trencher he shared with his wife, following it up with a generous helping of roasted pork and several flaky pastries stuffed with mincemeat and berries. Bypassing the whole swan, with its graceful neck, Gray chose portions of tiny sweet onion floating in butter. As a final thought, he heaped spoonfuls of spiced apples and peaches along the edge of their trencher.

Gray noticed that Elise sat still as a statue, pale now, while he arranged their food. However, her gaze kept drifting nervously to the arched doorway through which her brother had disappeared, as if she awaited his return. It annoyed Gray to realize that she seemed unaware of how considerate he was being. She couldn't know, of course, that he'd never even allowed another woman to share his trencher, no less to serve her.

But Alban knew. His friend was seated across from them, not far down the table; Gray saw that from the moment he'd begun selecting foods to share with his wife, Alban had paused mid-motion in his eating, his hand halfway to his mouth.

Gray cleared his throat and gave Alban a look that made clear he was to behave as if what he'd just witnessed was commonplace. The awe-struck look faded from Alban's face under the attack of a merry grin. His friend wasted no time in raising his cup in salute, nodding and calling for a drink to bless the union between the Lord of Ravenslock and his new bride.

When the entire hall followed suit, Elise looked

as if she might faint. Now that he'd spent some time
with her, Gray noticed that she seemed rather timid.
Almost roughly, he indicated that she should begin
eating. Elise wouldn't meet his gaze but gave him a
nod and picked at one of the pastries. It was obvious that she forced herself.

Gray frowned. At this rate, she'd starve to death
before they'd been wed a month. But before he
could address the issue, one of Eduard's pages came
up to the table; his master had been delayed in his
errand, the boy said, but he assured them that he
would return to the feast as soon as possible. Gray
nodded and turned to Elise again, intent on insist-
ing that she eat.

He never needed to utter the command. He
watched, stunned and appreciative, as she began to
polish off every last morsel of food he'd placed on
her side of the trencher. What had inspired her sudden change in mood boggled his mind, but he
wasn't about to interrupt her by asking.

She seemed to relax during the remainder of the
meal, even venturing to ask him several shy questions about his holdings. At one point she became
almost animated, her hands moving with the grace
of bird's wings as she described the beauty of the
willow fields near her previous home. Then she directed her gaze upon him, murmuring, "Is it possible that you have willow swamps here on your
land? 'Tis almost time to gather the withies, and I
could replenish my stock."

"Your stock, lady? And what do you do with
these withies, as you call them?"

She smiled, and the beauty of her expression took his breath away. He couldn't help but notice that she talked with what seemed an almost palpable excitement. "After they're boiled and dried, I weave them into all sorts of shapes and fancies. My last work took form slowly, but it turned out to be a fine, comfortable chair." She directed the full force of her gaze on him, suddenly, her face alight. "Mayhap I could weave another like it, as a gift for you?"

He was struck by the joy radiating from her blue eyes; it washed over him in a torrent, blinding him to everything but the desire to bask in it for as long as he could.

Without forethought, he answered, "'Twould please me well. I'm not certain if willow fields grow on these lands, but perhaps in a few days I can free some time to help you find them."

As soon as he said it he could have bitten off his own tongue, but by then it was too late. He looked away, silently cursing himself, unable to fathom what had possessed him to make such an offer. The woman had lulled him into a conversational mood, damn her.

Alban leaned in to offer them a platter of cheeses, wafers, and cakes baked in the shape of doves, smiling as he commented, "Your husband's holdings are vast, milady. He governs much more than this one estate, though this castle and its lands are by far his most valuable prize to date."

Alban seemed to ignore Gray's pointed glare. His friend continued blithely, "As a native of this region, I'm quite familiar with these lands. I'd be happy to assist you both in mapping out a route that provides the most thorough overview of the area, if you wish to look for willows with Lord Camville."

"Perhaps you should simply escort my wife yourself," Gray offered dryly.

"Nay, I couldn't." Alban feigned courtly surprise. "That pleasure is not mine to enjoy."

If Elise noticed the undercurrents of his exchange with Alban, she hid it well. Glancing at her to gauge her response, Gray felt a flash of concern; her face had gone ashen again, and those graceful hands were clenched still, as before, in her lap.

"My lady, are you ill?" he asked quietly. "Shall I—"

"Ah, my dear new brother by marriage. A thousand pardons to you and my sister for my absence."

Gray snapped his gaze to Eduard, who talked as he approached, his face sharp with an expression that for some reason made Gray's hand itch to slip down and grip the hilt of his broadsword. That Eduard would throw down a challenge here and now at the wedding feast seemed unlikely, but Gray knew from experience that anything was possible with the man. Hatred for him rose full in his throat again, along with a battle-honed instinct to gut him where he stood. Gray stood to face his rival, noticing that Elise pushed herself slowly to her feet as well.

Yet instead of issuing a challenge, Eduard thrust his hand forward with a brocade-wrapped bundle clutched in his fist. " 'Tis here, finally. The wedding gift that I wanted to give to my dear sister." As he swung the parcel toward Elise, its wrapping fell away, revealing a beautiful oil portrait of two blond children, clutching hands and smiling in their matching silken garments.

Elise sucked in her breath, reacting, Gray decided, as if her brother dangled a snake in her face. Eduard's lip edged up at one corner. "Come, sister, and accept your gift. 'Tis a fine copy of the twins, is it not? I had this portrait of Ian and Isabel commissioned earlier, as a memento of home, and it has only just arrived by messenger."

"Twins?" Gray asked, feeling the bottom drop from his stomach. Alban caught his gaze, concern written in his expression. Gray clenched his jaw, willing the painful memories of Gillian back; he concentrated instead on the portrait and his certainty that the children painted there must be related to his new wife and her brother. "Who are they?"

"They—they're—" Elise tried to answer, but she sounded breathless and shaky.

" 'Tis a portrait of our niece and nephew, Ian and Isabel. They are the children of our elder departed brother, Geoffrey, and Elise became quite attached to them. I thought 'twould bring her pleasure to be able to gaze upon their faces whenever she wished."

Grayson instinctively gripped his wife's elbow when she swayed and clutched the edge of the table. "Are you unwell, lady?" he murmured again, this time with more insistence.

After a strained pause, she shook her head. "Nay, I'm fine."

Looking to Eduard, she leveled her gaze at him. "'Tis just that this gift was unexpected. And I—I am overcome by the stunning likeness that the artist achieved." Gently shaking Gray's hand from her arm, she stood erect under her own power. "Would it be possible to grant me a few moments with my brother? I wish to . . . to thank him in private for his gift."

Gray nodded in silence, watching the purposeful rhythm to Elise's steps as she walked with Eduard to a more secluded area of the hall. Though he caught only glimpses of her profile, he couldn't miss the tight line of her lips or her sudden pallor.

Alban moved in close behind Gray. "'Tis a strange reaction from your wife." He glanced to the portrait that had been left partially wrapped on the table. "The gift is beautiful, yet she seemed none too pleased with it."

Gray's eyes narrowed as he studied the hushed conversation taking place between brother and sister across the hall. "Aye, 'tis odd indeed." He folded his arms across his chest. "There's more to all of this than either of them are letting on."

He settled his wife into his sight like a hunter marks his prey. Sitting down, he leaned his elbow on the table and absently rubbed his finger across his lip as he let his gaze bore into her, relentless. Penetrating.

Finally he saw a delicate shudder ripple up her back. Like a cat alerted to danger, she looked at him sideways, her glance barely connecting with his before shifting away again. After a few more murmured words to Eduard, she turned to inquire something from one of the lady maids who stood ready to accompany her to the bridal chamber. Then, in the space of a heartbeat, she skittered from the hall, casting one more anxious glance at Gray before she began to climb the steps that led to his chamber.

As he watched her go, realization stamped a burning brand across his chest and deep into his groin. Heat flooded him, for the time being masking the suspicion that had begun to cloud his mind. He understood with sudden clarity that his wife was going upstairs for a particular reason tonight, and it threatened to make him cease taking the deep, regular breaths that usually filled his lungs . . .

Because he realized that at this very moment, Elise was leaving the hall to ready herself for their marriage bed.

Chapter 2

⎯⎯⎯⎯⎯◦◦◦⎯⎯⎯⎯⎯

Darkness blanketed the chamber in velvet folds, mirroring the bone-deep weariness Catherine felt seeping through her limbs. Confronting Eduard had sapped the last of her strength, and seeing her children's portrait had ground her soul to nothingness.

She sank onto a bench by the fire, aware that for the first time since this morning she was alone. Thankfully, Grayson had squashed the revelers' plans for the customary, rollicking escort of men to their bridal rooms. She needed fear nothing now but her husband's entrance to their chamber.

Her arms hung limp by her sides, her hands resting on the cushion. Her body felt depleted, yet her mind burned feverishly with images of the day. It was finished, God help her, the advance and retreat, the posturing and pretense. For better or worse, she was Baron Grayson de Camville's new wife. His counterfeit bride.

Mustering the strength to look around, Catherine took in the comfortable arrangements of her husband's bedchamber—her bedchamber now, as well. The thought filled her with dread. All that saved her from collapsing under the atrocity of what Eduard wanted her to do was the knowledge that she wasn't expected to act against her husband for several months.

Eduard had instructed her on the long journey to Ravenslock; first, she must establish trust. Become the dutiful, loving wife. Then, when sufficient time had passed, Eduard would send word to her, and his hireling would strike; when it was over, none would dare suspect the loyal wife of complicity in her husband's death.

Quivers rippled through her stomach again, making her shudder. Slowly, deliberately, she reached up to unfasten the circlet from her brow. 'Twas time to prepare herself for the farce of her wedding night. She slipped her amethyst kirtle over her head. But she paused before removing her smock. Somehow the thought of exposing her skin to the night air made her cringe. She couldn't do it. Not yet. It would seem too final.

And yet she knew the time was fast coming when she must submit to Grayson de Camville, to her husband's most intimate caresses. To his touch and his possession. And it was going to be all she could do not to weep and beg him to leave her alone.

But she had no choice, she knew. She must play the innocent virgin and allow him all of the liberties a wife owes her husband. Pressing her palm to the flat of her stomach in a vain effort to still the trembling, Catherine reminded herself that this part of her foul bargain would not be the worst. Surely she could survive the bedding she faced with the man who was now her husband. He was handsome, almost to the point of profanity. His shape was finer than any she'd ever seen in a man, and he was clean and well mannered on top of it all. Nay, bedding Grayson de Camville would not be the most difficult part of her unholy agreement.

Helping to kill him would.

Catherine pushed herself to her feet as she forced that sickening thought from her mind. She paced to the window, pressing her forehead against the wooden shutters and feeling the night air seep through the cracks to cool her flesh. It might not come to that, she reasoned. There was still time. Time to find another plan, to outwit Eduard and save her children without having to aid in the murder of an innocent man.

Then, with a grinding jolt, she realized that more time was not necessarily a foregone conclusion. First she had to convince Grayson that she was a virgin. She fingered the tiny bladder of chicken blood that Eduard had instructed her to use when the time came, as proof of her broken maidenhead. Pray God it worked.

Other men had been known to kill their wives on their wedding night if they discovered that they'd been deceived in such a foul way. One look at her husband made Catherine certain that, should he be that kind of man, a discovery of her true womanly state might mean this night would be her last. And little as she cared for her own life, her children's safety depended upon her staying alive, with her wits intact so that she could think of a way out of this horrific nightmare.

Her musings were cut short by the creaking of the door. A faint whisper of air, carrying with it the clean, fragrant scent she recognized as her husband's, made Catherine's hands clench. God give her strength now, she prayed, to carry this night to its conclusion with dignity and skill.

Turning slowly to face him in the shadows of the room, Catherine struggled to smile.

Gray held back near the door, for the first time in years uncertain as to how he wanted to proceed. By the Rood, but his wife was beautiful. Not in the way women of his experience were attractive—nay, his warrior queen possessed an almost otherworldly quality, both ethereal and entirely physical at the same time. The incongruous blend of opposing forces produced an intoxicating result . . . lush sensuality that battled with a depth of spirit that seemed to spill out of her and light his chamber with a golden glow.

Gray took a deep breath and held the air in his lungs for as long as he could, striving to regain some bit of composure before he spoke. 'Twas not like him to be so struck by a maid. But then he wasn't accustomed to sampling the pleasures of virgins. Those years he'd spent in the filthy alleys working for Bernard Thornby when Gillian was still alive had ensured that his first sexual experience and many others thereafter happened with whores.

After he had escaped that hell to build a life of his own as a knight, he'd taken to bedding women of more noble status, but they too had possessed enough carnal skill to rival the best in Thornby's trade.

This woman was different.

He'd seen that from the moment he'd lifted her veil in the chapel, from the moment he'd gazed into those wide, uncertain eyes. 'Twas that knowledge which explained his strange reaction to her, he reasoned. That and the intimacy of having her standing before him half-clothed in the shadows of his bedchamber.

"Have I disturbed you too early?" His husky question broke the reverent quiet of the chamber, making him want to grimace at his own awkwardness.

Pink suffused Elise's cheeks, deep enough to be seen even in this dim light. "Nay," she murmured. "'Tis your right as husband to enter this chamber whenever you wish."

"And yet I would not disturb you on this of all nights." Gray's tongue felt thick as he spoke. Somehow, acknowledging what they were doing here even with such a vague reference made him feel more on edge. Made him feel the desire to possess her burn more fiercely, warring against his better instinct.

He turned away, breaking the contact of their gazes. Walking to the table, he placed his hands, palm up, in the cool water from the wash bowl there. His mind raced with a thousand thoughts of why he should simply do his duty tonight. Why he should consummate this union with his wife and nothing more. Any further involvement, any emotional attachment to her, would be damaging and foolish.

Bringing up his cupped hands, Gray splashed the water over his face. He hoped that the sensation of cold would aid him. Only this morning, he'd followed his ritual bathing with a plunge in the frigid waters of the river, to help clear his mind and brace him for the unsettling events of the day.

The icy shock didn't help him now.

He heard his wife step nearer to him as he dried his face with a towel. Her voice pierced the distance, its tone edged with a kind of quiet panic.

"Have I angered you by coming to our chamber too soon?" she whispered. "Please forgive me. 'Tis only that I wasn't sure—"

Concerned, Gray turned to face her, and with a sobbed intake of breath, she shrank away from him, half-raising her hand as if to ward off a blow.

He felt as if it was he who'd been hit. Taking several steps toward her, he gripped her shoulders and forced her to look at him. "Why do you pull away as if I would strike you?"

Elise stared up at him, eyes wide, luminously blue with tears that threatened to spill over at any moment. She only shook her head and tried to make him release her.

Something snapped in Gray as she struggled against him, making him hold her tighter in his determination to win their clash of wills. "Tell me why, Elise. I demand to know why you whimper and shy away every time I look at you."

"Please let go," she whispered. "You're hurting me."

Startled, Gray released her and took a step back. She recoiled a few paces and rubbed her arms, but he continued to stare at her, his gaze steady. "Strong I may be, lady, yet I know when I exert enough force to cause pain. If your flesh protests, 'tis not from my touch."

"Nay, I spoke true my lord," she said, glancing at him in that skittish, uncertain way he was coming to expect from her.

Exasperated to the point of frustration, Gray strode forward again and took her hand. "Then I must see proof of the damage I inflicted, so that in future I can restrain myself."

He lifted her hand toward him, at the same time pushing aside the long draped sleeve of her smock to expose her arm. For the second time in less than a minute, Gray felt as if he'd been struck, only this time his concern mixed with bewilderment and then with anger. Bright, angry red marks, made by the force of fingers—God, he hoped not his— slashed across a mass of bruises.

"What in Christ's name is this? Why didn't you

tell me of it before?" Without waiting for her reply, Gray pulled her to the padded bench near the fire and made her sit. "Did you meet with an accident during your journey? Have you sustained other wounds? I demand that you tell me!"

He didn't at first notice how his commanding tone affected her. But when he saw the deathly hue of her cheeks and the strange, haunted look intensify in her eyes, he went still. More softly, he said, "I need to know how this happened, lady, and if you were hurt elsewhere. If you cannot remember or will not comply, I will summon a physician to examine you, to ascertain that you are in no danger."

"There's no need to call an examination, my lord. The bruises were the result of my own foolishness, nothing more."

Gray waited in silence for her to continue, but she apparently felt herself finished. The only outward sign of her feelings came in how her fingers clenched in her lap. Her throat worked convulsively, as if she tried to hold back some strong emotion. Placing his fingertip under the silky curve of her chin, he guided her gaze back to his again. "Are there more bruises than those I observed?"

He thought he saw a glimmer of unshed tears beginning to build again, but then she just blinked and nodded. Gray found himself wavering between a desire to comfort her and the urge to force her to explain. The conflicting feelings annoyed and angered him. She had no right to come into his life and upset the delicate balance he'd worked so hard to achieve.

He'd not allow it. He needed to get to the bottom of his wife's secrets, and he intended to uncover this particular mystery right now.

"Show me."

She pulled away with an abrupt motion, standing and pacing to the other side of the chamber. "Nay. 'Tis of no matter. I will heal in time." She half-turned, her eyes downcast as she clenched her fingers again. "I swear that I will not allow it to interfere with your pleasure this night, my lord."

Shadows masked her face, but not enough so that Gray couldn't see the tightness there. *Fear*. Aye, he'd expected as much. She was virgin, after all. He'd already reminded himself of that fact, cursing his inexperience in handling one such as she.

But whether she was his virgin bride or one of Thornby's most seasoned whores, nothing mattered as much right now as making sure that she was well.

"Lady, I'll wait no longer for your compliance."

Gray covered the distance between them in the space of a heartbeat. Against her soft protests, he led her toward the fire; taking a candelabrum from the mantel, he tipped it to the flames.

The tapers ignited with a popping hiss, and he set them on a small table perched near the hearth. Elise faced away from him, motionless; the mellow candle-glow bathed her hair, turning its lighter brown strands to gold.

Sweet Jesu, but this was more difficult than he'd expected. It took all of his strength not to bury his hands in her hair, to feel its silky weight against his cheek and breathe in her sweet fragrance. Desperate to quell the desire, Gray pulled his dagger from his belt and sliced through her smock in one quick motion.

Elise gasped as the fabric of her underdress slipped, but she couldn't prevent Gray from seeing what she'd obviously been trying to hide from him. The bruises that flowered across the smooth expanse of her back showed even more brutality, if that was possible, than the discoloration on her arm.

No accident under heaven could have resulted in this. It had been caused by the pounding force of some kind of animal. *A human animal.*

Fury swept through Gray with the swiftness of a winter squall; he beat back the surging memories that the sight of her injuries invoked. Memories of pain, darkness, misery, and impotent fury. A muscle in his jaw twitched as he stepped forward to push his wife's hair gently from her neck. She shuddered, and her shoulders hunched forward protectively.

By all that was Holy. Cursing softly, Gray let its silky weight fall back down to shield her. "Tell me who did this." His voice echoed quiet and deadly, and he felt the all too familiar battle rage begin to build in his blood. Whatever man had dared to touch Elise, had dared to touch *his wife* like this, would pay dearly. Before morning, the wretch's blood would soak the earth below the walls of Ravenslock.

She swung around to face him, eyes wide. Her mouth was even more drawn and pinched than before. "Please, my lord, 'tis of no matter. I beg of you to let it pass."

Gray's anger burned hotter, and a dark, destructive need for vengeance flared in his blood. "I'll excuse your request on the grounds that you've known me but a few hours, lady. Do not ask it of me again. Just tell me the name of the bastard who did this to you. Now."

"I can't," she whispered. Her eyes had filled with tears, and her voice sounded choked.

"Why the hell not?"

"Because, I . . . because I can't let you take action against him, or—" She broke off mid-point, choking back another sob and clenching her fingers so tightly in front of her that Gray felt sure they must snap from the pressure.

His temper broke instead, and he stalked to her, gripping her hands. "Why all the secrets? Why the heavy silences, the mysterious glances? Have you a lover whose seed already grows in your belly? Is that why you take such pains to protect his name?"

Elise's face turned ashen, and she gasped. "Nay! I've taken no lover, now or at any time in my life!"

"Who, then, would dare to visit such abuse upon you?" But even as he uttered the question aloud, its answer burst upon him with startling clarity. Only a man who had access, power, and the right given him by law to exert such force could be responsible for the deed. And only one man fit that description, so far as Gray knew.

"Christ, it was Eduard." He murmured it half as a statement and half as a question. His wife's silence gave him the confirmation he needed.

Releasing her, Gray stalked to the door, preparing

to hunt down and drag the bastard from his bed, King Henry's sanctions be damned. But before he could pull back on the wooden slab, Elise cried out and threw herself against him to block his access. He stared at her, stunned. Though she was tall, he'd not expected her to wield such strength.

She gazed at him, her eyes blue and glistening as the dew-soaked flowers that dotted the meadows near Ravenslock; she'd pressed back against the door, so caught up in the grip of emotion that she didn't seem to notice how the cut edges of her smock slipped from her shoulders.

Gray did.

His gaze drifted almost against his will, picking up every nuance, noticing how the creamy fabric bunched around her hand where she continued to clutch it to her breasts. The sight enticed him beyond reason. She looked wanton in a purely innocent way, which only added to the spiking shafts of desire and rage that lanced through him at the moment.

The soft linen provided sensual contrast with the smooth contours of bare flesh above it. In the firelight her skin took on a deeper glow, a silky warmth that made Gray burn with the desire to stroke his palm over the exposed places.

And other, more hidden places as well.

Jerking his gaze up to her face once again, he tried to thrust the thought from his mind. He nudged her, hoping to ease her from the doorway. But she didn't move. Her free hand had tangled itself in the cloth of his cloak, and she squirmed and pushed back in her effort to keep him from leaving their chamber.

"Please, my lord. Take no action against him. It is enough that he no longer has rule over me, and that I can hope for greater mercy at your hands. I beg of you, let it be!"

"Nay, lady. I cannot." Gray looked down at her, exasperation filling him at her stubborn defense of a villain. "No one may harm you with my knowledge and then continue as if naught occurred."

Elise looked horrified. She searched his face desperately, as if seeking some measure of mercy. Finding none, her expression went blank, then took on a reckless, bitter cast. She blinked back her tears. "Yet you may continue the righteous hypocrite! Can you say that *you've* never corrected a woman in anger, my lord? Now that you hold dominion over me, do you not intend to beat me whenever you deem it necessary?"

Every muscle in Gray's body tightened. "Regardless of what other men may do, lady, since I was but a lad of fourteen, I've never suffered another to harm a woman in my presence. And while there's no denying that I dislike the slashing barb of your tongue, I do not intend to beat you for it. Now or ever."

Dead silence greeted him. Elise blinked twice more and then the fight seemed to leave her, seeping away until she went limp and pliant against him. Yet Gray found that he couldn't continue his plan. He couldn't just push her aside to go after Eduard.

He felt the warmth of her palm, still resting, forgotten, on his chest; it burned through his cloak and shirt, holding him captive far more effectively than any steel shackle or metal bars might have. The curve of her breast and hips, pressed so intimately along his body in her struggles, branded him with heat. His desire jolted to full awareness, and he tried to shift away to curtail the swelling need that rose from being so near to her soft curves and enticing warmth.

But his abrupt movement made him pitch forward, and he came into complete, overwhelming contact with the length of her body. The erotic heat burgeoned, sending waves of pleasure through him and making him want to groan aloud with the sensation.

A soft moan broke from Elise's lips; her face tipped to his, and he was startled to see an answering awareness in her gaze. Without further thought, he bent his head, taking possession of her mouth, savoring the soft, salty taste of her lips. His tongue flicked into the honeyed recess, need for her burning hot and heavy in his groin.

She didn't resist, and so he deepened the kiss, taking his time, tasting fully of her. Her mouth slid smoothly across his, and he felt the soft sounds of pleasure she breathed against his lips. Every fiber of his being screamed for him to take her to their bed. To strip away her ruined garments, to satiate his hunger deep inside her moist heat.

It took all of his willpower to remain still as he kissed her; his palms were pressed to the door at either side of her head, and the muscles in his arms twitched as he fought against the urge to let go, to pull her body into him and the molten force of his desire.

But another part of him reveled in the teasing, the tantalizing sensation of holding back. Her body burned him like the kiss of a thousand fiery butterfly wings, making him loath to end the erotic tension that was rapidly spiraling out of control.

Deep in the recesses of his mind, Gray knew he should stop. He knew that he was casting years of self-discipline to the winds as he tasted of this pleasure. But he also recognized that he could as easily harness a storm right now as he could walk away from the temptation that was his wife.

With a groan of defeat, Gray slid his hands from the door to cup her buttocks, cradling her against the heat of his erection. She leaned into him, yielding and warm, and the soft pressure of her breasts, the sweet fit of their bodies, made him groan again. He lavished nibbling kisses down the side of her throat, pausing to breathe in her delicate floral scent as he captured the lobe of her ear with his lips. But when he moved his hands up her back, lifting, preparing to carry her to their bed, her sigh of pleasure ended on a hissed intake of breath.

Pulling back, Gray saw her bite her lip as tears sprang to her eyes. *Christ in heaven.* Releasing her immediately, he stepped back. But it was too late. He couldn't take away the hurt he'd just caused her by touching her bruises.

Elise shook her head without speaking, trying to

reassure him, but he could see the suffering on her face. Her fingers clenched as he'd seen them do so often in the hours since their wedding, and the sight made him feel sick and helpless.

Damn Montford. Cursing aloud, Gray turned away from Elise. He raked his hand through his hair and took a deep, shuddering breath until control ebbed back, thickening his blood with slow, painful beats of his heart. He allowed anger to replace his desire, let the cooling force of it drown the liquid heat that had filled him moments ago.

Averting his gaze from his wife, Gray turned back to the door, intending to go past her and find her bastard of a brother this time, pleading or no. But the feather-light touch of her hand made him pause.

"Nay, my lord," she murmured. The pain seemed to have receded, leaving her expression open and vulnerable. "Grant me one boon in this, I beg you. Do not seek out Eduard this night."

Desire battled in Gray—the need to beat her abuser to a pulp, warring with a sudden, unaccountable wish to please her, to give balm to the suffering he'd caused her. His hands fisted, even as she tried to lead him back toward their bed. Forcing his control to remain firm, Gray pulled away from her grasp. "Nay, lady. I cannot—I will not—join with you this night."

Elise stopped, and her face went ashen again. "But—but we must consummate our union."

"Aye, we will. But not tonight. I would not be

able to complete our joining—" He broke off, uncertain how much he needed to say to her about the intimate act between men and women. He cleared his throat. "I do not wish to hurt you, and so I will not share our bed until your bruises have healed."

"No, please," she grasped his arm. "I do not care. We must finish this." She looked stricken, even more fearful than she'd looked when she'd thought him about to strike her. "Sweet Jesu," she whispered, as if the words were wrenched involuntarily from her, "If Eduard were to discover that 'tis not in truth . . ."

Anger swelled anew in Gray. The wretch had far too great a hold on her, he decided; the sooner he broke that connection, the better. As his wife, she needed to learn that she had no more to fear from her brother or anyone else. But until that happened, he saw no reason for her to agonize over Eduard's reaction. Not when he could easily provide the proof that she seemed to seek so desperately.

Grasping the corner of their bed linen, Gray yanked it from the ticking. At the same time, he slid his dagger from its sheath at his waist, ignoring Elise's gasp as he sliced a small cut at the edge of his palm. Making a fist, he spattered blood on the sheet's pristine white; after he dabbed the flow to a stop with it, he tossed it to the floor.

"There. Now no one will question the validity of our marriage. 'Twill serve as proof that I breached your maidenhead." His cut throbbed, and he welcomed the burning sensation as he stalked to the door. "I'll not be forced into barbarity by anyone, for any reason."

"Wait! What . . . where are you going?"

Pausing for one moment, he swung to face his wife, willing himself to keep his emotions in check. Her eyes were huge in her face, and the frightened look made him clench his jaw before he was able to answer her.

He took a deep breath and attempted to gentle his tone. "Allay your fears, Elise. None will know of my absence from our chamber to gossip about it."

"But what of Eduard?" she whispered, as if she could scarce find the courage to voice her request.

Gray felt his lips curl almost against his will into a mocking grin. "Your wishes shall be respected on that account as well, my lady. For this night, at least." He yanked the door open, adding, "But on the morrow I host a tournament in honor of our wedding. Your brother will not fare so comfortably then, I assure you."

Gray steeled his heart to the simultaneous rush of relief and renewed anxiety he saw in her eyes. She seemed about to speak more to him, but then she simply looked to the floor, her hands clasped again before her.

"Good night, lady," he finally murmured, taking one long, last look at his bride. Then, before he could change his mind, he slipped out the door and disappeared into the cool, welcome embrace of the night.

Faegerliegh Keep, Somerset

Heldred's breath rasped in his throat. The old man leaned his hands on his knees, trying to force his heart to slow, so that he could continue his work. As he rested, he glanced around, concerned more about the possibility of seeing one of Montford's soldiers than of crossing any evil spirits that might be lurking in this shadowy crypt.

Only two generations of Montfords rested here; the others were back in Normandy, whence the current, corrupt brood sprang. As a man of science, he had no reason to fear the reappearance of their disembodied souls. They were all surely damned to eternal hell for the lives they'd led.

A sudden, fierce pain gripped Heldred's innards, making him wince and sink to the earthen floor of the vault. Damn his weakness! He muttered and gasped, even as he reached for the bag of herbs around his neck. Taking a pinch of wild cherry bark from his pouch, he ground it between his teeth and swallowed.

There. The pain subsided; the prickly feeling on his neck faded, and he breathed easier. At least for the moment. But he had to hurry, he knew. The scent of morning already seeped into the tomb, urging him on and reminding him that the sun would bring new guards to replace the night watch. If Montford's men caught him lurking in the crypt, they would capture him and present him into Lord Montford's bloody hands.

Yet he couldn't leave now. He had to know.

Heldred's gaze darted around the dim confines of the earthen vault, searching for the spot. He'd recognize it, once he saw it, of that he was sure. Scuffling his rag-covered feet over the stone and dirt floor, Heldred approached a tomb. It looked like the place. No carved stone figure reposed on its top, so it was either a new burial or the resting-place of a less significant member of the Montford family.

With a groan, Heldred pushed at the lid of the stone case until it grated off-center a forearm's width. He lifted his torch with a trembling hand, his lips pressed tight as he prepared to see if the horror of his suspicions was true.

A clammy vapor rose from the tomb, bathing his face in chill. He held his breath against the fetid stench of decay he expected to follow soon after. But when he peered into the recesses of the stone case, he saw rotted cloth, topped by the grinning head of a skeleton. A few wisps of hair clung to patches of scalp left upon the unfortunate's head, but it was obvious that this man had been dead for a long time.

With effort, Heldred pulled the lid shut again and shuffled to another tomb, not far off. This time he paused and scrutinized the area, squinting and trying to visualize the place as he'd seen it in the light, on the day of the burial, when all of the villagers had been allowed to pay their respects.

Carefully he swung the torch along the edge of the stone, searching for some sign. Curse his sight for failing him now! Why couldn't he see more? Recognize some clue? The torch sputtered and popped, throwing a flurry of sparks that bounced off the edge of the platform to flicker out on the dusty floor. And then he found it.

With a gasp, he knelt as quickly as his old knees would allow him, bringing the torch closer to the base of the bier that supported the stone coffin. Scuff marks marred the dirt round the sepulcher, the result of scores of mourners who'd filed past the resting-place of their beloved lady on her burial day.

This was it. Her tomb. Setting the torch aside, Heldred put his back into his labor, pushing the heavy lid from its mooring with a strength belying his years. The stone grated and scraped, and he felt blood ooze, stinging, from his knuckles, as he dragged them across the harsh surface in his haste to see what lay inside.

Torchlight flickered from the rough-hewn ceiling as he raised his arm and leaned over to view the corpse. The stench hit him immediately, and he sucked in his breath, holding it and feeling his head reel. His eyes strained, and tears rushed behind his lids, blurring the horrible sight before him. With a growl, he threw down the torch, shoved the tomb closed, and slid down the side of it to crumple in a heap on the floor.

Grateful sobs bubbled from his chest, and he caught the faint, metallic odor of dirt and blood on his hands as he leaned his forehead into them. When the emotions passed, leaving him empty and dry, Heldred dragged his sleeve across his eyes. A smile wrinkled his wet cheeks. He'd been right, by God. She was alive. That bastard Eduard had done evil in the most terrible way. He'd killed his own sister, and she, not their beloved mistress, lay here in the tomb. The poor Elise hadn't even been granted her own identity in death.

A rusty laugh escaped Heldred's throat, mixing with a joy and hope he hadn't felt since that awful day. But it wouldn't be awful in his memory any more. Never again.

Because his lady was alive, by the saints. And he, Heldred the weaver, was going to find her.

Chapter 3

 ornamental divider

Catherine shifted in sleep, catching herself with an aching jolt an instant before she would have toppled off the edge of Grayson de Camville's enormous bed. Stiffening as she came to full awareness, she pushed herself up on one shoulder and squinted at her surroundings. 'Twas nearly dawn, by the lead-gray light that seeped in the shutters.

She'd survived her wedding night.

Twisting to look behind herself, she saw that she'd moved little from where she'd finally curled in exhaustion hours after Gray had left her last night. The blood-stained linen still lay across the bed where she'd thrown it before she slept, fearful lest someone enter the chamber while it was on the floor and realize the ruse for what it was.

Now she looked at the sheet with distaste.

Though she was thankful for the reprieve it had granted her, the soiled linen represented the lie that had become her life in an undeniable, tangible way.

Forcing herself to stand, Catherine limped to the wash basin. Her limbs protested against the ache that had worsened over the course of the night. How long had she slept? 'Twas difficult to tell. Still, she needed to perform her toilette before a maidservant arrived who might see her bruises and talk of them to the others at the castle.

She'd just slipped on a mulberry linen kirtle when the door creaked open. Catherine glimpsed an older woman's face a moment before it disappeared again behind the portal.

"Pardon, milady," her voice came gruff from the hall. " 'Tis Mariah. I've been sent to attend to you as lady's maid, if you'll allow it."

"Aye. Come in." Catherine adjusted the fitted wrist of her smock so that it peeked from beneath the kirtle's long, pointed sleeve. "I've dressed already, but I'd welcome help with my crispinette."

Catherine watched Mariah enter the chamber, noticing the sharp expression that creased the small but able-looking woman's face. She looked to be nearly two score and ten years, with black, silver-streaked curls that framed her face and set off eyes the color of steel. Though obviously roughened from hard work, her hands were gentle as she gathered up Catherine's hair and arranged the delicate netting of the crispinette over it.

"Thank you, Mariah. 'Tis a welcome boon to have

your assistance. At home I always had to tend my hair myself."

Mariah pursed her lips, tucking the last curl in place. "I've served in noble households my whole life, and in all that time I never met a lady who fixed her own hair." She scowled and added, "I'd not have thought Lord Montford the kind of man to allow it."

"And yet I've spoken true," Catherine said, startled to find the woman so querulous.

"Pardon, my lady," Mariah said stiffly, though her expression remained sharp. "I meant no offense."

Catherine nodded her acceptance of the apology, meeting Mariah's gaze with as much calm as she could muster. 'Twas unexpected, this obstinate regard from a servant. Prickles of warning inched up her back. Could Mariah suspect something amiss? What if she knew, somehow, that Grayson had spent the night elsewhere and because of it questioned the validity of Catherine's marriage to him? And what if Eduard learned of it as well . . . ?

A sickening twist gripped her belly. Pushing herself to her feet a bit too quickly, she said, "Thank you for your help, Mariah. 'Twas thoughtful of you to come without my bidding."

"I deserve no thanks, milady. 'Twas Lord Camville that asked me to peek in on you, to see what you might need." Her eyes softened a bit. "Though in truth, I know too well how hard the wedding night can be on young women," she added, nodding to the bloodied sheet that still lay crumpled on the bed where Catherine had left it.

"Oh." Catherine felt a flush fill her cheeks. "Well. I—I should be going down to chapel. It must be nearly *prime*, and my husband is surely waiting for me to attend mass with him."

Mariah simply nodded, the same pointed expression on her face. Catherine felt the woman's gaze on her, boring into her back until she'd left the room. As she descended the stairway, she tried to shake off the feeling. Mariah's stare hadn't been unkind, after all. Just watchful, perhaps. Even penetrating.

Aye, but that could be dangerous, too, she reminded herself, considering her borrowed identity and evil mission.

The caution sounded its dull warning, adding to the burdens she'd carried with her since the day Eduard had forced her to take part in his plots. Mariah was the least of her worries right now, she reminded herself. First, she had to face her husband in the cold light of day. Had to use every ounce of her strength to appear serene and calm when she looked into his eyes, rather than as she truly felt.

In all of her life, even through the years when Geoffrey had pounded the knowledge of her failings into her every night, she'd never loathed herself as much as she did right now. Thanks to her agreement with Eduard, she felt like a horrible spider, waiting to trap her victim in a web of deceit and death.

With that thought ringing in her mind, she entered the chapel for morning mass. Her husband, however, was nowhere to be seen. Through the course of the service, she somehow found means to

let the peace of the atmosphere soak into her, allowing her a few moments of escape from her tortured
thoughts. But as soon as she left the cool chapel they
converged on her again. She walked faster, letting
the sun warm her as she paced herself against their
onslaught.

"Lady Camville!"

Catherine turned at the sound of the voice. Sir
Alban Warton strode toward her, a grin lighting his
boyish features. She tried to muster a smile in return; her husband's friend seemed like a cheerful
man who wore his good humor like a favored garment, often and well.

"Lady, I saw you at mass but had no chance to
speak with you. I trust that this morn finds you content?" Alban offered her a slight bow.

"Aye, sir. And you?"

"Hale and hearty." He closed his eyes and tilted his
face to the sun. "Ah . . . the breeze is fragrant and the
sky a sparkling blue. 'Tis a day fit for a king, is it not?"

A more honest smile tugged Catherine's lips. "It
is, sir, though I'd hazard to guess that you find
every day as pleasing."

Alban laughed. "Quite true. One learns to appreciate the simpler aspects of life when faced with the
loss of them."

Catherine tipped her head, trying to guess his
thoughts. "You refer to the Crusade in Egypt?"

"Aye. I have many tales to tell of it. Your husband, however," he added, his eyes crinkling at the
corners, "tells every one of them far better than I."

"I didn't realize that you and Lord Camville had

known each other for so long." Catherine nodded to a serving boy who bowed as she and Alban strolled by the herb bed he was weeding.

"Oh, Gray and I met when we were lads. We squired together, received our dubbing three years later and rode out to face the infidels side by side not five months after that. He's the one responsible for getting me back to England in one piece." Alban gestured toward the great hall. "But that story must needs save for another time. Will you accompany me to break your fast?"

"Aye, 'twill be welcome." She paused and glanced at Alban, uncertain as to whether or not she should voice her concerns about her husband's whereabouts. In the end, the knight's kind expression helped her to make the decision. "Have you seen Lord Camville yet this morn, Sir Alban? I had thought to meet with him during mass."

Alban looked surprised, but he masked the expression quickly. "There's no need for alarm. 'Tis not Gray's habit to seek daily mass. Your wedding was the first time I've seen him in a church since his last sojourn with King Henry."

"Oh, I didn't realize."

" 'Tis of no matter. There's no shame in knowing less than all about a man you met only yesterday."

Catherine nodded, troubled nonetheless. Her husband avoided the comfort of God and church? It boded ill, flaunting against the most basic rules of society. Even Eduard, as sinful as he was, attended mass daily. She'd had to look at his hypocritical face all through the service this morn.

Just then a cloud shifted from in front of the sun, and the full force of light made Catherine squint. "'Twill be brighter today than yesterday, it seems," she murmured, almost to herself.

"Aye," Alban answered as he escorted her onward toward the hall. "Gray will be pleased that no rain will mar his tournament—less mud usually means fewer injuries."

Catherine frowned. "Does he expect many men to be wounded?"

"'Tis not uncommon." Alban shrugged. "In *mélées* bruises and broken bones are to be expected. 'Tis much the same as regular battle, which is why the king doesn't always view it with favor."

"Is my husband not concerned, then, of incurring the king's wrath with his *mélée*?"

"King Henry indulges Gray more often than not. War is a dangerous enterprise, and tournaments serve as our best and only preparation for real battle."

Catherine was ready to ask another question, but before she could say anything, a hand gripped her arm, clamping down hard on the worst of her bruises there.

She stifled a gasp as Eduard's voice hissed in her ear, "Sweet sister, I've had to run a merry chase to catch up with you." Then louder, for Alban's benefit, he added, "You left the chapel too quickly for me to bid you good morn."

Standing still where he'd been near the door, Alban glanced warily back and forth between them. Catherine struggled to look unconcerned at Eduard's interruption. "How silly of me not to have waited," she murmured, "but I was so interested in hearing Sir Alban tell of the tournament today that I paid no attention."

"Ah, yes, the *mélée*. It should provide us with some lively sport, eh, Warton?"

"Indeed."

Eduard smiled, though the look was more predatory than friendly. "I'm hoping to take ransom from Camville on the field today. 'Twould be a fine jest to trounce him so soon after his wedding to my dear sister." Grinning now, Eduard pulled Catherine against him as if giving her an affectionate hug.

A muscle twitched in Alban's jaw. "I wouldn't wager my spurs on besting Gray. 'Twould be unwise to attempt it." Then, as if dismissing Eduard, he directed his gaze to Catherine. "You'll be coming in soon, then?"

"Aye, we'll be in directly," Eduard answered for her. "I plan to eat hearty in preparation for battle."

Alban gave them a curt nod and stepped into the hall. As soon as he disappeared, Eduard renewed his punishing hold on her and walked her across the yard. In a few moments they'd rounded a corner of the main building, secluding them in the shadows between the castle wall and the stables. Gripping her shoulders, Eduard shoved her hard against the stonework, forcing a cry from her.

"Be silent, woman," he snapped, "lest I assist you in the endeavor with my fist."

"You wouldn't dare," Catherine ground out, straightening to level a hate-filled glare at him. "You no longer have the right now that I am another man's wife."

Anger flared hot in Eduard's eyes, and for a moment, she thought he would follow through with his threat anyway. But he released her. "Aye, your correction is Camville's pleasure now." Stepping away, he growled, "Still you must needs answer me. What happened last night with him? What went awry?"

"Nothing was amiss."

"Nay? Then why did your husband ride out so early this morn? He saddled his mount and set off as if the devil himself chased at his heels." Eduard leaned in, digging his finger under her chin. "The mongrel learned you'd been used before, didn't he, Catherine?"

She jerked her head from his touch. "He discovered nothing. The sheet was bloodied, and all was as it should be."

"Then why the hell-bent ride at dawn?"

"Perhaps 'tis his habit to ride early."

"The morn after his marriage?" Eduard scoffed. "'Tis more like you failed to keep him interested enough to remain abed with you."

Catherine kept silent, unable to refute Eduard's jibe and unwilling to add to his animosity by trying. Pushing herself away from the wall, she clenched her fingers and faced him. "Whether that be true or not, I do not know. But 'tis likely that you and I will be missed at table if we tarry longer. I'm going back to the hall."

Eduard looked surprised for an instant. Then he smiled. "Ah, the titmouse has a bit of hawk in her.

Marriage to Camville has added some backbone to you, foolhardy though it may be." Gripping her tightly by the back of the neck, he hauled her close enough so that his mouth brushed against her ear. "Just be wary, sweet Catherine. I know two very precious ways to keep you groveling, and I'll take great pleasure in using both of them against you if you force me to it."

Yanking herself from his grip, Catherine pressed her lips together and pushed past him. She headed for the hall, but Eduard fell into step right next to her, mocking her with a whistling tune that sounded profane coming from his lips.

As they neared the building, he slipped a brotherly hand under her elbow, and though she wished to pull away, she knew such an obvious movement would be noticed by the many eyes that now witnessed their approach. Yet she couldn't stop herself from muttering a curse against him under her breath, ordering him to release her.

Her oath had an effect opposite to what she'd hoped. Eduard let go of her elbow only to reach out and encompass her waist, pulling her tightly and painfully close to him as they walked.

And though she forced herself to endure his embrace without outward reaction, it was all she could do to shut her mind against the sound of his laughter, ringing soft and malicious in her ear.

Gray looked at the array of swords on the table before him, alternately lifting and swinging one and then another as he tested their weight and balance in his hand. The selection of practice blades should have been sufficient, but he found himself dissatisfied with every weapon. 'Twas an annoyance and not like him to allow himself to be so distracted. Yet the image of his wife kept coming to him, taking his thoughts away from his work.

He'd avoided her successfully so far this day. But in his mind's eye he saw her as she'd been last night, pressed against his chamber door, her eyes beseeching, her skin golden honey in the firelight. She'd begged him not to hunt down her brother then, and he'd agreed. But no such constraints bound him today.

Pacing to a window of the nearly barren chamber, he glanced out of the open shutter. It was not yet midday and already the heat oppressed, undulating over the fields in waves. In less than an hour the *mêlée* would commence; he could see preparations taking place at the edge of the grounds, saw patches of brightly colored silks shining in the sun, pitched by traveling knights who'd come to try their luck at winning the tournament ransoms this day. His reputation as the best of King Henry's champions always seemed to attract droves of young men eager to try their mettle against him.

Gray frowned, wondering how many of those same men would be carried from the field of battle on pallets. Turning on his heel, he strode back to the table and stripped off his shirt. He hefted one of the swords, swinging it in wide arcs, then lunging and jabbing in a few practice passes. But as he warmed to the task, his movements became more intense; soon he was repeating the series of motions over and over, driving himself with relentless focus until he ran with sweat. Yet it wasn't enough. The familiar beast grew inside him, thirsting for the feel of his blade hacking through flesh, for the slippery heat of blood spilling over his hand.

Gray pushed himself harder, moving faster, as he swung his sword with greater precision and violence against his invisible foe, the adversary who'd made every battle he'd fought in the last seventeen years a struggle for life or death. He struck at the guilt and anger that had been eating him from the inside out since that horrible day . . . since the moment he'd lost Gillian forever.

Gillian. His mind breathed her name as he swung and sliced with his blade. The images flooded back, assaulting him, pummeling him with fury. He'd choked on her name then, unable to speak it aloud after he'd found her, his twin, his second self, knowing that it was his fault. His unimaginable error.

Gray. Oh, Gray, it hurts . . . make it stop hurting. Her whispering voice haunted him, sharpening his rage and twisting his gut until he felt sure that he too must bleed from the pain. But he'd never escape the guilt, never be absolved of the sin or the memory. He'd left Gillian alone, and the son of a bitch had gotten her. Thornby had broken her with his fists, leaving nothing but a bloodied, bruised shell. And as he'd held his beautiful sister—his equal—in his arms that day, she'd opened her eyes one last time, looked into the depths of his soul . . . and stopped breathing.

The red haze of agony and rage swelled, bubbling and building to a wordless roar that filled Gray's chest and burst free in a sound to rival the howling of the damned.

With one, swift movement, he swung his sword into the air and slammed it point first into the table. Then he sank to his knees, burying his face in his hands. His breath rasped painfully, straining his sides. His body felt numb, and he fought against the flood of emotions, even as he ached for the cleansing relief of tears that wouldn't come.

After a moment he became aware of sight and sound and touch again; he heard the heavy hilt of his sword rocking back and forth atop the blade he'd embedded in the table. His hands fell limp to his sides as he pushed back the darkness and the fury. But it was there anyway, always lurking close to the surface and waiting to spread bloody destruction.

Pushing himself to his feet, he moved slowly to the door. His time was up. The *mélée* was about to begin, and yet he dreaded its start almost as much as he despised waking each day. It wasn't the danger he feared. Clashing swords, grinding bones, pain, injury, even death—none of it held any power over him. Nay, 'twas just the opposite. He was bound by an understanding of the dark forces that drove him; somehow he needed to find control, to rein in the raging beast that clawed for release whenever he was on the field of battle . . .

Because he knew that if he didn't, Eduard was going to need the protection of God Himself to walk away from the tournament this day with his life.

Catherine felt sick as she climbed the raised pavilion that had been set up at a safe distance from the field where the *mêlée* was being assembled. Several ladies and the few older lords who sat as spectators viewed her surreptitiously as she passed. Because of her husband's position, she knew that none would use outward ill manners, but it was clear that they were curious about the woman who'd wed the powerful Baron Grayson de Camville.

She recognized a few guests from the brief introductions she'd received during the wedding feast yesterday. Lady Mandeville sat at one end of the pavilion. She was surrounded by her ladies, all in varying hues of pink, while she herself was swathed in what seemed to be yards of heavy crimson fabric. Only the force of a breeze that had developed in the past half-hour seemed to prevent the lady, draped in excessive silk, from succumbing to a swoon.

The Countess avoided Catherine's gaze, but a younger woman nearby smiled shyly. Nodding in return, Catherine tried to remember her name. Lady Margaret of Haverford, that was it. She murmured some pleasantries to her as she edged past toward her seat in the front of the spectators.

Catherine settled onto the padded bench, uncertain what to do next. She'd never witnessed a tournament before; both her father and Geoffrey had been too ashamed of her to allow her attendance at them. As she glanced discreetly to her right, she saw Eleanor de Valianne waving a silken cloth at a knight riding past. Fascinated, Catherine watched as the gallant stopped to acknowledge the gesture. With a flourish, he tipped his spear, accepting the bit of silk from Eleanor, before riding off to join the ranks gathering on the northern side of the field.

The chivalric display made a pit open in Catherine's stomach. Quickly, she sat up straighter, scolding herself for a fool. 'Twas futile to wish for what could never be. She'd learned long ago that she'd never be first in any man's heart.

Someone nudged her arm, sparing her further self-disparagement. "Have you a token for Lord Camville, lady? He will undoubtedly take the field soon."

Turning, she looked into the wrinkled, kind face of William de Bergh, one of the king's assistant justiciars. He'd taken the seat next to her, and for some reason, seeing him made her feel more at ease. As with all of Ravenslock's guests, she'd met him briefly during the wedding feast, and she'd noticed that Grayson had seemed fond of the old man. "I'm sorry," she murmured. "What did you say?"

He smiled and patted her hand. "You should prepare a token, Lady Camville. Ready a favor to present to your lord husband when he comes onto the field."

Catherine's throat felt like it was going to close. "Me, offer him a token?" she croaked. "But what shall I give? I brought nothing—"

The sound of trumpets broke into her speech, followed by a rumbling so fierce, she thought the pavilion must fall with the reverberation of it. Three score knights thundered onto the far end of the field, led by a magnificent figure atop a steel gray stallion. The squire riding next to him held high an azure banner that flapped in the wind.

As the pennant unfurled and snapped, Catherine squinted and caught sight of an emblazoned gold eagle with wings outstretched, a thunderbolt clasped in its hooked beak. The same design decorated the blue samite tunic the powerful knight wore over his hauberk, as well as the shield strapped onto his left forearm.

A thrill of shock went through her. 'Twas her husband's device—and it was Grayson himself who led these warriors across the green. He was still too distant for her to see his expression clearly, though Catherine could now identify his form. His powerful stature and dark hair gave him away. Many of the men who rode behind him wore mail coifs and helms that left only their faces visible, but Grayson's head was bare, allowing his hair to flow free to his shoulders and whip in the wind.

"Lord of the Storm," William murmured next to her. "That's what they call your husband. 'Tis a tribute to both his device and his reputation. On the field he's as fierce and unpredictable as the furies themselves, and often as deadly." William cackled softly. "If these old bones allowed me to engage in the sport as I used to, I'd not want to be opposite him. Nay, not if the gates of heaven beckoned me from the other side."

"He—he's coming this way," Catherine said, the words catching in her throat.

"Aye," the old man laughed again. "Your favor, my lady. Prepare your favor!"

Frantically, Catherine looked down at her clothing. She'd not known enough of tournaments to bring a scrap of silk with her, and her mulberry kirtle bore none of the fripperies that decorated the necks and sleeves of the other women here. Desperation gripped her; Grayson would reach the pavilion in a few moments, and she'd shame him if she had nothing to offer in tribute.

The edge of her smock. The thought burst upon her, startling her to action. The undergarment had been a cast-off of Elise's, and when one of the maids had lengthened it for Catherine's greater height, she'd sewn a bit of scarlet ribbon to the hem.

Leaning over without thought of propriety, Catherine flipped up the end of her skirt. Her fingers felt clumsy as she fumbled with the stitching, tugging and twisting to yank the ribbon free. It finally came loose with a ripping sound, but the force of her pulling made her hand slam into the pavilion's waist-high enclosure wall. She almost toppled from the bench, managing to right herself just in time for her husband to rein his steed to a stop in front of her.

Clutching the ribbon in numb fingers, she stood to face Gray. His expression was inscrutable, but his sea-mist eyes held her gaze. Something about the way he looked at her made her feel as if she stood with him alone, no longer surrounded by the dozens of spectators, hushed now, in the pavilion.

With a soft clicking sound, he nudged his mount forward, all the while keeping his gaze locked to hers. Her lips felt dry; she licked them and swallowed against the tight feeling in her throat, hoping against hope that she'd not also be required to speak as part of this unfamiliar ritual.

Gray seemed to sense her hesitation; with a slight nod, he indicated that she should hold out her token to him. As if in a dream, she leaned over the edge, arm outstretched to reach him. Though her hand shook, the stiff breeze made the ribbon flutter, masking her trembling. Gray lifted the point of his sword to her, and somehow, she managed to fasten the token to its tip.

When he took the scrap of scarlet from his blade and tied it to the emblazoned *ailette* at his shoulder, Catherine felt a burst of pride the likes of which she'd never known. Then he raised his gaze to hers again, his eyes glowing with the same passion he'd shown last night when he kissed her in their bedchamber, and she was sure her heart would burst from the force of its thudding in her chest.

"For your honor alone, my lady."

His oath, murmured in husky cadence, caressed her like the stroke of his hands over her skin. It wrapped her in a tingling cloak of intimacy, its power taking her so by surprise that it knocked the breath from her lungs.

Dimly she recognized that she wasn't alone in her reaction to his gentle vow. A hum rose from the ladies around her, their envious sighs mingling with soft exclamations as they watched the most powerful knight in the kingdom offering homage to her.

But in the next instant he was gone, nodding to

the crowd as he wheeled his stallion about and spurred him to a gallop. His men followed close behind, all of them thundering across the green to position themselves with the other warriors, both on foot and mounted, at the southern end of the field.

"You carried the moment with a fine show of grace, my lady," William said, patting her hand.

She nodded her thanks, somehow finding her seat again. The buzzing in her ears began to recede, and she tried to focus on what the old man was saying. His voice rose and fell as he prattled on about how fine a day it was for a tournament and about how evenly matched both sides seemed to be. Then he shook his head and smiled, wondering aloud how she would be able to choose sides in the contest, since her brother's forces held one end of the field while her husband's defended the other.

William's last comment cut through the happy fog in her brain; she tried not to gape at the old man. "Lord Montford and Lord Camville are on *opposing* sides of the green?"

"'Tis customary, my lady. Your husband and his men will hold the field against all comers to the tournament. That includes your brother and his forces."

Dread circled Catherine's throat as she considered the possibilities of that scenario. No one knew better than she of Eduard's hatred for Gray. And though she hadn't really understood what he'd meant when he'd boasted that he planned to collect ransom from her husband today, it hit home now with a vengeance.

Gray held no fondness for Eduard, either, she

knew; after witnessing her bruises last night, he'd vowed to seek retribution against him at this tournament.

For your honor alone, my lady.

The squeezing sensation increased in Catherine's chest. That Eduard would try to kill Gray seemed unlikely; before the wedding, he'd rejected her suggestion of defeating him openly on the field, calling such an action useless as far as obtaining the position and lands he sought by his rival's demise.

But what if Gray managed to slay Eduard? Her odious brother by marriage had as much as told her that he'd already ordered his men to murder her children should she be foolish enough to attempt to expose his evil plots. And regardless of the method, his men might well assume it was her doing if Eduard turned up dead.

Sweet Lord in heaven . . .

Suddenly William leaned forward, his eyes sparkling with excitement. "Ah, look, lady. 'Tis what we've been waiting for."

Time seemed to stop as she raised her gaze slowly to the field spread out before them, to the dazzling array of knights positioned on either end of it. A horn sounded in the distance, and the great expanse erupted into a deafening chaos of hurtling bodies, charging steeds, and flashing weapons.

"'Tis the moment of truth, my lady," William shouted above the din. "The battle has begun."

Chapter 4

Until the numbness began to invade her wrists, Catherine didn't realize how tightly she was clasping her hands. Releasing the grip, she winced at the burning, prickling sensation flooding her fingers. But for the past quarter-hour she couldn't drag her gaze from the sight in front of her. Couldn't pull her thoughts from the worry that gnawed with increasing ferocity at her heart.

The tournament field was a scene of pure bedlam. Great gouts of dirt lay scattered across the green, kicked up by hooves of war mounts that careened and reared at their masters' commands. Colors flashed, men shouted, and weapons clashed against shields and armor in a metallic clamor that Catherine thought must harrow the soul of the most stalwart in the crowd.

Yet taking a swift glance in either direction, she realized that the people around her seemed to be enjoying themselves. It startled her almost as much as the action on the field. She looked at William. He was leaning forward, cheering what she assumed must be acts of valor or prowess by the small packs of knights, some on horseback and some not, who occasionally broke away from the large group to fight on the edges of the green.

"'Tis difficult to see what's happening," she called to him, trying to be heard over the crowd. "Can you find Lord Camville anywhere?"

"Aye, my lady," he answered, tilting his head to her, though his gaze remained fixed to the field. "There he is, directly in the center." William pointed. "The eagle on his device catches the sun. 'Tis the golden flash you see now and again."

Catherine struggled to find what he described. To her, the field looked like a writhing mass of animals and men, the horror of it compounded by the din of battle. But what William said was true. If she focused on the center group, she could see an occasional glint of gold backed by sapphire. Yet she couldn't tell how her husband fared, or if he'd dealt Eduard any blows.

Of a sudden the crowd surged to their feet, a collective shout marking some momentous happening. Catherine shot from her bench as well, straining to interpret the sight; she tugged on William's sleeve. "What is it? Why is everyone so excited?"

"'Tis almost over, my lady," he shouted. Then he began to stamp and cheer as loudly as the rest of the spectators. She saw that many of the knights seemed to be turning their steeds and charging off the green, hotly pursued by opposing warriors. Even the smaller clusters seemed to dissipate as the combatants ceased their struggles and headed toward either end of the field.

"Some of the men are giving over, fleeing to the safety of their side. They will be captured by their opposites, then forced to pay a ransom in order to regain their freedom," William explained.

"But how will we know who was injured—or which side won the tournament?"

"The wounded will be counted and aided after the battle, while the side that captured the most men and obtained the greatest amount in ransom will have the right to claim victory." William nodded toward the green in approval. "From the looks of it, though, I'd say that your husband's forces won the day. See? There is Lord Camville even now. He's chasing that group of knights to catch them before they reach the safety of their own side. And 'tis very likely he will succeed, I'd say!"

As she watched, Catherine saw the knights William described. There were three of them, riding their mounts so hard that, as they neared, she could see foam flying from the horses' mouths. Gray rode close behind them. He was hunched over his steed's neck, his face a mask of chill concentration as he pursued his quarry. His expression sent a shiver up Catherine's spine, and she suddenly understood William's comment about not wishing to be opposite her husband in a battle.

The cheering crowd grew louder as Gray charged after the men, coming closer and closer to pass in front of the pavilion. Yet he seemed not to notice the reaction of the spectators, keeping his gaze fixed with deadly purpose on the backs of the knights who fled him.

Suddenly, from the corner of her vision, Catherine noticed another knight hurtling across the green; but rather than heading for one of the positions of safety, this man cut an angled path across the field that would lead him to sure collision with either the escaping knights, or with Gray.

Her heart leaped into her throat, and she shifted forward, her fingers clutching the edge of the enclosure wall until her knuckles turned white. Others in the crowd saw, too, she realized, as a tense silence settled over the area. When the charging knight howled a battle cry, the crowd gasped, and Catherine gripped the wall tighter to prevent herself from crumpling back onto the bench.

God preserve her, it was Eduard.

The hairs prickled up on the back of Gray's neck an instant before he heard the blood-curdling roar. Whipping his head toward the noise, he saw a flash of red and white and felt the bone-jarring impact as the knight's steed slammed into his mount at almost full tilt. His stallion gave a shrieking whinny, and then the sky and the earth tumbled together in a sickening whirl. When it stopped, he found himself flat on his back on the field; the fall had knocked the wind from him, but he knew he couldn't wait to recover. Struggling to stand, he cursed at the shooting pain that went through his right thigh, even as he raised his sword to ward off the blow that swung in hard from his opponent.

It only took an instant to recognize Eduard's device—and even less for raw hatred to spill through his veins to mix dangerously with the battle lust he already felt. He'd done everything he could to avoid confronting his rival directly on the field today, trying to protect the fool's life. Now he couldn't hold back, even if he wanted to.

Gray spun around to fend off another blow and was knocked off balance by the pass of Eduard's steed. But as he started to pitch backward, he reached up and dragged Eduard from his mount. They landed together in a crashing heap, and Gray bit back a growl as the impact jarred his injured leg again.

"Damn you, Camville," Eduard snarled, pushing and grappling with him as he righted himself. "Give over and agree to ransom!"

"Never!" Gray took deep breaths, trying to keep rage from gripping him too tightly, from blinding his vision with the red heat that made his mind shut down for the kill. "'Tis you who'll be damned," Gray muttered, "if you don't cease now, while you still can."

"I'll take my chances." Eduard lunged forward, and their swords clashed. Neither would give ground, but when Eduard stumbled back, it seemed as if he'd had enough; then with a bellow he attacked again, using his knee as a battering ram. He slammed into Gray's wounded leg with a sickening thump, and Gray's vision erupted in flashes of light as pain engulfed him.

Everything seemed to slow. Gray felt every breath of air rasp into his lungs, heard the grinding screech of his armor as he crashed to his knees. Still Eduard came at him, yelling like a madman, swinging his blade down in a stroke meant to kill. At the last second, Gray raised his weapon to deflect the blow, and Eduard's blade sliced sideways, gouging into his shoulder rather than his head. Burning warmth cut through him, hot blood seeping into his sleeve even as the strength drained from his arm.

All was quiet for a moment, as Gray absorbed the shock of his wound. He looked up slowly, feeling dark, dangerous emotions swelling, coming to life. He gripped his sword tighter, willing power to return to his muscles. And then the beast inside him thundered out of control.

Shooting to his feet, he hurtled at Eduard, heedless of anything but the need for answering blood. Through the haze of red he saw Eduard's eyes widen, saw him trip over himself as he floundered back, trying to avoid the powerful sword thrusts. But Gray was relentless, driving and slashing. A long, drawn out roar burst from his lungs, and he pushed his enemy back and still back.

It was all Eduard could do to block the blows raining down on him, each one seeking to spill his life's blood. But then he tripped, arms wheeling as he crashed to the field; his sword popped from his grip with the impact, and he lay there, helpless as a fly on its back.

Battle lust coursed hot and thick through Gray as he stood over his adversary and raised his weapon in both hands, point down. He heard nothing but the rush of his own blood in his ears, felt nothing but the gnawing hunger for vengeance, saw nothing but the faceless enemy he needed to crush.

With a battle cry, he prepared to drive his blade home into Eduard's chest—when a woman's voice pierced the well of his rage like an icicle plunged into his heart.

"Gray, please don't! In God's name, I beg you, please don't kill him!"

It took a few seconds for the plea to penetrate his mind and a few moments more for awareness to come back and shake him from the throes of his battle trance. He felt as if all the pieces of his body were disjointed as he turned his head stiffly to the side to see who had spoken to him.

The blurring in his vision began to fade, and he recognized his wife. She stood less than ten paces away, tears streaming down her face. His gaze locked with hers. Dimly, he realized that she must have climbed from the pavilion, exposing herself to grave danger by running onto the field. Now her hand reached out to him, and she sobbed softly. All else was silent.

Almost against his will, the warmth of life began to seep back into his limbs, into his mind and his heart. He glanced back to Eduard, who lay still and helpless at the point of his sword. He struggled internally, thirsting to drive his blade home and finish the barbaric deed, while at the same time finding himself unable to ignore Elise; her entreaties pulled him away from the violence, tugging at the last vestiges of his compassion.

"Please, Gray, no more. Let him go, I beg you."

The last was whispered, yet it resounded through his soul as if pealed on all the bells of heaven. Of a sudden his rage ebbed away. He closed his eyes for one, brief moment. Then he looked back at his wife.

"Christ," he muttered, throwing his sword onto the field. He tilted his head back, took a deep breath and unclenched his fists. Without another glance at anyone, he turned and began to walk away from the scene of battle.

But in that instant, Eduard sprang up and rushed at him, dagger drawn.

Even as Gray whirled around to face him, Eduard's cool blade pierced below his ribs and withdrew with stinging force. Surprise mingled with shock. Vaguely, Gray realized that it was his own blood spilling hot and slick over his tunic and hands. It splashed onto his legs, and he looked down at the gushing wound in his side as if he was apart from it, viewing it from a distance.

When he glanced back up, his head felt light from loss of blood. He took a few steps back, but his vision whirled, and he thought he might fall to the field. Gritting his teeth, he forced himself to stumble forward again. He grasped the front of Eduard's tunic, yanking the bastard closer, even as he cocked his arm back for the blow.

And as the darkness closed in on him, Gray tensed every muscle with whatever strength was left in him and slammed his fist right into the middle of Eduard's sneering face.

Catherine bit the inside of her cheek, reminding herself to stay calm and in control as the men laid Gray on a pallet in a chamber off of the great hall. But from the moment that Eduard had attacked her husband, all she'd wanted to do was scream until she went hoarse.

"Bring me some water, hot wine, clean cloths, and my needles," she managed to command.

Some of the servants departed to do her bidding, and she began the task of loosening Grayson's clothing. *Hurry.* Her mind raged in frustration as she fumbled with the unfamiliar knots and clasps of his armor.

"Here, my lady, allow me," said the knight who'd helped to carry Gray from the field. Grateful, she took over holding the cloth he'd kept pressed hard against Gray's wounded side, while he made quick work of removing Gray's bloodied surcoat, hauberk, and tunic. Then he stood and carried the ruined garments from the chamber. Everyone else had already rushed out in search of a priest and Sir Alban.

She was left alone with her husband for the moment. Shock and fear made every second seem like an hour, heightening her senses. Catherine looked down at Gray, her heart wrenching at the sight of him lying so still, eyes closed, his handsome face drawn and pale. The powerful muscles of his chest and arms were smeared with blood. Even with the pressure she exerted against it, the dagger wound still seeped. She knew that they needed to stop the flow or risk his dying from it.

A sob began to build in her throat, and she pressed harder against the puncture. Gray groaned and turned his head, though his eyes remained closed. His massive chest rose and fell in barely perceptible movement.

"Quickly!" she shouted as two squires came running in with the hot wine and linens she'd requested.

"How bad is it?" Alban asked when he burst into the chamber a moment later, followed by another squire who carried her needles. Blood covered Alban's face, and she saw that his right hand was wrapped in bandages. He rushed to kneel next to the pallet. "Holy Mother Mary, he's unconscious."

"Take this," Catherine commanded, and Alban pressed his weight into the cloth at Gray's side so that she could more easily dip the linen in hot wine. "You," she nodded to the third squire, "Heat the metal rod near the hearth. Then hold this needle to a flame until it's blackened. Let it cool, and thread it with that silk there. I need someone else to fetch herb pots. Marjoram and fennel will do. And bring some nettle juice as well."

Everyone scrambled to obey. One of the servants put more wood on the fire, making the room heat to an almost unbearable temperature. Catherine used her shoulder to wipe the sweat from her eyes as she waited for the iron to be prepared. She knew that there'd be no time to dally once the pressure was removed from Gray's side.

Finally, all was ready. At her signal, Alban released the cloth, and she used the wine-soaked linen to catch the flow of blood and swab it away, revealing the extent of the wound. When it was clear enough to see, she poured hot wine over and into the two-inch wide puncture. Gray came awake then, cursing and thrashing. Alban held his friend still as Catherine murmured a prayer and then an apology; she hefted the wool-wrapped handle of the iron rod, glowing red-hot now, and pressed it into the bleeding gash.

Gray roared in agony and tried to throw himself from the pallet, but Alban pinned him down, cursing along with him. "Get him something to ease the pain," he barked at a squire, who nearly tripped in his effort to fetch a goblet and strong, herbed wine.

"Nay," Gray muttered at first, turning his head aside when the cup was brought to his lips. Someone pressed it to him again, and he dashed it aside, growling, "No wine! Just some water."

A beaker was brought. Gray sipped from it and then fell back, his face ashen, mouth tight. "Saints, Alban, did you need to scorch me with the iron?"

"If you wish an honest answer, my lord, yes," murmured Catherine, nudging Alban aside to inspect the cauterized area. "The wound was bleeding heavily enough to take your wits from you, and we had to stop the flow." She saw now that the flesh around it looked red and sore, but the puncture itself had turned to a blackened scab. Nodding in satisfaction, she stepped aside and began to prepare a poultice for it from the herbs the serving boy had fetched for her.

Now that the worst of the danger seemed past, a weakness flooded her limbs. Her breath caught in her throat, and she forced herself to blink back tears of relief. Concerned that someone might notice her reaction, she moved farther from the pallet and sat at a stool to work the poultice.

From that position, Alban blocked much of her view, but she couldn't stop herself from glancing toward her husband as she mashed the marjoram and fennel together. Gray showed improvement already. He had Alban prop him to a half-sitting position with cushions, and though 'twas obvious that his wounds still pained him, he was managing to carry on a hushed conversation. Someone brought more water, and Catherine was surprised to see her husband dutifully sipping from the beaker. When he'd emptied it, he handed it back to his friend.

"You're being almost agreeable for a change," Alban chuckled. "Mayhap I ought to arrange for you to be knocked about the field more frequently if I can get such cooperation from you afterward."

"Knocked about? Ambushed is more like. Where did they take the whoreson after he stabbed me?"

"They carried him, senseless, from the field; he's

being tended in another chamber, bleeding from nigh on a half dozen slices. 'Tis said you broke his nose for him, too."

Gray scoffed. "He deserved no less. I should have killed him when I had the chance."

Catherine looked down with deliberate concentration as she poured hot wine over the herbs she'd crushed, but she saw from the corner of her vision as Alban gestured toward her with a murmur.

Her husband fell silent, obviously not wishing to offend her, and her heart welled with regret and grief. More than anything she wanted to beg his forgiveness for staying his hand on the field. But unless she exposed the lie of her identity, 'twould be impossible. She could never tell him that she hated Eduard even more than he did, but that his death would have placed her children's lives at greater risk.

"Aye, well, I owe you thanks for seeing to my wounds, friend. I'll not forget it," Gray finally said.

"'Twas not my doing. Your wife made the decisions for your treatment before I knew which direction to turn. 'Tis she who saved your skin this day."

Silence reigned again. Alban stood and moved toward the door, and suddenly Catherine felt Gray's stare on her.

"My lady?"

She looked up, meeting her husband's penetrating gaze and telling herself that the sudden heat in her cheeks was only from the warmth of the chamber. "Aye, my lord?" Catherine kept her gaze constant, though the sight of Grayson reclining nearly naked on the pallet was most unsettling. Some of the usual glint had returned to his eyes, and she tried not to notice the way his powerful muscles rippled as he shifted to a more comfortable position.

"I require your assistance, wife. And more of your tending, if it so please you."

The heat in her face intensified, and she clutched the mortar and pestle as she rose from her stool to make her way to the pallet. Alban coughed lightly and mumbled something about checking on the other injured. Then he was gone, leaving her alone again with Gray.

"I was just finishing with this poultice for your wound, my lord. It should speed the healing and take away some of the pain from the burn." She tried not to look directly at Gray, now that she stood less than an arm's length from him.

"And this?" he asked, indicating the cut on his shoulder. "I see you have your needles at the ready. Will you be stitching it so I may keep what little remains of my blood inside my skin?"

Catherine hazarded a glance at him, uncertain whether or not he mocked her. He appeared in earnest, his focused gaze eliciting another flush of heat in her cheeks. She turned away to fuss with a new strip of linen, soaking it to prepare it for the poultice.

"Aye, my lord. That wound was not so urgent as the other, though I did intend to close it as well."

"And glad I am that you'll be using a method other than scorching to heal it."

Catherine's mouth tightened as she sat next to

him. She stared down at the cloth as she smeared the ointment over it. "Truly I did not wish to pain you with the iron, but I saw no other way to stop the bleeding. And if the flow continued, I was afraid that you might—" She paused in mid-sentence when his finger gently caught under her chin and lifted, raising her gaze to his.

"Nay, truly, my lady, I wish to thank you for your care of me. The hurt you inflicted was not so much."

" 'Twas enough to make me regret the giving of it."

"Aye," he murmured. "And yet I've suffered much worse at other hands. My own included." He released her chin and looked away.

His enigmatic words intrigued her, at some level even frightened her. That he'd been wounded before seemed likely, considering the battles he'd fought as a knight. But when he spoke now he seemed to recall a particular suffering, a defined instance in his memory, and she couldn't help but wonder at the cause of it.

"My lord?" She waited, uncertain whether he intended to speak further on the subject. But he only shook his head and breathed deep, which made him wince as the movement stretched his wound.

"Mayhap you should apply the poultice now, lady, and stitch the other gash. I'll not be lying abed long."

"You'll not be rushing about anytime soon, either. The wounds need time to heal, and I'll not have you tearing them open to taint and fester." As she spoke, she began to wrap the strip of linen around his waist, centering the poultice over the burn. She punctuated the last of what she said by yanking his bandage tight, drawing another wince from him.

"I've a feeling that if a festered wound didn't lay me low for stirring too soon, you would, lady," he answered with the hint of a smile. "Do you always nurse those in your care so aggressively? You're like a mother hen, pecking at her chick when it gets too near the stable cat."

"Aye, well when you're used to tending chicks who are always skinning their knees and romping underfoot—" Catherine abruptly swallowed the rest of her words and stood to fetch her needle. *Heavens above.* How could she have been so foolish as to let such a memory slip?

Gray remained silent, though she could tell that he studied her. She tried to keep her hands from trembling as she knotted the end of the thread, in preparation to stitch him.

"So you've had children in your care, then? I didn't realize you—" His questioning came to an abrupt end when she jabbed the needle into his shoulder.

"Aye. My niece and nephew often stayed with us." She tried to sound unconcerned. Pulling the stitch through, she tugged it secure and then stabbed again, before pausing. "Are you certain that you don't wish to drink some of the herbed wine the serving boy brought? 'Twill at least dull the sensation while I finish the stitching."

"Nay," Gray muttered, obviously rigid with discomfort. She was relieved that her effort to divert his attention, deplorable as it was, had born fruit.

"I prefer to keep my wits intact," he added. "'Tis why I don't partake of strong drink. Why I haven't for nigh on seventeen years."

Catherine contained her surprise. Most men she knew relished their ale and wine, preferring intoxication to almost any other pastime. She fixed Gray with an intent look. "Do you also object to herbed cider, or water that's mixed with healing extracts?"

"Nay," he admitted, "as long as the herbs don't dull my wits. 'Tis the clouding effects of alcohol that I won't abide."

"Then here." Letting the needle swing from the thread in his shoulder for a moment, Catherine sprinkled some of the crushed marjoram and fennel into a water vessel, then added a few dollops of nettle juice. She swirled it together and handed it to Gray. "Drink it down in one gulp. 'Twill ease the pain, as well as speed the healing inside. The taste would improve with honey, but if you quaff it quick enough, it will not matter."

He drank it down with a grimace, coughing and shaking his head once it was swallowed. "Saints, but the stuff wouldn't taste better if you poured an entire bowl of honey on it. I'm beginning to think that you enjoy tormenting me, what with the iron, then the needle, and now this."

Catherine suppressed a smile. "And you, my lord, sound more like an unruly boy than the fierce warrior you showed yourself to be on the field today."

"I doubt that anyone will even think me skilled in

the fundamentals after today's spectacle." He looked at her askance, and she was relieved to see that his good humor hadn't completely disappeared. "'Tis not my custom, you know, to swoon at a tourney."

"Aye, but 'twas not a lack of skill that led to that." She paused, weighing her next words carefully and knowing that while she might not be able to tell Gray the truth of why she'd asked his restraint against Eduard, she could at least try to make some amends. "I—I wish to beg pardon for Eduard's cowardice against you, my lord. 'Twas his weakness and my interference that led to your wounding, and I regret it most heartily."

When she mentioned Eduard's name, Gray's eyes darkened. Once she finished, he remained quiet for a while. Not a muscle of his face moved. Finally he answered, "Then don't compound the error by taking on the guilt of it. You may have asked me to spare your brother's life, but 'twas I who chose to comply. Let us agree to leave it at that."

She nodded. Turning her attention back to his shoulder, she finished stitching the cut; in silence she knotted off the silk and cut the needle free. Gray cleared his throat but seemed lost in his own thoughts, so she continued to prepare a cloth to wash away the dried blood around the stitching. When she finished cleansing his shoulder, she moved to the rest of his torso, wiping the stains away with smooth strokes.

As she worked, she recalled the battle between her husband and Eduard in her mind's eye, remembering the look on Gray's face as he'd turned to her, and seeing again the emotional struggle in the depths of his gaze when she'd begged him to listen to her.

But in the end he'd walked away. Gray had looked into her eyes, and at the moment when he might have plunged his sword into Eduard's heart, he'd walked away. *For her sake.*

Warmth rushed through her even more potent than what she'd experienced in the pavilion when he'd attached her ribbon to his armor. It welled up and filled her; sudden moisture bathed her eyes, and she murmured, "My lord?"

Gray glanced to her. "Aye?"

"I know you wish to leave it be, but I need to say one thing more about this afternoon, if I might."

He nodded, his expression both cautious and questioning.

Catherine took a deep breath and forged ahead. "I think that you are a truly noble knight, my lord. You showed fairness and honor today, far more than anyone could expect, and I—I wish to thank you for it. 'Twas a lesson in nobility that I'd never glimpsed before in my dealings with men."

Her face flamed as she spoke, not only from the voicing of her most intimate sentiments, but also from the liquid heat that had begun to unfurl inside of her as she pulled the warm, wet cloth across her husband's chest and abdomen. It suddenly occurred to her that she was ministering to a virtually naked, completely virile man. A man with whom she would eventually join in the most intimate of ways.

A man who was staring at her right now, by sweet

heaven, as if she was the most beautiful woman in the world.

Her breath came more shallow. Her fingers clenched the cloth, and drops of water trickled down his belly. She caught the spill quickly, but silence stretched on as she worked over him, winding her tighter and tighter inside; she felt the heat of his gaze on her, adding to the heightened atmosphere. Finally, she could bear it no longer, and she pulled away to wring out the cloth.

"Wait," he murmured, his voice husky as he gripped her wrist. "You missed a spot."

The words sent tingling warmth up Catherine's spine, and she glanced up. His sensual expression devastated her, making the linen drop from her hand to land with a faint plop in the basin. "There's a little more right . . . there," he added, twisting toward her to show a rusty smear that ran from the flat just below his navel, downward, where it disappeared beneath the rolled edge of his *braies*.

Catherine licked her lips, realizing that her mouth had gone dry. To stall for time, she said, "I— I think the water has cooled overmuch. Let me freshen it." Hands trembling, she emptied the basin into a waste barrel near the door. Then, walking to the fire, she dipped out several ladles of simmering water before adding some cool cups full from a pitcher.

"Here," she murmured as she sat next to him again. "Tell me if this is too warm. My hands are used to it, but your stomach and . . . well, what with that part of you being covered all of the—or at least, most of the time—" Catherine came to a stuttering halt, and a flush crept up her neck again. She pressed her lips together. "I just meant that you might be sensitive to the heat."

While she spoke, a slow smile had spread across Gray's face. "Aye, lady, I'm sensitive enough to it. And I'll be sure to let you know if 'tis too hot for me to bear."

With a curt nod, she stroked the linen across the muscled planes of his abdomen. The dusting of ebony hair there thickened below his navel; she tried not to notice how the wet cloth made his hairs whorl together, or how his hips seemed to tilt slightly back, revealing a sudden, unmistakable swelling beneath his *braies*.

Her pulse quickened, and she paused in her ministrations to look up at him in uncertainty. But his eyes were closed. He leaned back against the bunched up blanket that served as his pillow, seeming completely contented. Even relaxed.

Heat flooded her cheeks again. Relaxed was the last word she'd use to describe her own state right now. She kept her gaze trained to the area she washed, pointedly ignoring the spot below his waistband as she rushed to finish quickly; her cloth skimmed along the edge of the garment, dampening the fabric as she gently rubbed to remove a particularly stubborn bit of blood.

She lingered there, fighting the urge to delve beyond that barrier, trying to ignore her desire to see if he looked as impressive to the naked eye as he appeared with the layer of fabric covering him.

She was just mastering her emotions enough to pull away, when he subtly lifted the rolled edge of his *braies*, causing her hand to slip beneath it on a downward stroke. She gasped and Gray groaned as the force of her motion slid the wet cloth—and her palm—across the hot, rigid length of him.

At that moment the door swung open. Catherine jerked back, and Gray shifted with a wince. The serving boy turned red as he looked from his master to Catherine and then back again. Finally, he averted his gaze, staring straight at the wall behind them, announcing, "My humblest apologies, my lord, my lady." The boy's voice cracked as he continued, "But I come with report from the sentries. A caravan has been spotted, approaching from the East. Sir Alban thought it best to inform you, my lord."

Gray sat up a little, holding his side and grimacing. "Are they outfitted for war? Look they ready to attack?"

The boy shook his head, so nervous and embarrassed that Catherine could see his knees quaking; the tops of his ears glowed scarlet. "Nay, my lord. Sir Alban said naught of that."

"Then why the summons? Tell Briggs to have chambers readied to accommodate them if they're nobility, or victuals served and a place to pitch their tents if they're but passing travelers."

"But my lord, I—I think you should come down yourself, if 'tis possible. The caravan—they be nobility all right, my lord," the boy stammered. "Sir Alban recognized them by their pennant."

"Well, son? Who is it then, that needs bring me

from my chamber when I'm being tended for my wounds?" Catherine could tell that Gray was trying hard to keep his temper in check. But when the boy answered, he came bluntly to the point, and Catherine thought that her heart might stop in her chest.

"Why, 'tis the king, my lord!" The boy finally met Gray's gaze, his eyes wide with the wonder of a child. "King Henry himself has come with his caravan, and he's about to gain entry to Ravenslock!"

Chapter 5

⁓⚬♽⚬⁓

Gray gripped the edge of the table, balancing himself. All of his wounds throbbed, but at the moment the torn muscle in his thigh pained him the most. He knew that his wife had noticed the hidden injury when he'd stood after hearing about the king's arrival at Ravenslock, but he'd foregone wrapping it to avoid being late to the great hall.

Now she stood a little behind him on the dais, silent. They both faced the arched doorway, but still he felt her gaze upon him, sensed the worry emanating from her clear, expressive eyes. The hall was filled with his own people, as well as many of the visiting tourneyers, yet the only sound came from whispers and hushed comments as everyone awaited the arrival of England's young king.

Alban flanked Gray's left. Eduard was nowhere to be seen, and Gray wondered if his wife's brother would dare to make an appearance. As if he'd read his thoughts, Alban leaned in to murmur, "Eduard was still being stitched when I checked on him a few moments ago. 'Tis not likely he'll come out of his sanctuary soon. I doubt he'll want to face the king, looking as he does."

"That bad, is it?" Gray grimaced as he shifted his weight partially onto his wounded leg.

"Aye. His nose is swollen twice its size. One of the women had to pack it with wool to stop its bleeding. 'Tis so distended from the stuff that he looks like a sow caught rooting in a patch of milkweed."

Hearing a smothered laugh, Gray twisted to see Elise; her hand covered her mouth, and his breath caught at the sparkle of humor in her eyes. Yet he couldn't question her unexpected reaction to the news of her brother's condition, because at that moment trumpets sounded in the courtyard.

The doors swung wide, and His Royal Highness Henry III, King of England, strode into the chamber, followed by his retinue of flag bearers, armorers, vintners, men at arms, wardrobe attendants, grooms and ladies. The entire assembly of Ravenslock Castle sank into bows and curtsies as the king passed. By the time all of his retainers had filed into the vaulted hall, the room looked more like a crowded marketplace than a spacious chamber in the greatest estate ever gifted to one of England's knights.

Gray pulled himself to his full height as he faced his Sovereign. At six and twenty, Henry was a tall, impressive man, yet he was not well liked by all of his barons. In the seventeen years he'd worn the crown, he'd chosen numerous and often unpopular favorites as political advisors. Many of England's nobles whispered of rebellion, angered by the constant stream of foreigners he welcomed to court. Gray, however, had decided to bide his time. Until the need arose, he saw no reason to act out against the man who ruled the land.

"Welcome, Your Highness," Gray called loudly, though the effort sent a burning lance of pain through the dagger wound below his ribs. "You honor us with your presence. Care you for some refreshment after your journey?"

He felt more than saw Elise move closer to him, her skirt whispering against his legs as she positioned herself at his side. Her hand slid, warm and comforting, beneath his elbow, supporting him as he bowed his greeting.

"Lord Camville." Shifting his gaze to Alban, who also bowed, King Henry nodded, "Sir Warton." He waved off the courtiers who had rushed forward to help him to a seat upon the dais. He chose to stand directly in front of Gray, scowling as he took in the physical state of his favorite champion. Without speaking further, he reached for the cup of wine a servant held ready for him, drinking deeply before he fixed Gray with another frown. "We see that you've been engaging in something more demanding than the pleasures of your marriage bed. Might it be another one of these tournaments We've forbidden you to host?"

Elise's hand tightened on Gray's arm, but he stood firm. "'Tis true that I sought a bit of sport to celebrate the nuptials you were so gracious to arrange for me."

"Aye, well, in light of the occasion We will over-look the transgression." A thin smile creased the king's cheeks. "Now that you're wed, you must admit We made a fine choice of brides for you." His gaze swept over Elise, but he paused, mild confu-sion replacing his smile. "Yet lady, We must say that you've changed greatly in the years since We saw you first at your brother's knighting ceremony."

Elise dipped into a curtsey, murmuring, "I was but a child, then, milord. I had not yet reached my twelfth year, if memory serves me." Her voice shook ever so slightly, Gray noted, and she cast her gaze to her hands, clenched in front of her.

The king frowned. "Aye, you were small. And ex-ceedingly pale, as We recall." He tilted his head as if to study her, a quizzical look on his face.

"I—I regret that time has not been overkind to me, milord," Elise mumbled.

Gray glanced to his wife, feeling the same twinge as when he'd lifted her veil in the chapel. But she bowed her head, refusing to meet his gaze.

"My wife hadn't mentioned her acquaintance with you, Sire," Gray said evenly, swinging his gaze back to the king.

"We met but that one time," King Henry com-mented, pausing to drink from his wine again. "It must have been . . ." he gestured in vague circles with his cup, ". . . some eight or ten years ago, now.

Isn't that right, Lady Camville?" Henry's gaze pinned her, and Gray noticed that she squirmed uncomfortably under the scrutiny.

"Aye, milord."

"'Twas a fine dubbing ceremony your brother had that day." King Henry laughed as a new, obviously fonder memory came to his mind. "Montford stood stoically in the heat, refusing even to sip some water to refresh himself. A staunch warrior even then. He's served as one of Our best knights since. Second only to you, of course, Camville," Henry acknowledged, raising his cup to Gray.

He drank again, then looked round the chamber, searching among the guests. "Where is Lord Montford, by the by, that he comes not to greet Us upon Our arrival at Ravenslock?"

After a moment of uneasy silence, Gray answered, "He rests in another chamber, being stitched."

The king went still before raising his brow. "Ah." His gaze swept over Gray again, pausing for an instant on each of his visible wounds. "And who, We must needs ask, found means to injure a seasoned warrior like Montford?"

"'Twas I." Gray admitted the truth boldly, looking Henry straight in the eye.

It was as if an icy wind swept through the chamber; every voice hushed, and each gaze seemed trained on the dais. "How unfortunate," King Henry clipped with deceptive calm, "in light of Our command forbidding the two of you from ever taking weapons to each other again."

Gray clenched his fists at his sides, reminding himself to be careful in what he revealed of Eduard's craven attack or his feelings about it.

"Your disobedience aggrieves Us, Camville," the king continued, enunciating each word with cold precision. "It calls your loyalty into question and makes Us wonder at your sincerity in defending Us against Our enemies on the field of combat."

"I have never lost a battle of honor for you, Sire, nor will I, unless the life be taken from me. I am as always your true subject."

"Then I must needs ask why you persist in trying to slaughter Lord Montford against Our command!"

Elise gasped, and Gray stiffened before answering, "'Twas not my wish to fight him." He stepped away from the dais, anger helping him to ignore his painful wounds. "But I could do no less without forfeiting honor."

"He speaks true," a voice called from behind them. Everyone nudged and jostled each other to see more clearly who had spoken. Gray knew without looking that it was Eduard. Yet the bastard's admission was so unexpected, he wouldn't have believed it without proof of his own hearing.

Eduard walked closer; a path opened before him as lords, ladies, and servants backed away to allow him free passage. His movements seemed slow and stiff; it looked as though his back pained him, and several bandages marked the places where Gray's blade had found its mark. However, the packing had been removed from his nostrils; his nose was still swollen, but it would heal cleanly.

Eduard stopped within a few paces of both the king and Gray, so that the three of them formed a sort of triangle as they faced one to the other.

"Montford . . ." the king said, tight with rage. "What have you to say about this forbidden fray?"

"I can say little, other than to confess to receiving a well-deserved drubbing."

Gray looked askance at him, doubting him more with every word that fell from his lips.

"And 'tis Your Highness's humble apology I wish to beg before this assembly, as well as that of my noble brother by marriage, for goading him into battle. 'Twas in sport that I approached him on the field, hoping to collect ransom as a jest so soon after his wedding to my sister."

The king looked ready to explode, but whatever he was feeling, it was only half of what Gray himself experienced. "What mean you by this?" Gray growled under his breath. "If you play another mockery with me, Montford, I warn you, 'twill be answered in blood."

Eduard turned full to face him, his expression so contrite as to make the very angels of heaven welcome him with an embrace. Gray's eyes narrowed, and he saw the king's gaze shifting back and forth between them.

"Nay, brother, 'tis no jest." Eduard bowed his head. "I must needs beg your pardon for the injuries I did to you, and hence to my sweet sister," his gaze swept over Elise, "when I pursued you on the field. I fear I was overzealous. And when you threw down your sword and walked away after besting me, 'twas to my dishonor that I leapt up and used my dagger against you."

The king turned, incredulous, to Gray. "You threw down your blade and walked away?"

"Aye," Gray answered, never breaking his gaze from Eduard's face, "though I can assure you that it will never happen again."

Silence settled thick over the crowd. The king stared and scowled, while Gray fought against renewed rage bubbling hot in his blood. That Eduard worked another travesty here was clear, but why? What could he gain by admitting his guilt before the king?

Finally King Henry made a scoffing sound and spun to face the assembly. His cloak billowed around him in regal folds. "We will rest here for the remainder of the day," he called, his voice echoing tight off the great chamber's stonework. "Seek you a place and prepare for the banquet. We leave on the morrow, at sunrise!"

Then turning back again, he muttered, "Camville, Montford—come with Us." He stalked away toward Gray's private solar off of the great hall, leaving the men to make their way after him.

Gray glanced at Elise, whose face was ashen, her eyes trained on the floor. But Alban met his gaze, his brows raised in an expression that echoed his own uneasiness. 'Twas a time for diplomacy, his friend seemed to say, not for the settling of scores. Nodding agreement, Gray strode forward, his jaw clenched, and his steps stiff but purposeful. Anger at Eduard still gnawed his gut, but he forced himself to suppress it.

Alban was right. More important matters than a desire for vengeance needed to be addressed right now. The signs were all there, God help them, and Gray knew as well as any that the next minutes might well determine certain key aspects of his future and the achievement of his goals.

As much as he despised the political games required on occasions such as these, 'twas the harsh truth that the Royal Lion of England needed soothing. Unless reparation was made, some kind of concession given, Gray knew that his Sovereign's razor-sharp claws were extended at the ready—and prepared to scratch their measure of blood from his already battered flesh.

A quarter of an hour later the solar door remained firmly shut. Catherine had been sitting at her place on the dais, hands clenched in her lap, as she waited. She'd struggled unsuccessfully to quell the fears that kept assaulting her. Meeting the king had terrified her beyond reason, and the dread still encircled her chest like a band of steel.

She nodded to one of the ladies who caught her glance, forcing a smile to her lips. Grasping her goblet with trembling fingers, she took a sip of its potent brew to calm herself. It didn't work.

Sweet Mother Mary, the king had noticed her appearance enough to comment on it in front of the entire assembly. She'd felt, at that moment, that she might not possess strength to take another breath of air into her lungs. When she'd found voice to answer, 'twas with the first response that sprang to mind. She only hoped she'd remembered Elise's age correctly. That she hadn't exposed herself to more scrutiny, more noticeable discrepancy.

Curse Eduard for leaving her out to dry again. In those weeks before the wedding, he'd tutored her and fed her details that he thought might be useful concerning Elise's life and experiences. But she couldn't learn everything about his dead sister or her habits in so short a time. Now he was closeted in the solar with the king, her husband and Alban.

What if Henry remembered something more about Eduard's knighting ceremony, recalled some detail and questioned him about it, and he unknowingly gave the true facts, glaringly different from those she'd blurted but a few moments ago? His Highness might become suspicious about her, as she sensed her husband already was.

By the Saints, if the lie she lived was exposed, all was lost. Aye, the discovery of Eduard's plots might save her from having to assist in a foul murder, but what then? Her children would surely perish at the hands of Eduard's men. At the very least the king would have her imprisoned for her part in the plot to kill his most powerful, favored champion. Then there'd be no one left to protect her babes, no one to shield them from brutality and avarice.

Sickness clenched her belly, and she forced herself to breathe slowly and evenly. Panic would gain nothing here, she reminded herself. She'd not survived men's cruelty this long by falling to pieces every time she felt threatened. She would be strong. She'd wait and watch, as she always had. And then she'd find a way out of this nightmare, or any other that might come her way to torment her.

The solar door opened. Catherine's gaze flew to the faces of the men emerging from behind its polished panels. The king came out first, his expression inscrutable. She felt a tiny flare of hope. He didn't seem angry.

Then her husband walked through the portal, and her hopes withered. He looked like a thundercloud ready to burst. *Lord of the Storm, they call him . . .* William de Bergh's comment echoed its warning in Catherine's mind as she stood and forced her legs to carry her toward the men. For once she was glad of the many eyes that watched her as lady of Ravenslock; several servants fell into step behind her, awaiting her command for attention to the king.

But her husband spoke first. He motioned for his steward to lead Henry to the large bedchamber. For this night at least, he and Catherine would move to a room down the hall. Henry said something about a rest before the feast, then swung his arm in command of his own servants, before following the steward to the door.

Catherine's fingers twisted in her skirts as she caught Gray's intense expression.

"Is something amiss, my lord?" she murmured, trying without success to pull her gaze from the mesmerizing force of his stare.

"Aye, lady. Much is amiss."

She felt as if she were going to be sick. She looked desperately to Eduard, sure, now, that something dangerous had been said in chambers with the king. But he failed to notice her, having moved stiffly to the table to gulp down a cup of ale even as he gestured for another.

Gray's next comment dragged her attention back.

"King Henry leaves on the morrow for a journey to London, to preside over an ordeal by battle. I was to be his champion in the fight against the traitor who's been charged." A muscle in Gray's jaw twitched. "But the king has elected to use another instead, due to the severity of my wounds."

Clenching his fists, he shifted to give the man responsible for his injuries a look that was half scowl, half wolfish glare. A shudder slipped down Catherine's back as she felt the leashed power in every muscled inch of Gray's warrior-hard body. Even wounded, he was a force to be reckoned with, and it vividly reminded her of the violence that her husband was capable of committing. Of his unsurpassed ability to kill, and how it had earned him his title as the king's High Champion.

"'Tis most unwelcome news," he said, sliding his gaze to her again. "Yet I cannot but choose to obey." She thought that he might say more, but then he simply nodded brusquely and stalked from the hall.

Where he was going, Catherine couldn't tell. He needed time to cool his temper, no doubt. Her guess was that he'd saddle his huge silver stallion and ride. Such jarring would pain his injuries, she knew, but somehow mere physical discomfort suddenly seemed unlikely to affect this man who had transformed before her eyes from flesh and blood to hardened steel.

Alban stepped up from behind her. "Fear not, lady. Your husband will take care not to pull his stitches or strain his wounds overhard. But he'll not be fit for the feast this night until he's burned away some of the demons that sting him."

She turned to face her husband's friend. "Is it that keen of a disappointment to him, then, to be kept from a court battle?"

"Aye, though 'tis not just that. The king also fined him for hosting this day's *mêlée* and issued new sanctions against both him and Eduard for their fighting. He declared that if they ever disobey him in this—if they ever come to blows again—'twill be at risk of all that they have, including their rank as his personal champions."

"I'd have thought that being denied the privilege to engage in constant battle would be a relief, not a punishment."

Alban shook his head. "I cannot speak for your brother, but I know Gray. His purpose in life is to fight and fight well. For King Henry especially, but whenever and wherever he finds opportunity and cause. The king's decision to leave him behind tomorrow is bound to be a sore distress to him."

"But why? It seems so reckless for a man of his wealth and status. 'Tis why there are knights, hundreds of them, to serve in place of a great lord such as he!" Catherine struggled to quell the shrill quality of her voice. If she wasn't careful, she'd lose all composure and go hysterical on him. After the events of the day, her nerves felt tight enough to play like a harp. Mastering her overwrought emotions, she added quietly, "Why does he continue to risk himself time and again if not for the petty sake of more acclaim, more glory?"

Alban seemed to consider how to answer. He gazed long into her eyes, as if reading her ability to hear the truth. Finally he glanced away. "The reasons are deep that drive him, lady, and 'tis for him to tell you the full of it. But know that he burns to see justice done. 'Tis why he craves the position as Sheriff of Cheltenham. 'Tis what keeps him breathing."

With that, Alban nodded his leave and followed Gray's route from the hall. She was left to stand bewildered, trying to make sense out of that which seemed to have neither rhyme nor reason.

None, at least, worthy to explain the commanding, formidable enigma embodied in the man who was her lord husband.

Chapter 6

~~~~~~~~~~~

The feasting was well under way that evening by the time Catherine received a call to the kitchens. A waifish page had darted up to her at table, begging her aid to test the roasted duckling sauce she'd ordered specially prepared, according to her recipe. The cook had fallen ill just the day before, unable to rise from his bed, and his assistant was a young lad, terrified to make a mistake lest he disappoint not only the master and mistress, but also His Royal Highness, the King of England.

Gray had given his consent, and she'd been glad to rise from the formality of the feasting table to attend the duty. Never had she faced an occasion such as this. Her very breath came shallow from the anxiety. Yet Gray's ride of the afternoon seemed to have done him some good, even if his stiff movements

113

belied that he'd strained his injuries. She'd insisted on checking his shoulder and rib dressings before the feasting began, and he'd reluctantly complied. She'd been relieved to see that the stitching and bandages had held.

But with the physical examination had flooded back heated memories of how she'd tended to him right after the *mêlée* and of how he'd encouraged her touch in a much more intimate way. Her cheeks still burned with the thought. Yet she knew that the strange warmth of her feelings for this man she'd married, the man she'd pledged to help destroy, were far too dangerous to indulge.

Now she sighed as she made her way back to the hall. The sauce had needed nothing more than a few more sprinkles of ginger to make it perfect. Catherine smiled as she remembered the look of gratitude that her praise had brought to the boy's face. He'd probably sweated full as much as the casks of chilled sweet wine she'd seen the brewers carry in from the cold cellar. Ravenslock was truly a castle of wonders, she thought, with the most current amenities, including a cooling chamber. She'd never imagined such luxury would exist in all of her life.

Catherine reached the empty, narrow hallway that would lead to the grand opening into the great hall, but a hissing sound drew her back. Eduard stepped into the light of the anteroom, his ruddy, bruised face sharp with contempt. He moved forward like an evil tide, forcing her back until the hard surface of wall stopped her retreat. Then he stroked his finger down the curve of her cheekbone in silent mockery.

"My dear Catherine," he muttered. "'Tis near impossible to find you alone these past hours."

Catherine tried to stand tall, struggled not to cower before him as every inch of her flesh longed to do. She'd faced Eduard's abuse so often in the past months that it seemed second nature to tremble as she awaited the punishing blow that should come next. But she reminded herself that she needn't fear that kind of danger from him any longer . . . only the greater threat of his harming her children if she failed to do his will.

"I believed you to be abed already," she managed to say. "You're usually full into your cups by this time of feasting."

"I cannot drink overmuch this night, thanks to King Henry."

"Why? Does he disapprove of foul-mouthed drunkards?"

Eduard's face tightened, and his hand clenched to a fist. "Your tongue is getting rather sharp these days, Catherine. Would that I could quiet it into pleas of mercy as I have in the past." He glared at her a moment more before adding, "Yet you're still as ignorant as ever. I cannot imbibe too heartily because I leave with the Royal Caravan at sunrise. The king has commanded that I join him on his expedition to observe the ordeal by battle in London. He hopes that separating his two best champions will cool the animosity between us."

"You're leaving?" Catherine echoed quietly.

"Aye." Eduard placed his palm on the wall beside her head, making her cringe. He leaned his weight into it, pressing closer, his sheer size and sour stench intimidating her as it always had. " 'Tis an unforeseen event. I'll not be here to guide you in the next weeks of your task with Camville. The king may decide to keep me for a month or more, but I expect you to continue our course. Work your way into your husband's trust. Into the deepest chambers of his heart." A wolfish smile creased his cheeks. "Prepare him well for the kill, sweeting."

She felt herself blanch, and he laughed, his breath riffling the hair at her temple. Hot pricking jabbed behind her eyes. The bastard was devoid of feeling. Of even the most basic human emotion. But as she stared at his chest, gazing at the immovable slab of muscle and bone that protected his heart of stone, she couldn't stop herself from uttering what she'd vowed never to let him hear again.

"I beg of you, Eduard, by all that's holy, release me from this nightmare. I will give you whatever I have, I will humiliate myself in any way that you wish, but please don't ask me to help you kill this man. 'Tis cold-blooded murder. An abomination to God and mankind and . . ."

Her words faded to silence as he touched her again, sliding his finger along her bodice to stroke a path up her neck, so gently that it seemed a profane reminder of the pain he'd so often inflicted on her. His finger ceased its journey below her chin, digging into the tender flesh there. He jerked hard to make her meet his gaze.

"Did I neglect to mention that I've had your children brought home from fostering at Denton?"

Catherine arched back, feeling as if he'd buried a dagger in her belly. "Oh God, why? You promised not to harm them!"

He grinned wider, the look mocking the Archfiend himself. "They were none too pleased, I'm afraid, to see their dear Uncle Eduard. Little Isabel even wept a bit." The corner of his lip curled. "Rather reminded me of you."

Tears flooded her eyes and she began to struggle against him. "You bastard! What have you done to them?"

"Calm yourself, Catherine." He looked down at her, gripping her wrists to prevent her from striking him. "The twins are safe enough in their old chambers at Faegerliegh Keep for now. But 'tis right that you remember what will happen to them if you thwart me in any way. Several of my people lie in wait here for the sole purpose of watching you in my absence. I'll be kept informed if you're stupid enough to try anything."

She gazed at him uncomprehending for a moment. When realization began to dawn, Eduard smiled and nodded. "Aye, Catherine, sweet. Spies. Neither you nor anyone at Ravenslock knows who they are. It might be the baker's apprentice, or the lady's maid who draws your bath. Mayhap even the squire that serves you at table. This is a huge and prosperous estate. My spies are many, and they are everywhere. Falter in any way, Catherine, attempt to tell Camville of our plans, and I'll learn about it swiftly. And then, my dear, your children will suffer the consequences." He stopped talking and drew his finger quickly across his throat with a slicing sound.

Suffocation squeezed her and welling tears spilled hot onto her cheeks. "How can you do this? You're their uncle, for God's sake. Their blood . . ."

Eduard's expression hardened, and he leaned closer. "No one is sacred, Catherine, remember that. It doesn't take much to snuff the life from children. Their necks are delicate, like baby birds fallen from their mother's nest. All it takes is a flick of the wrist—"

Gasping, she shoved against his chest with all of her strength. He barely budged. Instead he chuckled softly at her renewed struggles, the sound magnified in her ears like the howling of the damned. She pushed against his powerful weight in earnest, trying to raise her fists to beat against him. It had no effect except to make him laugh harder.

A split second later, however, he went utterly still against her, and his smile faded.

"Get your hands off of her Montford, or I swear you won't live to regret it."

Slowly, Eduard turned to face the owner of that inexorable voice—and the deadly tip of his sword. Catherine had thought Gray looked menacing on the field earlier, but it was nothing compared to the expression in his eyes now. His gaze had sharpened to cold, green ice. Eduard backed up, Gray's blade pointed at his chest, until he was pressed against the wall.

"A wise choice," Gray said. Catherine stood a few paces away. She dashed the tears from her cheeks as she gazed back and forth between the two men, feeling the almost tangible hatred rippling tense and hot around them. Eduard looked coiled and ready to spring at Gray, who seemed in turn to be waiting for even the slightest reason to rip Eduard open, belly to chaps.

She clenched her fingers tight to still their trembling. Though Gray stood a little taller, the men were dangerously similar in build and strength. Seeing them in this adversarial pose, wounded as both were, made it easy to understand how they'd risen to the status of the king's champions. They looked like gods of war, their bodies hardened and trained into weapons of destruction.

She shuddered anew, thinking how fortunate it was that they'd not managed to kill each other on the field. Surely 'twas only an act of the Almighty that had prevented what would have in turn brought death to her children.

"Care to explain what you were doing to my wife?" Gray's voice sounded deceptively quiet. Unmistakably lethal.

Eduard's expression shifted, suddenly, and he shrugged. "I was giving my sister a bit of brotherly advice on conducting herself as your lady. That and wishing her farewell in private before my journey of tomorrow." He smiled, though she saw that the look didn't reach his eyes. "'Twas nothing sinister, I assure you."

It was clear that he wanted to strike Gray away from him; he was barely restraining himself, and it gave Catherine a burst of satisfaction to know that for once Eduard was being forced to rein in his brutal temper.

"My lady," Gray murmured, calling her attention back to him, though he kept his gaze and his blade squarely pointed at Eduard. "What say you to this? I would feign believe otherwise, but tell me he speaks true, and for your sake I'll forswear."

Eduard tried to twist his head to look at her, no doubt to glare her into submission, but Gray immediately shifted his stance to prevent the contact. She was left as so oft of late to make her own decision in the matter. The power of independent thought frightened her. She felt unsuited to the task, having rarely been allowed to indulge in decision-making before coming to Ravenslock.

"I—I don't know what to say, my lord."

"Just tell me the truth."

Catherine clenched her fingers tighter together. What could she say? Oh, but she would love to see Eduard suffer for his sins against her. For his threats against her children. But the twins were the very reason she needed to protect him from Gray's retribution. Sighing, she unclenched her hands and pressed her palms flat to her skirt. "'Tis true that Eduard was giving me parting advice in private, for fear he'd have no other opportunity before his departure on the morrow."

"'Twas no more than that?"

She paused briefly. "His ways are not yours, my lord, but that is all that happened."

Gray paused, obviously wavering. Finally he murmured, "Then I am forced to abide by your avowal." He slid his sword back into its sheath and stepped away from his rival, though he continued to position himself as a buffer for her. He indicated the portal to the great hall. "Go, now, Montford, before I change my mind."

Eduard looked ready to explode. He flashed a hate-filled glare at Gray, his gaze flicking over to slice Catherine as well. Then, with a growl, he gritted his teeth and stamped down the corridor. The door to the great hall swung open and slammed shut behind him.

Gray faced Catherine once more and warmth flooded her. She felt shock tingle up her spine, not unlike the sensation she'd had the first time she looked into his startling, beautiful eyes at their wedding. But when he spoke that sensation faded under a wave of regret.

"I had hoped that you would expose Eduard for the brutal wretch he is, my lady," he said softly. He gazed into her eyes, reaching to her very soul, it seemed. The way he looked at her was making her breathless, and she struggled to find some answer for him. Something that wouldn't sound as awful and insincere as she felt. But before she could muster a sound, he looked away. "I'll expect your return to the feast shortly." Then he walked away down the corridor, disappearing into the great hall as Eduard had done a few moments earlier.

She sagged against the wall after he left, bitter emptiness engulfing her. Her chest tightened as she remembered what he'd asked of her during the confrontation. *Just tell me the truth.* By the Saints of heaven, she knew the value of that practice, now more than ever. If only she could follow through with it. She'd prided herself on her honesty all of her life. She'd taught her children to revere it as one of the best Christian virtues. But that had been before Eduard had trampled over her and threatened everything she held dearest with destruction.

Nay, there was no help for her deceptions. Not now at least. Though it galled her to her soul, though it went against every fiber of her nature to continue it, she'd have to maintain this enormous lie that had become her life. Two other far more precious lives depended on it.

She shook her head and turned to begin walking back to the great hall herself, but a tingling up her spine made her pause in her steps. Someone was watching her.

Slowing, she reached out to the wall to steady herself and hazarded a glance over her shoulder. The tingling intensified to a rush of fear. A shadowy figure lurked in the doorway at the opposite end of the hall, back toward the kitchens. The person crouched in the portal to the castle spice chamber, not moving in muscle or breath, it seemed. Only watching.

It was a man, or at least she thought it was. Her heart pounded, and her hands felt icy. 'Twas difficult to tell, he was stooped so low and swathed in so much dark fabric. He looked to be lame, perhaps. Or afflicted with a humped back. Only his eyes showed, glittering dark and intense through the space in his head covering. Her heart leapt into her throat again.

Merciful heavens, he was staring right at her . . .

Gasping, Catherine turned and fled the rest of the way to the great hall. Gripping the heavy door, she pulled it open and then shut it firmly behind her, leaning against it for a moment to regain her composure before forcing herself to reenter the din of feasting still underway in the hall.

She didn't dare, even once, to look back.

Gray watched his wife reenter the hall, making her way timidly around the clusters of people who feasted, drank, and sang with the minstrel who played a rollicking song near the hearth. The king had already retired to his chamber, as had Eduard directly after the incident in the corridor. But many others remained awake, and the revelry still went strong.

Gray knew that he couldn't sleep. Not if his life depended on it. He'd been reliving what had happened in the corridor, shifting between condemning himself for not beating Eduard to a pulp, sanctions be damned, to reassuring himself that he'd done what was right by giving Elise the final say. But as she approached him now, he almost wished he'd gone with his urge to throttle Eduard. She seemed more upset then ever. Apparently allowing her to stay his hand hadn't been the right choice.

When she rounded the end of the hall, one member of the Royal Caravan, a squire to a lesser knight, leapt from the table near her, shouting with laughter at one of his friends. The young man was well into his cups, oblivious to much around him, and Elise shrank away from his abrupt movement and noise. Her skittish reaction might have gone unheeded by anyone at the feast.

Anyone but Gray.

"My lady," he said, his voice even as she regained her seat next to him on the dais.

"My lord."

She was still pale. Her hands trembled when she raised her cup, and he watched with displeasure as her gaze strayed immediately to Eduard's place at table.

When she noted her brother's absence, she seemed to calm a little, but anger spiked within Gray nonetheless. Damn Eduard. Damn every man who ruled those in their care with their fists. He, too, knew what it felt like to be so thoroughly dominated. He'd lived his childhood in fear, always watching and trying to read each expression, each word from his master's mouth. Yet even at the tender age of fourteen, he'd had his masculine strength and size to bolster him against Thornby's threats.

Elise was tall, but she was most definitely female and therefore more vulnerable to abuse. *Just like Gillian had been.*

The thought raked him with claws of steel, and he tried to push aside the images that never failed to lurk close to the surface of his thoughts. He tried to repress the vision of Gillian, gasping his name as he held her. She'd been beaten and broken. Defenseless. And Gray had been unable to stop it. Unable to save his own sister.

But he could help his wife. He'd already vowed to protect her with his body and blood, both as knight of the realm and as her husband. True, the king's command forbid him from killing Eduard, as deserving as the bastard might be. Yet there was something else that he could do to safeguard Elise. Something he would have done for Gillian, if he'd only known how, then.

"My lady?" he murmured. Considering the din of the feasting around them, he'd spoken softly, and yet she startled at the sound of his voice. When she looked at him, the timidity and caution in her gaze sent an aching stab through his heart.

"Aye, my lord?"

"Have you ever held a sword?"

Surprise widened her eyes, their soft hue reminding him again of the blue flowers sprinkled across Ravenslock's meadows.

"Nay, my lord. Never in my life."

Gray paused to weigh what he was about to say, knowing that it would sound daft. He wanted to be logical, but intellect wasn't part of what he was feeling. This sprang from some deep, primal place in him that urged him to protect and shield this woman from anything that might harm her.

He clenched his jaw and forged ahead. "Do you dislike the thought of wielding a weapon, lady?"

"Aye . . . I mean, nay . . . I—" She stumbled over her answer as her face suddenly bloomed with color. "I cannot say that I ever considered the possibility."

"Yet you seem strong, and you have your height to aid you. Do you think it possible? If not, we could begin with daggers and work our way up."

"My lord?"

Now she seemed truly confused; she'd gone completely still, and she was looking at him as if he'd grown a third eye. Gray felt a twinge of remorse. Of course she had no idea where he led with this conversation. In truth, what he envisioned doing with her was as unorthodox as his own donning of gown and veil.

It would be better, he decided, just to spit it out. "I wish to train you, Elise. I want you to learn how to use weapons for defense, to give you enough skill so that you need not fear physical harm from any man, ever again."

She gazed at him, unmoving, not uttering a sound. She was shocked. Mayhap even mortified. Gray tried to read her thoughts but found that they were closed to him. He was preparing to clarify himself, wondering if she'd understood what he meant, when she spoke.

"'Tis a noble gesture, my lord, your desire to teach me these skills. Yet 'tis pointless. Under English law a woman cannot take arms against a man."

"In the act of protecting oneself, 'tis allowed."

"And yet many women have been punished,

nonetheless, for daring to do just that, especially against men bearing title."

Gray stared at his wife, surprised at her quick intelligence and pleased with her stubbornness; this show of spirit boded well for her success in the training he planned for her.

"You argue aptly, lady," he said, "but I must counter that England is still a land of justice and truth. And I vow that I will allow none to punish you for defending yourself against tyranny."

She seemed to hold her breath for a moment. Her gaze slid to her hands, folded tightly in her lap. When she looked at him again, he saw a flicker of interest in her eyes. "'Tis not likely that Eduard would approve of such training. Is that why you wish to pursue it?"

Gray's jaw tightened. "I would have already punished your brother for what he did to you had the decision been mine to make. But barring my own action, I must find other means to protect you from his or any other man's violence. If that means training you in weaponry and defense, then so be it."

Elise's cheeks flooded pink again, and she looked away. "I understand, my lord," she murmured, "and I am humbled by your care of me. 'Tis more than I deserve."

"Nay, lady, you deserve all that honor and respect can afford. 'Tis sinful that you have not received more of both in the past." Gray heard the gruffness in his voice, even as he tried to ignore the warmth that had begun to swell outward from his chest at her praise. He stemmed the unfamiliar feeling by adding, "You agree to the training, then?"

She nodded, her eyes grave as she lifted her face to him. Trusting. Accepting. Another surge of warmth engulfed him. He allowed himself a moment's indulgence to stoke the delicious embers of emotion she inspired in him. He knew that it couldn't last. It never did. But God, how good it was to taste this pleasure again. To let himself feel needed by a woman, if only for a short time.

Too soon it slipped from his grasp. Like an arrow fired true and deadly, the memory of what had happened the last time a woman placed her trust in him pierced his heart.

"We will commence your training as soon as your bruises are healed," he said, clenching his jaw as he tried to push back the memories and the fear of failure that accompanied them. "I leave it to you to inform me when that time arrives."

"Aye, my lord," she murmured.

A shout of laughter from the feasting tables and the arrival of several jesters on the floor prevented any further discussion. Gray tried to concentrate on the antics of the fools. He forced himself to look amused when one of them hit the other on the head while juggling apples. But he felt incredibly distracted, and it wasn't only because of the nearness of his voluptuous bride. He was a man, after all, and such carnal thoughts were to be expected, especially considering that their marriage would remain unconsummated until she was healed.

Nay, his anxiety went much deeper, stemming from a source not so easily dismissed as physical desire. He couldn't help but acknowledge that he'd taken a giant leap off the path he'd planned to follow here, a leap away from safety into the most dangerous arena of all.

He'd promised to keep his emotional distance from Elise. To leave his heart unaffected. But he'd already begun to break his own word, for his vows to stay clear of entanglement seemed to have melted into a sapphire mist. It had billowed up and surrounded him, muddling his mind and making him want to stay wrapped in its seductive embrace forever . . .

Mist the same soft, compelling shade as his lady wife's beautiful eyes.

Chapter 7

Though he'd known she'd come eventually, Gray was still unprepared for his reaction when Elise appeared in his solar a fortnight later and admitted that her bruises were healed. He could commence her training on the morrow, she'd murmured. Then she'd stared at the floor for a moment, cheeks blazing, before glancing up at him again and scurrying away. He'd been left sitting in his chair, engulfed by an almost painful sensation, as if someone tugged invisible, taut threads connected at strategic points to his belly.

He'd spent the remainder of the day roaming the grounds of his castle, restless and sharp-tempered. Nothing had pleased him. He'd felt on edge. Tight as a bowstring. As the shadows deepened to darkness over the lush fields of Ravenslock, his tension had only wound tighter. He'd come late to the evening meal in the great hall to learn that his wife had already supped and retired to their chamber for the evening.

At the news, he'd swallowed his food mechanically, downed the rest of his mulled cider, dismissed his jesters and his courtiers, and stalked up the curved stairs after her.

Now he stood outside their door, filled with the same uncertainty he'd felt the first night he'd come to her. 'Twas ridiculous, he knew. What other man had ever waited more than two weeks to bed his lawfully wedded wife? And yet something still nagged at him as he pushed open the door and stepped into the chamber's gloom.

Moon shadows played a pattern across the floor as he moved closer to the bed, close enough to touch her as she slept. She looked innocent, almost like a child in slumber. He unclenched his hand and reached out, his fingertips pausing but a whisper away from her hair spread out on the bolster. He could almost feel the silken texture of it against his skin. But with a grimace he pulled back and pressed his hand to his side.

He'd fought this same temptation every night since they'd wed, and each night he'd made himself walk away, made himself sleep on a pallet before the fire so that no one would question his absence from their chamber. He'd succeeded in his restraint thus far, spurred by the knowledge that joining with her might bring more pain to her injuries.

But there was nothing to hold him back now.

Nothing, that was, except the haunting shades of his own past.

Elise sighed and shifted, turning away from him. One arm crossed over her chest protectively; the other cradled her head. Just looking at her made Gray's breath catch in his throat. He was struck again by that incongruous, seductive blend of sensuality and spirit that seemed to emanate from her. His heart thudded slowly, and threads of heat tingled through him, spiking shafts of desire that tightened and wound from his belly out to the rest of him as he gazed down at her.

God, how he wanted her. Wanted her with a need so great that it sometimes hurt to breathe. It boggled his mind how it had come to this. Before the wedding, she'd been nothing more than his enemy's sister. He'd trusted that, like Eduard, she'd be easy for him to hate. That he'd simply take her to his bed, do his duty in consummating their irksome marriage, and then promptly dismiss her for all intents and purposes from the rest of his life.

But the opposite had happened. Each day that had passed, every moment that he'd spent with her, witnessing her quiet strength, her intelligence and her beauty, he'd desired her more.

And it was tearing him up inside.

Somewhere in the back of his brain a warning clanged, telling him that once again he played the fool. He'd planned to hate Elise de Montford. Hell, he'd *wanted* to hate her. But he couldn't, no more than he could hate his own eyes or bones. In truth, he was beginning to care for her, and he of all people knew how dangerous that was. Feelings like these could divert him, weaken his purpose—cripple him with guilt for daring to have them at all. He wasn't fit for such emotions. Not he with his stained history and the blood of innocence on his hands.

And yet Elise was his. This was their marriage for better or worse, and it waited only for him, now, to make it a union in truth.

Closing his eyes, Gray tilted his head back and held tight against the pain that washed through him. He let out the air from his lungs slowly, unclenched his fists, and looked down at his wife one more time before pulling off his tunic and sliding into bed beside her.

She stiffened, and he heard a catch in her breathing. It lasted but an instant, and yet he knew that she was awake. She lay on her side, facing away from him, and he gently placed his palm on her waist, sliding his hand forward until it rested on the flat of her belly.

"Elise?" he murmured. He caught the sweet fragrance of her hair and fought the impulse to bury his face in it. Leaning closer, he breathed in her ear, "Let me see you."

She lay still for another moment before rolling on her back, clasping the blanket tight under her chin. She gazed up at him, eyes wide and solemn, and he stroked a wispy curl from her forehead.

"I'd share our bed, this night, lady, if 'tis meet with you."

At first he wasn't sure she'd answer. Then she

whispered, "Aye, if 'tis your will," before averting her gaze and biting at her lower lip. She clutched the coverlet tighter to her chest, her knuckles white.

Gray paused. He'd never bedded a woman who seemed so nervous. Her apprehension surprised him after the passion she'd shown the night of their wedding. Of course, then her actions had stemmed from fear that Eduard might learn their marriage remained unconsummated. She'd needed the bloodied sheet as proof for her brother and the rest of the guests, and so she'd pursued their joining. Now no such pressure goaded her. She was free to act as she truly felt, and it was clear that she was frightened.

'Twas natural, he supposed. He was a larger man than most, and she was a virgin. He couldn't forget that. He needed to go slowly and gently, to use all the skill he possessed to make her desire their joining before he took her in body as he had in name.

Breathing deep, Gray willed himself to patience. He cupped her cheeks in his palms, bringing her gaze back to him before pressing a kiss to the tip of her nose. He moved his mouth in a gentle path along her cheek and to the delicate hollow beneath her jaw, feeling encouraged when she made a soft sound in her throat and reached up to rest her fingers tentatively on his shoulder.

Even that light touch sent a jolt of fire through him. He moved over her and kissed the sweet temptation of her mouth. Her eyes fluttered closed and she sighed again. But she seemed to tilt her head up a bit, as if offering herself more fully for his taking.

He didn't hesitate. He deepened the kiss this time, gently coaxing her to return the caress. She seemed to respond in kind, but when he stroked the tip of his tongue along her lips and into the honeyed recess of her mouth, she pulled back; her eyes snapped open, and she blinked up at him, alarmed and uncertain.

Innocent.

Aye, innocent—he'd forgotten again. Damn his need. He'd allowed it to overwhelm him, and it had caused her to stiffen fearfully against him; both of her hands once more gripped the blanket as tight as if it were a rope to salvation.

Pulling back, Gray held his breath. *Slow*, he reminded himself. *Go slow. You'll fright her if you push too fast.* He leaned his forehead on hers for a moment, then pulled away to kiss lightly along her cheek again before moving on to nuzzle her earlobe.

"'Tis all right, Elise," he murmured, hoping to soothe her. "There's naught to fear. I'll be gentle with you." He stroked his fingers rhythmically along the side of her face and over her shoulder and arm, trying to dispel her anxiety and ease her back into their lovemaking.

He breathed in her sweetness, feeling a heady swirl of sensation wind through him. Brushing his lips over the tender spot below her ear, he pressed more fully against her and feathered kisses down the side of her neck as his passions began to swell.

And it was then that he noticed it.

She was trembling. Tiny shudders that shook her body like a leaf in a storm, rippling, it seemed, from the very center of her. Gray lifted his head, concern jabbing him with tiny pinpricks. Her teeth were clenched together, her eyes squeezed shut.

"What is it, Elise? What's wrong?"

She gave no answer, though a single tear slid down her cheek. His gut felt hollow as he moved his fingers to brush it away. But it was followed by another and still another, until she sobbed softly and turned her head. The pit in his stomach opened wider.

"Sweet Jesu, lady, why are you crying?"

She didn't speak at first, only shaking her head. "Forgive me," she whispered at last, her voice ragged. "But having you touch me so . . . I—I can't think of anything but—"

She stopped talking when he gently used his finger to tilt her face to look at him. Fresh tears wet her cheeks, seeming to flow without end.

He gazed at her, his heart wrenching. He felt lost and powerless in the face of this sadness. After a while he sat up and shook his head, running his hand through his hair. "I cannot continue this if the very act of lying with me in our bed terrifies you to tears."

"Nay, my lord, 'tis not fear of you," she said, her voice catching as she sat up next to him. "'Twas only that your touches made me remember . . ." She swallowed hard. "They made me remember how Eduard would stroke his fingers over my cheek as you just did. Only he did so right before he beat me. He said it pleased him to caress me first, so that I might experience the fine contrast of sensation when he struck me." She looked down at her hands clenched tight in her lap. "He repeated that phrase each time he beat me, until I could hear the words without him speaking them. Until I could not escape them."

"Each time?" Gray asked hoarsely. He watched the shadows playing over her face, knowing they reflected darker emotions lurking inside. He felt the sudden urge to pummel Eduard to a bloody pulp. "He abused you other times, then, beyond what I saw the night of our wedding?"

"Aye," she whispered, struggling to meet his gaze. "He struck me almost daily at Faegerliegh Keep." In the moonlight her eyes looked wet and full, vulnerable with remembered pain. When she tried to muster a smile for him, his heart broke a little more.

"'Tis perverse, I know, but because of him, cruelty and tenderness are strangely twined for me. When you were so gentle a moment ago, all the memories rushed back." She shook her head, her pallid face suddenly resolute. "And yet I promise to try harder to overcome it, my lord. I will work to control it and make myself—"

"Nay," Gray broke in harshly. Then he gentled his voice. "Nay, lady. I will not have you anything more than you already are."

"But I—"

"I'll not allow it. Your ease with me will come in time. Think no more on it until then."

She looked as if she might protest again, so he moved his head until he held her gaze, adding,

"Make no mistake, Elise. We *will* consummate our union—but I am not so bound to my own pleasures that I cannot wait until you are ready to share this with me, without fear or remorse."

Even in the dusky light, he saw her face regain some of its color; a delicate flush spread across her cheeks, and she looked away. But to his dismay, she seemed ready to cry again.

His mouth softened to a smile, and he shook his head in mock reproach. "Ah, lady, we'll be floating away on a stream if every thing I do and say keeps releasing that wellspring of your eyes."

A soft, throaty chuckle escaped her, and she blinked, smiling back at him even as she swiped her hand over her cheeks. "You're right, of course, my lord. I will cease immediately."

"Gray."

He saw a flash of white teeth, and her gaze dipped again. "Aye, my lord." The pink of her cheeks deepened. "I mean, Gray."

Warmth flowed through him, and for a brief moment he reveled in the bittersweet sensation. By heaven, but she possessed a beautiful smile. He wanted to bask in its light a little longer, but the weariness in her eyes made him gesture to the pillows. "Come, now, wife. No more talk. You must be tired, and you'll need your rest if we are to begin your training tomorrow."

She gazed at him in silence a moment more, her haunted expression intensified by the room's shadows. But then she nodded and lay down facing away from him, offering no protest when he stretched next to her and pulled her back into his arms. She even nestled against him, shifting until he too was forced to move so that she wouldn't feel the rigid swelling of his manhood in response to her buttocks curving so sweetly against him. Soon her breathing settled into the regular rhythms of slumber.

Closing his eyes, Gray held very still. She felt so warm, so good in his arms. As he watched her sleep, felt the gentle rise and fall of her breast, breathed in the delicate fragrance of her skin and hair, a pang twisted his insides. He waited for it to pass, but it remained there, a steady, dull throb of emotion that he felt as ill prepared to face as he had the prospect of this marriage when King Henry had first commanded it of him.

Christ, but just holding her like this was difficult. It taxed him in a new and unexpected way. He'd fought in hundreds of battles, laid siege to countless foreign lands and wielded his sword in an infinite number of bloody conflicts, but he'd never faced anything quite like this. It was a war against himself this time—a savage combat waged in his own soul.

Walk away, his logic told him. *Save yourself, before 'tis too late.* But he couldn't. Something deeper forced him on. God help him, but he wanted to protect this strange, lovely creature that was his wife. Wanted to comfort her and make her feel safe . . .

Wanted to love her.

Gritting his teeth, Gray sucked in his breath and pushed the thoughts back. He rested his chin on the top of Elise's head, feeling the silken texture of her hair as he struggled with the moment.

'Twas near impossible to try to sleep with her curled against him like this; along with his other torturous thoughts, his mind raced with images of what he'd planned to do with her this night. Ways he'd wanted to touch her, passions he'd hoped to make her feel. And yet for all of the delicious torment it caused him, he knew that he'd be loath to relinquish their embrace.

Before long, he acknowledged defeat. The bliss of dreamless, easy rest would not be his this night. He opened his eyes and exhaled. Elise made a little sound of contentment and, moving her head where it rested on his arm, she reached up and sleepily gripped his hand, clasping it to her chest as if it were a favored poppet.

Gray froze, barely suppressing a groan at the sensations shooting up from his palm and fingertips, cupped now over the soft warmth of her breast. Against every instinct he tried to pull his hand away, but she only nuzzled closer, rubbing her cheek against his shoulder and pulling his arm to her bosom more tightly. He held still in shocked silence a moment more. Then he tipped his head back with a soft, chuckling groan.

Nay, sleep would not be his this night.

With a murmured prayer for strength, he used his free arm to pull the coverlet secure around them; then he held his wife close, settling in for the long, quiet passing of the hours. He waited in the hush, watching the dark outside the window deepen to midnight, then to sapphire blue. He watched and waited, saw stars burst to life and wink out, followed the rising moon in all of her splendor until she dipped as slowly again beneath the curve of the horizon. And still he lay, soaking in the calm and peace he found cradling Elise in his arms.

He, Baron Grayson de Camville, man of action, war, and bloodshed, Champion Knight of King Henry III, scourge of every tournament and battle-field in England, lay very quiet and still in those hours before dawn, simply holding his wife and waiting . . .

Until pink clouds tinged the golden dome of the heavens, signaling the start of the new day.

When Catherine awoke, she felt the sun streaming in on her, warm and comforting. Something lingered in the back of her mind, leaving her strangely content. Without opening her eyes, she stretched until each joint of her arms, legs, fingers and toes rebelled in happy protest. And then she remembered.

Eyes snapping open, she looked around the chamber. By the sun's strength she guessed it to be well past *terce*, which probably explained why the room was empty but for herself and a small mound of clothing perched on a chair near the fireplace. A jagged scrap of parchment rested atop the garments.

Scrambling from the bed, she padded to the chair. Beneath the note lay a pair of breeches, a shirt and tunic. The message scrawled on the vellum instructed her to don the garments for her weapon's training this morn. She was to go to the clearing just beyond the castle wall shortly before *sext*. It was signed simply, "Gray."

Gray.

His name echoed through Catherine's mind, leaving a swirl of warmth in its wake. He'd been so kind, so patient last night. Why hadn't he pressed his rights with her? She'd never known a man to show such restraint. It had been unusual enough when he'd forgone their joining on the night of their wedding, but this . . . this exceeded all bounds. He'd denied his own pleasure again, and for her sake. Because she hadn't been able to stop herself from weeping in his arms.

She sat down hard in the chair, pulling to her chest the garments he'd left for her. She'd felt so confused last night. At first she'd been nervous— aye, and with the same worries she'd borne from her first night here. But before long, Gray's kisses had made her feel . . . well she didn't quite know how to describe it. She'd never felt so before. 'Twas different. All she'd ever known when Geoffrey kissed her was disgust and fear.

But with Gray silky warmth had swept through her, and she'd realized that she wanted more of the feeling. That it felt wonderful. And when he'd stroked his tongue so gently inside her mouth . . .

Liquid heat settled low in Catherine's belly at the recollection. Her cheeks felt hot, and she jumped from the chair to pace across the chamber. Lord have mercy on her, but when Gray had kissed her like that, she'd almost forgotten the horrible reason she'd agreed to wed him. She'd wanted to forget.

'Twas only when he'd brushed his fingers across her cheek that the spell had been broken. She hadn't lied to him; his gentle touch had sent images of Eduard hammering into her thoughts. The pain and fear of those times had ripped through her in the darkness, unmerciful and harsh. Their onslaught had left her feeling exhausted, empty and aching.

But miraculously, Gray had seemed to understand. He'd comforted her, held her as she slept without complaint or guilt. She'd felt safe in his arms. And he'd asked for nothing in return. Nothing. He was like no man she'd ever known before.

But is he the kind of man you can trust with your secret? A man you can trust with your children's lives?

The question taunted her. She put down the clothes and swallowed the nausea that rose in her throat. Dare she consider that possibility now, with Eduard gone from Ravenslock and Gray sure to be alone with her all during her weapon's training?

Nay. 'Twas too soon to decide. She'd known him but two weeks.

Many men were capable of going to great lengths to hide their true and often foul natures. What if Gray was a man of that ilk? Aye, he'd been kind to her, but he was still a fierce warlord—the king's best champion, a man capable of great brutality on the field. What if he secretly harbored a darkness that exceeded even Eduard's hate? 'Twas possible, she knew. Many men had proved their baseness to her time and again.

She didn't need to decide right away. There was still time. Eduard wouldn't return to Ravenslock for another month at least, and perhaps once she knew more about Gray, 'twould be easier to know what to do. Until then, she'd trust nothing and no one.

She busied herself with getting ready for the day, trying to calm her mind. Except for old Heldred, the village weaver, who was the nearest thing to a friend that Catherine had known during her years at Faegerliegh Keep, there'd been no one to confide in, no one to believe in but herself, for as long as she could remember. And for now, at least, she resolved to be content to keep it so.

Pulling the shirt and tunic over her head, she sat and began to roll the unfamiliar breeches up over her knees. Compared to her usual layers of smock and kirtle, the fitted garments felt peculiar. But she managed to lace them up and take a few paces across the chamber.

She lifted her leg, kicking and swinging it back and forth. 'Twas an odd sensation. She supposed such free movement was necessary for learning to handle a sword, but she wasn't sure that she liked it. The tightness of the breeches left her feeling almost . . . well, almost naked.

Catherine stood up straight and ran her hand down her leg, smoothing her palm over the fabric. Strange or not, 'twas part of her life now. Her training would commence today. And with it, she'd cross another new threshold.

Raising her arms, she combed her fingers through her unruly hair and began to plait it, thanking Jesu that time, at least, was still hers to command. For a little while, anyway. As for the rest? She'd leave it to God to help direct her to the path she should take in saving her children from Eduard's evil . . .

And in coming to some lasting decision about the unusual, powerful man she was bound to, body and soul.

Gray almost sank to his knees when his wife came striding into the clearing beyond the castle's outer wall just before noon. She'd done exactly as his message requested, he noted, his mouth going bone dry. He reached for his water-skin, making a mental note to take care that no one else saw her like this. Adding to the allure of her form-fitting garments, she'd pulled her hair into a single braid that hung down her back. It swung in provocative rhythm over the curve of her buttocks, enticing all sorts of thoughts into his imagination.

Swallowing hard, he cursed himself for his bright ideas. That they'd need to prolong consummating their union indefinitely had become more than apparent last night, when she'd dissolved into tears in their bed. He'd resolved himself to wait, planning to be patient and give her time to adjust. To let the destructive memories of Eduard fade a little.

But now, seeing her dressed in the garments he'd left for her, he suspected that maintaining his physical distance from her was going to be even more difficult than he'd anticipated.

He shifted the sword he'd chosen for her use

from his right hand to his left before balancing it against a tree stump. He'd trained more than his share of squires in the arts of war, but none of them had possessed a voluptuous shape and legs as long and graceful as a doe's. His wife's breeches encased every subtle curve, right to where his sight was halted by her tunic at the tops of her thighs.

Gray swallowed again, dragging his gaze from that spot and subduing the heated image that sprang into his mind, suddenly, of those long legs wrapped around his waist in the throes of passion. He looked in desperation to her face, seeing the uncertainty clear in her eyes. Her heightened color told him that she experienced uneasiness about her unorthodox clothing as well, though he doubted that her thoughts traveled the same, heated paths as his.

He cleared his throat. "Perhaps we should begin." Gesturing toward the sword, Gray indicated that she should take it up. He'd chosen it as one that would be best suited for her training, since it was light, and its hilt flowed in leaner lines, making it a better fit for a woman's smaller hand.

As she approached, he added, "Once you're used to the feel of the sword in your grip, we'll master some of the common strokes and then practice the training skills used daily by the men."

She nodded, lips tight, as she reached out to grasp the hilt. "'Tis heavy," she murmured, almost to herself, as she balanced the handle's weight in her palm, though still without lifting it.

"Aye, but a light blade compared to many. 'Tis

the size used most oft by a squire, though I warrant it feels more ponderous to you than it would to a well-muscled lad of sixteen. You'll grow accustomed to it as the training brings strength to your arms."

She glanced to Gray, hesitant.

"Go ahead," he tried to reassure her. "'Twill take time, but you'll learn to handle the blade. You must become one with your weapon before you can use it effectively. And you must learn to respect its power." He nodded again. "Lift it up, that I may judge how best to proceed with your training."

Feeling awkward and silly, Catherine hefted the sword with both hands, gripping it by the metal hilt. *By the Saints, but it was heavier than she guessed!* Somehow, she managed to lift it waist high. Staggering for balance, she tensed her arms, fighting to keep the blade aloft even as the tip began to veer earthward; she lurched forward as it slammed home, its point digging into the soft ground near her feet.

Her breath came out in a rush, and she felt more than saw Gray frown from his position behind her. But when she turned to catch his expression, he altered it to one of concentration and continued to watch her, arms crossed in front of his chest.

Heat flooded her face, and she looked back at her metal opponent. This was proving to be more difficult than she'd imagined. But Gray had told her that she was suited to this kind of training, even though she was female. She recalled the rush of pleasure she'd felt at his words. It had been the only time in her life that she could remember feeling anything but shame about her unnatural size.

Catherine narrowed her eyes, glaring at the deadly weapon dangling from her grip. Gritting her teeth, she dragged it upward again, straining and holding her breath until she managed to balance it at chest height. It wobbled there for a moment or two, and she threw Gray a small grin of triumph. But then suddenly the blade shifted in her hand.

It crashed to earth again, and an exasperated cry burst from her. Defeat balled in her throat, and she gouged the dirt with the sword's tip, wanting to fling the cursed weapon away as far as she could. Only the knowledge that her puny show of strength would undoubtedly embarrass her further stayed her hand.

Just as she was trying to muster enough energy to attempt hoisting it again, she realized that Gray had moved in behind her. Surprise blossomed to shock when she felt him press against her back to enfold her in his arms.

When he slid his hands down from her shoulders, placing them over hers where they gripped the hilt, jolts of sensation surged through her. Her eyes drifted shut of their own accord. She felt his palms, warm and hard, caressing her hands; she sensed his strength behind her, supporting her, protecting her, guiding her. And then he whispered in her ear . . .

"Save your anger for your enemies, wife. It serves no purpose to direct it at your weapon."

Catherine's eyes flew open, and she twisted to look at him, her mood sparking to ire again at the thinly veiled amusement in his damnably green gaze.

"Aye, well, my enemies will have a fine laugh at my fumbling, my lord. I'll nary find means to lift this weapon, and they'll lop my head off for me."

She felt his entire body tighten—all but for his hands, which stroked the tops of hers more gently round the hilt. The warmth of his breath wafted soft against her cheek. "Nay, lady. By the time I finish with you, I warrant you'll be able to keep even me at bay. 'Twill take hard work to get there, but we will make it happen together, I promise you."

Together. That word sent a strange thrill of longing coursing through Catherine, until it settled deep in her heart. But she had little time to nurture the feeling; he lifted her arms, her hands still gripped by his to her sword. Then he took a few practice strokes, and she felt the swish of the blade, reveled in the tantalizing play of his chest muscles along her back.

"Spread your legs wider."

His soft command made a warm blossom of heat unfurl in her belly, and she was appalled for one sinking moment when she thought that he'd heard the catch in her breathing. He paused before continuing with the movements of their arms, but other than that he didn't seem to have noticed. Yet it was all she could do to concentrate on the strokes and arcs he guided her through in the next minutes.

She couldn't seem to focus. All she could feel was the warmth of his body behind hers, his arms circling her with their strength, the powerful muscles of his legs pressed into the backs of her thighs from his own wide stance . . . the delicious sensation of his breath tickling her ear on each exhalation.

Her muscles felt like butter and her belly a fluttering swirl of sweet, hot liquid, when he finally released her a few minutes later and stepped away. Though she'd exerted herself but little in the exercise, her breath came as fast and hard as if she'd raced up a hill.

When the reason struck her, 'twas with stunning force. What had happened last night was but a taste of this unbelievable feeling. This was raw, full-blown desire, and it took her so much by surprise that she crumpled to her knees where she stood.

"Are you unwell, Elise?" In one swift motion, Gray knelt next to her, taking her hand to chafe at her wrist. "Here." He reached for a water skin, untied it, and held it to her mouth. "Take a drink."

She tried to protest that she was fine, but he pushed on until she took a quick swallow. It was probably for the best, anyway. Certainly better than telling him the true reason behind her moment of weakness.

"I feel much better now," she said, rising to stand.

"Don't move so quickly."

"I'm fine," Catherine protested, dusting off her knees with her hands. " 'Tis just the heat. The sun shines bright today."

Gray shielded his eyes and glanced up. "Aye. 'Tis near midday. We began our training too late. You'll need some refreshment before we continue." He gestured to the shade of a nearby tree. "Come and sit you down where 'tis cooler, while I fetch the basket."

Catherine frowned. Basket? She'd thought they'd be going back to the castle to eat with the others. But she had to admit that she was hungry. Her stomach rumbled as she sat beneath the tree, reminding her that she'd yet to take any food or drink today. And Gray was right about one thing. It was much cooler here, and it *did* feel good to sit.

She watched him return from his stallion with a woven basket. The lid was attached to the ragged sides with a frayed strip of willow, and she raised her brow as he sat beside her with it.

"That basket looks as if it could use some mending."

His mouth quirked up on one side. "Aye, I suppose it could. I've had it for years. 'Twas with me on Crusade."

"I amend my remark, then. 'Tis in better shape than I guessed if it survived the war in Egypt."

"Yet it has seen better days." He caught her gaze as he unwound the tattered silk that held the lid on tight. "At our wedding feast you talked of searching for willow swamps. Do you possess skill enough in weaving to repair the basket for me?"

Now it was Catherine's turn to smile, though she hid it in the act of smoothing the ground for their meal cloth. Of course he couldn't know that she'd been weaving willow of much finer texture than his basket since she was a seven years child.

"I think I might be able to manage it, my lord, provided we find an ample supply of withies to harvest in the next weeks."

He handed her the cloth, and she spread it in front of them, adding some smaller folded linens for wiping their fingers and mouths later. As he busied himself with pouring wine into her cup and cider into his own, she stole another glance at him. "You must have had many adventures while Crusading for the Holy Cause. Sir Alban talked of the battles you fought together while in Egypt, and he swore that you'd saved his life."

Gray laughed. "Alban tends to exaggerate. I didn't actually save his life. And 'twas hardly heroic."

"Nay? Alban made it sound so, though he suggested that you tell the story better than he does."

"He did, did he?"

"I would like to hear it."

He ran his hand through his hair. " 'Tis of no matter, really. Nothing you'd find of interest, I think."

Catherine looked down at her lap. "If you don't wish to tell me, I understand. 'Tis just that I so rarely heard news of the Holy Crusade, and I had hoped to learn more about it."

Gray remained silent for a moment, and she felt his gaze on her. Finally he looked away. "I only hesitated to tell you, Elise, because this particular story is less than savory. I don't object to your hearing of it if it is what you wish."

She nodded. "Aye, please."

"Very well. Alban and I were on our way home,

passing through Turkey. We stayed for a while in a village not far from the border, thinking to give ourselves some rest before undertaking the rest of the journey home. Instead, we found trouble. A local man charged Alban with raping one of their women and getting her with child. Alban was arrested and brought to trial under Turkish law, which meant that he faced almost certain execution."

"How terrible! What did you do?"

" 'Twas a difficult case. Alban had never even seen the woman, and yet no matter what either of us said, the man who'd charged him refused to be dissuaded." Gray took a swallow from his cup and shrugged. "So I made some inquiries, discovered the truth, and took care of it."

Catherine waited for him to explain, but he remained silent. "Well?" she finally burst out. "What happened? How did you save Alban from execution?"

"Once I knew the truth I just tracked the—" Gray paused. Then he shook his head. "Nay, perhaps I'd better not say more. I fear the rest of the details are not fit for delicate ears."

Catherine raised her brow. "We're here because you're training me to wield a *sword*—hardly a delicate pastime. I think 'tis safe to say that I can endure the full telling of your story."

A beat of silence passed. Still without comment, Gray reached into the basket and took out a leg of roasted fowl and a hunk of bread. He handed them to her, his generous mouth flirting with a smile. "I concede your point. But before I'll go further, you

must eat something. I'll say no more until you do."
He gestured to the food, adding a plump yellow
apple to the mound.

Seeing that it was hopeless unless she cooper-
ated, Catherine picked up the chicken and took a
bite. She chewed deliberately, tempted to glare at
him for making her wait to hear the rest of his story.
But after swallowing the first mouthful, she forgot
her ire. The roasted bird was delicious. Perfectly
seasoned and moist. Her stomach growled again, almost as if in thanks.

She took several bites of the bread and a few
more of the chicken, interspersed with swallows of
her wine, noticing that Gray polished off his portion
as well.

When she'd finished the last bite of apple, she
sighed and leaned back against the tree, patting the
unusual fullness of her stomach. Contentment
flowed through her like an elixir, enticing her to
close her eyes for just a moment. Ah, if only she
were a cat right now, free to nap in the warm caress
of the sun . . .

With a groan, she forced herself to sit up and
open her eyes. If she napped, she'd never hear the
rest of the tale. She tidied the cloth that had served
as their table, wiped her cup clean, placed it back
into the frayed basket, and then faced Gray with an
expectant look.

He'd tipped his head back to drink his cider, and
he paused in mid-swallow, catching her stare from
the corner of his eye. When his playful gaze met her
far more stern one, he jerked the cup down and

wiped a drop that trickled onto his chin. Then he coughed as if he were choking, but the effort was so feeble that she knew it was a performance for her benefit, and a weak one at that.

"Is something wrong?" He asked in a raspy, exaggerated voice.

Oh, but he was maddening. "Aye. You promised to finish the story about Alban once I ate something. I've done as you asked, and now I'm waiting to hear the rest."

"Ah, yes. The tale." He took his time using his small square of linen to wipe his fingers and his mouth, before swabbing his cup dry and tossing it and the soiled cloth back into the basket. Then he looked at her again. "I can't remember where I left off."

She almost rolled her eyes. "You were going to tell me how you freed Alban."

"Well, I didn't free him, exactly. That took care of itself, once I exposed the liar whose sin had brought evil down on Alban's head."

Liar. Sin. Evil. The words sent a jolt through Catherine. She stiffened, but he continued to talk, seemingly unaware of her agitation. "I told you that Alban was imprisoned, awaiting trial, and that he was certain to be convicted." He paused. "This is where the story turns indelicate. Are you sure that you want to hear the rest?"

She managed to nod, not trusting that her voice wouldn't give away her own guilt.

"As you wish." He picked up a twig, twisting it in his fingers as he talked. "In many cases of deception, I've found that he who protests most loudly often bears the most fault. 'Tis a quirk of human nature. And this man who'd charged Alban was most vocal about the damage done to the young woman. Naturally, my search for the truth began with him."

Catherine fiddled with the edge of the cloth. "How did you get him to admit his guilt?"

"I didn't. I learned where he kept his liaisons with her, arranged for the village justices to come with me one night to the spot, and then quite literally, exposed the man with his braies down." Gray frowned with the memory. "'Twas not pleasant, especially when the council sought justice against him. He was punished not only for defiling the woman, but for swearing to a falsehood on top of it."

"He was executed?" Again, her voice seemed to come out in little more than a squeak.

"Nay," he shook his head. "He was the child's father, and so they let him live to provide for it. But they ensured that he'd never father another child again."

She swallowed hard. "Oh."

"Alban was released with reparations, and we continued on our journey home." Gray tossed the twig aside and looked straight at her. "And so you see, lady, 'twas the truth and not I that freed Alban. 'Tis a much more powerful force than mere man."

Catherine's stomach rolled, and her meal suddenly felt very close to reappearing in a most unpleasant way. She lurched to her feet, reaching out a hand to steady herself against the trunk. "I see.

Thank you for telling me the whole tale. But now I—I feel the need to move around a bit. Perhaps we could continue our training."

Gray rose to stand next to her, and again she was overwhelmed by his sheer size, by the rippling muscle across every inch of him. " 'Tis a good sign, your willingness to press on," he said, shaking out the blanket, then folding it and placing it back in the basket with the remains of their food.

When he faced her again, encouragement and pride lit his eyes, making her want to wither to the ground with shame. "And I have a few more strokes I'd like to teach you, only this time with a child's wooden sword. 'Twill allow you to practice on your own between our meetings."

Catherine nodded, weak-kneed, as she followed him back into the clearing. She picked up the wooden sword he handed her and tried to concentrate on the strokes he began to demonstrate. But her mind kept straying, even as her arms performed the motions of the practice.

There's naught to fear. He knows nothing. She repeated the phrases in her mind like a prayer as she moved through the strokes. For now everyone was safe. As long as Eduard believed that she would carry out his evil plans against Gray, her children would remain unharmed. And as long as Gray knew nothing of the truth—of who she really was, and of what game she played with him—her life could continue secure and unscathed.

And yet somehow she sensed that 'twas not her

life that was in danger here at Ravenslock Castle. 'Twas a far more serious risk she took, with each breath, every minute, each day she stayed in the company of the castle's great lord. Aye, evil plots or no, she needed to tread very carefully . . .

Because she sensed that Baron Grayson de Camville might well possess the power to steal her heart and soul away from her forever.

Chapter 8

The sun was just coming full above the edge of the horizon when Gray strode up the stairs to his bedchamber the next morn. He felt invigorated by his ride, full of energy and anticipation.

And hope.

For the first time in years, he'd risen from bed looking forward to something other than battle. The new day was fresh with possibilities, not the least of which was another opportunity for private weapons training with his wife.

Memory of yesterday's lesson with Elise still burned in his mind. Whenever he thought on it, a strange thrill shot through his body and up to his face, making his mouth want to edge up into a smile. Just last evening he'd had to subdue the impulse with force; he'd been overseeing his squires'

159

efforts at polishing armor, and one of the lads had caught him grinning at nothing while he rubbed down a rusty helmet.

Such strange behavior wouldn't do, especially around the men. But it had been difficult to maintain a serious expression. Pleasant thoughts seemed to overwhelm him without warning: thoughts of Elise's eager efforts to maintain her sword stance, or the feel of her graceful body pressed against his when he'd guided her through that series of strokes. Or the sight of her in those breeches . . .

He grinned again, taking the last three steps to the landing in one bound. When he'd left her this morning, she'd been sleeping peacefully. Now he hoped to awaken her with a kiss and ask her to prepare for another round of training before the sun rose too hot in the sky. A quick lesson in lunges, perhaps, after breaking their fast. Aye, that sounded like a plan.

But as he approached their chamber, a strange noise made him pause. His grin faded under a tingle of warning. He heard crying. Soft, heart-wrenching sobs that made him scowl as he got closer to the room's portal.

Lifting the latch quietly, Gray nudged the door open with his toe and peered inside. The chamber sparkled with morning light, illuminating a scene that took his breath away. 'Twas the embodiment of a stained glass window he'd once seen in a great cathedral in France, depicting the Virgin Mother, praying as the angel Gabriel descended to tell her of her Immaculate Conception.

Like Mary in the picture, Elise knelt by their bed, a shaft of sun streaming in on her and imbuing her flowing, turquoise robes and rich brown hair with celestial radiance. But unlike the Blessed Virgin, his wife wasn't praying. She was weeping over something she held clasped in her hands. Something small and oval, compassed in a golden frame.

'Twas the portrait of the twins, the same likeness that had produced such a strange reaction from her when Eduard presented it at the wedding feast.

Gray pressed his lips together, the tingle in his belly intensifying. Why in hell did it disturb her so? This weeping, this grief over something so simple seemed unnatural.

He nudged the door open wider and stepped into the bedchamber. "Elise?" he called.

With a gasp, she twisted to look at him, scrambling to her feet and leaving the portrait lying half-covered by the folds of blankets. She swiped her hands over her wet cheeks. "My lord—I mean, Gray! I did not expect you soon. I—I thought that you would be sending for me at a later hour."

"I wanted to surprise you."

She looked as though she wished to say something more, but then she only exhaled softly and remained silent, casting her gaze to the floor.

Gray tried to keep his suspicions from overwhelming him as he glanced to the oval likeness still hidden in the bedcovers. After a pause, he asked, "Your niece and nephew, I've forgotten what they are called."

"Ian and Isabel," she whispered, as if saying their names pained her in some way.

He nodded, keeping his expression even. "Aye. You were crying over them. I wish to know why."

Elise paled, standing before him as still as a statue. But then she blinked, and her gaze seemed to search him for a moment before veering away to stare again at the floor.

"'Tis nothing but a woman's weakness, my lord," she finally murmured, "to weep over what she has left behind. 'Tis the way for every new wife, is it not?"

"Perhaps. But 'tis also a husband's duty to ensure his wife's comfort and happiness, in so far as he may," Gray answered, even as he questioned her explanation in his own mind.

She seemed not to breathe as he walked over and picked up the portrait, running his finger over it. As before he was struck by the likeness these children shared with her. Of course, that was explained easily enough; they were of her blood—her brother's offspring.

He suppressed the twisting in his gut and handed the portrait back. "Why is it that you feel the absence of these children more keenly than any other person from your life before we wed?"

Her gaze remained steady on him. "There is no one else for me to miss. I was never close to Eduard. And Geoffrey and . . . and his wife I but saw infrequently these past years. As I told you whilst I stitched you after the *mélée*, the twins often came to visit, and I grew close to them. I cared for them," she said, clenching her jaw and looking away, "as if they were my own babes."

"And that is why you were weeping just now?"

She nodded, her lips trembling.

"Then 'tis simple enough. If it distresses you so to be parted from them, I will arrange a visit to Faegerliegh Keep, so that you may see them and put your heart at ease."

"Nay!" Elise gasped, blanching as her gaze snapped back to him. " 'Tis not possible, or at least 'tis not wise to do that."

"Why not?" he asked quietly, studying her.

"Because the twins do not reside at Faegerliegh Keep any longer." Her fingers squeezed tight round the gilded frame. "For the past year they've fostered at Denton, another three days ride beyond Faegerliegh. Too far to go for the sake of my foolishness." Abruptly, she walked over to the chest and deposited the portrait beneath its lid. " 'Tis of no matter, my lord. I'm sure that I will see them soon enough, without a special trip."

Her back was to him as she spoke the last bit, but he saw the stiffness of her spine and the way her hands clenched down on the trunk until her knuckles turned white. Yet when she spun to face him again, she'd wiped all signs of sadness from her face. All except for the haunted look in her eyes.

Gray frowned. " 'Twould be no hardship, lady, to arrange such a journey, even to Denton, should you wish it. Do not hold back for fear of cost or time."

She only shook her head and struggled to fix a heartbreaking, wobbly smile on her face. "I'm only being silly. I must learn to govern myself better as your wife, not as a childish maiden. The past must be left behind to live in the present, is that not so?"

Another pang cut through him, inciting him to action. He crossed the room and, reaching up, brushed a golden-brown curl from her cheek. He fought the same helplessness that had overwhelmed him two nights ago, wanting more than anything to take away this sadness that seemed to fill her.

He threaded his fingers through her hair, cupping her face and leaning closer to brush his lips over her brow. "Ah, Elise. I only wish—I would only that I could make you happy, lady."

She sucked in her breath, her eyelids fluttering down. "I am, my lord," she whispered, finally. "In truth when you are near me, I am happy in a way that I have never known."

He pulled her to him, then, pressing her cheek to his chest, and she wrapped her arms around his waist with a deep sigh. He held her there for a long while, uncertain what else to do or say.

In the end, action seemed better than words. After a few moments more, he released her gently and said, "Then be it as you will, lady, concerning your niece and nephew. For now, I ask that you meet me in the clearing after you break your fast. We should begin your training early today."

"Aye, my lord."

He nodded and walked from their chamber. But her sadness seemed to follow him, filling him with shadows that he knew would be difficult to shake. Once again he'd failed to assuage her pain, and it bothered him. He'd wanted to soothe her. To make her happy, as she made him.

He descended the rest of the steps to his solar and pushed aside the tapestry on the wall. Using the key, he strode out of the castle, into the lists and the clear light of day, resolving to put thoughts of Elise and her pensiveness out of his mind for now. After all, 'twas but a small matter, really. Not something he should spend overmuch time trying to understand. He had offered to make the trip to see the twins with her, and if she chose not to go, there wasn't much he could do about it.

And yet as he strode toward the stable, he couldn't stop himself from thinking about his wife's sad eyes. Or wondering if he'd ever learn to understand the workings of her enigmatic heart.

Catherine pressed her hand to her breast, trying to still the thundering there. That had been close. How stupid of her, to allow herself those moments of grief for her children. But she'd had that horrible dream about them. About Eduard closing them away in a dark, cold place. Their little faces had been twisted in pain as they cried out to her, reaching out and calling her to save them . . .

Sucking in a ragged breath, she ran her hand over her eyes and shook her head. She wouldn't think about it anymore. She couldn't. 'Twas too dangerous. It left her feeling exposed, vulnerable. She'd almost blurted the truth to Gray when he'd asked her why she was crying over them, and that might have been a terrible mistake. Anyone might have been listening.

"My lady? I've brought you some warmed cloths and water for the morn—and this jar of salve from out in the hall."

Catherine jumped at the brusque voice, whirling to face its owner. Mariah came in the door without waiting for acknowledgement, one strong arm piled high with folded squares of creamy linens and the salve pot, the other gripping the handle of a steaming pitcher. She glanced sideways at Catherine with a penetrating, almost knowing look, as she set down the towels and pot to pour the scented water into the washbowl. Threads of doubt wound up Catherine's back at the attention.

"Can I get you anything else, milady?" Mariah asked, straightening and placing her hands on her hips.

"Nay, thank you," Catherine answered, reaching to pick up the jar of salve, glad to have it for some of the blisters that already reddened her palms from yesterday's training. Perhaps Gray had anticipated her needs and sent it up. But then why hadn't he just given it to her himself when he came to their chamber?

She frowned. "Where did you say you'd gotten this ointment?"

Mariah scowled. "I didn't get it anywhere, milady—'twas forgotten in the hallway, on the little table outside your door." Mariah shook her head and mumbled something about it not seeming meet for the lady of a castle to leave her things carelessly here and there. Then she glared once more at Catherine before sweeping through the door and shutting it behind her.

Catherine stood, stunned, uncertain what to think. That this mysterious jar of salve wasn't hers at all seemed the least of her worries; Mariah and her apparent dislike provided more concern. The woman was rather bold for a servant. This wasn't the first time she'd made pointed view of her, and her expression was never the least bit submissive. It had been the same that first morning, when she'd come at Gray's bidding to help Catherine with her hair.

Could Mariah be one of the spies Eduard spoke of? Might she have been listening outside the chamber when Gray questioned her about the portrait, to see if she would reveal information that Eduard had forbidden her to tell?

Sinking to sit at the edge of the bed, Catherine hugged the jar to her chest and stared at the unyielding silence of the door Mariah had closed so soundly behind her . . .

Left, as so often of late, to face her fears and worries alone.

Chapter 9

"Come now, 'tis not so difficult. Just cast to the water and pull back smoothly. The motion must be fluid if 'tis to bear fruit."

Struggling to follow Gray's suggestion, Catherine bit her lip and squinted at the offending string dangling from the rod in her hand. A snip of blue feather fluttered near the metal tip at its end, seeming to mock her efforts. The cast-off plumage was supposed to lure the fish, enticing them to bite, though why they'd choose to eat something so awful Catherine couldn't guess. It didn't look very appetizing to her.

Giving her pole a few practice flicks, she eyed the dripping feather again. It was a sad sight indeed. Aye, she'd warrant her bedraggled bait had more to do with her lack of success so far this morn than want of proper technique. But she'd not say as much to Gray. To do so would only invite him to devise some practice even more outrageous, she was sure. As it stood, her muscles and joints already groaned from his inventive methods of training these past weeks. When she wasn't in the clearing practicing sword strokes, she was doing other strengthening skills that he conjured up.

Just two days ago, he'd told her to drag baskets full of dirt back and forth across the tilting yard; last week he'd insisted that she raise buckets of water from the well until she could lift no more. Before that, he'd had her climb a gnarly tree to fetch each of a score of linen strips that he'd tied among the upper branches.

And now this.

Yet she couldn't deny the success of his methods. Her hands were developing protective calluses from wielding her weapon, and she could sense the growing power in her arms, back, and legs. For the first time in her life she felt strong instead of merely awkward and clumsy.

Still, she'd debated begging off of this exercise today, thinking the better of it only when she realized that, unlike some of the other activities he'd put her to, this task had another purpose; theoretically, there would be fish to eat at the end of it.

Bolstered by the thought, she shot Gray a look, pulled back her arm and cast the line again, jerking it toward the water. She followed his direction to the very point, and was rewarded with naught but disaster; she succeeded only in catching the line in a thorn bush that jutted from the stream. Biting back an unladylike curse, she yanked the pole, ensuring that the string knotted itself more securely on the branch.

"Saints preserve us, but this is useless!" Stomping over to the bush, she began to snatch at the string to untangle it. Thorns jabbed her as she worked, and she gritted her teeth.

The fact that Gray stood there watching only fueled her temper further. She felt his gaze, calm as always, boring into her back. Even without looking, she knew that he stood with his arms crossed, legs slightly apart, with that familiar, mildly amused expression on his damnably perfect face. One brow would be arched, the corner of his mouth lifting in that way that maddened her beyond reason.

Curse him, but he seemed to revel in her struggles—all masterminded by him, she reminded herself—and to take pleasure in her feeble shows of resistance when she found enough courage or daring to show them.

"Aren't you going to help me?" she finally yelled over her shoulder.

"Nay." Gray shook his head and smiled. "One of these days you're going to learn to harness your anger. It can serve as your best or worst enemy, depending on how you handle it."

Catherine ground her teeth not wanting to give him the satisfaction of a reply, but in the end she couldn't resist mumbling, "*You'll* become my worst enemy in a moment, if you don't help me with this."

Gray made a clicking noise of reproach as he

strolled closer. She could still feel his smile on her and, rankled by it, she stiffened. He leaned in, reaching his arm over her head to clip the string from the branches. His breath tickled her ear, sending a delicious tingle down her neck. But she'd not let him know it.

"That passion of yours, lady," he murmured, "will get the best of you if you cannot learn to govern it. Try to focus. Channel it. Use it to your advantage."

"And how might I do that, pray tell?" she snipped, turning to glare at him; it was a mistake. He stood dangerously close, and the glint in his eyes made her go still. Sweet heavens, but he was handsome. And when he gazed at her like that . . .

"You should channel your passions, milady," he said softly, "into endeavors like this." All thought ceased when he brushed his lips over hers; he came back to taste again, drawing her into a maelstrom of sensation. She felt like she was falling, drifting to a place both strange and wonderful. Reaching up, she gripped his shoulders to steady herself and found that she couldn't stop her traitorous hands from moving up to tangle in the dark waves of hair at his neck.

With a growl of pleasure Gray pulled her to him and deepened their kiss, taking her mouth this time with sweet urgency that left her breathless.

Finally, he pulled back a little, smiling. "Hmmm. It seems you're capable of learning *some* pursuits rather quickly. I'm relieved, considering your dismal show at fishing."

Laughing, Catherine shoved at him, but the motion threw her off balance; she started to tip back, heading toward a good dunking in the stream. Gray laughed too and grabbed her, swinging her around to land with him instead on the mossy bank.

The fall knocked the breath from her, though she felt certain that if it hadn't, her husband's physical proximity would have accomplished the same result. He lay half over her, his lips hovering a breath away from hers. Grinning, he moved to kiss her again, but a bloodcurdling yell from the meadow made him stiffen. In the space of an instant, he leaped to his feet, clearing his sword from its sheath.

Three boys charged over the knoll, shouting mock battle cries and brandishing wooden sticks at each other. They fell silent and slid to a halt when they saw Gray, his upraised blade glinting in the sun, his massive warrior's frame silhouetted in the golden rays.

Catherine recognized the lads as some of the pages who served them at the castle. One of them was named Tom, she thought. Aye, that sounded right. She didn't know the other two, but she'd seen them near the kitchens carrying trays or scrubbing pots. All three lads looked to be no more than nine, and they were as pale as ghosts as they faced their fearsome master.

Brushing grass from her skirts, Catherine pushed herself to her feet. There was no need to make anyone feel worse by remaining in her indelicate position.

Tom was the first to break the silence. "My—my lord! My lady! Forgive us!" he shouted. His voice cracked on the last word, and Catherine winced in sympathy, biting her lips to keep from smiling when he dropped to one knee, his chin tucked and his forearm thrown over his chest in tribute. The others just gaped, wooden swords dangling useless from their grips. Aye, she'd peg young Tom as a natural gallant in the making.

"Tom, arise. Charles, William, at ease." Gray nodded, eyeing the boys sternly as he sheathed his sword.

They began to fidget, and Catherine stepped up to Gray and touched his arm. He glanced to her and caught her playful expression. Almost immediately, she felt his muscles relax under her fingers. Still, he maintained his fierce aspect as he turned to the boys again.

"What have you three to say for yourselves, then?"

She knew he was trying to sound firm, but she recognized the lilt of humor in his tone. Clearing her throat, she tried to keep the mirth from her own voice when she added, "In truth you gave us quite a start when you scrambled over the knoll."

Tom's face crumpled. "A thousand apologies, my lady, my lord. We were practicing and little knew that you were taking your ease by the river. If I had thought you here, I'd have cut out my own tongue before I disturbed your peaceful moment!"

Catherine choked back a giggle, and Gray's mouth twitched. Aside from Tom's extravagant speech, taking their ease and enjoying the peace were not how she would have described her calamitous attempts at fishing—or their heated kissing afterward. But Gray saved her from losing her composure and the boys from further discomfort by speaking again.

"'Twas an honest mistake, Tom, and one that gave me leave to better view your skills. Your practice has been well taken, if what I witnessed is the result," Gray said. "'Tis a fine ambush you made. And that yell . . . why, 'twas enough to inspire terror in a man's heart."

Pride lit Tom's face, burnishing his freckled cheeks, and he swaggered a little. "'Twas I who made the yell, my lord," he said. "William here has mastered the waving of the banner, and Charles is the fastest of us at a charge. We've been practicing these last weeks, since Sir Alban came to stay and lead the men in the drills."

"Ah." Gray crossed his arms over his chest and leaned back on his heels. "So Sir Alban is the inspiration for all of this fervor, is he? He has a way of inciting riots, I'll give him that." Moving to take up Catherine's abandoned pole and tackle, Gray nodded to the boys. "I'd warrant Sir Alban is in the midst of running the men through exercises right now."

"Aye, my lord. He trains with a dozen of them in the lists, practicing sword strokes and hand to hand combat," young William offered in a wobbly voice, his initial concern that Gray might slice them in half apparently subdued for the time being.

"Good. Wait but a moment, lads, and I'll go back to the yard with you. You can watch and learn another stroke or two while I join Sir Alban and the others in the sparring," Gray said, laughing when the boys whooped with pleasure and raced a little ways off to battle again with their sticks.

After gathering the last of their equipment, Gray glanced at Catherine with an expression that made her go weak in the knees. "'Tis a disappointment, my lady, but it seems we must resume your lessons later."

She nodded and dropped her gaze, trying not to grin like a fool. Taking the tackle box from him, she said, "'Tis time for me to return to the castle anyway. I need to overlook the weavers and view their work, though they've made much progress in their skills these past weeks."

"The result of your apt guidance, no doubt," Gray said, his gaze warm on her. They began to walk, the boys shouting and playing on the path ahead of them. "You'll meet with me after the noon meal, then? The village fair begins today, and I'd like you to accompany me and the others to it."

"Aye." She still smiled, filled with pleasure at the thought of spending the entire afternoon with him.

Hurrying to keep up, she kept pace with him and the boys as they headed back to the castle, laughing at their antics and thrilling to the feel of the wind in her hair. It whipped in wild gusts round her legs, making her scarlet gown snap and flutter like the pennants atop Ravenslock's massive towers.

The early morning sun shone down, lighting the autumn air, it seemed, to shimmering gold, and all was right with the world for this brief moment. The afternoon promised more of the same. More happiness and sweet memories to sustain her through the dark days ahead.

But she'd try not to think of the future now. It would come soon enough, she knew, for her decision had been made. Soon she'd take action to bring Eduard's evil plotting to its end. She had to, for with every day that passed, every moment that brought Eduard's return here closer, the danger to her children seemed more real.

Aye, soon she'd see this nightmare to its end, only it would not be in the way that Eduard had planned. Not like that at all. Because she'd decided that she only had one real choice in this matter, though its outcome frightened her almost as much as the thought of murdering Gray had. In truth, her heart nearly stilled from fear when she allowed herself to think on it . . .

For she'd decided that her only real hope lay in telling Gray the truth.

Gray wiped the sweat from his eyes and continued his methodical strokes, relaxing as he moved through a sparring sequence with one of the younger knights. Derrik was developing well. The young knight's stamina had improved since the last time Gray worked the men. Still, this exercise had proved more of a show for Gray than a challenge to his abilities.

"Break!"

Alban's shouted command caused them to cease

and back away from each other. Gray was surprised at the call to halt, but he knew Alban must have good reason. 'Twas true that young Derrik looked as if he needed a respite. As he took a long pull from his water skin, Gray saw Alban approach. By the swagger in his friend's step, Gray knew he had something brewing. As soon as Alban spoke, he knew what it was.

"You look a little winded, Gray." Alban obviously tried to look concerned, leaning in as if to avoid anyone else hearing his comment. "Could it be that the rumors are false? Might a simple mortal frame compass the famed warrior of steel?"

Tossing the water skin back to his squire, Gray raised his brow. "I don't know what wind's been blowing in your ears, old man, but 'tis not my labored breathing you heard."

"If you say so." Alban shrugged, playing his role to the hilt. "But I only called break to spare you the indignity of suffering a cut at the hands of a new blood. 'Twas a foregone conclusion, the way you huffed and puffed through that last set." He looked hurt. "It wouldn't be amiss, you know, to show a little appreciation for my quick thinking."

Grinning now, Gray leaned on his sword. "I'll appreciate you more when you lift your blade and get to work with your arms instead of your mouth. 'Tis tedious to hear you keep braying like an ass on a barren field."

Shouting a laugh echoed by the boys surrounding them, Alban caught the sword Gray tossed to him and moved to the center of the yard, shifting his weight back and forth. "A challenge from my old friend? I'd hoped your creaky bones would be up to it. Come, then, let us begin!"

"At your service." Gray smiled again and took his stance opposite him. He kept his gaze fixed on Alban, calling out to the young men, who were gathered in a circle around them, "Observe this set well, lads. 'Tis a prime example of how to out-thrust your opponent and keep him controlled on the field."

Alban grinned. "Or a lesson in how quickly the tables can turn when you think you're in control."

The young knights tightened their position around Gray and Alban, jostling each other for a better view. Humming excitement swelled in the yard, and Gray felt the familiar pulse of it in his blood, heightened by the knowledge that this fighting would be less in earnest and more in fun. He and Alban circled each other; he swung his blade in two half-arcs, laughing when Alban swirled his blade over his head in kind, nodding in mock court fashion.

They stopped, and all went still for a single, energy-charged instant; then with a roar, they leapt at each other. Metal clanged on metal as they came together, falling into a pattern of sparring that by now seemed as familiar as breathing, thanks to so many years of training with each other.

They fought hard, and Gray pressed forward, using his height to full advantage. Alban only stood a few inches shorter, but it was enough to make a difference in the angle of his thrusts. Gray slashed and met each of Alban's strokes, throwing his weight into the blows he dealt with his blade.

But Alban moved quickly, his smaller build allowing him freer movement through the series of strokes. He charged Gray several times, trying to knock him off balance with the leverage of surprise. If it wasn't for the extreme concentration required in displaying skills like this, Gray felt sure that at least one of Alban's efforts would have resulted in success.

After a few minutes, the sword began to feel heavy in Gray's grip. Still he swung and dodged, and Alban did the same. Neither gave ground as each worked his advantage; the area was silent except for the harsh rasp of breathing and the grating, metallic sounds of their blades.

"Care you to give, old man?" Alban called to Gray, feinting to the left to avoid a powerful blow that might have cut his shield in half had he stood still.

"Nay!" Gray laughed, swinging and ducking himself to avoid Alban's parry. "Not until one of us falls down or bleeds."

"A show of blood, eh? I'll try to arrange it!"

Grinning, Gray doubled his efforts, allowing the white heat of battle to take over, masking the pain weighing down his sword arm and dulling the ache in his shoulders, back and legs. He drove forward, his press finally successful in forcing Alban back a step. Then three more.

A few more paces and he'd be pushed out of the

circle, which would be as good as a victory. Just two steps, now . . .

A flash of scarlet moved at the edge of Gray's vision, up on the ramparts of the castle. At the same time, a gust of wind whipped through the yard, causing a billowing curtain of golden-brown hair to float above the scarlet figure. Gray's heart skipped a beat. 'Twas Elise, leaning on the stonework as she watched their sparring. She looked concerned, and warmth filled his breast to know that she was worried about—

Pain sliced Gray's arm, just above his elbow, and his breath hissed in with the flow of anger that followed it. His gaze snapped back to Alban. His friend's eyes were wide with amazement, his sword held frozen in position. All was silent.

"Blood!" Alban suddenly called, a mischievous twinkle replacing the shock that had initially filled his gaze. He danced around in a little circle, strutting and hooting, much to the laughter of the knights in training.

"Bloody hell," Gray growled, examining the cut to his arm. But Alban's capers soon drew a grin from him as well. "Gloat all you want, friend," Gray said. " 'Tis but a scratch. Less deadly than what I might earn from a fishwife's nails."

"Still so cocky?" Alban reached for his water skin as he handed his blade to his squire. "See you, lads," he called loudly, gesturing around them, "Distractions can prove deadly on the field. Particularly those of the feminine kind."

Alban's gaze lifted to the ramparts, and two score

eyes followed the path of his vision until all of the young knights were staring up at Elise, still perched at the crenellation, watching them. When Gray met her gaze, a bewitching blush covered her cheeks, visible even at this distance. He smiled and gave her a flourishing bow before her lashes fluttered down, and she scooted out of sight.

"Women make men's legs weak, lads. Remember that at your next tournament."

Alban's statement dragged Gray's attention back to the yard, and he walked up to his friend, slapping him on the back hard enough to make him cough. "Aye, you're right, Alban. Distractions may be deadly—but pray don't forget that without a distraction this day, you wouldn't have had a prayer at defeating me."

The boys all laughed again, spreading to gather up their equipment, before they all headed back to the castle for a change of clothing and the noon meal.

But Gray's mind really wasn't on their friendly banter. It kept drifting to more country matters, thoughts awash with scarlet linen and billowing silken tresses—and he found himself glancing often up to the ramparts as they went, hoping for another glimpse of the tempting angel who was his wife.

Chapter 10

Gray didn't appear at the noon meal. Catherine picked at her food, waiting for his arrival, but eventually she was forced to accept that he wasn't coming. None of the men she'd seen in the yard were in attendance either, so she knew she shouldn't feel concerned. Still, she hadn't been able to keep her focus on anything else. With or without her eyes closed, all she could see was that terrible moment when Gray had been cut—and then the wicked, sensual promise in his eyes when he'd looked up at her and bowed afterward.

She didn't know whether to feel anxious or shameful. 'Twas most upsetting.

But there was no more time for thought now. The hour of their journey to the fair approached, and it was time to get to the yard to mount up with the others. She picked up the bunch of autumn wild-flowers that had mysteriously appeared at her place on the table this noon—no one seemed to know who had brought them, though they were the third such bouquet in as many weeks—and put them in water before heading for the courtyard. Her excitement swelled with each step toward the portal. Soon she'd see Gray again. She would ride with him to the village fair and spend a whole, carefree afternoon basking in his company and his smile.

Just before she reached the yard, a wild impulse took hold of her. She ducked into the shadows of the portal and peered around guiltily before pinching her cheeks. Then, laughing at her own misplaced vanity, she strode out into the sunlight and the company of the others who would attend the fair.

As always, the inner yard teemed with people. But in addition to the peasants and laborers who milled about, performing their tasks, a score of men and women mingled on foot near horses that waited, saddled and impatient, for the journey to begin. Alban was among the group, as were several of the young knights from the morning's sparring, she noticed, but Gray was nowhere to be seen.

Catherine's smile dimmed, as disappointment crowded her. Nodding, she took the reins handed her by a stable boy and mounted.

"Good afternoon, my lady!" Alban said, smiling as his stallion sidled up to her. "With your arrival, we're ready to depart." But before she could ask him about Gray's whereabouts, he urged his mount to a gallop and called out to the others to begin the ride.

Her horse cantered into an easy rhythm as they passed through the outer wall and gate; she tried not to think about her husband, concentrating instead on the colorful autumn sights during the ride. Soon they approached the edge of the village, and she saw telltale signs of the fair in the increase of blustering activity.

The harvest had yielded much bounty this year if the caravans were any indication. Wagons creaked as they rolled by, piled high with pumpkins and gourds. Meat-sellers prepared their wares, displaying plump geese, legs of lamb, or whole pigs for roasting. And just inside the Village Square, Catherine spotted several women setting up tables to display fine woven fabrics and woolens. It showed the makings of a fine festival, with goods from far and wide.

She slowed with the others, preparing to ride closer to Alban as they entered the main portion of the marketplace, but a sudden movement off to the side made her pull her mount to a halt. Her heart bounded with happiness when she saw Gray emerge from the crowd to canter up to them. He looked exhilarated, and his eyes sparkled as he nodded to her and rode past to intercept Alban near the front of the riders.

She didn't have to wait long to discover what had delayed him. After exchanging a few words with Alban, Gray wheeled his horse around and cantered back to her, indicating that she should follow him away from the rest of the group and outside the village gates.

"I trust you are well, my lady," he said, when they stopped, smiling at her again as if he savored a pleasant secret. As always, she lost her breath when he looked at her like that. He seemed to see only her, and when he grinned in that charming, boyish way, with one side of his mouth tilted up, 'twas difficult to think of anything logical.

"I am, my lord. But why are we leaving the others behind?"

"I have something that I'd like to show you. We can rejoin the group later if you will accompany me now."

"Of course. What is it that I am to see?"

"You'll know soon enough."

With another grin, he guided his steed toward the wide, leafy fringe of the forest. They left the clearing, ducking into the cool recesses of the wooded path. She gazed around her as they traveled, feeling as if she'd entered a magical land.

The season was full upon them, and sun peeked through the intertwined branches and leaves overhead, painting the thick canopy with strokes of brilliant orange, red and gold. Pockets of warmth lit her head, and the branches dipped and swayed in the breeze, making the air smell fertile and ripe.

She breathed in the fragrant, almost smoky scent, savoring the crackling of the leaves under their mounts' hooves. Though the day was sunny, the air was crisp, reminding them that winter's breath would soon frost everything in glistening layers of white.

After several minutes of riding, Gray pulled his

steed up short and twisted to look at her. "We leave the path here. Do you need to rest before we go on?"

"Nay, I feel fine," she answered, realizing that her training had done more than just help her to wield a sword. Only weeks ago such a jaunt might have tired her, making her long for the comfort of her chamber, but now she felt exhilarated and ready to ride all day. She patted her mare's neck to make sure she fared as well. "Bella feels warm, but she's not sweated yet. She'll need to take water and rest soon, but I think 'tis safe to go farther for now."

Gray nodded and pushed off the path into the woodland, picking his way through the brush and holding back large branches so that Catherine and her mount could pass by unhindered. Their travel slowed here without the trail. The horses stepped carefully to avoid tripping on uneven ground or stumbling on a rock. But Catherine enjoyed their leisurely pace, as it gave her more opportunity to study her husband without his knowing it.

She watched him riding in front of her, forging the way for them with his own body and the movement of his steed. The sun winked through the trees, burnishing his hair to blue-black and dancing over the broad, well-muscled expanse of his back and shoulders. Every now and then she heard him murmur something to his steed, talking him around a treacherous root, or guiding him under a low-hanging branch with soothing tones.

'Twas his way, she realized, feeling a ribbon of warmth unfurl through her. Gray took others into his care and tried to calm and settle them. It seemed as natural to him as breathing.

She'd seen him do it countless times during the weeks she'd lived at Ravenslock—with the children who played round the castle like happy ants, with his men, who respected his command and authority as if he were a brother rather than their lord . . . and especially with her. He'd worked with her every day, helping to make her stronger, to make her feel worthy.

To make her feel safe.

And many nights he'd come to their bed and simply held her close, telling her with his actions far more eloquently than words ever could that she mattered. That her feelings and needs meant full as much as his.

"We're here," he called to her, interrupting her thoughts as he reined in his horse. He turned in his saddle, his eyes alight with pleasure. Whatever he wished her to see was making him as excited as a little boy.

Was it ground for a new castle, perhaps? Or the site of an existing ruin that he wished to show her? Regardless, she realized that his desire to share his excitement with her pleased her well.

Dismounting, she tied her mare and approached where he stood waiting for her. Gray took her hand and led her the last few paces through the wood to the edge of what seemed to be a clearing.

"Come, lady. I discovered the spot this morn, during my ride."

Pushing aside a thick bough that blocked her view, Catherine stepped into the clearing and gasped. A broad, green field sprouting with thousands of slender willows stretched before her. Swelling hills rose on three sides of the flats, providing the wetland with the protection and water needed to nurture the growth.

Speechless with pleasure, she stepped forward into the clearing. Her foot promptly squelched into the soft earth, and she jumped back with a shriek.

"Careful," Gray said, laughing as he reached to balance her.

She stilled, suddenly aware of the way his palm cushioned the small of her back, supporting her. Warmth radiated through her clothing and sent a heated shiver up her spine. He was so good to her. His eagerness all during the ride hadn't been over something he'd found for himself, but for a gift that he wanted to give her.

Tears stung her eyes, but she smiled through them. "This field is large enough to supply the castle for an entire year's weaving." Swinging her gaze to meet his, she was surprised to see an answering tenderness that made quivery feelings settle in her belly. "Thank you for this," she whispered. "Thank you for *everything* you're doing—everything you've already done for me."

He was silent as he gazed down at her, his eyes soft with some nameless emotion. "'Tis nothing, lady. I'm happy to have pleased you." He cleared his throat and stepped away, breaking their physical contact. "But tell me, how do you judge these withies for their quality and readiness for culling?"

A sudden sense of loss overwhelmed her excitement for a moment. Yet it bubbled up again when she envisioned all of the beautiful pieces she would be able to weave from the harvest of this field—chairs and tables, baskets, platters, bowls. 'Twas a dream come true. More carefully, she took a step onto the field, motioning for him to follow as she picked around the lesser of the soggy spots.

"Here," she said, reaching for a supple strand. She bent it in toward them, pulling and testing its strength so that Gray could see it as well. "See the texture?" she asked, holding it for him to touch. " 'Tis nearly ripe, and yet it must grow longer before 'tis ready for cutting. Then, once the strands are harvested, they must be boiled and peeled, which leaves them a deep golden color as they dry." She let the rod go, and it swung back to dance gracefully with the others in the breeze.

"How much longer?" Gray murmured. "Until they can be cut, I mean."

"Another week or two, when they reach above our heads. Willow ripens last of all, so that when the farmers are sitting back and surveying the wealth they've worked from the land, weavers are just beginning their harvest. 'Tis difficult, oftentimes cold work, with winter nipping at your fingers."

"And yet you seem to relish the thought of doing it."

"Aye," she smiled as they walked further along the edge of the field. "Though 'tis not the harvest itself that I take pleasure in, but the fruits of that labor. I can spend the winter months creating beautiful things, thanks to it."

"You're quite skilled, from what I've seen of your work at the castle," he said, stepping closer to inspect another frond.

"I love to weave. I've been practicing since I was a child."

"Ah. No wonder you seemed so amused, then, when I asked if you possessed skill enough to repair my basket that first day I took you to train."

Heat rushed to Catherine's cheeks. "I didn't mean to be so obvious. I hope you don't think I was making light of your request. In truth I was pleased that you asked me to help you."

"'Twas not your fault," Gray said, smiling and shaking his head. "You masked your reaction well. I, unfortunately, have the galling habit of watching people too closely. I seem to do it without even trying, most of the time."

Catherine nodded, glad that his perceptiveness hadn't revealed some of her other secrets to him. Not yet, anyway. He would learn about her sins against him all too soon, she thought—as soon as she could muster enough courage to tell him. They were alone here, after all. No servants, no knights or ladies . . . no spies. 'Twas the perfect opportunity to tell him the truth. But a part of her held back, craving just a few more moments of happiness with him.

At his suggestion, they began to make their way back to where they'd left their horses tied. Anxiety tightened her belly. 'Twas almost time, then; she'd have to make her confession before they rode away from this solitude and back into the danger-filled community of the castle. They'd reached within several paces of their mounts, when a flutter of red-tipped wings startled them.

"Look!" Gray called, pointing to follow the silktail's path. It flew into a tree just past the field's edge. Nestled in a deep crook there, the bird had built a shelter of twigs and leaves. It was unusually late in the season for chicks, but peeping over the top of the nest, Catherine could see two shiny heads; the nearly grown birds were so plump that they filled their modest home to bursting. At their mother's approach, they still craned their necks up greedily, their beaks gaping open for food.

"Oh, look at them," she said, trying to creep nearer for a better look. She walked slowly, keeping her gaze trained on the birds to avoid startling them with her movements. As she stepped on the edge of the swampy field, her foot slipped and she began to pitch headlong into the muck.

Her eyes shut instinctively, her arms flailing as she fell, when she suddenly felt a strong grip on her elbow, swinging her around. She slammed into Gray's chest, and the force of her momentum toppled them to the ground.

When she opened her eyes, she realized that she lay atop him, her face hovering inches above his. It was the reverse of how they'd fallen on the bank of the river during her fishing lesson, but the effect of his body pressed to hers was the same. He gazed up at her, his eyes beautiful, clear green and fringed in those impossible lashes. Their breath mingled in the chill air, and his chest rose in opposite rhythm with hers, making her breasts push against him with each inhalation.

She blinked, and a slow smile lifted Gray's mouth, sending a stab of longing through her.

"We seem to be making a habit of this, wife. I trust that I make a useful cushion."

His comment startled her into action. She tried to scramble off of him, murmuring apologies about his getting muddy for her sake, but she stopped her squirming when she realized that she wasn't going anywhere. His hands held her hips firmly to him, and her struggles only succeeded in causing delicious sensations to blossom, forcing her into unavoidable, teasing contact with the hard length of his body.

Every inch of him seemed to touch her, tantalizing her senses and releasing a flood of warmth through her belly and to the tingling points of her nipples where they rubbed against his chest. When she stilled, his smile eased away, leaving his expression open, vulnerable and utterly sensual. His gaze flicked from her mouth to her eyes, and he shifted suddenly, dry leaves crackling as he rolled so that she lay half beneath him.

Gray's arm cradled her head, but when his thigh slipped between hers, she gasped. Need curled hot and sleek through her, swirling up to ignite a desire that rippled to the ends of her fingers and toes. Her eyes fluttered shut and then opened again as he cupped her face with his palm.

His breath whispered over her jaw. Lifting one hand, he stroked her cheek with his thumb. "There's no mud here, lady. In truth, I'd wager our leafy carpet as soft as the finest bed of feathers."

Catherine couldn't breathe for a moment. The very birds seemed to cease their chirping, the rustling of the leaves faded into silence. Everything seemed to still around them, all but for the warm flutter of Gray's breath on her cheek, and the exquisite, gentle caress of his thumb on her skin.

"The leaves are soft, my lord," she managed to say, struggling to keep the husky note from her voice. "Yet the ground beneath is very . . . hard."

"Aye, lady. 'Tis hard, indeed."

Another wave of warmth swept through her; she couldn't help but feel the swollen, rigid length of him that burned through her skirt against her thigh. A tiny moan escaped her before she could stop it, as with a tenderness that almost shattered her, Gray bent his head and kissed her.

Then he rested his cheek on hers, closing his eyes and whispering into her ear, "'Tis a hard and soft that God made to fit together, lady." He brushed his mouth over her again, this time tantalizing the delicate spot at the tip of her jaw. "Let me teach you how perfect it can be. Let me love you as a man is made to love a woman. As a husband is made to love his wife."

Desire curled up to surround her, filling her with

cravings, with wants and needs she'd never known. "I wish it more than anything," she whispered, caution fleeing under the heated onslaught of emotion. She broke into a throaty moan when he moved to tease the sensitive spot beneath her ear. "Ah, Gray, teach me to be your wife in truth. To be yours in every way."

Catherine wound her hands round his neck, threading them into his hair, pulling him down to meld her mouth to his. With a groan he leaned into her, slanting his lips across hers with passion that left her breathless and hungry for more.

He shifted over her more fully, and instinctively, she opened to him, cradling him between her thighs. Her breath came shallow, his kisses spilling across her cheek and nibbling down her neck. She clung to him, in turn raining kisses along the stubborn line of his jaw, reveling in the tickle of his stubble against her lips. His skin tasted faintly salty, his scent utterly masculine. Intoxicating.

Vaguely, Catherine realized that she should stop; they were good and truly alone here in the glen. She should stop this now and tell him everything while she still had the chance, even knowing that it would enrage him and break her heart. And yet a few more minutes wouldn't hurt, would it? Not when she'd waited so long already. What he was doing to her felt so good, and . . .

Another moan broke past her lips; the last of her rational thoughts fled as Gray sank his hips between her legs and moved against her slowly, emulating the act of love. Only their garments served as a cruel barrier to keep pleasure at bay. His motions teased her, making her arch against him with a need so new and sweet, she felt that she might splinter from the intensity of it.

Breathing his name almost as a plea, she slipped her hands beneath his tunic and shirt, wanting more of him, needing to feel the heat of his skin next to hers. Gray loosened the laces at the neck of her kirtle as she touched him, pushing the edges down over her shoulders. He bared her breasts, easing her back onto the soft bed of leaves, and she sucked in her breath as her nipples tightened to scarlet peaks in the chill.

But the cold vanished when he stroked his hand around her exposed flesh, gently teasing her nipples between his finger and thumb before leaning down to capture one of them in the wet warmth of his mouth. She cried out with the pleasure and pulled his head closer as he laved his tongue back and forth, never moving away from the sweet prize. He suckled and nipped at her other breast in turn, stroking his fingers around its fullness and keeping her warm with the heat of his body.

Catherine reveled in the pleasure of his caresses until she could contain herself no longer. From somewhere deep inside her raged an urge to tempt him in the same way as he did her, to feel every inch of him and stroke and fondle him to a fever pitch that matched her own.

She took his face in her hands, guiding his lips to her mouth and kissing him with all the longing and emotion that swelled in her. Loosening his shirt, she kissed down his neck and pressed her lips to the places she'd bared, even as her fingers stroked down his chest and sides to splay over the strong, warm contours of his ribs.

"Ah, love, you'll unman me," Gray breathed in her ear, when she slid her hands down to his hips and around to the front of him. She brushed her palm over his rigid length, reveling in her new-found power as she grasped and massaged him firmly through the thin barrier of his breeches.

As if in sweet retaliation, Gray shifted her skirts and slipped his hand beneath, stroking his fingers up between her legs. She opened to him without thought, her cry mingling with his groan when he found her slick, wet heat.

"Elise," he whispered, the muscles of his arms and chest corded with need as he stroked her, "God help me, but I want you. All of this time I've wanted you, even when I tried not to feel it."

Catherine's heart contracted at the sound of her false name on his lips; it filled her with an aching sadness that made her turn her face away, even as her body responded with surging, traitorous rapture to his touch. But when he slipped his finger into her, she moaned aloud, unable to stop herself from pressing into his hand at the rush of pleasure.

"I've dreamed a thousand times of touching you like this," he murmured, gliding his finger in and out of her in an intoxicating rhythm, "but by God, I swear that none of my imaginings ever came close to the beauty of this truth."

Catherine gasped and writhed with the intense

feeling; she struggled to keep control of herself, not to disappear into the swirling ecstasy that his stroking touch promised.

"Now," she begged, shifting desperately under him. "Take me now, Gray. I want to be yours, in every way. Please, I can wait no longer."

"Aye, love. We'll wait no more," he said, bracing his hands to lift himself over her. Then he eased himself into her slick opening and rocked slightly, closing his eyes and tipping his head back as he pushed gently into her.

Intense pleasure rippled through her when he sank completely inside. The smooth, hard heat of him filled her, and, responding to instinct as old as the ages, she lifted her knees to coax him deeper, losing herself in the mindless ecstasy of motion. He rocked in and out of her, pulling back to the very brink, and then delving inside as deep as he could go.

Catherine wrapped her arms tightly around his shoulders, her legs locked to his waist as he stroked into her. The seductive intimacy of their joining shocked her. Never had she felt such rightness— such *sanctity*—in this act. Tears of joy sprang to her eyes as she rose up to meet each of Gray's thrusts, moaning the sweet music of his name into his shoulder. The salty taste of his skin was primal on her lips, and she nipped at him, writhing with passion and need beneath him.

Just when she thought it was impossible to feel more, she began to tense with an exquisite tide that started to overwhelm her, a gathering storm of sensation that threatened to tip her over the edge and into mindless bliss. Her fingers clutched Gray's back under the assault of this new and wonderful feeling. With a low cry, she arched up to pull him more deeply inside her.

And then suddenly, her body wasn't hers to control any longer; she screamed aloud as she climaxed, pulsing around him, coaxing him to rapture along with her. Roaring her name, Gray thrust once more and sheathed himself to the hilt, filling her with his hot, liquid flow . . .

And delivering her at long last into a paradise of love and completion she'd never dreamed she'd find.

After a few moments, Gray rolled away from his wife. Reaching to his side, he grabbed his long cape and tucked it around them against the chill. Then he just lay back and allowed the feeling to seep through him. Warm and sated. He shielded his eyes with his forearm, willing his breathing to slow. But no matter how his body rested, his mind continued to churn. Something was amiss. Something important. It had shadowed his thoughts while they were making love; now it returned with a vengeance.

His wife wasn't a virgin.

There'd been no barrier to break. No innocence to shatter. She'd been smooth and achingly sweet when he took her. So sweet that even now the thought of what they'd done, of the pleasure she'd given him, caused his groin to tighten again in anticipation. But hurt lanced through him as well;

she'd lied to him. A lie of omission, by keeping the truth of her lost virginity from him.

Lifting his arm a little, he peered from beneath its shelter to gaze at her, wondering what she was thinking. How she was feeling. She hadn't uttered a word since their explosive climax. She rested next to him in silence, still but for the even rise and fall of her breast. Her eyes were closed, her face inscrutable.

She didn't look guilty. She wasn't acting afraid or nervous, or like a woman who was deceiving him. But then how to explain her lack of innocence?

Suspicion began to wind dark tendrils into his heart again, bringing with it memories of all the other times he'd felt this twinge in the past weeks, of all the other disparities he'd ignored because of his deepening feelings and his need for her. But they glared through his brain now, relentless, taunting.

He'd felt them from the start, from the moment he'd lifted her veil on their wedding day. There'd been her people's false description of her and King Henry's pointed comments about her changed appearance. And then the portrait. He remembered her strange reaction to it when Eduard presented it as a gift, and again later, when he'd caught her weeping over it. So many inconsistencies . . .

Elise opened her eyes. "Gray, there's something I need to tell you. Something I should have told you long ago. 'Tis awful, and I pray you can forgive me for keeping it from you."

Gray lowered his arm slowly, still looking at her. The tone of her voice had sent a shock up his spine; her expression was deadly serious. She turned to stare at him, eyes huge in her face, and he couldn't keep back the renegade thought that those eyes were pleading with him, silently begging him to understand something that meant life or death to her.

Christ. He'd suspected right. She'd been hiding something, and she was about to tell him of it. Pain and doubt cut through him anew. That she'd lied to him about anything was serious; aye, especially if it had been a deliberate deceit on her or Montford's part to shame him. But she was acting as if she feared for her safety now, and that hurt him almost as much as her deception. She should know him better than that by now.

He began to speak but then stopped, so bothered by her stricken expression that the words lodged in his throat. She looked as if she was about to cry, or get on her knees and pray, or throw herself at his feet and implore his mercy. It made his skin crawl the way it did right before a deadly battle. It was damn unsettling.

Both to stem his feeling and to ease her anxiety, he reached out and grazed his thumb across her kiss-swollen lips, heat rising again in a heady swirl at the feel of her, at the warm, lush sight of her. Her scent lingered on his skin, reminding him of their lovemaking and sending a pleasant twist into his belly. He tried to push the warmth aside. He needed to stay focused. Stay clear. "Elise," he said quietly, "just tell me who it was and why it happened, and we'll—"

"Gray! Gray, where the hell are you, man?"

The deep voice rang through the clearing, accompanied by a crackling, banging noise as if from a hundred stomping feet. Gray reached for his sword, cursing under his breath, even as he moved to shield Elise from the intruders' gazes.

Alban and three young knights came crashing into the glen atop their steeds; Alban jolted his stallion to a halt when Gray glared up at him from his position concealing Elise on the ground. Reining his mount back, Alban shooed the younger knights from the glen, muttering something about taking care of it himself and ordering them to return to the village to await Gray's arrival there. Then, red-faced, he dismounted and walked toward his friend.

"I'm sorry to have disturbed you both," he muttered, "but it could not be helped. You must come back to the village with me, and quickly."

"What the hell is it?" Gray snapped, tucking his cloak around Elise, who sat up, silent and wide-eyed, as he stood to lace his breeches and slip his shirt over his head.

"'Tis a bloody brawl. A half dozen lads from beyond the valley, newly-knighted, I'd say, from the looks of them, took insult at something young Drake said. Before anyone could intervene they were at it with our squires and young knights, swords drawn and fists flying." Alban leaned down to pick up Gray's surcoat, which had been thrown in a heap at the far edge of the clearing. His brows lifted, and he whistled appreciatively, shaking his head as he tossed it back to him.

Gray scowled and pulled it on, indicating that they should move farther away to give Elise some privacy to dress. From the corner of his vision Gray saw her stir from beneath the security of his cloak. Pulling Alban more deeply into the brush, he asked, "How bad is it?"

Alban shrugged. "Bad enough to convene a manorial court. At least five are wounded. One might not live. Many of the sellers had goods destroyed. Tables were knocked over and produce trampled. We've got it contained for now, but 'twill need your judgement as Lord of Ravenslock to dispense justice." Reaching into his tunic, Alban withdrew a sealed parchment. "And then there's this. A message arrived for you from the king."

Gray took it and broke the seal, reading it quickly before cursing aloud. "I'm to depart without delay for a grand assize in Cheltenham. King Henry wants me there as a representative of the Crown." He tucked the parchment into his shirt. "I'll go as soon as the problem in the village is cleared. Elise?" he called over his shoulder. "Come, we must hurry."

"I'm right here," she murmured behind him. He almost jumped with her nearness. Mother Mary, but his wife was quicker at dressing herself than any woman he'd ever known. He covered his surprise with a command and action. "We must mount up and return to the village. Fighting's broken out and I must call a manorial court to deal with the accused."

He moved to follow Alban to the horses, but Elise tugged his sleeve, pulling him back. "Wait!" she whispered, sounding almost frantic. "Please, Gray, just a moment more. I must tell you before 'tis too—"

"We'll have to talk about it later," he broke in. "I cannot tarry here or lives may be lost." Clenching his jaw, he guided her to her mount and helped her up. He struggled to mask his emotions, hiding them behind a stony expression. And he seemed to accomplish what he intended, effectively stopping any further conversation. They mounted up and headed for the village without another word between them.

Scowling as they rode, Gray tried not to think about what his wife was preparing to tell him. About the man who'd taken her virginity or why she'd kept it from him for all of this time. He only focused on the path ahead, glad that there was something tangible awaiting him in the village. Something he could handle and solve.

His secretive wife was more than he could deal with right now. For Elise, with her wide blue eyes, her sweet disposition, and her soft body was beginning to get the best of him . . .

And he'd be damned if he'd allow himself to accept defeat that easily.

Chapter 11

Catherine hunched over her mare's neck, clutching her reins until the blood left her hands as their mounts crashed through the woods. 'Twas fortunate that Gray and Alban led the way back to the village. Even at their breakneck speed, she couldn't seem to focus on the trail ahead; she barely managed to duck when a fir branch snapped back at her, and just a moment ago she'd almost lost her seat when her horse had stumbled on the rough terrain. Her thoughts kept dwelling on one, festering point.

How could she have been so selfish? She'd had a chance to tell Gray the truth with no one near to report of it back to Eduard, and yet she'd put her own wants, her own decadent, carnal desires, ahead of her children and their safety. Her face felt hot and her stomach rolled with guilt and dread. She'd waited too long to tell Gray and beg his aid, and now the opportunity was lost. Such a chance might not present itself again for days. Perhaps even weeks, and by then it might be too late. Eduard might have returned to Ravenslock to demand her fulfillment of their foul bargain.

She bit the inside of her cheek until she tasted blood, relishing the bone-jarring pace and alternating between reviling herself for her weakness and trying to plan what she could do to make it right.

They passed through another clearing and more woodland before reaching the village, which consisted of two score rough, thatched-roofed cottages clumped here and there among several larger buildings. As they entered the main thoroughfare, chickens ran squawking out of their way, but before they reached the square, Catherine saw telltale signs of the fighting that Alban had witnessed.

Ale barrels lay overturned, their rich, golden brown contents trickling onto the road. As they rode farther, the damage looked worse. Two or three wooden display stalls were cracked in pieces on the ground, and blood clotted the soil, staining it dark red. At first she thought it gory evidence of the brawl, but a closer look calmed her fears.

'Twas animal blood, she was almost certain. One of the broken stalls must have offered poultry, since fowl carcasses were strewn about the area; several dogs growled over the birds, snatching them in their jaws to lope off and rip them apart without interference. Catherine frowned, her mind straying from her own troubles for a moment as she wondered why none of the villagers made any move to stop the beasts from gobbling up the goods. Then she saw what held their attention so inexorably.

The angry mob surrounded nearly two dozen young knights who stood bound in pairs or threes to stakes in the middle of the square. Even with many of them slumped over from exhaustion or pain, Catherine recognized some of the lads as being from among those Gray and Alban were training at Ravenslock. Four of the remaining knights were strangers to her.

All of the men were bound, but someone had tied the unknown knights' hands behind their backs. These four looked more disheveled than the rest from what must clearly have been vicious fighting, and yet they stood rigid, their faces wary against the snarls and insults thrown at them by the crowd. They tried to hide it, but they were frightened. Aye, so much so that it made their skin gleam pasty in the late day sun.

All but one, anyway.

He was the largest of the captured knights, and he also seemed to be the oldest, appearing to be of some nineteen or twenty years. He stood firm, his blond head held at a regal angle, his bloodied face a mask of hate and derision that blasted the villagers all to hell. Catherine shuddered, unable to dismiss the thought that if this young man could have disemboweled those taunting him with a look, he would have done so without a second thought.

The shouts and jeering began to die away when

Gray strode into the circle. He stood taller than everyone, knight or villager, his head easily visible above the crowd; everyone backed away and made room for him as he passed. Alban stayed close by him, but Catherine lingered at the edges of the crowd, allowing two of Gray's men to help her dismount so that she might stand within their protection to witness the proceedings.

Gray didn't speak for a moment, seeming to assess the condition of those bound before him. Catherine saw his gaze flick over some of the lads he knew so well—among them Matthew Osgood, Bernard de Varienne, and wiry Derrik Lowes—before settling with stern concentration on the four unknown men.

Without looking away, he called for Stephan Baker and Clyde Potter to step forward. The two men, both freeholders of Ravenslock land, pushed through to stand proudly next to him. But in the next instant, someone from the crowd hurled a rotten apple into the square; it hit the blond knight in the chest, spattering his face. He threw himself forward against his bonds, sneering and calling out curses upon all of them as cowards.

"Enough!" Gray roared, his command ringing through the village and bringing everyone to silence. He cast his gaze around before coming to rest again on the captured knights. A shiver tingled up Catherine's spine.

"This will be settled peaceably. As Lord of Ravenslock, I hereby convene a *hallmote*. A jury will decide the guilt or innocence of each accused man. Clyde Potter and Stephan Baker will serve as manorial officers to choose the remaining ten witnesses of the court. Once we hear both sides of each case and the jury passes verdict, I will dispense justice."

A low murmur of approval rumbled through the crowd, though Catherine saw the blond knight scowl and spit off to the side. But the other young men seemed to relax a little, the panicky look easing from their faces.

Soon the remaining ten witnesses were chosen from among the freeholders and knights, and the accused men, whether they were lads from Ravenslock or the strangers, were brought forward one by one. Each had witnesses stand to represent him and argue his case; for each a verdict was delivered and, if necessary, a fine imposed. In some cases, the young knight in question agreed to make restitution with work, rather than with money, to those whose property had been destroyed, while in others, the jury determined innocence of the charges.

Catherine watched Gray where he stood at the makeshift table that had been set up for the jury. She saw him working with his people—freemen, lowborn, or noble—lending his view, or nodding and observing with serious concentration, but always serving as a powerful, stable presence in the center of the gathering. She marveled at his skill, his composure. It was amazing, really, his ability to arrive at this scene of chaos and wrest a civilized proceeding from the midst of it.

Pride burned in her breast. And love. Aye, she could deny it no longer. She loved Gray in a way she'd never thought it would be possible for her to love a man. He'd won her heart with his goodness and passion, with his sense of right and wrong, and his determination to see justice done.

She brushed her finger over her swollen lips, remembering the feel of his mouth taking hers as he stroked deep inside of her this afternoon. Her cheeks burned as she stared at him now, here in the square, gazing at his striking face, his powerful body . . . those graceful hands that were strong enough to kill with one pass of his sword, or gentle enough to caress her into mindless ecstasy.

She ducked her head as the memory of their lovemaking washed over her again, filling her with renewed heat. Darting her gaze to the people surrounding her, she prayed her expression hadn't given away her thoughts.

A jolt went through her. Someone was watching her. He crouched, motionless and furtive, about ten paces away through the crowd. 'Twas the deformed man, the one she'd first seen peering at her from the shadows of the corridor the night of the king's feast weeks ago. He wore the same, swathed garments that obscured his face from full sight, but she knew by the chill up her spine that he stared nonetheless.

Just like that first night, his gaze sliced into her, hard and penetrating. Then, suddenly, he looked away and ducked into the shifting masses of the crowd. No one else seemed to have noticed his presence—or her discomfort. All eyes were trained on the proceedings.

Catherine craned her neck to try to see where he'd gone, but he'd disappeared as if he'd been no more than a figment of her overwrought imagination. She suppressed a shiver, cursing that there was nothing she could do about him, or anyone else she might suspect as one of Eduard's spies, other than to be more careful than usual about what she said or did.

She glanced back to the jury table. The last of the accused was being readied for trial; it was the blond knight, but as he was led from the stake to face the council, he shook himself free of those who held him and walked to the table unaided, his gait cocky.

"Your name?" Clyde Potter asked, nodding for him to stand nearer to the scribe.

"Gilbert de Clare."

"Clare?" Gray's gaze snapped to the young man. "Be you kin of the king's former regent, William Marshall?"

"Aye," the knight answered insolently. "William Marshall was my father's cousin."

Another low murmur swept the crowd, and Catherine took a step forward to see the man better. If what he said was true, he was aligned with one of the most powerful houses in all of England. William Marshall had been dead nearly fifteen years, and yet both the country and King Henry still reaped the benefits of his great influence. Henry had been crowned at the tender age of nine, but in the three years William served as his Regent, he'd guided the boy-king through the intricacies of fair and noble rule.

"Any kin of William Marshall is welcome at Ravenslock. However, you'll still need to answer to this day's charges against you, the same as any other," Gray said, nodding to Stephan to release the young knight's bonds. "What brought you so far from home, son?"

"I am no green boy to be addressed so," Gilbert scoffed, shaking his hands and rubbing his wrists to restore the feeling in them. "My travels lead me on the same path as my renowned cousin. I intend to make a name for myself."

"I met William Marshall several times when I was a young knight, Clare. He used violence when 'twas necessary, not for the kind of lawless brawling that took place in our village this day," Gray chided.

Gilbert's face went white in anger. "So you say, Camville—yet what know *you* of acting within the bounds of law?"

"Enough to ensure that you'll receive justice here today," Gray answered sharply. "I've handled many disputes as lord of my estates, with results deemed just by those who received them. Fear not. You'll be judged most fairly."

"I do fear the kind of justice I'll receive," Gilbert muttered, his eyes narrowed on Gray. "And you know why."

Gray went silent for a beat. "I've given you my word, Clare, and that should be enough." He glanced to the bailiff. "Proceed."

"Nay! I will not accept your word for my fair treatment. Your word means nothing, for I know what is spoken of you at Court—tales of your lawlessness and crimes of the worst kind, committed when you were even younger than I!"

Several of the villagers gasped, their gazes shifting from Gilbert de Clare to Gray. Catherine felt a flare of outrage. How dared this youth accuse Gray of wrongdoing? His audacity bordered on dangerous, she knew. One look at Gray and she realized that it might well prove fatal.

"Watch your tongue, lad." Gray's voice was deceptively quiet. "You know nothing of what you speak."

"Think you to keep it secret, then?" Gilbert's face screwed into a mask of derision. "For the love of Christ, man, you slew your own sister! You've no right to pass judgment on me, or any of these men who have been brought before you today!"

The entire square fell silent at his horrible accusation. Catherine felt as if someone had sucked the air from her lungs, and she watched, stunned, as several of Gray's men leapt forward, obviously intending to throttle the young knight senseless. But Gray waved them off. Catherine could see the war he waged in himself for control, and she found herself holding her breath, awaiting the outcome.

Finally he cast a sarcastic smile at Gilbert. "You

continue to live right now, *boy*, thanks only to your tender age. Regardless of what some say, I am not a murderer of children." His hands fisted at his sides, and a muscle in his jaw twitched. "You will be tried by this jury and a judgment assessed to you for any damages you caused here this day. After that, 'tis my will that you be gone from here. Never darken my lands with your shadow again."

Gilbert looked ready to explode, yet Catherine thought his silence meant that he would abide the ruling. But then his chin jutted out again.

"I refuse to be judged by you or by any of these fools!" Gilbert growled. "Let God serve as my arbiter. Face me in an ordeal by battle and let us see who will emerge victorious!"

The crowd burst into an uproar, and Alban grabbed Gilbert by the back of his tunic, shaking him. "You insolent whelp. Think that you may command the king's High Champion to combat and be *obeyed*? You'll command nothing but a view from a cell while we await ransom for your worthless hide."

"Is Camville a coward, then, as well as a murderer?" Gilbert shrieked, struggling and kicking as Alban began to drag him toward the path to the castle.

"Wait." Gray's voice cut through the noise in the square, but Alban seemed unable to hear it; he kept going, forcing Gray to yell, "Wait, Alban!"

Giving the youth another shake, Alban ceased his progress and stared dumbfounded at Gray. "You don't mean to entertain the thought? Do battle with this wretch of a . . ." His voice trailed off and he shook his head in obvious reaction to the look he saw on Gray's face. "Oh, nay, this is not good. 'Tis not good at all."

Gray walked the distance to Gilbert with rigid, even steps. Almost methodically, Catherine thought. His movements reminded her of something. Something unpleasant. The recollection flashed suddenly into her mind. Aye, that was it. It was the same as the day of the *mélée*—that horrible moment on the field when he'd seemed so stiff and detached, like an instrument of death . . .

Oh, sweet heaven, he was acting just as he had in the moments before he almost drove his blade through Eduard's heart. Icy cold washed over her, but she had no chance to speak. Gray had reached Gilbert and a new hush descended over the crowd. Even in the stillness, Catherine had to strain to hear what he said.

"You wish to fight with *me*, Clare? Right here and now, in an ordeal by battle?"

"Aye," Gilbert spat, straightening and glaring up at him. "If you're man enough to take my challenge."

Gray looked as if he was going to laugh, but then his face regained its preternatural, rigid lines. "If we fight, you'll die."

" 'Tis a chance I'm willing to take."

"Then make your peace with God and arm yourself, boy, because your insults will be answered in blood."

Without another word, Gray turned and stalked a few paces away. He drew his sword and the crowd

pulled back, leaving space for the fighting to commence. Catherine pushed to the front of the throng,
trying in vain to catch Gray's gaze. But he refused to
look at her. He just stood there, staring straight
ahead as he waited for Gilbert de Clare to enter the
fighting space.

Uncontrollable tremors radiated from her stomach, and she laced her fingers tightly together. Her
lips moved of their own accord in a soundless
prayer, interrupted only when someone came close
and touched her elbow. She met Alban's gaze, seeing her own worry reflected in his eyes.

"Is there nothing you can do?" she whispered.
Nausea rode up into her throat, choking her. From
the side of her vision, she saw Gilbert walk stiffly
into the clearing, his sword held tight in his grip.

"Nay," Alban answered. "'Tis gone too far to
stop. We must trust Gray to do what is right."

She nodded wordlessly, too overcome with dread
to say anything more. In the next instant the fighting began; with a howl, Gilbert raised his sword
over his head and lunged, but his blade glanced off
of Gray's as if his blow held no more force than the
weight of a gnat.

Gray made no sound as he faced the youth,
though his eyes shone like green ice. He hardly
shifted his stance as he delivered two swift strokes in
return. The first hooked Gilbert's sword and sent it
sailing out of his grip; the second sliced down to just
above the young knight's knee, cutting through his
chain mail and deep into the tender flesh beneath.

Blood spurted and Gilbert went down screaming,

gripping his leg as Gray raised his sword again. The crowd gasped, women covering their mouths or shielding their children's eyes as they prepared to watch their lord deliver the death blow he'd promised. Swinging down in a stroke meant to decapitate his opponent, Gray shifted back at the last instant, slicing into Gilbert's cheek instead.

The young knight shouted in pain again and reached to his face, staring up with frightened eyes as Gray smoothly lifted his sword to the side and sheathed it, growling, "Let this be a lesson to you, boy. Be thankful that you kept your life this day. Now go, before I change my mind."

Gilbert gaped like a fish, terror seeming to paralyze his ability to speak. With a whimper he scrambled to his feet and stumbled as best as he could from the clearing to his friends, who helped him mount his horse before all of them rode away down the road as if pursued by devils.

Gray stood silent for a moment more. He breathed deep, fisting his hands at his sides; then without a word to anyone, he stalked away. Catherine watched him stride with a purposeful gait toward the outskirts of the village.

The buzz of the crowd swelled again as she watched him go, uncertain whether or not she should follow him. People began to disperse, and she realized that Alban would be no help in deciding; he'd already gone to gather some knights to follow Gilbert, to ensure that he and his friends left Gray's lands after paying their fines.

She was on her own.

Biting her lip, she considered her options. She knew that she played with fire to approach Gray now. And yet she couldn't be a coward. Setting her gaze ahead, she followed his path, stepping gingerly around piles of animal leavings and debris as she went.

When she finally caught up to him, she found him standing at the limits of the village, gazing out at a clearing where the rye had recently been cut. Birds lit on the stubble in quest of grain, chirping every now and then and lifting in a graceful mass before settling to earth again. It was a peaceful scene; the sun shone warm in the late afternoon sky. And yet even with some of the villagers milling about, Gray looked very alone.

His broad, powerful back was tense with emotion, his arms crossed like bands of steel over his chest. As she approached, she saw his face in profile. He wore that familiar, troubled look, his jaw and neck rigid. She stepped a little closer.

"'Twas a fine thing you did just now, sparing Gilbert de Clare's life," she said softly, coming up beside him.

Gray hardly shifted a muscle. "He was a raw knight, barely in his spurs. I could not kill him."

"Aye. And yet his falsehoods were enough to make any man yearn for blood. None would have blamed you for killing him. You gave him every chance to recant his lies, and he refused."

"His lies?" Gray said, twisting to glare at her. "Play you a farce with me, lady, to say so?"

"Of course not." Catherine looked at him in confusion. "His accusations brought him what he deserved. Anyone who knows you could never believe you capable of committing such a horrible deed as that which he accused."

She met Gray's fierce expression head-on, searching his gaze with hers and watching his anger fade to surprise before his eyes darkened with pain. But in the next moment he tilted his head back, a sardonic chuckle rumbling from his chest. "You don't know, do you? You truly have no idea what Gilbert de Clare was talking about today."

"Nay," she said softly. "I only know 'twas a shock to hear him speak so of you."

"Ah, this is rich," Gray murmured, shaking his head. "Eduard brought you here and wed you to me, and yet he neglected to tell you. How perfectly perverse—and how very like him."

"What? What didn't Eduard tell me?"

"About my sister and my past." Gray's gaze captured hers, searching her in a way that made her breath catch in her throat. "It seems that you have been misled, lady. I am not the man you thought me to be when we married."

"Nay, my lord, you are much more. In truth I've never met someone like you in all of my life. I never knew such goodness could exist."

His expression tightened. "I am not so different from other men, Elise. Worse, if anything."

"Most of the men I've known were animals. You are not like them."

The poignant simplicity of her statement made Gray go still. The aching well in his heart cracked open, sending warmth flooding through his chest. He sucked in his breath against the bitterness, against the pain that swelled and left him feeling exposed, raw and vulnerable.

His hands trembled, and to mask it, he raked them through his hair. "You would not think that if you knew the whole truth, lady," he murmured.

"What is it? I pray you tell me so that I can show you how meaningless it is. It holds no weight compared to all of the good you do every day. To all of the kindness you've shown me."

Calm descended over Gray. A calm like that he remembered from childhood, before the darkness had swallowed him and destroyed Gillian. His wife had inspired that calming feeling in him from the first, though he'd denied the gift, believing such a blessing undeserved by one such as he. Virgin or no, her soul had shone clear and sweet from the moment he'd seen her face on their wedding day. Only then he'd thought she'd known the truth about him. He'd thought that she'd accepted him in spite of it.

He tried to laugh again, but it sounded more like the choked rattle of a dying man. "Gilbert de Clare spoke true on more than one point this day, lady. I did have a sister. She was my twin. And she is dead because of me."

Ignoring Elise's startled gasp, Gray plunged ahead, committed now to his path of self-destruction. "Gillian was as beautiful and sweet as she was pure. I was supposed to protect her from harm." His fingers clenched against his thighs as he forced the words to form on his lips. "And instead of keeping her safe, I killed her."

This time Elise's hands flew to her mouth and her gaze filled with horror.

He lifted his hands, palms up, pain shooting into his brain as he saw Gillian lying in his arms, saw the welling wounds on his own flesh, earned in his rage-filled attack on Thornby—watched his blood course over his fingers to soak his garments, the floor, her hair. His blood. Her blood. Mingled together as it had been from their conception.

Dropping his hands to his sides, Gray shifted his gaze to his wife. "I didn't kill Gillian myself, lady, but 'twas the same as if I did. She died because of my sin. Because of my weakness."

"What happened?" Elise whispered. Her eyes seared him with their innocence. "How—how did she die?"

Gray looked away again, the images firing through his skull. "We were still children when *Maman* caught the pox. In order to ensure Gillian a home and food, I worked as an errand boy for Bernard Thornby, the whoremaster who'd led my mother to ruin. He all but owned me. I was young and stupid, and I began to drink as a way to forget. As the years passed, I started stealing from him, selling what I took in order to satisfy my growing thirst. When he discovered my thefts, he took revenge by hurting Gillian."

Gray's voice wavered, but he went on. "We were only fourteen, but that didn't stop Thornby from beating her and violating her. He put his filthy hands on her and hurt her in ways no woman should ever be hurt—" His voice broke, then, and he had to pause before he could finish. "By the time I found her it was too late. My sister died in terrible pain, gasping my name with her last breath."

Gray had watched Elise turn ashen as he spoke. Now she faced him, speechless, though he couldn't tell if it was pity or disgust that he saw in her gaze. It didn't really matter. She knew the whole truth about him now. Now she would cease this talk of goodness and see him the way he really was. Corrupt. Sinful. *Irredeemable*.

But instead of being relieved, he couldn't help but feel as if he'd just jabbed a red-hot knife into his own gullet and gouged out what was left of his heart.

Gray pasted a mocking smile on his lips. "Less than a year ago, your brother learned of my past— how, I don't know—but he found out the sordid details and used them against me, spreading the tales at Court. Only he claimed that it was I who had killed Gillian in a drunken rage. We came to blows over it. The king was not amused to find his two best champions at war. He forbade any further fighting between us. 'Tis why he arranged your marriage to me, as a union of peace between our houses."

"I didn't know."

He remained silent for a moment before adding, "In truth, I despised your brother for trying to ruin me, and yet I cannot deny that he was right in a way. I did kill Gillian, through my weakness. I am not a good man, Elise. Justice and honor are but the trappings I wear to hide the sin beneath." Gray looked away, unable to bear the weight of her gaze on him any longer. "Do not count on outward appearances when you judge a man's worth, lady. I am proof that you will oft be deceived."

Turning on his heel, he strode away, sure that if he stayed he might buckle from the pain. For in the past weeks, he'd watched his wife grow in confidence and freedom, watched the spring come into her step and seen the smiles come to her face more freely. Curse his soul, but he'd even tasted the sweetness of holding her as she shattered with passion in his arms.

And yet just now he'd earned a far more dismal response from her. One that damned the others all to hell . . .

For today, in one, fell swoop, he'd managed to gather all of the sadness and pain Elise had worked so diligently to abandon, and he'd poured it right back into the clear blue innocence of her eyes.

Chapter 12

Catherine watched him go, too stunned at first to say a word. But then something snapped inside of her, and she lunged forward, racing to catch up with him as she called, "Gray, wait! *Please!*"

He slowed and finally stopped, but he wouldn't look at her. She felt his muscles clench beneath her palm as she grabbed his arm, tugging him around to face her.

Several villagers and knights who stood nearby struggled not to gape at the strange sight of their lady accosting their lord in public, but Catherine paid no heed. All that mattered right now was making Gray understand that his past meant nothing to her. That it was the man he'd become in the days since his tragedy that made her feel truly happy.

That made her feel loved.

She gripped his arms and looked up at him, trying to make him understand. "I don't care what you did, Gray, or didn't do, when you were a boy. Aye, I ache for the loss of your sister and the pain it must have caused you, but I don't blame you for her death. No one could. Her murder was a horrible deed committed by an evil man who abused women as a way of life. The fault of Gillian's death lies with him, not with you!"

"'Tis in your nature to be generous," he said, finally meeting her gaze. "That is why 'tis hard for you to believe that I bear fault in this, Elise. And in truth, these past weeks with you, I've felt . . ."

He stopped and looked away, seeming to subdue his emotions by force before he was able to bring his gaze back to hers. "As much as I'd like to, I cannot change reality. I must accept the fact that I almost allowed myself to forget my part in Gillian's death."

"But—"

"Nay, lady," he said, touching his finger gently to her lips. "Let me finish. Every hour I continue to breathe must be lived to make up for her loss. I vowed that long ago. 'Tis why I never let anything cloud my mind again, be it drink or remedy. 'Tis why I must continue to fight whenever possible as the king's champion."

"But how can that honor Gillian's memory?"

He paused, and she sensed his withdrawal from her, though he didn't move in a physical sense. "I must curry favor with King Henry," he continued quietly, "so that he will continue to grant me lands and appoint me to positions of power. Positions like Sheriff of Cheltenham. Only then will I be able to see justice done for others in a way that was denied me. This I vowed on the day that Gillian died, no matter what the personal cost to me, no matter what the pain. I cannot be deterred or distracted from that goal. I cannot forsake it lest I fail Gillian, and myself, again."

He spoke as if he'd uttered that statement many times before. As if he struggled to remind himself again now of its importance above all else in his life.

A horrible thought took hold of Catherine. She stood facing him, feeling the warmth of his skin under her hand, sensing the powerful play of muscle beneath her fingertips, remembering their lovemaking near the willow field. And understanding struck her with the force of a gale wind, sucking the life from her with its impact.

She'd never considered their marriage from any other point of view but her own. Not until now.

Whatever the cost, whatever the pain . . . ?

"Sweet Jesu, our union was forced upon you, wasn't it, Gray?" she whispered. "And you endured it, joining yourself to a woman you knew you would hate. Someone whose very presence couldn't help but remind you of your enemy and your sins every time you looked at her . . ."

She tried to see into his eyes, needing to read the truth in the one place he couldn't hide it. She stood on tiptoe, shifting until he could avoid her gaze no longer, and recoiling with almost physical pain when she saw her answer there.

"I'll not lie to you," he answered, raggedly. "It was like that at the start. But not now. It hasn't been so for—" He broke off and clenched his jaw, emotions full in his eyes.

Then he shook his head and seemed to become almost angry, shaking her hands off of him to grip her arms fiercely with his own. "Damn it, don't you understand? I can't allow myself to feel like this about you. I can't let anything cloud my direction or get in the way. Not now. Not ever." He let his hands drop from her arms as he looked away. "Gilbert de Clare's accusations today reminded me of that. 'Tis the way it must be."

"Nay. You only make it so by believing it. If you would just—"

"'Tis not just belief. 'Tis the truth that makes me stay this course—the only truth I've known for years."

The truth. Catherine's stomach clenched and she felt like screaming aloud. If only he knew the complete and horrible truth. The truth about her lies and her identity. She wanted to tell him right now. She wanted to blurt it out and the rest be damned, but Gray's next words stopped her as cold as if he'd shot an arrow through her heart.

"I have to leave, Elise. Alban brought a message from King Henry, ordering me to ride immediately to Cheltenham. I'm to take part in a grand assize there to judge a land dispute between a powerful abbot and a prior, both vital for their support to the Crown."

"What?" Terror shot through her, masking all else

for the moment. "But you can't go now! Please—you must wait a little longer, so that I can—"

"I can't stay," he broke in. "'Tis the king's wish that I settle this problem without delay, and I'll not risk my appointment to Sheriff by ignoring his command."

She wanted to say something, anything, to make him stop what he was doing, but she couldn't get past the grim purpose in his eyes. He looked away. "I'll return as soon as I can." Without meeting her gaze again, he stalked away toward his men, who stood clustered, awaiting him by their steeds. She heard him give the order to mount up, saw him swing astride his stallion . . .

Taking two running steps forward, she started to call out for him. She felt him slipping away, and she wanted to make him stop, even if it meant shrieking out the secret that had been bottled up inside of her for all of these weeks, gnawing at her insides. But the words lodged in her throat.

She swung her head, gazing around in desperation; a hundred eyes of villagers, knights, villeins, and lasses seemed to stare back at her. Curse his soul, but Eduard had done his work well. She imagined suspicion in every gaze. Sly awareness. They were like vipers waiting to strike and destroy her.

Just like the deformed man, any one of them might be Eduard's spy.

Or all of them.

Her fists clenched and her breath rasped painfully. Nay, 'twas too dangerous to speak out. Her own destruction she could bear, but not her children's. She'd not risk their lives more than she already had by committing another selfish act. She'd do what needed to be done in the right way, at the right time, when there might still be hope of Gray's help and protection from Eduard.

Silently, she watched her husband spur his heels into his steed's side and wheel toward the castle. Saw him lead his men away from her in a thundering cloud of dust. He didn't look back.

Wrapping her arms around her middle, Catherine walked across the Village Square and back to the servants who held her horse for her. With a few words of explanation, she mounted and allowed them to escort her back to the castle by the same trail Gray had taken moments earlier.

Her heart felt heavy, and her head ached. She didn't want to move. Didn't want to think any more. Only one thing stood out clear and apart from the confusion and the pain: now more than ever she knew that she needed to tell Gray the truth, but it had to be far away from here. Somewhere secluded, where she could confess without fear of anyone listening and reporting back to Eduard.

She made a clicking sound, urging her mount faster on the trail to the castle. How long did it take to complete a grand assize? A week? Two? A month? Sweet Mother Mary, but she hoped that Gray meant it when he said he'd be back soon. He had to be. Because it appeared that she was going to have to wait until then to unburden herself of all the lies that had grown these past weeks, flourishing into vines that had risen up to strangle her.

So she'd wait.

And pray.

Gray wheeled his stallion to a halt several hours later, calling for his men to make camp. 'Twas not quite dark, but they'd made good time from Ravenslock. It wouldn't hurt to allow them some extra rest tonight.

While the five knights who'd accompanied him on this mission moved off to gather wood and secure shelter, Alban dismounted with Gray and helped him lead the horses to drink from a nearby stream.

"All right, my friend," Alban said. "What's the plan? I know you wouldn't have interrupted my training of the squires to join you in this unless you had a damn good reason."

"You're right. 'Tis of the utmost importance."

"Something to do with your assignment from the king?"

"Nay. 'Tis a matter of the heart," Gray answered, cupping some water from the stream. "*My* heart."

Alban scowled at him. "Christ, man, I knew you never wanted to marry, but I can't believe that you'd allow yourself to get involved with another—"

"My wife is the woman in question."

A long moment of silence passed before Alban finally broke into a grin. He slapped Gray on the back. "Well, why didn't you say so? I'd hoped it would all work out. She's a fine woman and a good match." His voice faded when he caught Gray's expression. "There's more to it, I gather."

Gray nodded and clenched his jaw, stroking his mount's nose as the stallion raised his head from the water. "I think Elise is hiding something from me. Something important. It lies like a shadow between us."

"I'll be the first to admit your ability to sniff out secrets," Alban murmured, and Gray knew that his friend was remembering how he'd saved him from his nearly fatal imprisonment so many years ago. "What makes you think your lady is keeping one?"

"Just a feeling, mostly. But I have reason as well. Elise . . . well, she wasn't untouched when we consummated our union." Looking off to the side, he mumbled, "Which was this afternoon."

"*Today?*" Alban asked, incredulous. "You waited until today to bed her? Why in hell did you put it off for so long?"

" 'Tis involved," Gray said wryly. "Suffice it to say that my wife was not virgin when I joined with her."

"You think she's taken a lover, then?"

"Nay—hell, I don't know. Not since we've wed, at least. I'm not sure about before. But I get the feeling that there may be more to all of this than that."

"It sounds serious," Alban said, shaking his head as he loosened the bridle on one of the horses. "What do you plan to do about it?"

Gray reached into his saddlebag and retrieved a purse full of coin. "I want to gather some information about Elise. About her life before we married. Only I suspect 'twill be a few days until I'm able to leave Cheltenham and devote my full attention to it."

He tossed the purse to Alban. "And that's where you come in, friend. If you're willing to help me, then take this. On the morrow when the rest of us continue on to the assize, veer off toward Somerset and start nosing around for me. I'll meet you there in a few days to see what you've found, and to add my own efforts to the task."

Alban whistled, weighing the purse in his palm. "God's bones—there's a small fortune in here."

"Aye. And we may end up spending every last farthing of it to get to the truth. I want to know all that I can about Elise and her past. But we must work quickly. I need to return to Ravenslock by week's end."

"That's not much time."

"'Twill be a challenge, no doubt, but one that I must undertake." Gray held out his hand. "Will you begin it for me, Alban?"

His friend clasped him by the forearm, gripping him tight. "You know I will. I'll get started at first light."

Gray nodded and looked back toward the clearing and the orange flames winking at them through the wood. "The men have kindled the fire. Come. We can discuss the particulars of your journey later."

"After we eat, I hope?"

Gray allowed himself a smile. "Aye, Alban. God knows you think better on a full stomach."

As they made their way back to the clearing with the horses, Gray jested with Alban about the reliable voracity of his appetite. But for all of his apparent calm, he felt a knot of anxiety twisting tight inside his belly. Because he knew that what he learned about Elise in the next few days would likely spell his heart's salvation—or mark the beginning of its final demise.

Chapter 13

◯◯◯

Squinting, Catherine blew a strand of hair from her eyes. Her knees ached from sitting in a cramped position for the past three hours, even though she'd been using the padded weaving mat that had mysteriously appeared in her chamber a few days ago. Worse, her fingers felt as if she'd dipped them in boiling water. But she couldn't stop now. 'Twas almost done.

There. Slipping the final strand of willow through, she deftly wove it among the other supple rods until it held. Then she pushed herself to her knees on her mat to better survey the finished product.

The chair was her best yet. Its large, curving back was graceful, the arms sturdy looking, but with an intricate woven design along the edges that set it

232

apart from others she'd made. 'Twas a kingly chair, fit for a noble knight or a great leader.

Fit for Gray.

She stood abruptly, gripping the chair's back as his name resounded through her mind and soul, flooding her with all of the thoughts she'd done her best to keep at bay for the past six days.

Time was running out. Eduard wouldn't wait forever to take what he wanted. He'd been with King Henry for nearly two months already, and she had a sinking feeling that her luck wouldn't hold much longer. Soon he'd be breathing down her neck again, demanding that she help him to finish their evil bargain or allow her children to suffer for her inaction.

Her hand tightened on the chair until the long, graining weave imprinted on her already sore fingers. Her skin was stained with tannin from the boiled rods, and her fingertips had long ago gone numb. She'd been weaving night and day, it seemed, since Gray had left for the grand assize. But the simple act of creating had calmed her, as always. Had helped her to think.

Now she knew what she must do, though it was breaking her heart. For as much as she loved Gray, and as much as it would destroy her never to see him again, she had to leave Ravenslock. She could wait no longer to save her children from Eduard.

Her stomach rolled with the thought of what she planned. Rescuing the twins without help was risky at best. Her skills in swordplay were barely enough to carry her through rudimentary drills, not to mention defending herself and the children against Eduard's trained knights. But with Gray in Cheltenham for God knew how much longer, it was the best she could offer.

Foolish twit, waiting like a lovesick maid for your prince to return. Such nonsense was the stuff of dreams. It never happened in real life. Not for someone like her, anyway. But she'd clung to the fragile hope that Gray might return in time to hear the truth. That she'd somehow manage to keep his love, despite her lies and her sins against him.

It had been a dream built on air, one that had served no purpose but to place her children in more danger.

Silently cursing herself, Catherine blinked back tears. Ian and Isabel needed her, now more than ever, and she'd sat here doing nothing for them. The time had come to act.

Tonight.

Aye, she'd leave tonight. The Punkie Night celebration would be under way by sundown. 'Twas an evening of freedom and wild revels, when the castle gates opened wide for a flood of people descending to the village for the harvest festivities. If she was careful, no one would notice her slipping off onto the dark down the road back to Somerset. They wouldn't raise the call that she was missing until much later, after she'd made good distance from Ravenslock.

A tingle of fear went through her as the reality of her decision sank home. What would she need to

take with her? Her boy's garments, of course. And
her sword. Her jaw tightened at the thought of actually using it on anyone, but she tried to concentrate
instead on what else she should gather before sunset. A large, dark cloak to conceal herself. And a
swift mount. As much as she hated the thought of
adding horse theft to her list of sins against Gray,
she'd never reach the twins by morning unless she
rode to get to them.

It was settled, then. Yet those things needed to be
gathered at the last moment, to minimize the chance
of anyone noticing. What provisions could she gar-
ner now without raising undue suspicion?

Food.

She'd need as much food as she could carry with
her, for both herself and the twins. Enough to last
them all for a few days, at least. By then she hoped
to have traveled nearer to London, where the three
of them could more easily disappear into the
crowds and where she might hope to earn even a
meager living through her weaving.

After taking a few deep breaths, Catherine poked
her head out the door of the weaving chamber and
looked around. 'Twas quiet in the corridor. She
headed toward the stairs, preparing to sneak down
to the larder to fill a sack that she could hide in her
room until tonight.

She could hear the sounds of preparation for the
Punkie Night festivities increasing as she got closer
to the gallery above the great hall. She stopped a
few paces shy of the stairway, keeping back in the

shadows. From her position near the rail, she could see people scurrying back and forth, scrubbing, cleaning, setting up wooden trestle tables and shaking out linens. They darted about, trying to avoid colliding with servants who were in the process of laying fresh floor rushes sprinkled with herbs.

Several women moved through the confusion, giggling as they pushed a handcart piled high with fat orange pumpkins toward the courtyard door. One of them shrieked and veered around a boy replacing torches; at their movement, a few of the pumpkins rolled from the barrow and cracked on the stone floor. Peals of laughter mingled with grumbling while the women jostled each other to scoop up the mess of seeds and stringy pulp.

Taking advantage of the distraction, Catherine swept down the staircase and out of the hall. She only stopped when she was in the cool dark of the corridor leading to the kitchens.

Pressing her hand to her stomach, she leaned against the wall, trying to still the nervousness that radiated through her entire frame. It was then that she realized that she stood in almost the same spot where Eduard had cornered her so many weeks ago. The same spot where Gray had come to her rescue and made her loathsome brother by marriage pull in his claws and retreat.

Grief threatened to overwhelm her, flooding her with a thousand sweet memories of Gray. Sweet Jesu, it was going to be hard to leave him. Clenching her jaw hard, she pushed away from the wall and continued to the larder, managing to nod and murmur something about a picnic to the page and two cook's assistants she passed on the way.

Young Tom, the gallant who had accosted her and Gray near the stream with his friends, looked up from his pot-scrubbing duty as she passed. He grinned and waved, and she mustered a smile for him. Another pang cut through her. Everyone had been so kind to her here. But she couldn't think about that now. She fought to keep the image of Ian and Isabel at the front of her mind, reminding her of what she needed to do.

Finally, she reached the larder. After glancing to see that no one watched, she slipped into the cool chamber. Her eyes adjusted to the gloom as she scrounged for an empty sack. Like every other part of this wondrous castle, the food stores here exceeded imagination. Provisions of every kind lined the shelves and filled the barrels stacked on the floor. And it all smelled wonderful. Eight freshly baked loaves lay cooling on a board near a pallet of cheeses with thick yellow rinds.

She tossed three of the loaves and two circles of cheese into her bag, adding seven or eight crisp apples, topped by numerous handfuls of walnuts from one of the barrels. She allowed herself a tiny smile while she scooped up the hard fruits; Ian always adored cracking open their shells with a stone to get to the meat inside. Pray God she'd find him well enough to take the same pleasure in dissecting these.

A few onions followed the rest. As a final thought, she added a parchment-wrapped bundle of wax tapers from a pile that lay in the coolest part of the larder. They were a luxury, unsuitable for the life she and the twins would be living once they escaped, but they might be bartered, later, for more food. Taking a last look around, she pulled the string tight on the sack and gritted her teeth to lift it over her shoulder.

Saints, 'twas heavy. The trick would be getting it back to her chamber unnoticed. Then again, perhaps she ought to hide it somewhere nearer to the stables, so that it would be easier to hoist onto her mount when the time was right tonight.

Biting her lip, Catherine considered her options. There was a mound of clean hay, covered by a pavilion of sorts, just behind the stables; she could hide the bag there until night fell and the area emptied as most of the workers went to the Punkie Night celebration. She dragged the sack to the door, so caught up in her thoughts that she opened it and stepped out without checking first.

"Good morn, Lady Camville," a harsh voice rasped. "Planning a journey, are you?"

Catherine silenced the scream that bubbled up in her throat; her sack thudded to the floor as she snapped her gaze to the person who'd surprised her.

'Twas the deformed man, swathed in his customary black robes. He stood crouched in the shadows just outside the door, his mouth the only visible part of his face. His thin white lips pursed together, and though his eyes were hidden in the folds of his hood, she felt the strength of his stare on her.

"You seem to have packed a great deal there," he

said, nodding to the sack. "It must be a sizable journey you plan to undertake."

"I—I'm having a picnic," she blurted, despising herself for the fear that tightened her throat.

"Oh, aye, a picnic," he cackled. "All the way to Faegerliegh Keep, I'd warrant." She felt herself blanch, but before she could even attempt a denial, he shuffled closer to her, making her shrink against the wall. He started to say something, but then stopped as two laundresses opened a door down the corridor and started toward them.

The women chattered, unaware of anyone else, until at last they veered away and disappeared down another passage to the great hall. But their interruption seemed to change the man's mood. He swung his hooded head around, as if checking for others who might disturb him.

Finally, he leaned closer to her again, rasping softly, "If you wish to keep your children safe from harm, lady, then do as I say. Meet me after the *nones* bell in the abandoned crofter's hut beyond the limits of the fallow field. Fail me not."

With that he coughed, the sound rattling from his chest, and turned to hobble down the hall. She heard the portal to the yard swing open and bang shut behind him. And then her knees gave way. She gripped the doorframe to steady herself, her breath coming shallow, her eyes a blur of dancing black dots.

If you wish to keep your children safe from harm . . .

Holy Mother Mary, the man was Eduard's spy, and he'd caught her planning her escape.

Her babes. Sweet God, her precious babes. She'd done this to them with her clumsy, ridiculous ideas of a rescue. Would the spy tell Eduard about her transgression against him? And would her odious brother by marriage choose to take out his anger toward her on her children?

Her heart hammered with thick, painful beats. She released her hold on the wall, sinking to the floor as she clasped her hands tightly to pray. She begged God to help her, beseeching Him for the courage to face this nameless spy of Eduard's . . . and for the strength to deliver her children from the clutches of evil.

Pushing his hand through his hair, Gray strode into the village tavern in Somerset, bone-weary from the events of the past six days. The grand assize was over, thank God. He'd conducted himself in a way sure to please King Henry, but the whole time his mind had kept straying to the task awaiting him here; his chance to learn more about Elise and the secrets she was keeping from him.

His gaze swept the dim recesses of the inn. At this time of the afternoon, the place was predictably full of customers, all seeking a pint of ale or some watered wine to ease their day's toil. He'd sent a message ahead to Alban, informing him of his arrival, but it seemed that his friend remained occupied elsewhere for the moment. Ah, well. Waiting for Alban gave him good reason to sit and cool his own parched throat.

He walked to the back of the wattle and daub building, finding an empty bench near the hearth. He sank down with a sigh, stretching his back and trying to work the kinks out of his neck, noticing that several village residents favored him with curious stares. 'Twas nothing out of the ordinary. His size alone usually elicited such attention, but today he'd worn several of his finest garments for the conclusion of the grand assize, and it assured that many here would find him an interesting sight.

"Here you go, love."

A blond serving wench set a cup of ale in front of him, sloshing some of the brew over its rim. With a false mew of distress, she leaned over to wipe up the spill, ensuring that the full mounds of her breasts wobbled temptingly in his face while she cleaned.

Gray lifted his brow. Tavern lasses were a usually cheeky lot, but this one was bold, even by common standards. When she smiled and pulled away, ready to flounce her nether assets at him on her way to the next customer, he decided to smile back at her. It stilled her in her tracks as effectively as he'd hoped it would.

"I'd prefer some spiced cider, lass, if you have any," he said, lifting the cup of ale to hand it back to her.

The girl stared at him, her mouth gone slack. Finally she clamped it shut, seeming to regain her wits enough to run her appreciative gaze over him and dart out her tongue to moisten her lips. "The name's Cassie, milord," she answered in a husky purr, "and I'm not so sure Master Jack keeps much more than ale and wine in store."

"Cassie, then." He held the cup to her again, still smiling. "I'd be grateful if you'd look for me."

She smoothed her hands over her curved hips and tilted her head ever so slightly, fluttering her thick fringe of lashes at him. Ah, she was good. Too good, perhaps. It wouldn't surprise him if he came back here in a year to find Cassie full and ripe with a babe, courtesy of one of the men with whom she so shamelessly flirted.

"Are you sure you want to make do with cider, milord?" She blinked again, pulling his attention back from his meandering thoughts. "And not try something a bit more . . . potent?"

"Nay, Cassie. Cider will do fine if you can find it for me."

Disappointment flared for a brief moment in her eyes, but then she just nodded, a bit more shyly, he thought, before going off in search of his drink.

By the time she returned with it, he'd worked most of the stiffness from his neck and was even beginning to relax a little. He took the spiced brew from her with murmured thanks and drank deep. He was readying to take another healthy swallow, when the hissing, slurred voices of two men hidden on the other side of the jutting hearth gave him pause. He leaned forward to look. They appeared to be common soldiers of some sort, engaged in drunken conversation.

"'S blood, Francis, I'm sick to death of hearin' it! You didn't bury the wrong corpse! 'Tis a story the like of which you've told a hundred times. Only if Lord Montford hears you tellin' this one, it'll be the long sleep for you, it will!"

Lord Montford?

Gray set down his cup. Eduard was lord of these lands, and had been since his elder brother's death some five or six months past. The soldiers could mean no other man.

"Christ Almighty, I'm tellin' true, Rolf!" the man named Francis hissed, before dropping his voice so low that Gray strained to hear.

"May Saint Peter strike me down if I'm false! Lord Montford made me sneak in and put her in our lady's tomb. 'Twas the dead of night. He had her wrapped up real good, so's I couldn't see her, but I'm telling you, 'twasn't mistress Catherine! I knew our lady as well as anyone, and 'twasn't her! This one was 'alf her size. Like a little bird, she was. And I saw a lock of hair peepin' out the top of the shroud—not brown like our lady's, but pale as spun gold!"

Golden-haired? Like a little bird?

Montford kept her so secluded within the keep, 'twas impossible for me to gain an audience with her. I told you the only information I could gather from the people of the village. They described Elise de Montford as small and fair-haired. One of the villeins even likened her to a tiny sparrow.

Alban's apology from the day of his wedding shot through Gray's brain like fire. Without even realizing that he was going to do it, he surged to his feet and lunged across the hearth, grabbing Francis by the front of his tunic and pushing him up against the wall.

Francis gasped and sputtered, his eyes rolling wildly in his head. "What—what the devil?" Before he could say more, his gaze fell on Gray's fine garments, took in his masterful height and the iron-muscled arm gripping him, and then he fell to blathering like an idiot.

"Please, milord Montford! God save me, oh Lord, sweet Jesu in heaven spare me, milord Montford! I didn't mean any of—"

"I'm not Lord Montford!" Gray muttered, giving him a shake hard enough to rattle his teeth, while he jerked his other arm to remove the loyal Rolf, who'd attached himself with drunken fervor to Gray's elbow in an effort to protect his friend. Rolf slid to the floor, a boneless heap, crossing himself repeatedly and moaning that they were both doomed now, for sure.

Gray scowled and leaned into Francis, talking slowly, so that the man couldn't help but understand him. "Tell me everything you know. Who was the woman you buried? And if she was a lady, why was she buried in secret? I want to know everything, damn you, and I want to know it now!"

"Gray, for Christ's sake, let up on the wretch. He's senseless already."

With a growl, Gray released the swooning Francis and twisted to face Alban. His friend's expression was stony, and a chain with something round and metallic dangled from his fist. Alban held out the object. "I think this will go a long way in explaining what you want to know."

Taking the offering from him, Gray squinted at it in the dim light, trying to see it more clearly. 'Twas a locket, fairly new. He popped the clasp to see the miniature inside. A thread of shock wound through him. He looked back to Alban in question, not understanding how this could explain anything.

Rolf had been kneeling in desperate prayer on the floor near Gray, but now he dared enough to peer around him and catch a glimpse of the tiny painting. "Ah," Rolf murmured softly. " 'Tis our beloved mistress Catherine, God bless her soul. A fine lady and a good woman she was." He crossed himself again. "May she rest in peace."

And in that instant all of the strength seemed to leave Gray's limbs. He sank down to the bench like a stone, wondering if he'd ever find means to rise again.

Chapter 14

~~~⁓O〇⁓~~~

A breeze caressed Catherine's fevered skin as she made her way across the clearing, toward the path that cut through the fallow field. With each breath, she inhaled the fertile scents of fallen leaves and sun-warmed grass, but she had no will to enjoy autumn's bounty this day. Her stomach felt sick, the echoing notes of the *nones* bell matching the relentless thrumming in her ears.

In a few moments she was going to reach the abandoned crofter's hut and come face to face with Eduard's evil spy.

Her fingers tingled, and she kept flexing her hands to keep them from going numb. Trying to force herself to focus, she patted the handle of the sheathed dagger she'd secured at her waist as protection. 'Twas little comfort, considering the ordeal that lay ahead, but 'twas better than nothing.

The wind seemed to pick up, gusting through the trees as she approached the old cottage. It crouched like a troll in the woods, with chunks of thatch missing from its roof and several boards hanging askew. A fitting choice, she thought, for Eduard's misshapen spy.

She paused at the portal, trying to gather her courage to go in and face the man. But then the door creaked open, and she forced her trembling legs to carry her into the cottage's dim recesses.

It was quiet inside. A film of grit seemed to blanket everything in the oppressive atmosphere, and a damp, musty smell assaulted her. Rubbing her eyes, Catherine squinted, trying to make them adjust from the light of outdoors. Where was the wretch? He'd arrived first, the open door made that clear. Was he hiding to frighten her? Was this some perverse game he played, worthy of his evil master?

A grinding crunch sounded to her left, and she swung her gaze to the spot. The hunched man stood half in shadow, his form partly illuminated by daylight streaming in from the shutter he'd just opened. Dust motes danced in the slash of light, swirling round him. He stepped closer, and Catherine forced herself not to shrink back. As before, only his thin, pale lips showed beneath the folds of his hood.

"Have you come alone?" he asked in a low rasp.

"Aye," she whispered.

"You're certain that no one followed you?"

She nodded mutely this time, feeling what little courage she'd mustered beginning to fade. This man, this *spy*, held her children's lives in his hands. Holy saints, what could she do to stop him from making them suffer for her mistakes?

"Please," she blurted, "please don't let Eduard hurt my babes. I'm begging you, do not to tell him of—"

"Hush, Catherine," the man said softly, and she stilled, feeling a tingle go up her spine at the change in his voice. There was something about it. Something that struck a chord at the very center of her . . .

"There's no need to fear," he continued, his tone gentle and melodious. "I'll not be telling Lord Montford anything, except to go straight to hell where he belongs, to roast with all of the other demons and villains."

With that the man slowly straightened until he stood miraculously transformed, just as tall and true as any other healthy person. When he lifted his hands to his hood, Catherine gasped; her heart skipped a beat as he swept the dark material back to expose his face and the silvery waves of hair atop his head. After staring for several moments, her voice finally squeaked past the tightness in her throat.

"Heldred? Sweet Mother of God. Heldred, is it really you?"

"Aye, my lady, 'tis me," he answered quietly. "Blessed be, but 'tis good to speak with you at long last."

Shock dissolved into happy tears as Catherine threw herself into the old man's arms. He hugged her tight to him, and she heard the catch in his breathing as he stroked her hair softly.

In all of her years as Geoffrey de Montford's wife, Heldred had been the only person, other than her own children, to show her kindness and love; the old weaver had been the first in her life to treat her gently, with courtesy. Though their stations in life were different, they'd become friends. She remembered how his sun-browned cheeks had wrinkled with smiles every time he helped her, teaching her new skills to perfect her weaving, and she'd never ceased to feel grateful for his care of her.

Now she pulled back, gazing at his dear old face and spilling questions at him in a confusing stream. "Why did you—how did you know where to find me, and what do you know about all this—?"

Heldred shook his head, smiling. "Ah, lady. I suspected something foul from the moment Lord Montford announced you dead." He stroked his finger over her wet cheek. "When I slipped past the guards and found Elise's body in your tomb, I saw the truth of his evil deed. I decided then that he had brought you here as his own sister, though at first I didn't understand why he would commit such blasphemy. I came here to watch over you and to be sure that he planned no other harm."

Suddenly, everything seemed to fall into place. Gripping his hand, Catherine smiled at him through her tears, "'Twas you all along, wasn't it?

You were the one who sent me that pot of salve for my blisters. And those bouquets of flowers—and the padded weaving mat that appeared in my chamber just last week. All this time, it was you! But why did you not reveal yourself to me? Why did you let me think you were one of Eduard's spies?"

"For the fears that I caused you, my lady, I am heartily sorry," Heldred murmured, bowing his head. "But I needed to keep my disguise to be sure that none other might recognize me and report of it. I didn't want to endanger you in any way, so I watched and waited." Shadows deepened his brown eyes. "And I learned. I think I understand, now, my lady, why Lord Montford sent you here. It has to do with your husband, does it not?"

Catherine released his hands and stepped away. "Aye. Eduard wants me to prepare the way for Gray's murder, so that he can assume Gray's power and lands. If I refuse, he's vowed to kill Ian and Isabel as punishment."

Heldred cursed under his breath. "'Tis as I suspected." He looked back to Catherine. "When is the deed to be committed?"

"I do not know. The order is certain to come soon, though. Eduard has been away with the king for nigh on two months already. 'Tis why I planned to escape tonight."

"But why have you not—" Heldred paused, studying her. "I mean no offense, my lady, but why have you not confided in Lord Camville? I've noticed in these weeks of watching that he seems to be a kind man. A powerful man, in a position, surely, to help you."

Catherine felt her cheeks heat. "Gray is a good man, Heldred. The finest I've known. I had resolved to tell him, and in truth, an opportunity to confess presented itself but a week past, when we were away from both the castle and Eduard's spies. But I let the chance slip by."

Heldred frowned. "When was that?"

"The day of the village fair."

"Ah, yes," Heldred said. "I remember. Sir Alban left to find you and Lord Camville in the forest after the brawling began at the marketplace."

Catherine nodded, the heat in her cheeks intensifying. She remembered all too well those moments in the glen and the passion she and Gray had shared. But she couldn't bring herself to tell Heldred, dear as he was, the full reason behind why she'd remained silent.

Finally, she settled for an explanation of a different kind. "Gray left that same afternoon at the king's command. He went to Cheltenham, to assist in a grand assize there. It's been six days already, with no telling when he'll return." She looked away, so that Heldred wouldn't see the pain in her eyes when she added, "And that is why I must leave tonight. I cannot continue to risk my children's safety by waiting longer. I am only indulging myself if I do."

Heldred drew her gaze again, his dark, wise eyes searching hers. "You feel deeply for your husband, then, lady?"

She tried to blink back stinging tears, but in the end, she just nodded and forced a watery smile. "Aye, Heldred. I love him. My heart aches to think that I must leave him. But my children must come first. I know that, and yet I—"

Her voice cracked, and with an oath, Heldred gathered her to him like a wounded child. All the anxiety of the past week seemed to overwhelm her, and she let herself weep into his kind embrace, clinging to him for strength. It felt so good to have the comfort of this old friend; he knew her true identity and could share her burden, even if only for a little while.

When the worst of her crying had passed, Catherine hiccuped and wiped her nose with the scrap of linen he offered her. "Thank you," she murmured, trying again to smile. "The only bright spot in all of this is finding you, Heldred. That, and knowing I'll see my children again tonight, God willing."

"Aye. If there be any justice in this world, you and they will live safely together once more." Heldred stood straighter. "I want to help you to it, my lady."

"What?"

"I wish to go with you, to assist you in freeing your children from Faegerliegh Keep."

"Nay, Heldred. I'll not have you risking yourself more. Coming here and taking a disguise to watch over me was danger enough."

"And what of the twins' safety, lady? Will you be

content to pass by what help I can offer? Are not two rescuers better than one?"

Catherine frowned at her old friend, taking a breath in preparation to argue with him, then clamping her mouth shut when she realized that he was right. She sighed. "You have a point. But attempting a rescue at Faegerliegh will be dangerous, as you well know. The intricacy of the corridors alone will daunt us, not to mention the guards Eduard has surely posted everywhere."

"That doesn't change my wanting to aid you." A familiar glint sparked in his eyes. "Besides, if we find trouble, you can always stun the guards with a few passes of your blade. You know, your first day of training with the sword was inspirational." He grinned and made a feinting pass at her before letting his imaginary steel tip thud to the floor.

She rolled her eyes and smiled. "You saw that too, did you?"

He shrugged. "I followed at a safe distance. 'Twas but a short while after I'd arrived at Ravenslock, and I had to be sure that your new husband meant you no harm by taking you out dressed so strangely and with weapons in tow."

Catherine's smile dimmed. Gray had never meant her any harm in the entire time she'd known him. All he'd ever done was care for her and make her feel safe and loved. Shaking her head to push the thoughts away, she said, "I'll have you know I'm much improved from that first day."

"Aye, lady, I know," he said, still smiling. "I've

been watching." Then he gestured toward the door. "But perhaps we should go now so that you may get back to the castle. It wouldn't do for you to be missed on this of all days."

Catherine nodded, clasping his wrinkled hand in hers. "I had planned to leave after dark, once the Punkie Night festivities were full under way. My maidservants told me 'tis a night of wild revels. The confusion will provide a chance for us to make our escape."

"'Tis a good plan. We can leave with what we need before anyone even knows we've gone. Where did you stow the sack of provisions I saw you gathering?"

"I hid it in the straw behind the stables. I thought it would be easier to retrieve when I needed to get it onto my mount."

"Clever, my lady. But riding will make it necessary to steal a horse. Two, if I am to go as well."

"Aye, Heldred, I know. I regret the theft, and yet I cannot see much choice in it. Not if we're to get to Faegerliegh and spirit the twins away before a search finds us."

Heldred nodded. "'Tis a boon, then, that I sleep in the stables. I've been passing myself off as a groom. In disguise my back looks crippled, but I've proved to them that my hands work well." He grinned, wiggling his fingers. "I can prepare the mounts for us. All you'll need to do is meet me at the stables as soon as most of the revelers have left the castle."

"I'll be there," Catherine said, opening the door

and peering out of the cottage to ensure that the pathway was quiet. All looked bright and deceptively calm. She ducked back inside for a moment to give Heldred a hug and a murmured farewell. But before she could embrace him, he winced and drew in his breath sharply. Startled, Catherine pulled back.

"What is it, Heldred? What's wrong?"

"Nothing, my lady," he said through gritted teeth, reaching for the pouch on his neck. After fumbling to open the drawstring, he took a pinch of the dried contents inside and pushed it past his lips. In a moment his spasm seemed to pass, and he breathed easier. Apologetically, he looked at her. " 'Tis but an old malady of the chest. Nothing that a little cherry bark cannot cure."

"But it pained you so," she said, still worried. "Might it not be better to have the castle healer examine you to be sure 'tis nothing more serious?"

"Nay, I'm fine," he said, waving her off. "I'll not forestall the rescue of your children for the sake of my aches and pains."

He smiled tightly again and shooed her toward the door, but she resisted. "I wish you would reconsider, Heldred."

"Nay, my lady. Please. Speak no more of it."

She paused, lips pursed at his obstinacy. Finally she just shook her head and said, "If you will not do as I bid concerning this, then you must grant me one other boon."

"What is it, my lady?"

"To be careful in your preparations for this night.

Horse thieving is a serious crime, and I do not know if I could live with myself if anything happened to you because of me."

He patted her cheek. "Aye, you have my word, lady. I will be fine. I plan to do my work in the shadows, as always." He smiled, crouching back down into his former, hunchbacked pose, startling her again with the swiftness of his transformation. "People often overlook cripples, you know, my lady. 'Tis easier for most to pretend deformity doesn't exist."

She nodded, squeezing his hand before moving to the door.

"Until tonight, then, Mistress Catherine," he called gruffly.

"Aye, Heldred." She gave him one last look over her shoulder. "Until tonight."

Eduard tilted a stick of sealing wax to the flame and let it drip onto the fold of parchment he held. When the liquid had accumulated to a thick, blood-red pool, he turned his hand and pressed his signet into it. There. 'Twas done. Nodding for his messenger to approach, he handed him the sealed document.

"I want this delivered posthaste. No delays. It must arrive at Ravenslock on the morrow. I myself will follow by no more than two days. See to it."

The man nodded, fear etched in the tight lines of his face. The messenger's expression pleased Eduard, made him more comfortable. His will would be obeyed, as always. Because if it wasn't . . .

Smiling to himself, he strode back to his tent at

the center of camp. His men, the nearly five score of whom he'd forced to join him for his travels with King Henry, were settling in for the night in their lesser shelters, dotted around him in circular formation. The very position of their tents protected him as their lord. 'Twas his right, as was his own sumptuous canopy, occupied by no one but himself.

Aye, 'twas his right—as Ravenslock Castle would also be his by right, before the week was out.

Pushing aside the flap to his tent, he ducked in and squinted at the thin veil of smoke hanging in the air. That blasted boy, Compton. He'd forgotten to leave an opening at the tent's peak again. Eduard resolved to speak to him about it, to ensure that he'd remember next time. Just as soon as—

"My—my Lord Montford?"

The soft, dread-tinged voice tingled up Eduard's spine like the stroke of fingernails. *Ah, she was here.*

At least Compton had obeyed one of his commands. He stepped further into the partitioned area of his tent and approached the mound of pillows and furs that served as his bed. A woman huddled beneath the coverlet, obviously naked. And trembling. Her auburn hair curled over her shoulders, spilling onto the blankets; her eyes followed his every motion, as a hare watches the approach of a wolf.

Eduard smiled again, excitement flaring in his blood. She was afraid. Deliciously so. As well she should be.

After disrobing slowly, so that she might gain full view of his impressive size and strength, he yanked the covers off of her and sat on the bed. Then, taking the back of her head, he pulled her hard to him for a deep kiss. She tasted of cinnamon. He delved deeper into her mouth, pleased. Again, his wishes had been obeyed.

Soon the woman—Juliette, was it?—began to struggle, whimpering and pushing against his bare chest as she fought for air. Laughing, he shoved her away and reclined on the pillows, flicking his wrist to indicate what she should do for him next.

Her lips looked slightly bruised from his kissing, her eyes wide brown pools, so expressive, so shocked at what he was demanding of her. And yet she did as she was bidden, crouching over him to grasp his erection and take it into her mouth. She moved tentatively at first, then with a choking cry as he dug his fingers into her hair, forcing her into a rhythm that pleased him.

He sighed and leaned back into the pillows, abandoning himself to sensation. Ah, yes, 'twas just what he'd needed. He craved release to soothe the tensions of this last week with the king. All of the bowing and scraping he'd been forced to do—it had sickened him, but he'd done it, done everything needed to ensure his continued privilege and rank in the kingdom. To ensure his high status with King Henry.

And yet even the mighty king didn't know how much Eduard de Montford's power was about to increase. Aye, it would swell by no less than a third of the cursed Camville's estates. And after that he'd take the wretch's latest plum on the vine—his imminent appointment as Sheriff of Cheltenham. Pluck it himself, once that milksop Catherine completed his instructions, as he'd directed her in his letter. Then it would all fall into place. Just a few more days . . .

His groin began to tighten, pleasure rippling into his belly, mounting and growing. He gritted his teeth, savoring his coming triumph as he watched Juliette's head bob up and down on him with smooth, even strokes.

It was good to be obeyed. To know that those he commanded would scramble to do his bidding, would struggle to please him and serve his will. He closed his eyes, pressing into the pillows as the delectable tension began to overwhelm him. He felt it building to a fever-pitch . . .

Suddenly he exploded, releasing the hot flow from deep inside. Sensations swirled and throbbed, mixing with his angry thoughts until they were almost indistinguishable in his mind.

Blind obedience. So sweet, so necessary to the smooth progress of life.

And his right, by heaven and hell.

His bloody right.

As darkness fell over the land, Catherine stood in the torch-lit opulence of the bedchamber she'd shared with Gray, trying to put the constant, wrenching thoughts of him from her mind. She'd waged a silent battle against her emotions all day, her heart leaden at the thought of leaving, even knowing that she had no choice.

Setting her jaw, she twisted her plaited hair into a knot and paced to the window. Rain spattered the costly glazed panes and a chill seeped through the cracks between window and wall, but the storm seemed to be waning. Thank the saints that the foul weather had had little effect on the Punkie Night revelers beginning their celebration below. Bonfires winked merrily across the hillside, glowing in defiance of wind and weather.

With a sigh, Catherine turned away, resolving to make her final preparations. She'd already changed into her breeches and tunic, and strapped the sharp sword she used for training to her side. *A cape.* Aye, she still needed something dark and hooded, like Heldred wore, not only for warmth, but to hide her features and shield her feminine shape from the world.

Making her way into the small room attached to the bedchamber, she lit a wall torch. Gray kept most of his clothing here, stored in trunks or in the two tall wardrobes standing against the wall. Her garments were here too, though they weren't what she sought now. Nay, all of her things were too feminine and colorful. She'd have to use one of Gray's cloaks for her escape.

After rummaging a little while, she found what she sought. A hooded cape of thick, black wool, brushed soft, with no edging or braid to distinguish it. Taking it from the trunk, Catherine shook it out and draped it over her shoulders. It was big, cut for Gray's powerful frame, but that would serve to hide her more effectively. She only hoped that her height and build would help her to carry it well enough to avoid suspicion.

Snuggling the fabric around her, Catherine closed

her eyes. A biting pang stabbed her. Gray's scent, fresh and masculine, drifted to her from the folds of the garment, teasing her as if he stood there with her, wrapping her inside his embrace. She breathed deep, letting the feeling wash over her, unable to stop herself from prodding the fresh wound.

Gray. Oh, Gray, my love.

Squeezing back tears that welled again, Catherine turned and walked into the main bedchamber. She forced one foot in front of the other, making herself keep moving. 'Twas time to meet Heldred in the stables. No more dawdling with childish hopes and memories.

She gazed round one last time, every object, each shadow seeming to burn itself with aching clarity into her mind. 'Twas here that Gray first came to her after their wedding, here where he'd soothed and cared for her. Here where he'd simply held her, safe and warm, until dawn on the night they finally were to consummate their union.

These and so many other memories throbbed with a life of their own, making the ache swell until she thought it would swallow her up. But it couldn't. She must consign her memories to the dust now. Those and all of her secret dreams of a future with Gray.

Dashing her hand across her eyes, Catherine moved toward the door. It was over. She was leaving.

But as she reached the portal, she heard a loud noise in the corridor. Startled, she stepped back; at that moment the door crashed open and slammed against the wall. Gray stood framed in the opening, rain-soaked, his chest heaving, his expression feral.

He went still and gazed at her for what seemed like an eternity. His shadowed eyes burned, dark and vulnerable, his muscled frame outlined in stark relief by his wet shirt and breeches. Finally, he just shook his head.

"Damn you, lady," he growled softly, "but I want to know who the hell you really are, and what kind of game it is that you've been playing with me."

Chapter 15

❦

S he stood frozen in place, dwarfed by his ridicu-lously large cape. Gray clenched his jaw. Hell, she looked more like a naughty child caught raiding his closet than a deceitful imposter bent on his de-struction. Her breeches clung to her legs as deli-ciously as ever, her eyes bluer than he remembered. And damn her, but she was gazing at him with a look he might have mistaken for love if he hadn't al-ready discovered the awful truth about her.

God, she was beautiful.

The thought came unbidden to his mind, and he shoved it aside angrily, striding into the chamber. The locket swung like a weapon from his fist.

"I stopped in Somerset on my way home from the grand assize, lady," he grated. "And I found this."

He stopped right in front of her, offering up the necklace. She moved nary a muscle, nor did she utter a sound in her defense.

"Well?" he demanded, thrusting it at her again.

She took it from him then, and the gentle brush of her fingers against his made him wince, made the ache he'd borne since that moment at the tavern lance deeper in his belly. He watched as she opened the pendant and looked at her own portrait. Her gaze was somber. Almost sorrowful. And yet still she didn't speak.

"By the Rood, woman, just tell me. For once, let me hear the truth coming from your lips."

She stood motionless, her expression filled with pain. "I'm so sorry, Gray. You're right. You deserve the truth. I've wanted to tell you for a long time, but I—I—" She made a choking sound and squeezed her eyes shut. "Nay! I cannot tell you. Not here. Eduard's spies—"

"*Spies?*" Gray broke in bitterly. "You mean other than you?"

She flinched, and the ache in his gut bloomed wider.

"Eduard hired spies to watch *me*," she said quietly. "To report of my every move, my every word, back to him."

"If that is true, then I can assure you, they are no longer a concern. When I arrived, I ordered all of the revelers back to the castle before barring every gate under heavy guard. 'Twill remain so, with none allowed to enter or leave Ravenslock until I am satisfied that there is no further danger to me or my people."

She remained silent, looking at the floor.

"Go ahead," he challenged her. "Speak! There's naught to fear now in revealing the truth."

Slowly, she lifted her gaze until it connected with his; a jolt of agony went through him, mocking him with its power. God, but he was a pitiful excuse for a man, a weak wretch to still want this woman—this betrayer—so much, even after all that she'd done to him.

"I never meant you harm, Gray," she whispered. "You must believe that."

"Must I?" he managed, his throat aching, tight. "Was it not you who came here under false pretences, you who feigned marriage with me, making our union and everything that came after it a lie?"

"I swear that I never wanted to deceive you."

"And yet you did. Every time you let me call you Elise. Every time you let me call you *wife*." His already hoarse voice broke on that last word, and he took her by the shoulders, forcing her to look at him. "For God's sake, tell me why! Did you and Eduard plan this to make a fool of me? To humiliate me further at Court?"

Exquisite pain shifted over her face, that face he loved so well, but she shook her head. "Nay. 'Tis worse than that."

"Then tell me, damn it."

Biting her lip, she paced a few steps away, her fingers clenched tight. Finally, she faced him again.

"All of this began when Elise died. She took her own life, driven to it by Eduard's cruelty. When he discovered that she had escaped him, he came up with his own solution to the problem. He forced me to marry you in her place so that I could aid him in committing the terrible deed that he'd already planned . . ." Catherine gazed at him blindly, her eyes pleading with him.

"God forgive me, Gray, but I married you in order to help kill you."

He didn't think he could breathe for a moment. Her words hammered through his skull with cracking blows. She stared at him now as if he might crumble to dust before her eyes. And he felt like doing it. Felt like disintegrating rather than having to face what she'd just said. He should have expected as much, but hearing her say it made it that much more real and painful.

His breath finally exploded from him in a rush, and he jabbed his hand through his hair, swinging away from her. He held himself very still, very stiff. What he'd stumbled upon in Somerset was true, then. His real betrothed, the woman he'd forced himself to accept to appease King Henry, was dead, and he'd been duped into a marriage whose sole purpose was to ease the way to his murder. And Montford had plotted it all . . .

His stomach rolled, his mind careening with the duplicity of it. With a growl, he slammed his palms into the wall above the fireplace, closing his eyes against the pain.

God it hurt.

The lies . . . sweet Jesu, the lies. Even with his eyes closed he could see her face, so beautiful and serene—on the altar, with his people, in front of his men. Aye, even cradled in his arms as they made love with a passion that had pierced him to his soul.

And it had all been a lie . . .

Desperately, Gray searched within himself, looking for some dark, dangerous emotion to swell and ease the pain of this betrayal. He'd always been able to summon such feelings at will, call up rage or battle lust to wipe out all else from his mind. But this time, nothing happened. This time, the hurt went too deep. No matter how hard he tried, it still seethed beneath the surface, vying for power and precedence.

And for the first time in his life, Gray feared that the hurt would win.

"I'm sorry," Catherine whispered. "I should have told you the truth long ago."

"Aye," he said finally, still leaning into the wall. "But you didn't."

"Because I was protecting my children."

For the second time in less than a minute, Gray felt like someone had impaled him with a bloody lance. "Your *children*?" he asked in a raw voice, swiveling his head to look at her. "You have children, lady?"

"Aye," she murmured, looking startled. "I thought you'd learned about them as well."

Of course. The realization of it sliced him like a blade. He should have made the connection back at the tavern, only he hadn't allowed himself to think beyond the excruciating point of learning that she'd played him false.

When he didn't answer, she looked down at her hands, still clasped tightly in front of her. Then, with slow, even steps, she walked over to the trunk by the bed, lifted the lid and retrieved the portrait that Gray had somehow known from the first would come to mean more than just a wedding gift. His heart throbbed, the ache inside him thrumming with each beat.

"I named them Ian and Isabel," she said softly. "They were born to me eight years ago, through my cursed union with Eduard's brother, Baron Geoffrey de Montford." She stroked her finger over their images, her lips tight. "They were the only joys of my existence, and that is why Eduard chose to use them against me, to get to you."

"How?" Gray couldn't seem to stop himself from asking.

When Catherine raised her gaze to him again, her eyes were shadowed by that same haunted look he remembered from their very first night together. "'Twas simple. Eduard forced me to comply with his schemes by threatening to kill my children if I did not."

"Sweet Christ." Even through his own pain, Gray couldn't escape the horror of what that must have meant to her. Montford was a sick bastard. As corrupt and evil as the devil himself, to be willing to threaten the lives of his own niece and nephew.

Gray shook his head, feeling blessed numbness begin to creep in. It was all starting to make more sense now. At least he was beginning to understand why Catherine had betrayed him. He couldn't blame her for going along with Montford's plots. Nay, not when her children's lives were at stake.

But that didn't change what had hurt him more than anything else in all of this. She should have told him the truth. Weeks ago. Christ, she should have trusted him enough to tell him the truth.

He pushed away from the wall, the heaviness in his soul near to choking him. "On the morrow, lady, I will lead my forces to Faegerliegh Keep and take your children back, by force if necessary. At the same time a message will be dispatched to the king, informing him of the situation. We will await his answer and direction here, with you and the twins safe under my protection."

She stared at him, eyes wide. "You would do that for me? Even now, after all this . . . ?"

"I would do no less for anyone, lady. 'Tis justice, pure and simple."

"But what of King Henry's sanctions against it? Will you not be risking everything if he does not see this thing in the same light?"

"Aye," Gray said, snapping his gaze to hers in exasperation. "'Tis a distinct and unhappy possibility. And yet do you think I could live with myself if I let any number of sanctions—or even the king himself—stand in the way when children's lives weigh in the balance?"

She looked as if she would answer, then. Perhaps assure him that, nay, she'd been foolish not to trust him. That she'd always known he would do what was right, regardless of what he risked or how he'd been hurt. But in the end she said nothing. She just stood there, pale and haunted, her gaze downcast.

"Ah, lady," Gray said at last, shamed to find his voice gone suddenly as husky as hers, "here you stand before me as you did on our very first night together, silent and frightened, uncertain of what the future may bring." He swallowed hard. "And still knowing me, it seems, not at all . . ."

Unable to say more, Gray walked to the door on legs of wood, hardly aware of leaving the chamber or pulling the heavy door closed behind him. He took several stumbling steps before the pain finally overwhelmed him and he jerked to a halt.

Then he just stood very still in the dark, listening to the rain beating its muted melody on the roof above him, and feeling sadness sweep through him in crashing waves; it weighed him down, defeating him. He sank slowly to his knees under its power, fists clenched against the agony tearing through his brain—against the inescapable knowledge that he had just walked away from everything in the world that would ever matter to him . . .

A woman and a love, God help him, that had never truly been his to begin with.

Catherine watched the door shut, feeling its echo reverberate through her soul. She waited until the sound of Gray's leaving faded into nothingness, until she heard naught but the cold wind rattling the panes in the window.

He was gone.

Wrapping her arms round herself, she gripped the twins' portrait tight against her, letting the metal frame dig into her flesh so that she'd know she wasn't some formless spirit, wrenched from her mortal body by the force of her anguish. The pain rocked through her, devastating in its power.

Sweet Mother Mary, she'd just lost the man she loved. Lost him forever because of her secrets and her lies.

And it was then that she began to weep.

Chapter 16

The hearth logs had burned to glowing coals before Catherine made up her mind. 'Twas well past midnight, she guessed. Hours earlier she'd sneaked a message to Heldred in the stables to relieve him of both his worrying and his waiting for her. Then she'd unbound her hair and changed from her boy's clothing into her long chemise to curl in this chair near the fire. She'd tucked her legs to her chest, absently wiping tears that seemed to seep from her eyes without end.

'Twas high time to stop crying and get on with it.

She'd wronged Gray, of that there was no doubt. But she loved him, too, and as she'd sat stewing in her misery, she realized that in all she'd told him when he'd confronted her earlier this night, she'd never told him how she felt. It was an error she planned to remedy right now.

Grasping one of the tapers from the mantel, Catherine eased open her chamber door and stepped into the corridor. She sucked in her breath as the stinging cold of the stones assaulted her bare feet, moving quickly to keep them from going numb.

She needed to find Gray.

Should she look in the tilting yard? Nay, the lists would be soaked from the rain. Besides 'twas too late for him or anyone else to be engaged in any kind of exercise outside.

Some corner of the great hall, perhaps? She chewed her lip, pausing in her progress until the chill made her pick up her pace again. Nay, not the great hall. He'd avoid company in his current state of mind; there would be too many people to see him there and remark on his presence among them.

His solar. Aye, his solar was the perfect place for him to be alone, though 'twas possible that by this time of night he might already be asleep. Still, she couldn't help thinking that if he managed to fall into blissful slumber after all that had happened between them, then she would have her answer and no more need be said.

There was only one way to find out.

She made her way to the stairs, creeping down them in silence, moving even more carefully when she reached the bottom and the entrance to the great hall. She snuffed out her candle, stealing round the edge of the huge chamber to avoid rousing any of the sprawling squires, servants, retainers and knights asleep on the rushes or benches.

The rain had ceased more than an hour before,

and a thick crescent moon hung in the sky, providing enough light through the arrow slits and windows high near the vaulted ceiling to allow her shadowy view of those sleeping below. She saw no sign of Gray anywhere.

After picking her way carefully around the groups of sleepers, none of whom offered more than a snore or cough to mark her passing, she reached the corridor leading to his solar. 'Twas darker in the passageway, especially without the light of her candle. Feeling silly holding an unlit taper, she set it down. Then, straightening, she wiped her palms on her shift, breathed deep, and pushed the solar door open enough to slip inside.

A fire crackled in the grate, banishing the chill of the corridor; it drew her gaze, and a joyful shock went through her. Gray himself leaned back in a chair before the blaze, dressed only in his shirt, boots and breeches. His long legs were stretched out to the heat, and he sipped from a cup as he stared into the flames, unaware, it seemed, of her entrance.

Catherine hesitated, wondering if she wasn't risking a beheading to startle him without warning, when suddenly he spoke.

"I see that you've found me."

The sound of his voice, deep and smooth, made her jump. But then she wondered if she'd imagined its echo; Gray hadn't shifted even a hair from his position. He continued to stare into the fire, drinking again, but otherwise moving not at all.

She took another step, and another before he turned his head and directed the full force of his gaze on her . . .

And then she knew that she hadn't imagined anything.

His expression was primal in the firelight, dangerous and untamed. Catherine swallowed. Now that she stood closer, she saw that his shirt was unlaced, and as he sat up and twisted to face her, the muscles of his chest and belly rippled. He rested his forearms on his thighs, his cup gripped loosely in both hands; the firelight shone through his open shirt from behind, glowing tawny on his skin and his ebony hair.

"Welcome to my haven, lady, such as it is," he murmured, his brow arching in time with one corner of his mouth. He lifted his cup to her in salute.

His haven from her. The dark thought pushed its way into Catherine's mind, shoving aside the curls of heat invoked by his stare. But she stopped herself from voicing her fears aloud, instead nodding to his hand. "What is that you're drinking?"

"This?" He glanced at the cup. "'Tis my usual brew—would you care for some?" Then he looked at her again and understanding dawned; his expression turned almost mocking. "Ah, I see. You were wondering, perhaps, if I'd forsaken my vow of so many years ago in order to indulge in something stronger tonight."

"Nay. I mean, I didn't think you would, but—" she stumbled over her words, feeling awkward and stupid. Finally she clamped her lips shut and looked away. By the Rood, what had possessed her to come here and intrude on him like this? She was a fool. Gray owed her nothing. She was naught but an imposter in his eyes. A cheat. Once her children's safety was resolved, he would probably send her packing, with good riddance.

"I—I'm sorry to have disturbed you," she managed to say around the lump in her throat. "I'll leave now." Her eyes burned and her stomach felt sick as she turned to go.

"Wait, lady."

She stiffened but didn't look back.

"Please, Catherine. Don't go."

The sound of her name uttered in his husky plea made her stop. She faced him again. His mocking look had vanished, leaving in its place the fullness of his emotions, raw pain and need, burning clear in the emerald depths of his eyes.

She took two steps toward him, uncertainty assaulting her anew. "Gray, I—"

"Why did you really come here?" he said quietly.

She stared back at him, realizing that she risked everything if she told him, but knowing that if she didn't, she'd spend the rest of her miserable life alone, wishing she had.

She swallowed hard again, her heart pounding.

"I—I came to find you because there is something else I've kept from you. One more truth that you deserve to know."

"Another truth, lady?" His gaze remained leveled on her, so cautious, so unsure, that her heart wrenched again.

She blinked, his face blurring in the flood of heat that swelled and stung in her eyes. Somehow, she managed to nod, and then the words flowed from her in a torrent. "Gray, I know that our marriage is false because of my deceit, and that it is your honor alone that has compelled you to offer your help in rescuing my children. For that I am forever grateful. But once their safety is achieved, I also know that I will—" her voice wavered under a fresh assault of pain, "I know that I will have to leave you and Ravenslock forever, and—"

Her composure was beginning to slip, but she struggled to stay strong through the rest of what she had to say. Choking back her tears, she finished, "The truth is that I love you. Through all this time, it is what has helped to keep me going, what has kept me strong." She fisted her hands, willing them to stop trembling. "I love you, Gray, and I couldn't leave until I'd told you."

While she spoke, Gray closed his eyes, sitting back as if she'd struck him a mortal blow. He remained still and quiet for a few moments. Then, without opening his eyes, he said raggedly, "Nay, Catherine. I do not accept it."

The grief that had been balled up inside of her unfurled into agony at his response. She felt it rising, suffocating her. She'd told him how she felt, exposed her innermost feelings to him, and he was rejecting her out of hand. 'Twas no less than she deserved, she knew, and yet she'd been foolish enough to hope . . .

She turned away from him, holding herself still

and trying to remember to breathe as she squeezed her eyes shut and let the hot flow course unhindered now down her cheeks. She had to go, had to leave this chamber. It hurt too much to look on this man she loved and know that he could never— would never—return what she felt for him.

"I do not accept what you've said, Catherine, because if you leave me forever, I think that I will die from the pain of it."

Gray added this last statement hoarsely, quietly, but Catherine felt the words clear through her soul.

"What did you say?" she whispered, still facing away from him lest he dissolve before her eyes like the traces of a dream.

"I said that if you leave me, I'll die."

His voice was very gentle, very close to her now. In the next instant she felt his hands slide around her waist from behind, splaying warm across her stomach as he pulled her against him and rested his cheek against hers. "God, Catherine, don't ever leave me."

A great dam seemed to break in her then, flooding her with almost painful sweetness. She closed her eyes and leaned back, releasing a deep, shuddering breath; when his mouth brushed her neck, it sent shivers of longing through her.

"By all that is holy, Gray," she breathed, "I never want to leave you. But I thought that I'd have to. That you wouldn't want me anymore."

At that he turned her around to face him, cupping her face in his palms, and the intensity—the love—in his eyes seared her to the depths of her being.

"Don't you know, Catherine? I want you with every breath I take. *You.* I don't care if your name is Elise, Margery, Ann, or Jane. It matters not, because 'tis *you* that I love. Only you."

"But I thought—"

"Hush," he murmured, brushing his thumb over her lips. "I was angry when I learned that you'd deceived me, I'll not deny it. And it hurt to know that you didn't trust me enough to tell me about Montford's plotting."

"I'm so sorry," she said, gazing at him, aching again for the pain she'd caused him. "I wanted to tell you, but I feared Eduard's spies, and—"

He shook his head. "I only felt so because I wanted to help you fight him, not because I thought you were going to do his bidding. I understand. You did what you believed you had to in order to protect your children from an animal who would have harmed them if he learned that you'd acted against him."

She nodded, closing her eyes and laying her cheek against his chest. "Aye, it felt like I was living a nightmare. A horrible, terrible nightmare, from which I'd never awaken."

"But it's over now, or it will be, as soon as I bring the twins to safety and deliver Montford to the justice he so richly deserves," Gray promised, holding her to him. "I swear to you, Catherine, you will never be alone again."

"I love you so much," she said, clinging to him just as tightly. "God in heaven, can you ever forgive me?"

"'Tis already done."

She pulled back to meet his gaze, and he smiled, sending another rush of love coursing through her. He brushed away the wetness near her eyes. "I just needed to know that you felt the same that I did. To know that what happened between us these last months was the truth. That it was as real as I'd believed it to be."

She smiled through her tears as he stroked his fingers across her brow and down her cheek. He slipped his hand gently behind her neck, his touch sacred to her. When he pulled her to him for a kiss, she responded with passion, reveling in the warm, salty taste of him, in the sensation of his arms around her, his heart beating firm and steady against her breast.

"Make love to me, Catherine," he whispered, "with no more secrets, no more lies between us."

She glided her hands up his chest and over his shoulders to tangle in his hair. "'Tis what I want, too, more than anything."

Gray felt a surge of joy at her answer. Kissing her again, he swept her into his arms. He moved to carry her to their bed, then paused, frowning as he looked around them. "I fear that my solar isn't well equipped for what we intend."

The beautiful sound of her laughter, low and sweet, sent a tingle of pleasure up his neck. He looked down at her, a smile tugging his lips as well.

"We needed no bed when you brought me out into the woods," she said.

"Aye, the leaves were better than a bed, if I recall correctly."

"Your memory has ever astounded me," she nodded with mock seriousness, dragging her nails lightly down his chest.

He grinned with her, then, a sensuous shudder rippling through him at her touch, driving him past the point of waiting. He wanted to have her for his own, now. To touch her, to taste her . . . to love her.

With a little growl, he carried her to the hearth and the thick, furred skin that lay in front of it, kneeling there to let her stretch out full before him.

Her hair spread like a fan of chestnut silk on the dark fur, tempting him to bury his hands in its fragrant abundance. Golden firelight wavered over her, swirling across her skin to create tantalizing shadows and hollows he ached to explore anew.

Leaning over, he kissed her, unlacing the top of her chemise to slip his hand inside and stroke the soft fullness of her breast. Her nipple hardened at his touch, and she moaned his name when he tugged it between his thumb and finger.

Pushing the fabric aside, he kissed her neck and across the delicate hollow near her collarbone before trailing his lips down to her breast. He paused over her delicate, pink nipple for a moment, not touching her, just letting the moist warmth of his breath tease her until she whimpered with longing and raised herself to his mouth. Then, with a low growl, he bent his head to suckle her; she gasped with pleasure, her fingers tangling in his hair as he breathed in the sweet scent of her skin and laved his tongue over her.

"God, I love you," he murmured against her softness, kissing her breasts again before moving back up the silken column of her neck. "So much, Catherine."

"No more than I love you," she whispered, arching under him. "Ah, Gray, I never want to be without you." She stroked her hand across his bare chest as he kissed the tender spot behind her ear, smoothing her fingers over his ribs and up to his shoulders before finally guiding his lips to hers for another kiss.

"I want to be one with you," she said between kisses, "One in truth—now. I need to feel you inside me, with me . . ."

"I want you too, love. All of you." He cupped her face, brushing his lips over her forehead, her cheeks, the crescents of her eyelids with their feathery lashes before nibbling again at the honeyed fullness of her mouth. "But I want to savor you too. Every inch of you, as I've dreamed of doing every night since our first together."

She moaned softly, stroking his arms as he lifted the hem of her chemise; he tugged it off over her head, gliding his hand up the warm length of her thighs. His fingers nestled in the silken curls at their juncture, gently stroking the slick folds there; he reveled in her slippery heat and in the way she spread her thighs to open herself further to his touch. Little jolts of feeling shot from his fingertips up to the rest of his body, darts of sweet, hot pleasure into his groin and the iron-hard stiffness straining against his breeches there.

" 'Tis heaven," he whispered, closing his eyes and suppressing a groan at the incredible sensation of touching her so. She was like an exotic flower opening to him. He wanted to lose himself in her, to breathe in the delicate perfume of her arousal and luxuriate in the lush, wet feel of her forever. Being with her like this was driving him to the edge of ecstasy, to a place of fractured thought and pure feeling.

He continued to stroke her as she moaned again, brushing his thumb over the tiny bud nestled in her folds, until she began to twist beneath him and press into his hand. He shifted, then, tracing a heated path with his kisses; when he reached her most intimate place, he tasted of her, swirling his tongue and lips over that sensitive spot.

She gasped, but he held her firm, relentless in his tender assault. He cupped his hands under her, lifting her, gently spreading, until the swollen silk of her was opened to him. He groaned with the beauty of it, the incredible gift of her, tasting her again and again, hot and tangy sweet, like honeyed apples to his tongue.

Too soon, it seemed, he saw the flat of her belly begin to ripple, tiny shudders that made her thighs tense; then she stiffened, crying his name and clutching his shoulders as her body pulsated with a powerful release.

After a few moments, he lifted himself up to hold her, and she turned her face into his neck while the last delicious shudders of her fulfillment eased away.

"You're crying," he murmured, brushing a tear from her cheek with the tip of his finger. "Are you all right? Did I upset you by doing that?"

"Nay," she said, looking at him. Her lashes clumped in adorable spikes, framing those wide, beautiful eyes that were fixed on him now in wonder. "'Tis just that I never—well, I never knew that such things could be done."

"Aye. There are many ways to give and receive pleasure."

Her cheeks bloomed with color, and she lowered her lashes. "Did you learn how to do that when you lived in London, with any of those women who . . ." Her voice trailed off.

"Women who did such things for a living?" he finished for her. "Nay, Catherine, I never touched a woman like that before. I never wanted to. Not until you."

She blushed again. "'Twas wonderful," she whispered, stroking her hand across his bare chest. Then she smiled and leaned up on her elbow to gaze at him, almost stilling his breath when she added softly, "And 'tis even better knowing that turnabout is fair play."

It was his turn to groan when she reached down to caress the straining, rigid length of him through his breeches. He felt her loosening the laces, her nimble fingers working swiftly; in an instant his erection sprang from its confinement, and she grasped him, caressing him with both hands.

He lost all sense of time and place when she bent her head to him, kissing him gently before taking him into her mouth. In moments he was arching with pleasure just as she had, only he pulled away at the last instant for fear of releasing too early.

"Did I do something wrong?" she murmured, frowning as she sat up to look at him. He tried not to laugh his denial. For a widow with two children, Catherine was more an innocent than most virgins.

Her tumbled hair shone lustrous in the firelight, the pink tips of her nipples just peeking through the silky tendrils. But when she nibbled her lower lip in distress, Gray feared that he might spill onto the floor like a green lad; her succulent mouth was full and rosy, her lips still moist from her ministrations on him. God help him, but the woman could set a stone statue ablaze with desire and she didn't even know it.

"Nay, Catherine, you did nothing wrong," he managed to choke when he could command himself to breathe again. "'Twas only too good to bear for longer without . . . well without—"

Her eyes went wide with comprehension. "Oh." A moment later, she beamed. "In that case . . ." Leaning down, she kissed him playfully, and he growled, nipping at her shoulder as he rolled her beneath him. Her surprised shriek quickly faded to a moan of surrender when he pressed himself, hot and hard, between her legs. She arched up to meet him, lifting her knees and pulling him in to stroke deeply inside her slick heat.

Stars danced before his eyes with the pleasure of their rhythmic movements; his hands clenched the fur on either side of her head, even as her fingers tightened on his buttocks, and she began to pulsate around him with another swift climax. She screamed aloud, and Gray groaned with each soft cry that echoed her fulfillment.

"Catherine, I love you," he said against her cheek when she'd quieted. He lifted himself on his arms to gaze at her, still rocking gently in and out of her. "With all that I am, I love you. Now until I die."

"And I you, Gray," she whispered, tears of happiness gathered in her eyes. "Forever." She gazed up at him, her face glowing with that seductive, angelic beauty that had captivated him from the very first time he looked at her.

He bent his head down to capture her mouth, lost in the erotic and ancient pulse of their hips and tongues, delving deeper, tantalizing, stroking in perfect time. Words of promise and redemption spilled from him, returned by her in soft, throaty whispers. He breathed in her scent, tasted her sweetness, felt her soft, writhing heat cradling each thrust of his hips.

Through heavy-lidded eyes, Gray watched Catherine arch back into the pillows, grasping his arms and sliding her hands up as he stroked deeper. Her fingers clenched his shoulders when their tempo increased once more. She kept murmuring his name, her moans becoming louder as she lifted her hips to his again and again.

But when she wrapped her long, beautiful legs around his waist, he lost control. She cried out again as they peaked together, and he found himself spiraling into bliss so intense that his mind shattered into a million colored stars. The love he felt for her washed over him, then, a shower of beautiful, perfect light that soothed him, healed him, made him whole . . .

And banished his painful past forever.

Gray still held Catherine nestled close to him several hours later. She was sleeping peacefully, but he couldn't rest. His brain kept churning, kept reliving every agonizing detail of what she'd told him about Montford's evil. Even now his skin crawled with disgust and anger over what the bastard had done, not only to Catherine, but to the real Elise as well.

He tightened his arm around her protectively, and she sighed, shifting and nuzzling closer to his chest. Damn Eduard de Montford to hell. He'd pay, by God. Montford would live to regret every moment of pain Catherine and her children had suffered at his hands. This Gray vowed in the silent darkness.

But first little Ian and Isabel needed to be rescued from Faegerliegh Keep.

Studying the ebbing moon patterns that shifted

along the wall, Gray reviewed the plan in his mind again. At first light, he'd rouse Alban and gather a contingent of men to prepare a siege on Montford's estate. He already knew that Eduard had taken his best knights with him to journey with King Henry. Gray's forces could overcome those left behind in Somerset without too much difficulty.

It should be simple, really. Once they'd subdued Faegerleigh's guards, Catherine could lead them through the intricate passages of the keep to find her children. They would scoop up the twins, ride out, and be back at Ravenslock before sunset the next day.

He'd already prepared a dispatch to send to the king, explaining their situation. With any luck, Henry's sense of justice would override the anger he'd feel at Gray's thwarting his sanctions again.

And if not . . .

Gray closed his eyes and breathed deep, determined to put it out of his mind for now. It was a moot point. Even if King Henry chose to exert his full power as sovereign and follow through on his threat to remove Gray's titles and estates as punishment for defying him, Gray knew it would make no difference.

A sweet rush of emotion flooded him at the irony of this sudden turn of events. It was almost as if he'd been given another chance. An opportunity to right a great wrong in a way that he'd never been able to do for Gillian.

And he wouldn't fail Catherine or her children. On his life, he swore he'd not falter. Never again.

This time, vengeance would be his.

"Milady!"

Catherine rolled over, pulling the coverlet over her ears at the buzzing sound. A fly, perhaps? In a foggy corner of her brain, she decided to speak to Gray about having someone come up to the chamber to search out the pest. It—

The fly suddenly sprouted arms and began to clutch her shoulder.

"Milady, you must awaken!"

Catherine sat up, heart pounding, to face Mariah, who bent over the bed, obviously distraught from her attempts to rouse her mistress. "What is it?" she mumbled, wiping her eyes and looking around her as she blinked away sleep.

She was in her chamber. The early morning sun glinted through the scores of tiny, glazed panes, lighting triangular patches of gold all over the walls and floor. But the room was empty, save herself and Mariah. Gray must have carried her up to bed, then, and gone to find Alban and set their plan into motion; if all went well, they would depart before noon to rescue Ian and Isabel. Then she would hold them close and smother their little faces with kisses as she explained away the nightmare of these past three months.

Happy anticipation swept over her in a torrent, making her bound out of bed in her hurry to prepare.

She was so excited that she almost missed the import of what Mariah was saying to her. But as she padded to the washstand, the servant's voice harped so persistently that it cut through her joyful daze.

"Milady, did you hear me? The reason I awakened you is that a missive has come. The messenger awaits you in the hall, and he's refused to leave until he himself places it in your hands alone."

"That's strange." Catherine frowned, pausing as she poured water into the washbowl. "Do you know who it is?"

"Nay, milady. 'Tis why I thought it meet to rouse you," Mariah explained. "But you were sleeping as sound as if you'd not closed your eyes in weeks."

"Not weeks, though I'd warrant 'twas most of the night," Catherine murmured to herself, smiling as she remembered the voluptuous pleasure of making love with Gray on the furred skin in his solar. And on the table. And sitting in the chair before the fire . . .

"The night was peaceful, then, for you, lady?" Mariah's silvery brow lifted, and Catherine could have sworn that she saw a softer look than usual in the maidservant's eyes.

She smiled deeper. "I wouldn't call it peaceful, but . . ."

"I had feared some trouble," the maid continued, shaking out the coverlet, "when Lord Camville came home last night in such a fury, ordering us all inside and the gates barred." She paused and looked at Catherine, before clearing her throat self-consciously and looking away. "In truth, milady, I was worried about you."

Catherine stilled. Color suffused Mariah's cheeks. If she wasn't mistaken, the maidservant was trying to be nice. Clearing her own throat, Catherine said, "Thank you, Mariah. But there is naught to fear. All is well."

Mariah glanced at her again, looking more unsure than Catherine had ever seen her. "'Tis glad I am to hear it, milady," she nodded brusquely, her chin wobbling, "Because I know that I've a few sharp edges, and I've not always made it easier for you here. By my soul, I'm not ashamed to say I've always tried to protect Lord Camville from any I think might mean to harm him—but in these weeks, I've come to see that you're not that sort. In truth, I like you right well, milady, and I wouldn't want any hurt comin' to ye either."

She shook her head emphatically again; then, without waiting for a response, she walked into the garment chamber to fetch Catherine's gown.

Catherine gaped after her in silence. 'Twas the most she'd ever heard Mariah say at one time, but she was glad to have been given the gift of it. 'Twas a boon indeed to discover that the older woman cared for her, and that her previous coldness had not stemmed from the fact that she was a spy for Eduard, but that she was simply a loyal and protective servant to Gray.

Mariah returned with the gown, helping her to dress in the now companionable silence that weighed soft between them. Soon, Catherine was ready, and she descended to the hall with Mariah in search of the messenger. They found him sitting at the great fireplace, sipping a cup of ale and breaking his fast with some bread and cold pork from the castle larder.

He sprang to his feet at Catherine's approach, wiping his mouth on his sleeve. She'd never seen the man before; he was finely dressed, though gaunt and pale, and she couldn't help but notice how his gaze darted around as if he expected something terrible to happen at any moment.

"Lady Camville," he said, bowing low. When he straightened he held out a sealed parchment. "I present this missive to your hand alone, according to instruction given me by the most esteemed Lord Montford."

Catherine's stomach heaved, and she thought her knees might give way. With a trembling hand she took the parchment. But as she read its contents her heart pounded harder, nausea rising up to choke her. She grasped the edge of the table for support, vaguely hearing the messenger's gasp as he leaped solicitously to her side; one of the hall servants quickly poured a goblet of wine and pressed it into her hand.

She pushed them both aside, in her haste knocking the cup to the floor. It clattered to the stones, and she watched the widening, bloody pool of wine with a kind of morbid fascination before she lurched to the doorway in frantic search of Gray.

Nay! Her mind screamed in protest to the message on the parchment. She'd wanted to destroy it, but the words scorched her brain, burning her thoughts like venom.

It was too late. Sweet heaven, but it was too late for them all.

God help her, but Eduard was on his way to Ravenslock.

Chapter 17

"**T**his changes everything." Gray tossed the parchment to the table, feeling a pit open in his stomach. "Damn Montford's timing," he added under his breath, leaning back in the willow chair Catherine had made for him and raking his hand through his hair.

"It does present problems," Alban said, looking back from where he stood at the window of Gray's solar. "You and Catherine can't possibly rescue the twins and get them back here before Montford arrives. You'll be gambling a battle out in the open if you try it and he intercepts you."

"'Tis a chance we'll have to take," Gray answered. "We have to get them out of Somerset before Montford's return. If the bastard catches us at it and wants a fight, then by God, I'll give him one."

"But that means the children will face the added risk of battle," Alban argued.

"No one will face any added risk if I go to Ian and Isabel alone and leave the two of you here to keep Eduard out of my way," Catherine broke in quietly from her position near the hearth. She'd been sitting silent since bringing Eduard's missive to him, but Gray could tell by her expression that she was worried.

Pushing herself to her feet, she came toward him. "I can steal the children from Faegerleigh and take refuge in one of the village cottages with them until you send word that you've secured Eduard and his forces."

"'Tis an idea, Gray," Alban said, turning completely away from the window to face him. "Eduard would never think her bold enough to attempt such a rescue."

"Nay," Gray shook his head. "'Tis too dangerous."

"No more dangerous than what my children have faced alone for all these months," she answered. Her eyes seemed to pierce him to his soul. "You trained me to wield a sword yourself, Gray. I'm no master, but you know that I can defend myself. If it makes you feel better, send two or three of your knights with me. We'll move quickly and quietly, perhaps without anyone even knowing we were there. 'Tis our best chance for getting the children to safety before Eduard's return."

A bolt of fear shot through Gray at the idea of Catherine sneaking into her old home and facing its countless dangers without him. To stall for time to think, he said, "What about Montford's message?

Your bargain with him accorded that you would be the one to clear the way for his man to slip the poison that would kill me into my food. If you're not waiting for him in the courtyard when he rides through these gates, he'll know something is amiss."

"There's no help for it," she countered. "We've known all along that I would have to take part in Ian and Isabel's rescue. No one else here can successfully navigate Faegerleigh's intricate corridors."

She frowned, adding, "'Tis true that Heldred knows Faegerleigh's design as well as I do, but his health has been precarious of late, and 'twould be dangerous for him to attempt the rescue." She shook her head. "There's no other way but for me to go while you stay here to take care of Eduard. I'll trust you to keep him contained so that I can get to my children without his interference."

"I don't like it," Gray said, getting up to pace around to the front of his table. "There must be some other way."

"There's not," Catherine said. "None that will ensure Ian and Isabel remaining alive and safe, and that must come first. 'Tis the only way."

He gazed at her, fear for her warring with love and pride. "What you plan will be dangerous, Catherine. Too dangerous." He clenched his jaw, battling with himself as he added more quietly, "I don't know if I can let you go."

Her fierce expression softened a little; the shadow of a smile teased her mouth. "If you're worried that you're going to lose me, Gray—don't." She stepped closer to him and cupped his cheek, stroking his skin with her cool fingers. "If the truth about my real identity didn't tear us apart, I'm certainly not going to allow Eduard or his men to do it. Trust me to be strong, as you've taught me to be. Strong as I know I am."

Gray placed his hand over hers, pulling her to him, and Alban pretended to be very interested, suddenly, in the wooden joints of the window casement. Turning her palm up, Gray kissed the tender, now lightly callused skin there. She leaned into him, and he held her close, soaking in the warmth of her touch.

"All right," he finally conceded, cursing softly as he released her. "I give up. You'll go with a group of my men to Faegerleigh to get your children, and in the meantime, I'll plan a surprise attack to contain Montford. We'll give him no time to suspect anything. We'll just charge in and restrain him until King Henry arrives. Montford has enough men with him that there will likely be a battle before we can subdue him, but at least we'll have the advantage of being on Ravenslock ground."

"What do you want me to do?" Alban asked, leaving his study of the window to join them at the table.

"Go with Catherine. Damn Montford for keeping me from her, but if I can't be at her side, then I'll feel better knowing that you're there." Gray dragged his hand through his hair again. "I wish there were another option. Letting you both go with so little protection—it seems wrong, somehow."

"I'd say 'tis the best plan," Alban countered. "We

cannot have too many with us, or we'll draw notice. Your task will be far more difficult, keeping Montford and his men contained."

Gray clenched his jaw, worry ripping through his gut as he considered all that could go wrong.

"Everything will be fine, Gray, you'll see," Catherine said, taking his hands in hers.

Gray met her gaze, saw the purpose and fire burning anew in their blue depths. Another burst of pride and love shot through him. When had she changed so completely from the timid, frightened woman he'd first known into this virago, ready to confront their enemies single-handedly?

As if she'd read his thoughts, she added quietly, "I'm not afraid of Eduard any longer. His tyranny over me is done, thanks to you. But my children remain at his mercy; they need me, and I intend to be there for them. I've waited too long already to bring them to safety."

Leaning closer, she brushed her lips over his. He felt the warm, sweet caress of her mouth and yearned to deepen it, to let it escalate again into the passion they'd shared last night. But what lay ahead couldn't wait.

Pulling away with a sigh, Catherine gave him one more loving glance, then gestured to the door. "Come and help me prepare for the journey. We must leave soon if we wish to travel at least part of the distance to Faegerliegh under veil of darkness."

Nodding, he followed her from the chamber. A short hour later all seemed ready for their departure. Standing in the courtyard, he watched Catherine,

Alban and two more of his best knights ride through the gates. The feel of her parting kisses lingered on his lips, haunting him with self-doubt. He fought back the panicked sensation that threatened to overwhelm him, the feeling that said he was making the biggest error of his life. He suppressed it forcibly, reminding himself that this was what they'd decided together. He and Catherine. Together.

She had a task to accomplish, and so did he. If she was successful in stealing back her children, it would damage Montford's position in the evil game that he played, but it wouldn't stop him. Capturing and destroying the wretch once and for all would be Gray's duty alone.

It was a moment he looked forward to with every breath that filled his lungs. A task he would take great pleasure in completing at long last.

A night owl called from the stable rafters as Heldred settled with a sigh into the fresh straw. His bones ached more than ever, curse them. And his heart . . . Jesu, his heart was skipping enough beats lately to make him see stars thrice daily. It was because of his damnable weakness that Mistress Catherine had not asked him to join her in rescuing her children.

Oh she'd discussed it with him, introducing him to her husband anew and acknowledging that they'd known each other for years. She'd even told Lord Camville that they shared a friendship, bless her kind heart. But in the end, when she'd needed help, when she'd needed allies and supporters, she'd been forced to leave him behind. He was naught but an old and useless man.

Good Lord Camville had tried to make him feel needed; he'd asked him to keep an eye open to discern who among those at Ravenslock might be Lord Montford's spies. But it seemed so paltry compared to all he should have been able to do. And yet he would do it. Anything to aid mistress Catherine in getting her children back.

Punching at the hay-stuffed ticking that served as his pillow, Heldred rolled over and breathed deep. The stable was quiet now, but for the occasional snuffle of horses and a few grunts from the other men sleeping inside. Lord Camville had done well in closing off the castle to prevent anyone entering or leaving; in fact the whole place had been almost unnaturally still since Mistress Catherine set off.

He heard Hugh the tacksman growl a warning to one of the stablelads, threatening to bury him under the straw if he snored again this night. Another man coughed, and Garth Digby, the blacksmith's apprentice, called out for quiet, as he did every night. Then all fell silent. Heldred began to drift off, lulled by the rustling sounds of the animals settling down in their stalls. The warm, earthy smells of sunshine-dried hay, horse and leather filled his senses, and he closed his eyes . . .

Not five minutes later, a sound on the other side of the stall startled him from the edge of sleep.

Heldred lurched to sit up, peering in vain through the darkness. Something wasn't right. The lads never moved around after Garth's call for rest. The hair prickled on the back of his neck at the sound of crackling straw. He listened more carefully and heard a man's voice crooning softly to a horse. There was still no light. Then came the creak of leather, as if from a saddle being cinched.

A horse-thief? It couldn't be; the castle gates had been locked against traders, travelers or anyone not of the castle since before Mistress Catherine left . . .

Pulling himself to stand in his hunched-over position, Heldred stumbled quietly to the edge of his stall, squinting as he ducked under the rope and into the aisle. His eyes had by now adjusted to the dimness enough to see the shadowy outline of a man in the next stall, furtively tightening the bridle of the mare he'd just saddled. Grabbing a shovel from where it leaned on the wall, Heldred raised it and prepared to strike.

But before he could move, the man spun around, grabbing the tool from Heldred and hitting him hard in the throat with a closed fist. The pain in his neck sent Heldred crashing to his knees; his hands gripped his throat as he gasped for air. With what seemed a Herculean effort, he managed to raise his gaze, trying to see the face of the man who'd struck him.

Shock sliced into him, even through the pain. 'Twas young Rupert, a stable hand of no more than twenty years. He was a lively youth, always whistling a tune and laughing as he dallied with the girls from the kitchen.

"Rupert, lad . . . ?" Heldred tried to croak, but no

sound would come out. Without a word or a change of expression, Rupert raised his arm, and Heldred felt the cold, angry slash of a dagger blade rip into his shoulder, felt his own blood spatter up warm onto his face. He fell back, palms out, flailing and gasping without breath, like a fish on the beach; the blade sliced into his hands and then jabbed past them to bury with a sickening thud in his chest. Pain washed over him in a wave, and everything slowed as if in a dream.

Rupert's bloodied face floated above his gaze a moment more, his expression almost regretful now as he pushed past him to go back to the mare. As from the end of a long tunnel, Heldred heard a soft whinny—the mare liked not the smell of the blood, his fading mind supplied—then he heard Rupert lead her quietly out of the stables, before closing the door behind him with nary a sound. None of those sleeping at the far end of the stables seemed to have been awakened by his leaving.

Heldred closed his eyes, fully expecting that these would be his last seconds on earth. But he didn't die. To his great surprise, pain continued to wrench him with each tortured breath, and his chest felt like it was squeezing down on his heart, but he didn't lose his senses. Saints, he wanted to. He wished for the cool peace of oblivion. But God apparently wasn't done with him yet.

After a few more ragged breaths, Heldred forced his eyes open. Everything was quiet again. All appeared peaceful. But he knew that nothing would ever be the same. It seemed that Rupert was one of

Lord Montford's spies, willing to kill in order to escape with news to his evil master.

A rapidly spreading pool of his own blood grew warm and slick beneath Heldred's prostrate body, as he tried to make himself think. He pushed his mind to work, to formulate a plan of action.

He decided that he must first try to calm his heart, then staunch the flow of blood from his wound. Rupert's blade had punctured a lung, Heldred was sure of it, by the unnatural weight and bubbling rasp of air he felt in his chest with each breath. He couldn't yell for help. 'Twould be a challenge to overcome the pain at all, but he would do it. He needed to retain his senses long enough to get outside. To get to Lord Camville.

He had to find his lady's husband and tell him that their plans had gone awry, that the security of Ravenslock was breached, and that Lord Montford would surely learn, now, of their design to rescue the twins. Then Mistress Catherine would be in far graver danger than anyone had suspected when she left for Faegerleigh Keep with only three men to aid her.

Groaning, Heldred rolled onto his side, his gashed hands trembling as he reached for the medicine pouch hanging round his neck. It dangled there, torn, likely from the thrust of Rupert's wicked blade. He found a few bits of cherry bark left in the folds of leather, and, pinching these between his thumb and finger, pushed the pieces past his lips, grimacing when the metallic taste of his own blood mingled with the bitter peelings. But the bark's medicinal properties soon eased his irregular heart-beats, quieting some of the pain wracking his chest.

Finally, he strained to grasp the edge of his cloak from where it hung on the stable post, pulling it down and bunching it up to press against his dagger wounds. He gasped with agony at the movement, holding himself very still until the white-hot burst of light in front of his eyes faded away. Then, holding the makeshift bandage firm to his chest, he began to drag himself, shaking and sweating, inches at a time toward the stable door . . .

And toward the one man who might prove to be Mistress Catherine's chance of survival.

Gray was at work in his solar planning out his strategy of attack on Eduard when he heard the shouts. It sent a tingle of warning up his back, like the feeling he got in the dead, eerie silence right before a thunderstorm unleashed its fury from the heavens.

Something was wrong.

Grasping the silken bag from under the table's edge, he pulled out his key and jammed it into the lock in the wall, pushing the hidden door open and lurching into the tilt yard. Though it was night, nearly a score of men filled the area, their torches providing flickering illumination.

"My lord! Sweet Jesu, Lord Camville, 'tis awful!" Gray's steward, Briggs, came rushing up to him, his hands smeared in blood, his face pale in the unnatural light. "The old hunchback from the stables has been attacked, my lord. One of the watchmen found him. Knifed, he was," the steward cried, even as he led Gray past the open stable doors.

A trail of blood soaked into the wood chips along the edge of the lists; Heldred had obviously been trying to cross the yard to get to the castle. Several of Gray's knights knelt next to the old man's prostrate form another ten paces away, trying to staunch the red flow that continued to seep onto the now slick grass near him.

"Is he alive?" Gray asked harshly, stalking the last few feet to Catherine's old friend. Concern gripped him so that he didn't know if he could speak at all.

"Aye, my lord," Briggs answered. "At least, he was so when I left him a moment ago."

Heldred's eyes fluttered open when Gray dropped to his knees beside him. Even through the pain Gray saw reflected in the old man's gaze, worry and intensity shone brighter.

"Easy, now. I'm here. Talk to me if you can. Tell me how this happened," Gray said gently, anger at what Heldred must be suffering churning in him as he supported the old man's head on his arm. "I vow to bring those responsible to justice for it."

Coughing, Heldred tried to sit up more. The movement made him blanch anew, while the horrible bubbling sound that wheezed from him increased. He grasped Gray's tunic in his bloody grip, pulling him closer. "Breached, my lord!" he whispered. "The security of the castle is breached. Rupert—" He gasped for breath again, blood showing on his lips. "He is a spy. You must go after my lady Catherine . . ." He coughed, a harsh rattiing sound that mixed now with a gurgle. "She is in grave danger. You must go to her—!" he choked, before falling back into Gray's arms. He took one, last, tortured breath before his chest stilled and his eyes fixed upon nothing.

Gray felt the world spinning around him as he stared at Heldred's now lifeless body. Gently, he laid him back onto the grass and pushed himself to his feet. Somehow, he managed to give a mumbled order that the remains be looked after and prepared for a noble burial. Then, half-stumbling, he crossed the yard, the loyal old man's dying words ringing their deadly message through his brain and soul.

Breached. The security was breached.

Catherine was in danger, and she had no way of knowing it. She would reach Faegerliegh Keep before dawn with only three men to help her—only three men to keep her from the harm of a madman and his entire army.

Christ, Eduard was going to get her.

A roar exploded from Gray's chest, and he burst into a run, bellowing for his master at arms to assemble all of his forces to leave for Faegerliegh Keep. There wasn't a moment to spare.

Everyone burst into a flurry of activity, shouts going up and people rushing back and forth as they scrambled to obey their lord. Gray threw himself into his armor chamber, yanking his sword and mace from the wall, as his squire dashed to gather his chain mail, chausses, surcoat and hauberk.

Gray dragged the mail shirt over his head, his thoughts racing. He had to get to her. He had to. Because for the first time in seventeen years he faced a battle that might spell death for someone other than himself, for someone he loved more than his own life.

And so for the first time in seventeen years, Gray prayed.

He asked God for the aid that had been forsaken him on the day Gillian died. He prayed and pleaded with all that he had, with all that he was, that he would reach Catherine in time . . .

Because the alternative would be a hell he couldn't even begin to contemplate.

The little whore. Did she think she could outsmart him? Did she really think he would allow it?

Eduard stalked away from his tent, tightening his sword belt as he went. He relished the feel of the sheathed blade slapping heavy against his thigh as he cut through the cool morning haze. Ribbons of mist floated over the encampment, obscuring his sight and adding to his rage as he searched the piles of sleeping men for his captain at arms.

The bastard was nowhere to be found. With a fierce kick, Eduard roused one of his knights from a drunken slumber. The man sputtered and coughed as he sprang to his feet, ready to attack his assailant until he realized his master's identity and saw the fury in Eduard's gaze.

"Mi—milord Montford," he stammered, dragging his arm across his mouth with a grimace. "How—how may I serve you this morn?"

"Find Robileau. Tell him to report to my tent immediately. As for the rest of the men, have everyone pack without delay. We leave for Faegerliegh Keep within the hour."

"*Faegerliegh*, milord?" The knight's brows knitted together in consternation. "Pardon, milord, but I thought we'd already traveled past Faegerliegh on our way to Ravenslock Castle."

"Imbecile," Eduard growled, his temper bubbling up again; he yanked the man by the back of his tunic and tossed him forward to sprawl in the dirt. "Never question my orders. I said Faegerliegh Keep, and 'tis what I meant. Now go!"

Without another word the knight scrambled to obey, hazarding a glance over his shoulder as he disappeared into the maze of tents. With another growl, Eduard spun on his heel and stalked back to his shelter, ignoring the dark, angry gazes of the men waking up around him as he went. Curse them all. Curse every one of them, along with their slothful captain.

And curse that bitch Catherine for attempting, for even one moment, to thwart him.

Yanking aside the silken flap to his tent, Eduard ducked in, sparing hardly a glance at Rupert, who sat, bloodied and exhausted, on the floor, still clutching his pouch of reward gold. Eduard focused instead on Juliette, crouching in the corner of the tent where he'd left her. She stared at him, eyes wide in her bruised face, wordlessly shaking her head as he stalked nearer.

"Nay!" She shrieked hoarsely, when he grasped

her arm and hauled her to her feet. Pulling back his arm he struck her twice, hard, before allowing her to fall to the bed with a cry as she buried her face in her hands.

"Get out," he snarled, not trusting himself to keep from killing her if he began to beat her in earnest as he longed to do. She meant nothing to him. Was worth nothing. But a dead woman would slow him down, or else make him a target for someone who might report of it back to the king.

Balling up her clothes, he reached down and grasped her arm again, dragging her from the bed and across the tent. Then, tossing her garments out in front of her, he shoved her through the flap and into the camp, not caring that she was wrapped only in the coverlet, or that the men's hungry gazes would be sure to find her, even in the mist-laden air.

Rupert stirred to the sounds of her sobbing outside, and with a shouted command, Eduard ejected him from the tent as well. Let the bloody wretch join the men if he wanted the comforts of food and drink. Rupert had served his purpose and was of no more use to him. Right now he needed to be alone to think. And plan.

Pacing back to his bed, Eduard wrinkled his nose and kicked the piles of fur and cushions until they lay in a tangled mound at the edge of the tent. They'd need to be burned, reeking as they did of woman; 'twas a scent he couldn't abide after his lust was sated.

Scowling again, he stalked to the magnificent, carved chair that he carried with him wherever he went and threw himself into it. Then, leaning back, he rubbed his finger across his lip, attempting to calm the fury that still boiled, it seemed, beneath the very surface of his skin.

Damn it, but he needed to concentrate. Needed to plot the day's events anew and revise his ruined plans. Closing his eyes, he breathed in, trying to focus, trying to bring back the icy calm he needed to accomplish his mission. He envisioned his army turning back to Somerset, saw in his mind's eye as they descended on Faegerliegh, saw himself crashing through the doors of the Keep and hunting down Catherine, with her two weak-minded whelps. And then . . .

Eduard's eyes snapped open as he sat up, a smile edging at his lips. A rush of cold, hard purpose slammed through his gut, bringing back with it calm and focus.

'Twas perfect.

He'd reach Faegerliegh within a few hours—long before Camville could ever hope to get there, even if he'd left immediately after Rupert's escape, which was unlikely, based upon the lad's report that the only man who'd seen him was dead and unable to sound the alarm. Aye, he would have ample time to take his anger out on Catherine, even kill her if he wished, before Camville arrived. And then he could trap and kill him, too.

When the king demanded explanation for the debacle, Eduard could simply explain that his beloved sister had sought refuge at Faegerliegh after fleeing Ravenslock and her husband's brutal rages—the same rages that had caused the man to beat his own twin sister to death years before.

But, Eduard could explain regretfully, Camville had followed Elise to Faegerliegh and killed her for her disobedience, an act that, once Eduard learned of it, required vengeance, resulting in his rival's destruction as well.

Eduard broke into a full grin. 'Twas perfect. He'd have Catherine *and* Camville dead, and rather than gaining the simple third of Gray's lands he stood to inherit otherwise, no doubt the king would grant him the bastard's complete estates and titles for the losses he'd suffered.

He almost laughed with the perfection of it all.

Pushing himself from his chair, he walked over to his armor, hefting his shield and stroking his finger over his thickly painted device, a Rampant Lion crushing a writhing serpent under its paw. Aye. He knew what needed to be done now. He knew well.

By God, it was his destiny.

Catherine ducked into the darkened chamber, motioning for Alban to follow behind her. He slunk in, as quiet as she, unencumbered by his usual armor; he and the other men had decided to forsake it on this secret mission, wearing only their hauberks for the sake of silence and speed. Sir Newell and Sir Payton stayed behind in the corridor, keeping watch to alert them of the approach of any Faegerliegh guards.

Everything was proceeding as planned.

'Twas no longer dark outside; dawn had threaded

pink and golden fingers over the land a little more
than an hour ago, just as Catherine and the men had
reached her old home. They'd tethered their horses
in the wood beyond the keep and crept the rest of
way into the estate on foot, sneaking through the
gate while the watchman's back was turned to relieve himself against the wall.

They'd had to wait for a long time for that
chance, but they'd been ready when it came. Now
the waiting was over. In a few moments she'd see
her children again. She took a deep breath where
she stood in the doorway of their room and then
stepped forward.

Her entire body thrummed with excitement, her
eyes straining as she moved closer to their bed.
Other than the low glow of last night's coals in the
grate, the room was black as pitch. The shutters had
ever been thick here; for all the light outside, the
room seemed shrouded in darkness. She reached
out her hand, unable to see well in front of her but
expecting to touch the wooden posts of the bed
frame at any moment.

"Do you see them yet, my lady?" Alban called
softly through the gloom. She felt his presence close
at her back, and she breathed another silent prayer
of thanks to Gray for sending his friend along with
her. 'Twas almost as if Gray himself stood by her
side, stable and comforting.

"Nothing yet," she whispered. Her toe suddenly
rapped into something hard, and she stifled a gasp.
The bed. Her hands trembled as she reached out to
feel the warm, solid little shapes that should be nes-

tled under the coverlet. She groped and leaned over further, propping her knee onto the mattress. But she found nothing. The bed was empty.

"They're not here." She twisted to face Alban in the dark, her voice still quiet but edged now with panic. "The coverlets are rumpled, but they're gone!"

Alban stepped away, checking the rest of the chamber before returning to her side. "The room is empty, my lady. Are you sure this is their chamber? Might you have taken a wrong turn in the dark?"

"Nay. 'Tis the twins' room. This is their bed," she said, touching the thickly carved vines and leaves that covered the wooden posts. "Geoffrey received this bed from Eduard, as a gift at their birth. 'Twas one of the few luxuries he allowed us to keep." She felt her throat closing as she considered other, less pleasant places that Ian and Isabel might be.

Or what Eduard might have done to them if he'd learned what she was up to.

Pushing that horrid thought from her mind, she paced back to the door. An idea bloomed suddenly, filling her with renewed hope. "Come! There is one other place to check," she whispered, crossing again to the opposite side of the bedchamber. She pushed aside a thick woolen tapestry on the wall, revealing a narrow door with a little latch set into the wood. "It connects to my old room," she whispered, pulling the latch and allowing the door to swing into the adjacent chamber.

Here the light shone a little brighter through the

crevices in the shutters, though no fire warmed the grate. 'Twas deathly cold. In the gloom, Catherine made out the contours of her much simpler bed—almost a pallet, really. Geoffrey had made her retire to it most nights, as a punishment for having displeased him in some way.

She'd been grateful for the respite, then, and she was overjoyed now, to see the huddled forms of her children sleeping under her old blankets, like puppies curled together for warmth.

Tears stung her eyes and her throat felt tight. Slowly, carefully, she stepped closer to the bed, until she was able to kneel on the floor next to it. She reached out and brushed her fingers across Isabel's brow, stroking aside a silvery blond curl. Her hungry gaze took in Ian as well, seeing how he cuddled close behind his sister, his little fist clenched and tucked under his rosy cheek.

The tears overflowed, then, accompanied by a rush of love so great that it hurt to breathe. It was all she could do not to reach down and sweep the both of them into her arms right now. But she had to go slowly, she reminded herself. They thought her dead, and she'd give up her freedom before frighting them with her unexpected return.

"They are beautiful, my lady," Alban said softly from behind her.

She looked over her shoulder at him, smiling through her tears. "Aye. They are my heart and soul. Truly, I do not think I would have survived to this day without them."

Turning back to her children, she placed her hand on Isabel's shoulder, murmuring, "Sweetheart. Awaken, now, darling. 'Tis time to get up."

Isabel stirred, sighing and lifting her arm away from Lily, the doll Catherine had made for her when she was only a babe, to rub her fist across her eyes. Raising her head, she blinked a few times, finally staring ahead with a gaze almost identical to Catherine's own.

Her delicate golden brows came together when she saw her mother, but she didn't cry or start with fear. Instead, she whispered, "Mummy?" before blinking again. She let her mother take her hand, before releasing it and reaching up to stroke Catherine's wet cheek. "Angels aren't supposed to cry, Mummy. Have you come to visit us from heaven?"

Catherine's throat squeezed tighter. "Nay, my love. Mummy isn't an angel. I'm here, a real person just like you, and I'm going to bring you and your brother away to somewhere safe, where you won't have to worry about anything ever again."

"Away from Uncle Eduard?" Isabel asked, hugging Lily close to her.

"Aye, sweetie. Away from Uncle Eduard and Faegerliegh Keep for good."

A brilliant smile lit the little girl's face. "'Tis what I asked God for, Mummy! I prayed and prayed that you would come back home again to take us away from here, and God listened, just like you said He would, if I was a good girl and prayed very hard."

Catherine laughed through a fresh swell of tears, and Isabel wrapped her arms around her mother's neck, pulling her tight into an embrace. At the motion on the bed, Ian grunted and sat straight up, alert and bright as if he'd not been soundly asleep moments before; since infancy he'd come awake so, with enough energy, Heldred had always said, to drive the village mill for a week.

"Mummy, 'tis you!" he cried, scrambling over his sister to attach himself to her neck as well. "I knew Uncle Eduard told us a tale. I knew you hadn't gone to live in heaven and left us here all alone."

"Hush, darlings," Catherine murmured, kissing their faces and hugging them hard to her. "We must needs be quiet and dress swiftly so that we can go from here with the nice men who are helping Mummy. Sir Alban will—"

A sudden burst of light and a strange whooshing sound filled the chamber, followed by a sickening thud and groan. Catherine sprang to her feet, whirling around as she gripped the hilt of her sword.

Her horrified gaze met Eduard's icy stare, lit in the blaze of torches held aloft by the half dozen men who loomed behind him. Eduard stood over Alban, holding a blade to his throat to keep him pressed to his knees; a dirk protruded from Alban's thigh, soaking his breeches crimson with blood.

"Ah, Catherine, my sweet. Sneaking about dressed as a man," Eduard drawled, his smile cold.

"Suitable raiment for a woman like you, I suppose. But assuming that you know how to use that sword you're wearing, I'd think long and hard before deciding to draw it on me."

Chapter 18

❝**E**duard." Catherine tried to swallow her terror. "How did you find me?"

"I told you what to expect from my spies, sweeting. 'Twas stupid of you to have ignored me."

"Where is Gray? What have you done with him?" she couldn't help asking, even knowing in her heart that something must have gone terribly wrong with their plan.

"Oh, I haven't done anything to him. Not yet," Eduard answered with a malicious smile. "I expect he'll be coming along in a few hours, which is why time is short. There's much you and I need to . . . settle, shall we say, before your loving husband enters my trap and finds his just reward. Now drop your sword like a good little warrior so we can get on with it."

"You bastard," Alban growled. "If you touch her, you'll pay."

Eduard answered his threat with a brutal cuff to the head, jamming the knife harder against Alban's throat as he commanded him to silence.

Catherine shifted her stance, trying to keep her children behind her as she strained to come up with a plan of action. Her heart thudded painfully, her breath coming shallow as her gaze darted to the open door that led to the twins' chamber.

Eduard saw her glance and his smile deepened. "If 'tis Camville's two other lackeys you seek, don't bother. They're already taken care of, as Warton here will be as well, unless you do exactly as I say." Alban grunted and flinched as Eduard dragged his blade along the exposed skin of his neck, making a thin line of blood well and trickle down to his shirt.

Catherine bit her lips to keep from calling out for Eduard to stop, knowing that was what he wanted from her in this perverse game of power he loved to play. Four more of Eduard's knights filed into the room behind him, fully outfitted in armor like the rest; one of them held a bloodied sword, and Catherine cringed to think whose life's flow stained the blade.

She looked quickly behind her to murmur soothing words to Ian and Isabel; they'd begun to cry, clutching the back of her tunic as they hid from their uncle's gaze.

"Aye, hush now, little lambs," Eduard said softly, never taking his cold stare from Catherine's face. "Mummy has an important choice to make. 'Twill ensure whether this nice man lives or dies in the next few moments." To punctuate his comment, he rammed his knee into Alban's wounded thigh, and Alban roared with agony.

"Don't do what he wants, Catherine," Alban gasped, his face ashen as he looked up at her. "Don't give up your weapon."

Without another sound, Eduard pulled back his arm and smashed Alban in the temple with the heavy hilt of his sword, and Alban crumpled to the floor. Kicking him aside, Eduard stepped closer to Catherine.

"I'll deal with Warton later. But you should keep in mind that he isn't the only one who will suffer my wrath if you don't begin to cooperate, Catherine, *very soon*." He flicked his gaze with unmistakable meaning to the twins.

Nausea shot through her, and she swallowed hard against it, forcing herself to concentrate. She licked her lips. "What do you want me to do?"

"Do?" Eduard cocked his brow and grinned his evil, mocking smile again. "Oh, there's much that you will do, Catherine. Much you must atone for, I'm afraid. You've put me through quite an ordeal, with your little escapade."

She felt herself blanch. Old fears and agonizing memories of Eduard's favorite methods of punishment sprang to mind, but she tried to stand firm as she faced him. "If I agree to your terms, you must promise not to hurt the children. Swear that you'll leave them alone."

"You're in no position to bargain, woman. Concede now or suffer the consequences, both for your-self and for my darling niece and nephew."

She gazed at him helplessly, at his men clustered in the doorway. Beyond them she saw more knights carrying in the limp forms of Sir Payton and Sir Newell. Finally her gaze fell on Alban's prostrate body, and defeat gouged her with claws of steel. Hands trembling, she unclasped her sword belt, let-ting it fall heavily to the floor.

In an instant, Eduard's men surged forward, re-sponding to his command to take the twins and lock them in the solar for safekeeping. Catherine bit her lips to keep from screaming as her children were picked up and carried from the room, shrieking her name and reaching out to her over the shoulders of the knights who held them. When they'd gone, the last of Eduard's men lifted Alban, still senseless, and dragged him from the chamber between them like a butchered animal.

The door closed to resounding silence, leaving her alone with Eduard. Slowly she raised her face to him, meeting his icy stare. He wore a look that she knew too well. The look that told her far more pow-erfully than words ever could how much she was going to suffer—how much he was going to enjoy making her hurt for her transgressions against him.

Tearing her gaze from his, she searched the room wildly for something, anything that she might use as a weapon. Anything to keep him at bay. But there was nothing. Her chamber was empty, as always. As he'd ensured it would be.

Her entire body began to quake with treacherous

weakness, with tingling dread as he stepped closer. And closer . . . until he stood near enough that his breath misted warm on her temple.

His smile was dark as he reached up and stroked his finger across the delicate, fragile line of her cheekbone. He touched her gently. Softly. Profanely.

A moan of fear escaped her and her knees threatened to buckle when he leaned a little closer to murmur, " 'Tis a fine contrast of sensation is it not, sweet Catherine? To experience such tenderness before such pain . . ."

He paused for a moment. Then, with a sudden, savage growl, he raised his arm and backhanded her, sending an explosion of agony rocking deep into her skull. When his fist sank into her belly, she dropped retching and gasping to the floor.

And then she was lost in a nightmare of violence and torment from which she knew there'd be no escape.

She hurt. Sweet Jesu, everything hurt so badly.

Struggling to open her eyes, Catherine tried to get her bearings. She was on the floor of the chamber, her cheek pressed into the cool, hard wood. Pushing herself to a sitting position, she gasped and cried out, sucking in her breath. Tasting blood, she spit it out, swiping the back of her hand across her lips.

He'd beaten her badly this time. Worse than ever before. He'd wanted to kill her. And he'd have succeeded, too, she knew, if something hadn't stopped him. If something hadn't happened, forcing him to cease kicking her after she'd curled herself into a ball on the floor.

The messenger . . .

Wincing, she sat up a little more and closed her eyes, trying to remember what the man had said. Her mind felt enveloped in a fog, paralyzed by the throbbing ache in her skull. She had to think.

It had been one of Eduard's knights. He'd come to the door, interrupting the beating. She remembered the man's brown eyes, thick with sympathy when he'd seen her lying on the floor. But then he'd looked away, clearing his throat and announcing that Lord Camville's forces had been spotted surging over the hill east of Faegerliegh. He'd arrived several hours earlier than expected, and the men needed Eduard to lead them against him in the battle to come.

Lord Camville's forces had been spotted . . .

Gray had come! The realization sent a joyful shock through her numbed brain. He'd led his army to Faegerliegh Keep to help her and the twins. She struggled to her feet, ignoring the pain as she stumbled to the door. She had to find her children. Had to try to lead them outside the keep's walls. Outside to Gray.

The solar. Eduard had ordered his men to bring Ian and Isabel to the solar for safekeeping. She tried the door, her heart leaping when she realized that it was unlocked. Eduard hadn't even posted a guard in the corridor. Most likely he'd thought her too weakened to stir from the floor. 'Twas his mistake, and she planned to use it to full advantage.

Murmuring a prayer of thanksgiving, Catherine limped down the corridor, willing better clarity to her muddled brain and bursts of strength into her weakened legs. With each step, she focused on her purpose, gaining power and resolve. And anger. She felt the welcome burn of it, recalling Gray's advice to her during their training, to focus her passions and rage into something useful. To work them to her benefit.

She grimaced, which only made her lip bleed again. Dabbing it gently with her fingers, she stumbled on. Aye, she'd use her anger well. She'd wield every ounce of it against Eduard. She'd been given a second chance to save her children, and she'd get them away from here if it took her last breath.

Catherine ducked behind a thick curtain as one of the keep's maidservants came running down the hall. The woman was pale and obviously frightened by the sounds of battle echoing outside the walls. After she passed, Catherine came out of hiding and continued toward the solar.

She concentrated on the hate she felt for Eduard, and it helped her to keep going, to push through her suffering. Her loathsome brother by marriage had made a great tactical error this day, an error for which he'd pay dearly. He'd underestimated the force of her will to survive and fight his brutality and evil . . .

And that, she vowed, jaw clenched as she trudged

down the seemingly endless corridor, was going to prove his most deadly mistake of all.

Isabel squeezed her eyes shut, clasping her hands tight around Lily as she struggled to pray. She felt her own breath misting warm on her chilled fingers, but 'twas difficult to concentrate on talking to God with all of the banging and shouting going on beyond the keep's walls. There were no windows to see outside the solar. No way to tell what was happening.

"It sounds like a big fight," Ian yelled, his breath hanging in white puffs in the air. He hopped from the tabletop to a trunk ten paces beyond it, finally leaping to the massive mantel, where he dangled for a moment like a monkey before dropping to the stone hearth. He clambered up onto the unlit logs inside, standing up so that his head disappeared from view as he peered up the chimney, hoping for a glimpse of the action.

"Get out of there," Isabel yelled, getting up from her prayers to yank him from the fireplace.

Ian coughed and scrubbed his sooty arm across his eyes, leaving black smudges all over his cheeks. "You didn't have to grab me like that! I was just scouting." He coughed again and scowled at her. "Now I can't see, and you made me breathe in a pile of cinders!"

"Well, look at you!" Isabel scolded, brushing flakes of ash from his blond hair and using her sleeve to wipe his eyes. "What would Mummy say if she saw you, Ian?"

"Mummy isn't here." His lower lip wobbled a little and Isabel sighed, putting her hands on her hips.

"Well she will be, just as soon as she talks with Uncle Eduard."

"Uncle Eduard doesn't talk, he hits," Ian muttered, kicking his toe against the hearth.

Isabel felt the sick feeling in her stomach too, but she couldn't show that to her brother. He might get scared again, and if she'd learned anything in the year that they'd fostered away from home, it was that you could pretend yourself into feeling any way you wanted. It worked most of the time, anyway.

"We need to do something," she said, pursing her lips and tapping her toe.

"Like what?"

"Like getting out of here to find Mummy."

"But we can't! Uncle Eduard told those two men to stay outside our door. If we try to leave they'll just throw us back in here."

"Not if we trick them, they won't." Isabel paced slowly to the fireplace again, sticking her head in to look up at the square of blue sky she could see at the top of the chimney.

"Hey, I thought you told me not to do that!"

"I'm not doing what you were," she retorted, leaning her head out to glare at him. "I'm thinking out our plan."

"Our plan?" Ian's face lit up and he clambered back onto the wood next to her. "What is it? Are we going to climb the chimney to freedom?"

Isabel crossed her arms over her chest and favored her brother with a look of disgust. "And what good would that do? We'd end up stuck on the roof."

He shrugged, squinting to peer up at the patch of blue. "Once we were up there we could wave and jump about until someone threw a rope to us."

"Or shot us with an arrow." Shaking her head, Isabel peered up again. "Nay, I think we should reach a stick up there and scrape down the ash."

Now Ian screwed up his face with derision. "And why in blazes would we want to do *that*?"

"Don't say blazes—Mummy said 'tis a foul word."

She ignored the even more foul sight of Ian's tongue sticking out at her, instead ducking from the fireplace and pointing at the large chamber pot in the corner. "We could gather the ash in that, then hang it above the door and begin shouting and jumping, as if something was amiss . . ."

Ian's scornful look faded. "And when the guards rush in to see what's the matter, the ash will fall on their heads and blind them so that we can escape!"

"Well, the pot might hit the first guard," Isabel conceded, "but I think we'll need something else to stop the second one."

Ian grabbed a large, knotted walking stick that was propped against the wall near the fireplace. "How about this? I can hide behind the door, and when the second guard comes in I can trip him with it."

Isabel frowned, not at all certain that these plans fit in with the virtues that Mummy had always taught them. They were to say their prayers, tell no lies, be good to each other, and treat no other living thing with harm. 'Twas that last part that would be a problem now, Isabel thought, grimacing. But they weren't really going to harm the men, just trick them so that she and Ian could escape.

Squeezing her eyes shut, Isabel sent a prayer up to God, asking Him if what they were about to do was bad. She stood very still, waiting for some kind of sign against it, anything to let her know that they should think of something else in order to escape.

There was no answer.

She whispered the prayer again, just to be sure.

Heaven remained quiet.

That was it, then. God must understand. Perhaps He even approved. With a sigh of contentment, she opened her eyes and gazed at her brother with a look of determination.

"All right, Ian," she said firmly. "We're going to do it. Now let's get to work."

Chapter 19

Gray swung his blade, hearing men scream and feeling the familiar resistance of flesh beneath his hacking charge. His mind blurred in the heat of killing, and his heart thumped madly. But 'twas not from bloodlust this day. Nay, this was something entirely different. For the first time since that awful day seventeen years ago, he battled his opponents with a sense of panic and desperation.

He had to get to Catherine.

Eduard's men fought well and hard, and there were over three hundred of them to Gray's nine score. Already the imbalance in numbers had taken its toll; many Ravenslock men lay sprawled, dead or wounded, across the grassy field leading to Faegerliegh Keep. It would take a blessing from on high to turn the tides in his favor.

Or perhaps a burst of pure will.

An opening appeared in the thick mass of warriors in front of him. Kneeing his stallion forward, Gray lent his fury to the attack, widening the gap. The path led directly to the gates of the keep, its entrance barred only by an iron portcullis. Whether out of rash complacency or lack of preparation, Eduard had left his defenses weak . . . and that was going to give Gray the only opportunity he needed.

"To the gates!" he roared over the din, ramming and slashing his way through Eduard's knights. His men followed close behind, scrambling up the walls and scaling the tower that housed the gears to the mechanism. Several of them began to fight with the guards there, while three others pulled the lever back, raising the metal gate with a groaning screech.

A new flood of Eduard's men stormed the area as Gray and his troops surged into the massive courtyard, filling the enclosure with the violent tumult of warfare. Gray pressed on. He'd almost reached the curved doorway leading into the main keep itself, when one of Montford's knights caught him with a lance-blow.

Gray tipped off his stallion, rolling to his side and springing up in time to block the man's charge and deal a killing strike himself. He watched his opponent fall and then, with one last glance at the battle raging behind him, he ducked through the entryway and into the cool, dark silence of Faegerliegh Keep's main corridor.

Yanking off his helm, he moved down the hall, his weight on the balls of his feet, his sword ready. Catherine hadn't exaggerated; the hallways were intricate, twisting and turning, with several smaller corridors jutting off at odd angles. He kept to the main gallery, hoping to gain his bearings so that he could more swiftly locate Catherine or her children.

His ears thrummed in the silence, still numb from the clamor of battle, but he threw open every door as he passed, his eyes straining, searching, desperate. Some of the chambers revealed naught but empty disarray, while others sheltered huddled masses of servants and children, their faces streaked with tears or eyes wide with terror. He resisted the urge to stop and help them. Catherine and the twins needed him more right now. Continuing on, he darted his gaze to the left and right, alert to any movement, any shifting in the shadows.

Suddenly, the hair prickled at his nape and he stopped mid-stride. Something had moved in the corner of his vision. He was approaching the juncture of another hall; dust motes danced in the stream of sun from the glazed windows, swirling in a pattern that revealed a person hiding in the shadows.

Gray stepped forward, cautious, alert. As he reached the turn in the corridor, he lifted his blade and swung it toward the man who lay waiting for him in the gloom.

Only it wasn't a man. It was a woman . . . a battered woman, whose hair hung in wild, tangled strands to cover half of her face. Her upraised hands clutched a makeshift weapon, a wooden leg she'd obviously broken from a chair or stool somewhere.

Sweet Jesu in heaven.

"Catherine . . . ?"

She stood there for a mere instant, staring at him, eyes wide with apprehension. Then, with a sobbing cry, she dropped the piece of wood and threw herself into his arms.

Gray embraced her with a groaning cry that echoed her own, his heart contracting with love and relief. He pressed a kiss to the top of her head before pulling back to cup her face very gently in both of his hands.

"How did you know?" she asked, her voice thick with tears. "How did you know to come here so quickly?"

Gray shut his eyes for a moment, wishing that he could spare her the pain of what he was about to tell her. But there was no way around it. "'Twas Heldred, love," he said quietly. "He intercepted a spy who was fleeing to Eduard. While trying to stop him, he was wounded. But he fought valiantly and managed to drag himself into the open before 'twas too late, to alert us of the breach."

Gray saw Catherine's eyes widen, fresh tears spilling over as she suddenly grasped the full meaning of what he was saying.

"Then Heldred is—?"

She couldn't finish, and so he just nodded stiffly, holding her close as she cried her grief into his embrace. He wanted to let his love seep into her through his palms, to take away all of the pain she'd already suffered, all the hurt she was suffering now.

"He was a dear and loyal friend," she murmured finally, pulling back a little. "I will never forget him."

Gray nodded again and smoothed her hair from her brow, breathing in sharply at the bruises he saw along her temple and cheekbone. He clenched his jaw against the renewed flood of rage that swept through him. Beyond her visible injuries, he knew that she must have been hurt in many places that he couldn't see just by the careful way she held herself in his arms. *That bastard. That hell-spawned, treacherous bastard.*

"God, Catherine, I'm sorry," he said, his voice rough with emotions that threatened to swallow him whole. "I'm so sorry I didn't get here in time to stop him from doing this to you."

"Nay," she answered softly, shaking her head. "Don't blame yourself. There was no way to know. I'm just thankful that you're safe and that you're here with me now." She pulled back again to look at him. "But we must hurry, Gray. We need to get the children. Eduard ordered them locked in the solar. I was going to them when you found me."

He nodded, still supporting her weight. "Aye. We need to get them out of here." He looked into the shadows behind her, seeing nothing. "Where's Alban?"

"Eduard wounded him when he caught us. The last I saw of him he was being carried from my chamber between two of Eduard's men. I don't know where they've put him." She swallowed and added more quietly, "Or if he's still alive."

Gray clenched his jaw, keeping his reactions in check. He nodded. "We'll have to trust him to take care of himself for now. Your children must needs be rescued first. Come."

Taking her hand, he helped her down the corridor, following her instructions for where to turn. By the time they reached the short jut of hall leading to the solar, he uttered another silent prayer of thanks. He knew now that he'd never have found the chamber on his own. Not through the maze of corridors they'd followed to get here. 'Twas undoubtedly why Eduard had chosen the place as ideal for securing the twins.

Only two men stood posted outside the door. From his position with Catherine down the hall, he could see that they looked very young and very nervous. He'd hazard a guess that these new-bloods were all that Eduard could spare as guards, once he realized that he'd be faced with an all-out battle beyond the boundaries of the keep.

Suddenly, a banging arose from within the solar, followed by shouts and screams. Gray lunged forward just behind the sentries, who'd turned to each other at the noise and scrambled to open the door.

But before Gray and Catherine could reach them, there was a loud clatter, and a cloud of soot billowed out of the now open door. Throwing himself into the chamber, Gray tripped over the prostrate forms of the guards. He waved his arms and coughed, unable to see anything. Ash filled the air, along with the fearsome shrieking of two very small warriors wielding knobby sticks at him.

They swung their sticks wildly, and one of the blows connected with his shin. He cursed, shifting his weight to grab the miscreants, one in each hand, by the backs of their shirts. He hoisted them into the air, carrying them unceremoniously into the corridor, where he put them down before spinning back to shut and bolt the door on the two sentries still lying, half-senseless, inside.

"Ian! Isabel!" Catherine cried, kneeling to enfold them into an embrace.

"Mummy!" they croaked simultaneously, coughing and sneezing as they wrapped their arms around her neck, both trying to talk at once.

"Oh, Mummy, you're hurt!" Isabel said, coughing again and blinking back tears from the ash as she cupped her hand gently over her mother's cheek. She pulled a grubby doll from her waist sash, where she'd obviously secured it to do battle with the guards. "Lily was worried about you too, Mummy. We were trying to get to you, to save you from Uncle Eduard. That's why we had to trick those bad men. But we didn't want to kill them, really. We only—"

"It was my idea to hit them with sticks, Mummy!" Ian crowed between coughs. "You're not mad, are you? I didn't hit them too hard, I just—"

"Oh sweethearts!" Catherine pulled both of them

tighter in her embrace. "I'm not angry. I just thank heaven that you're both all right."

"We must make haste," Gray said quietly, loathe to end their reunion, but knowing that 'twas dangerous to linger. Catherine nodded, pushing herself to her feet with a grimace.

"We'll go this way," he said, taking her hand and directing the twins to walk next to her as he led them all back down the hall toward the courtyard.

"Wait a moment." Catherine pulled back suddenly and squinted as she looked to get her bearings. "We're close to the buttery here. If we can reach it, Gray, there's a hidden door that leads to a tunnel out of the keep. It goes all the way to a field beyond the walls."

He frowned. "A secret passage in a manor house?"

"It served as an escape route nearly two centuries ago, during the Conquest. Geoffrey once told me that the family who lived here added it in case the Normans breached the walls during an attack."

"Then Eduard knows about it as well," he said grimly.

"Aye. But 'tis our only way out, other than taking the children through the battle in the courtyard."

Gray nodded, leaning out into the corridor she'd indicated, looking for any movement. All seemed quiet. The twins gripped each other's hands, staring at him, but doing exactly as he bid while he supported Catherine down the hall. Every now and then the shouting sounded nearer, and they were forced to duck into the shadows or behind a door until it seemed safe to continue.

Though she never complained, Gray knew by the way she limped and by the ashen cast of her complexion that Catherine was in a great deal of pain. He cursed silently, love for her mingling again with his rage against Eduard. He itched to get his hands on the bastard, to make him suffer tenfold for what he'd done to her.

At last she pointed to a door ten paces away. "There it is. The buttery. The passageway is hidden behind the shelves on the far wall."

Gray led the children into the large, cool chamber; Catherine stood with them while Gray worked to remove the heavy shelving that blocked the tunnel. There was no way to do it quietly. Barrels thumped to the floor and pottery jars crashed as he yanked the wooden slats from the wall.

But soon the ancient looking door appeared, its latchstring hanging out. Gray lifted the rotted leather carefully, and the door creaked open. Cobwebs yawned and stretched at the corners of the portal, the odor of decay spilling out of the tunnel to coat them with a chill blanket of vapor.

"Come," he said, herding the children into the opening. "We must hurry."

"Nay. 'Tis too dark and small!" Ian cried, pulling back.

"He's afraid because when we fostered with Master Dumont he used to lock Ian in a little chamber below the kitchen floor for being bad," Isabel said softly.

"Merciful saints," Catherine muttered, looking as if she was going to be sick.

"'Tis all right, Ian. There's naught to fear," Gray said, hoping to comfort the lad. "Your mother will lead the way into the tunnel. You can go right behind her."

"I don't think that I can, Gray," Catherine said. "Without a torch, I can't see well enough through this swollen eye. You'll have to go first and let me follow behind the children."

Gray considered that for a moment, uncertainty assailing him. Leaving Catherine last made him uneasy, but it didn't seem that he would have much choice. Leaning in, he brushed her lips with a kiss, murmuring for her to take extra care before he stooped to enter the tunnel, coaxing first Ian, then Isabel in after him.

"You're doing fine, lad," he murmured to Ian, who trembled and clutched Gray's tunic in a death-grip as they crept along.

Gray looked back to ensure that Catherine had ducked into the tunnel as well before he continued to lead them all on through the dark passage.

Suddenly, he heard Isabel gasp.

"Lily!" Isabel cried. "Oh, Mummy, I've dropped Lily!"

Gray turned to see Isabel scrambling past her mother, trying to crawl back into the buttery.

"Nay Isabel! We mustn't return. 'Tis too dangerous," Catherine said sharply, lurching to catch Isabel at the very portal of the chamber. She was just nudging the weeping little girl ahead of her into the tunnel again, when Gray saw her face stiffen in the dim light from the chamber. A tingle of warning shot up his spine.

"Ah, Catherine, my dear. How lovely. It seems that we'll get to finish our little meeting after all."

Eduard's voice echoed through the tunnel a mere instant before he reached in to grab Catherine and drag her, kicking and fighting, back into the buttery. With a shout, Gray twisted and threw himself at the door, trying to get to her, but the wooden slab shut on him and the twins, sealing them inside and leaving Catherine trapped with Eduard on the other side.

Thrusting the children behind him, Gray slammed into the door, rattling the scarred planks, then ramming it with his shoulder. Aged as it was, it wouldn't budge. Eduard must have put something heavy in front of it. The twins huddled in terrified silence, as through the wood the muffled sounds of scraping furniture and banging gave way to the unmistakable echo of a slap and Catherine's cry.

Cursing aloud, Gray leaned back and kicked again and again at the old door. It cracked, finally, under his assault. He burst through the splinters, shoving aside the barrel blocking his way as he fell into the room, his frantic gaze searching for Catherine.

She stood at the other end of the chamber. Somehow, she'd managed to get one of the buttery's worktables between herself and Eduard. But he was in the process of drawing his sword, readying to slash at her with it.

Flashing a dark grin at his rival, Eduard gloated,

"You're too far away, Camville. You'll never reach her in time to stop me. But do come and try anyway. Then I'll have the pleasure of killing you as well!"

Gray knew in that sickening moment that Eduard was right. He couldn't get to Catherine in time. But an idea began to form as he shifted to look at the woman he loved more than his life, and her frightened gaze locked with his. Gripping the hilt of his sword, Gray nodded slightly, praying that she understood his unspoken signal.

In the next instant everything slowed as if in a dream. Eduard roared with fury, tossing the table aside, even as Gray drew his own sword hissing from its sheath and hurled it toward Catherine in flashing, rotating arcs.

Instinct surged in her, blending with skill borne of their hours of practice; she reached up and caught Gray's sword by the hilt, in the same motion twisting and lunging to point it at Eduard as he charged her. His momentum slammed them both against the wall—and then he stiffened, his weight still pressed into her, his eyes widening in shock just inches from her own. Past the sound of her gasping breath, she heard his weapon clatter to the floor.

He tried to pull back, looking down awkwardly at the blade imbedded in his chest to the widening blossom of blood around it, before finally lifting his gaze to meet Catherine's again.

"You bitch," he rasped in disbelief. "You unnatural murderous bitch . . ."

Rage flooded her anew. Even here, at the point of

death, Eduard couldn't resist spitting his venom at her. Gritting her teeth, she fixed her gaze on him, this man who had caused her so much pain, so much torment in her life, and muttered, "Now 'tis your turn to feel what hell is like, Eduard."

Yanking her blade free, she pushed him away; with a choked gurgle he slumped to the floor and lay still, blood soaking the front of his tunic and trickling from his mouth. His eyes remained open, but they gazed at her now without sight. Flat and empty.

She stood frozen for a long moment, just staring at him. *He was dead.* God help her, he was finally dead, and it was she who had defeated him.

Her mind throbbed so that she hardly noticed Gray's approach. She staggered back to lean against the wall again as he crossed the room in several strides, quickly checking Eduard's body before turning to her. Then he cupped her cheeks in his palms, lifting up gently to make her meet his gaze.

"Are you all right, Catherine? Did he wound you before I got back inside?"

"Nay," she managed to whisper, shaking her head.

"Thank God," he said hoarsely, enfolding her in his embrace. Her breath came shallow, and she held herself stiff for a moment, still staring at Eduard's body. Then with a cry she dropped Gray's sword and buried her face in his chest, holding him tight.

Ian and Isabel had crept out of the tunnel once everything went quiet, and now they rushed forward, tucking themselves against her and Gray.

"Oh Mummy, I'm sorry," Isabel sobbed. "I'm so sorry I went back to get Lily!"

"Hush, sweetheart," Catherine murmured, stroking her daughter's hair. "'Tis over now, and we're all safe. That's all that matters. We're all safe."

"Aye, praise God," Gray added.

"Stand down in the name of the king!"

The shout rang from the corridor, making Catherine stiffen. Gray released her and the children to scoop up his sword and face the door, sheltering them behind him.

A half dozen soldiers wearing the orange tunics of the king's forces burst into the chamber, weapons drawn. The leader of the group skidded to a halt when he saw Eduard's body. Then his gaze flicked to Gray and the bloodied sword, and he held up his hand to bring the others up short behind him. His expression tightened, but he nevertheless jerked his head in recognition of England's High Champion.

"Lord Camville," he said.

Gray nodded back cautiously, still keeping Catherine and the twins tucked safely behind him.

The captain straightened before calling out in an official voice, "I am under orders to take you and Lord Montford into my custody and escort you both to London, to face charges of seditious action and disobedience against His Most Royal Highness, King Henry." He paused, glancing again at Eduard's body. "However, it seems that Lord Montford's fate has already been sealed, and that the charge of murder must needs be added to those tallied against you."

Gray clenched his jaw, maintaining silence in the face of the false allegation. Nausea flooded Catherine when she realized what he intended to do.

With a cry, she stepped away from him, avoiding his attempts to keep her back as she stumbled a few paces closer to the soldiers.

"Sir, why have you charged Lord Camville with the slaying? He is no murderer! He—"

"Catherine, be still," Gray muttered, grasping her hand and trying to pull her back. "The children need you. 'Tis for the best."

"Nay!" Catherine said, shaking herself free. "Eduard is dead, and I will lie no more."

"What are you saying, lady?" The captain scowled.

"I am saying that Lord Camville did not kill Lord Montford. He is innocent of the charge."

Gray cursed softly, but the soldier just stared at her as if she'd gone mad. He glanced around the chamber again to see if he'd missed the presence of another person capable of killing one of the king's best champions. Seeing no one, he spoke to her as if she were a child, in need of gentle care and handling.

"Lady, what you say makes no sense. Lord Camville was the only man here, the only one anywhere, many might say, accomplished enough even to commit the deed. If he did not, then who, pray tell, killed Lord Montford?"

"That is what I have been trying to tell you, Captain," Catherine said, pulling herself up to her full height and staring in turn at each of the soldiers before finally settling her gaze on their leader again.

"I did."

Chapter 20

London
The Royal Palace of Westminster

Gray stood surrounded by guards in the great chamber of King Henry's Court, forcing himself to remain still as he waited for Catherine to be brought in. The hours had been endless, every minute torture since he'd last seen her on the day of his arrest nearly two weeks ago.

Disbelieving as they were, the soldiers had finally placed her into custody along with him for Edward's murder; they'd had no choice after she'd stood like an avenging warrior queen over Montford's body and made her bold statement to the captain. And so they'd brought her to London too, to let the royal inquiry sort out the mess of their sworn confessions.

Since then, Gray had been consumed with worry over her, driven by a fierce desire to see her and know that she was all right. But his inquisitors hadn't allowed it. Instead, he'd faced their questions. Days of endless interrogation, sometimes for many hours, without food, drink or sleep. It could have been worse, he knew; they could have used some of their more infamous means of torture on him in their quest for the truth. He was grateful that they hadn't and prayed that it meant Catherine had been spared as well.

Through it all, he'd done his best to convince them of his guilt, of his action alone in the murder of his hated rival. 'Twas the only possible conclusion, he'd told them, and they'd listened carefully to his explanations, sometimes scribbling notes, other times just observing him. Day after day, he'd stayed true to his story, relentless in his will to convince them.

Today he would learn if he'd succeeded.

At last the door at the back of the massive chamber creaked open. All of the more than three score guards, knights, nobles and ladies filling the room craned their necks to see the second prisoner brought forth.

Catherine walked steadily between her guards, head held high. Gray felt a stab of relief; she looked unharmed. Even the bruises from Eduard's abuse had mostly faded. Her steps only faltered once, and that was at the moment she met his gaze. In that instant, her emotions shone on her face; intense longing and a love for him so powerful that it seemed almost otherworldly spilled from her, lighting her with that angelic radiance that took his breath away.

Vaguely, Gray heard the murmurs of the people in court who saw it as well. But his entire focus stayed on Catherine. All he wanted was to touch her, to hold her, to love her, and it took every ounce of his strength not to leap over the benches and people separating them to carry her from this place and never let go.

Before he could act on his impulse, he saw her breathe deep and direct her gaze firmly ahead. Then she took her place in court, standing with her guards only twenty paces away from him.

Following the line of her vision, Gray started. King Henry had entered the chamber previously; now he sat motionless on his dais, his stare hard and penetrating as he looked at them both. But the row of royal councilors sitting at long tables to either side of him leaned into each other, whispering behind their hands as they glared at Catherine.

Only at Catherine.

The hair prickled on the back of Gray's scalp. Their expressions were filled with hatred, their mumbled comments malicious.

"Man-killer," he heard one of them mutter.

"Liar," murmured another, shaking his head.

A third scowled and formed a soundless, damning curse into the ear of the man next to him. *"Witch."*

Sweet God in heaven . . .

Bile rose in Gray's throat as he gazed from the councilors to the woman he loved and then back again. He felt their malice rippling toward her in an evil, oppressive tide.

Nay . . .

Oh, God, he'd failed to convince them. He'd failed *her*. They'd already tried and convicted her in their minds; he could hear their verdict as plainly as if it had been proclaimed aloud in the chamber.

Because she is a woman, a shadowy voice hissed from deep in his brain. Aye, he wanted to shout. A beautiful, strong, courageous woman who had fought back and killed the wretch who was abusing her.

But Catherine's words to him on that day he'd first suggested training her to fight returned in the shadow voice to haunt him now and forced him to silence.

"Under English law a woman cannot take arms against a man."

"In the act of protecting oneself, 'tis allowed," he'd replied blithely.

"And yet many women have been punished for daring to do just that, especially to men bearing title . . ."

Oh God . . .

Catherine seemed unaware of the darkness, the slithering contempt these men harbored against her. She stood there unsuspecting of the danger, the death waiting for her if she continued to claim guilt in Eduard's murder.

Almost against his will, Gray's gaze flew to the grim-faced Court official shuffling a pile of parchments to the left of the king. 'Twas Lord Webster, the sour old man who'd come to his cell daily to observe the interrogations. Once he found the document he was seeking, the man would be called to speak. There was no doubt that he would bring forth the Council's judgement against Catherine in front of everyone assembled here.

And then it would be too late.

At that moment Gray knew that he had to stop this in any way he could. He had to stop these men, before they brought down their wrath on Catherine's innocent head.

"Your Highness!" he called, throwing himself forward. More than a dozen soldiers in orange tunics lowered their spears at him, while his guards grabbed frantically at his arms to hold him back.

He struggled to shake them off, yelling, "Your Highness, I cast myself on your mercy and publicly claim open and clear disobedience to you, as well as full responsibility in the murder of my sworn rival, Eduard de Montford!"

The Court erupted into chaos, but Gray shouted over it, forcing himself to avoid Catherine's stricken stare. "I surrender myself to your judgement and penalty, great king, and ask only that you release this woman, who is innocent of any wrongdoing in—"

"Nay! 'Tis not true!" Catherine cried. Spectators lurched to their feet, engrossed in the drama, and the clamor of voices rose.

"He bears no fault in this!" Catherine called above the din. "'Tis I who killed Lord Montford! I alone who bear guilt in—"

"Enough!" the king roared. His command cut through the furor, bringing everyone to a reluctant hush. He stood and glared at the assembly. Dark anticipation seethed through the chamber, curling about everyone's ankles, alive and snakelike.

"In all of Our years as sovereign," Henry grated, his face stiff with fury, "We have never been subjected to the kind of frenzy engendered this day by the two of you, each stubbornly clinging to a confession of guilt in the same villainous crime. We are almost tempted to order both of your foolish heads struck off for it!"

Renewed gasps and murmurs echoed through the chamber, but the king continued, undaunted in his anger. Placing both of his hands on the table in front of him, he leaned forward to speak deliberately, succinctly. "However, as England is a civilized nation, We prefer not to execute the innocent alongside the guilty."

Gray made a move to speak again, but Henry held up his hand, his fingers so rigid that they appeared made of stone. Stepping back, Gray clenched his jaw and waited, deciding that it would be in Catherine's best interest for him to obey for now.

"Lord Montford was one of Our most powerful nobles," the king said fiercely. "A seasoned warrior and champion. And regardless of what part he may have played in this affair—a part that he is forever deprived from defending himself against, We remind you—We do not take his murder or his loss to the Crown lightly."

Gray gritted his teeth, but the king continued, glaring at him. "Nor do We accept the constant and blatant disobedience of you, Lord Camville, Our equally powerful and hitherto most favored High Champion. Your repeated defiance of Our sanctions speaks ill of your allegiance to Our authority."

More whispers arose, increasing to a low buzz as the king next directed his harsh stare at Catherine. "And as for the deceits that it appears you have perpetrated, lady, We find that We have no words to express Our feelings of shock and dismay."

She flushed and dropped her gaze. Henry's expression softened a little, though he didn't say more to her, directing his next words instead to the gathered assembly. "It is time to resolve this matter once and for all."

He sat in a flourish of jeweled robes, making an irritated gesture with his hand toward Lord Webster at his left. "The Court Official will now present the Council's findings to the assembly."

Gray scowled at Lord Webster, trying to catch his gaze, but the man ignored him to stand and look round the chamber, obviously relishing his important role in these proceedings.

"We, the High Council," he began in a nasal drone, "have come to several conclusions regarding the murder of Eduard de Montford and the events leading up to it."

Gray saw at least five of the dozen men on either side of the king avert their gazes or look down. His chest tightened, and he strained at the guards holding him, wanting to stop this, to make them all see reason before it was too late.

"First, in response to the charge by Lord Camville that Lord Montford exercised abuses on

Catherine de Montford in excess of that allowed by law as her guardian—no *legal* husband being present," he directed a pointed glare at Gray, "we, the Council, find it to be unsubstantiated. In addition, we find that—"

"Unsubstantiated?" Gray growled in disbelief. Rage slammed through him, and he lurched forward, blind to all else but the need to make this wretch admit the truth. "You arrogant bastard," he shouted. "Did you see her when she arrived here? Jesu, he'd beaten her near to death! What kind of proof do you need?"

Out of the chaos of the court chamber, four additional soldiers were forced to scramble to aid Gray's guards in restraining him. He was fighting like a madman to get to the now pale-faced and gaping Lord Webster, itching to do to the man what Montford had done to Catherine, to see then if he thought her injuries unsubstantiated.

Suddenly, something smashed into the back of his skull, and with a grunt he went down to his knees. Through the numbness that threatened to overtake him, he felt irons being clapped over his wrists, binding his hands together with thick chain.

"Lord Camville, you will govern yourself," King Henry called over the noise in the court chamber.

Shaking the remaining stars from his vision, Gray pushed himself back to his feet, first glaring at the guard who'd dealt him the blow, then looking to the king. Fury still clouded his mind, pulsing through him in heated waves, but even through it, he perceived a subtle change in his monarch. He saw for the first time a glint of something, perhaps a kind of understanding, buried in Henry's steely gaze.

When Gray turned to Catherine, however, what remained of his anger curdled in his gut. She faced him, gazing at him with those solemn, sad eyes. Like a tangible force, he felt the strength of her love wash over him. It flowed to him in waves, mingled with the pain of watching him struggle. Finally, she just breathed in and shook her head, her sapphire eyes brimming as she pleaded silently with him to be still, to let this day take its course.

Never! he wanted to shout. *I will never allow them to blame you for killing Montford!* He felt consumed by panic, wanting to destroy everything, anyone that might harm her. But before he could act, King Henry stood. He waved Lord Webster back into his seat, and the man sank down gratefully, his sweat-beaded face ashen, his eyes sunken as he fixed them on Gray.

The king spoke, his voice firm. "We did not wish to involve others in our quest for the truth this day, but it seems that We are left with no choice."

He looked to the sentries at the rear doors of the chamber. "Bring forth the two remaining witnesses!"

Gray's stomach lurched when he realized whom the king meant. He glanced again at Catherine, who'd blanched even milkier than she'd been a few moments ago. She gazed at him, eyes vulnerable, wounded by this latest blow. She seemed ready to topple over, and he tried to go to her, only to be yanked back none too gently by his guards, who pressed a blade to his back to keep him still.

When the doors opened, she tore her gaze from

his to look there, pressing her palm to her heart and making a sound that was half joyful sob, half moan.

Isabel and Ian walked carefully into the chamber between the sentries, clutching each other's hands, their eyes wide and faces serious. When they caught sight of their mother, they broke into smiles and went running to her, much to the chagrin of their guards, who began to chase after them, stopping only when the king waved his hand against it. Gray's own eyes stung as Catherine embraced her children, and the court fell silent for the first time that afternoon, the only sound her muffled crying as she held them tight.

After a moment King Henry cleared his throat. "Lady Catherine," he called. She looked up, her expression stiffening as she straightened. At his nod, she turned the twins to face him and nudged them forward. "Pay your respects to King Henry, children," she murmured, and they shuffled closer, Isabel dropping into an awkward curtsey and Ian offering a wobbly bow.

The king nodded as if the gestures were executed to perfection, though several of the unpopular foreign advisors with whom he insisted on surrounding himself had the daring to snicker. Casting a sharp look at them, Henry stepped down from the dais. He looked to one of the court scribes to learn the twins' names before walking to place himself in front of the children.

"Ian, Isabel," he said, as gently as Gray had ever heard him speak, "do you know why you have been brought before this Council and your king?"

Ian took a deep breath, wearing an expression of

awe as he took in the impressive sight of King
Henry, from his masterful height, to his heavy
golden crown and jewel-encrusted cape. Clamping
his lips tight, the little boy shook his head. Isabel
swallowed and darted a glance at her mother, before attempting to answer the sovereign.

"Is it to win our Mummy home again?" she asked
tremulously.

Sympathetic murmurs rippled through the assembly, and the king looked as dismayed as if he'd
just stepped into a steaming dunghill with his bare
feet. "Nay, lass," he finally managed to say. " 'Tis to
help Us to understand what happened the day that
your dear Uncle was killed."

"He wasn't dear," Ian said with a snort, finding
his voice at last. "He was horrid to us and to
Mummy. More than ever on that last day."

Swiveling his head, Ian looked at Gray. "That
knight was with us too," he said, before addressing
Gray directly, his little face wrinkling into a man-
sized scowl, "And I believe you to be a good man,
sir knight, for trying to help us escape my uncle. Yet
'tis only fair to tell you that if you intend to hurt my
mother like Uncle Eduard and my Father did, then
as her only champion, I shall have to challenge you
to prevent it."

A few titters mixed in with the renewed murmuring that arose from the crowd, causing the king to
raise his hand again. Gray's belly felt hollow as he
looked at the lad, standing so small and defiant in
defense of his mother. What must these innocent
children think of men and their brutality if their

only real reference came from knowing Eduard and his equally cruel brother?

"Fear not, young Ian," Gray answered, loudly enough for everyone to hear him. "I will never harm your mother. And while there is breath in my body, I vow that I'll not allow any other to harm her again either. Never again."

"That will be all, Lord Camville." Henry's tone was quiet but no less menacing. "Not another word from you, lest We be forced to remove you altogether from this chamber."

Gray forced himself to bite back a retort; he breathed deep and willed his temper in check, knowing as he did the deadly consequences of tweaking the Royal Lion's tail further at this point. A few tense moments passed. The king's gaze remained hard on him, but eventually, his continued silence seemed to satisfy. Henry returned his attention to the twins.

"You understand, children," he said, "that you are under solemn oath as loyal subjects to Us and thence to God, to share what you know of the day your uncle died, or of any other day, should it be asked of you."

Ian and Isabel didn't answer, only gazing at their sovereign solemnly before swallowing hard and nodding.

Henry stared down at them. "We are asking you now. Who was it that killed your Uncle Eduard?"

Gray felt every muscle in his body tense as he waited for the children's answer. *Tell them it was me,* his heart raged silently. *Tell them I killed the bastard.*

Isabel looked like she was going to cry; she clasped her hands in front of herself and turned to her brother. He gazed back at her, clenching his jaw mutinously. Then he shook his head to show that he would not speak.

"But we promised Mummy," she whispered, a single tear spilling down her cheek. "We promised always to tell the truth."

"Not this time." Ian's small hands fisted at his sides. "I'm not saying anything. Not unless Mummy tells me I have to."

As if on signal, both of the children turned their heads to look at their mother. Catherine met their gazes; a calm, peaceful look crossed her features . . .

And at that moment Gray knew all was lost.

"Mummy?" Isabel asked, her voice choked with tears.

"Ah, my sweethearts. How I love you both," Catherine murmured, her eyes welling as she tried to smile for them. "But you were right, darling. You must do as I've always taught you. Tell King Henry the truth."

Gray's stomach clenched and his heart beat shallow. His gaze locked with Catherine's as Isabel clasped her brother's hand, faced the king, and finally said, "Mummy said I have to say it, so I will. She's the one who killed Uncle Eduard. He ran at her, and she stabbed him in the chest with that other knight's sword."

"Aye, it was Mummy," Ian agreed, his gaze downcast.

The chamber erupted into chaos at the children's proclamation; Gray wanted to roar with pain when Catherine mouthed the words, "I love you," to him, silent tears spilling down her face as the guards began to lead her from the tumult surrounding them.

King Henry resumed the dais, and the rest of the royal council stood. He and several of the others looked unsettled by what had just transpired, but he refused to meet Gray's gaze as he prepared to lead his cabinet of advisors out of the room.

"We will retire in private for sentencing!" one of the Court Officials announced. As if from a great distance, Gray felt someone click the lock on his manacles. A guard murmured, "You are free to go," and then Gray's hands fell limp to his sides. His breath rasped harsh in his ears, his vision cluttered with a myriad of colors and images as he gazed first at Catherine, then the king, then at the twins and the crowd that was moving en mass to the doors at the back of the chamber.

Stop! his agonized brain screamed. It couldn't end like this. There had to be another way. Something he could do to keep them from taking her away. Something . . .

"Wait!" He shouted, pushing through the crowd and racing toward the dais where King Henry still stood. "My lord, I ask a moment's indulgence, that I might offer a proposal." He looked up at the king, fisting his hands and pressing them into the rich fabric draping the dais near his sovereign's feet. "Please, Sire, I beg of you to hear me."

He added the last bit gruffly, not caring anymore that the eyes of all of the other nobles and barons in the court were on him. Not caring that such a public plea would humble him unforgivably in their perception, likely costing him all of the power and influence he'd managed to amass in his years at Court. Nothing mattered now but saving the woman he loved.

The chamber hushed again as Henry turned with a swish of his lustrous robes. "What is it, Camville?" His voice sounded flat, resigned as he looked down at Gray.

"I ask of Your Highness a boon. Allow me the right of *wergild*, my lord. I will pay whatever you deem fair for the loss of Lord Montford's services to the Crown, if in return you restore Catherine's freedom from the debt of his murder."

"Wergild?" Henry scowled, staring down at him from his regal height. "You wish to invoke that ancient and barbaric ritual?" He shook his head. "The paying of man-money for murder was a Saxon practice, Camville. It has not seen use in England in nigh on three centuries."

"Then restore it."

Henry waved his hand. "Impossible. Even if We chose to allow such an outdated code of law, Lord Montford's worth as one of Our High Champions is virtually incalculable. 'Twould amount to an enormous sum."

"Perhaps," Gray nodded, feeling more hopeful with every passing moment that kept Catherine from sentencing. "And yet I am willing to pay whatever you ask, here and now. Allow me that privilege, my lord, as your faithful servant."

King Henry had gone still. He looked at Gray and

then to where Catherine stood near the door, surrounded by guards. But Gray didn't trust himself to meet her gaze himself yet.

Not yet.

Desperate to have this one, last chance, Gray added quietly, "I have never asked a personal boon of you, Sire. Not in all of the seventeen years I have served you. But I do so now, before these gathered here to witness your justice. Invoke your God-given power, Sire. Issue the command for *wergild* in this case, and name me your price."

Henry's gaze narrowed. The crowd remained hushed, every person teetering on the edge of anticipation as they awaited the king's response to his greatest Champion's strange request.

All of a sudden, the king folded his arms across his chest, his expression shifting to one of cold cunning. The change made Gray's gut twist, reminding him again of his sovereign's penchant for fickle and often petulant behavior. He only prayed that he hadn't overstepped his bounds this time, for the results would surely be fatal.

"So you insist upon a man-price for Montford, do you, Camville?" Henry finally clipped. "Very well, then, you shall have it. You must forfeit all of your titles. *All* of them, along with all of your estates, lands, and the taxes and income they entail. Surrender your entire wealth, every last piece of gold that you've earned since the day that I knighted you as a youth on Danbury Field."

The murmurs in the chamber swelled with disbelief, mingled with a few scandalized gasps.

"Do this," Henry continued, "and Catherine de Montford will go free from the charge of murder."

Gray felt his heart beating steadily in his chest. Air seemed to rush into his lungs once more, pure and sweet. Even the chamber torches burned brighter, somehow. And for the first time since this whole nightmare began, his lips edged up in a smile.

Raising his arms, he lifted from his neck the thick gold chain that secured the disk of his baronial seal—the emblem that marked him as a powerful peer of the realm. Removing it over his head, he set it on the dais at the king's feet. Then he grasped the top edge of his surcoat, emblazoned with his device of a golden eagle clasping a thunderbolt in its beak. With one swift motion, he rent the garment in two, pulling it off to lay it next to his discarded seal.

"It is done," he said, his voice firm. "I accept your price, Sire, and I pay it in full, most gladly."

The king gazed down at his former High Champion as if he were sure that the man had lost his mind.

"Do you know what you are saying, Camville? If you do this you will be left a pauper. A man without title, without fortune . . . without power of any kind. You will be left with nothing when you leave here."

"Nay, Sire," Gray answered, shaking his head. "I will walk from this chamber the richest of men. For when I leave here, my lady will walk beside me."

Henry tried and again failed to keep the look of burgeoning shock and dismay from his expression. "*Your lady* is not even legally your wife, Camville, thanks to her duplicity. Do you not think such a sacrifice, noble as it may be, is excessive, considering the circumstances?"

A tender smile still curved Gray's lips. "The answer is nay again, Sire."

In that moment, Gray finally dared to shift his gaze to look at Catherine, to take in the vision of the woman who was the true wife of his heart, the woman to whom he'd long ago surrendered the keeping of his soul. Her trembling hands were pressed to her mouth, her eyes glistening with tears of joy and love. Love most beautiful and sacred.

Love for him.

An incredible sweep of emotion rushed through him, blocking all else. "In truth, my lord," he added quietly, still gazing at her alone, "for Catherine's sake I would give up everything that I possess, everything that I am. God in heaven, but I would give up my very life for her if you asked it of me."

The chamber echoed with renewed murmuring. Only King Henry seemed rendered completely speechless. Catherine, however, wanted to cry aloud with happiness, feeling that her heart must burst from the surge of love and pride that swept through her at that moment.

She gazed at Gray, at this magnificent man who was her destiny and her life, and she knew without a doubt that there was nothing more on earth that could ever again come between them. He had faced down the entire English Court and its king for her, pledging to forsake his vows as a knight in order to be *her* warrior, *her* champion alone. He was willing to renounce all that had ever mattered to him. To give up prestige, wealth, the positions of power that he craved—even his own body and blood, if need be—all in order to save her.

But oh, if only he knew . . .

If he only knew that he'd saved her long ago. From the very first day he'd taken her into his arms, he'd been saving her, one tender step at a time. Aye, he'd pulled her back from the brink of destruction, freeing her soul with the awesome gift of his love.

Straightening, Catherine shook off the hold of her guards. They released her without argument, almost as if they too felt the magic, the power, in this moment. She crossed the chamber to Gray, walking with slow, measured steps, until she stood tall and proud before him. Then she took his hands in hers, raised his palms to her lips and kissed each in turn before sliding her arms up around his neck and throwing herself against him with a happy cry.

He held her tight, and she reveled in the feel of him as he cradled her close, in his murmured endearments as he buried his face in her hair. When he finally pulled away, it was to let Ian and Isabel join in their embrace. But he didn't fully release her yet, keeping his arm linked round her waist as the twins nestled in.

Catherine held onto her children and to the man she loved, overflowing with emotion as they faced their king once more. Faced him together, as they were meant to be.

Gray's face shone with a supremely happy expression, she thought, considering that he'd just forsaken all of his earthly possessions for her. But in the next instant she realized that she'd underestimated him yet again. Her heart flopped in her chest and her breath caught when he arched his brow in that infernally devilish way of his, matching it to the tilt of his smile.

"Have we your leave to go now, Sire?" he murmured.

Still holding her breath, Catherine waited for the king's answer, relieved to see that his incredulous look seemed to have faded. More encouraging, even, was the warmth lighting his gaze as he looked at them now. His mouth looked softer, his face relaxed. He seemed almost . . . well, almost *happy*.

But then he surprised her by shaking his head and answering sternly, "Nay, Camville, you may not leave. Not until We have put to rest this messy business of *wergild* that you foisted upon Us today."

Gray stiffened. "What else needs be done?" he asked calmly, though she recognized the tone of steel in his voice, saw the gathering storm clouds that turned his eyes to green ice. "I have already surrendered all that I possess into your keeping. What more do you seek from me?"

In a magnificent swirl of capes, the king stepped down from the dais again to stand before them, this time unable to mask his repressed glee, like a child who thinks that he alone knows the answer to some great and wonderful secret.

"You seem to forget, Camville," Henry added, "that We have not settled the details of your property's disbursement. The ancient code of *wergild* that you invoked today requires the man-money be paid to the victim's family. 'Tis only if there are no living relatives that the funds go to the *Cyng* himself.

"In this case, two heirs—heirs who already gained possession of Lord Montford's primary estates at the time of his death—survive him. Under *wergild*, it is they who shall also inherit the sum of your wealth, not Us. Therefore, before you go, We must needs publicly pledge your fortunes to them, so that all of England will recognize and respect their claim."

Eduard's heirs? Catherine's heart contracted with disbelief as the king spoke. Her breath stilled, and Gray went rigid beside her as he too realized the full import of the king's statement.

"Aye, that's right, Camville," Henry said, breaking into a grin now at his own cleverness. "Montford died unmarried and childless. Not for any lack of effort on Our part, We must say, but unmarried he was, and with no living siblings. His only remaining heirs exist in the persons of his niece and nephew, young Ian and Isabel here." Henry ruffled Ian's hair and patted Isabel on the shoulder, before crouching down to look them both in the eye.

"Someday the two of you will possess a very large fortune, the sum total of both your uncle's and Lord Camville's estates combined," the king said gently. He lifted his brows. "We trust that you will choose to wield your power most wisely when the time comes to use it."

The twins nodded in unison, speechless again before the majesty of their king. But Henry just smiled and chucked them on their chins before standing to look at Gray, seeming even more pleased with himself than before.

"Of course until they reach their majority, We will entrust the care of their inheritance to your capable hands, Camville."

Shifting his smiling gaze to Catherine, Henry added, "And to you, as well, of course, lady—though perhaps before anything else transpires, the two of you should seek out a holy father to make your marriage an official one."

"Aye, my lord," Catherine murmured, ducking her head under a flush of warmth.

"Indeed, Sire," Gray added, smiling. "Before the sun sets this eve, I hope to make Catherine my wife in truth, so that no man, woman, or child in England will have reason again to deny our union."

Feeling the sweet pressure of Gray's hand on her own, Catherine squeezed back, basking in this new and unaccustomed sense of happiness. There were no more secrets, no more lies between them. Nothing more could harm them or keep them apart.

And so as she prepared to leave with the man she cherished and the children she adored, Catherine felt that their good fortune couldn't possibly get any better. She thought it couldn't, that was, until King Henry reached down and picked up Gray's baronial seal from where it rested on the dais.

The monarch weighed the solid gold disk in his palm, balancing it carefully. After a pause he held it out to Gray and said, "It is Our belief, Camville, that you should resume possession of this seal, posthaste. After all, only nobles of the realm may serve Us as Sheriff, and it is Our understanding that the region near Cheltenham is in sore and immediate need of someone to assume the prosperous estate there and administer justice to the people. You are Our choice for the post, if you will take it."

Gray just stared at King Henry for an instant, his face unreadable, his jaw clenched under the force of some strong emotion. Finally he bowed his head, fisting his hand as he crossed his arm over his chest. "I thank you, Sire," he murmured, his voice rough with feeling, "and would be most honored to accept this gift and duty from your hand."

Eyes twinkling, Henry looped the chain over Gray's head, by the act restoring him once more to his position as a powerful nobleman of England.

"Go forward, then, Lord Camville," the king said quietly, "and continue Our work in this kingdom." Then he waved his arm in a flourish. "And now, Godspeed to you both!"

They turned to go, Catherine's heart singing with joy. But as Gray grasped her hand to take her and the children down the long aisle that led out of the palace, she heard the first tiny rumblings. It was a rhythmic sound, a repeated thumping that bloomed all around them, reverberating off the chamber's thick wooden floor.

In confusion, she looked from one side of the aisle to the other, surprised to see so many smiling eyes and happy faces directed back at her. A tingle went up her spine when she realized that the knights, nobles, and ladies of this assembly were offering her and Gray tribute, a send-off of great approval with their applause. The crowd stamped their feet or pounded their fists on the wooden benches in front of them, the noise getting louder and faster with every moment.

Gray met her grin with his own and gripped her hand more tightly; they strode forward with the twins clasped secure on either side of them. The applause burgeoned as they passed, growing until it blended with joyful cheers that rose to the rafters.

Soon Ian and Isabel let go, skipping on ahead of them and swinging their arms as they too giggled and cheered in the excited atmosphere.

A few of the knights near the back bellowed "Huzzah!" as they neared the great, arched portal that led from the chamber, and grinning, Gray tugged Catherine to a stop. She gasped when he pulled her to him, and, leaning her over his arm, kissed her in front of everyone—kissed her tenderly and passionately, until the cheers rose around them and she was breathless and laughing in his embrace.

When he eased her back to her feet, they continued the rest of the way through the arched portal. The shouts of the crowd swelled to a deafening roar before finally fading to nothing as the heavy doors swung shut behind them.

Then they just stood there in the quiet, cool hall of King Henry's beautiful palace, all four of them, hand in hand.

Ian and Isabel still breathed heavily from their exertions in the court chamber, but Ian managed to lean in to his sister and ask in an exaggerated whisper, "Well, what are we supposed to do now?"

Isabel shrugged and scratched her nose, looking around. Finally she gazed up at her mother and said, "I don't know. What *do* we do now, Mummy?"

Catherine's lips twitched; her mouth refused to stop smiling, and she felt like joyful little bubbles had replaced all of the blood in her veins as she in turn swung her gaze to Gray and asked, "Well, my lord champion, what say you? Have you any ideas about what comes next?"

As she spoke, a slow, sensual grin curved Gray's mouth. He gazed at her for a few moments before he murmured huskily, "Aye, lady. I have an idea. But first I want to make new vows—vows to you, so that everyone will know that the love I feel for you surpasses all, beyond bounds of space and time."

His eyes seemed to pierce into her very soul, their smoky depths warm with passion and the promise of all that was yet to come. The way he was looking at her made her insides melt, and a delicious tingle shivered up her neck. Touching his finger under her chin, he gently lifted her face to his.

"I love you, my Catherine," he whispered. "More than life itself and for all eternity, I vow that I love you." He brushed his lips across hers, and even that light touch called forth an intensity of joy that sent her heart's blood soaring.

"Say that you'll marry me now, in truth, with all the secrets of the past behind us."

"Aye, Gray, I will marry you," she answered.

"And I will be yours forever, now until the end of time. This I vow with my whole heart and soul."

She stroked her fingertips over his cheek and along the firm line of his jaw, willing the power of her love to spill into that caress, wanting him to feel the same intensity of joy, the same sense of completion she felt. His smile deepened along with hers and, cupping his face in her palms, she kissed him again.

"Come, my love," she murmured, still smiling as she took his hand and led him and the children out of the palace, into the sparkling light of a crisp, early winter afternoon.

"'Tis a most beautiful day, I think, for a wedding."

Epilogue

The Year of Our Lord, 1234

I am Catherine of Cheltenham. A woman blessed beyond measure. A woman blessed, praise God, with all the gifts that truth and hope can bring.

I am surrounded by the love of a man who carries my heart in his hands and cherishes it as the most precious of jewels. I bask in the affection of my darling children and the devotion of many dear friends—loyal friends, like Sir Alban, who is recovered now, heaven be thanked, from his terrible wounds. My family feels the warmth of true acceptance, given by the countless good people who live with us and around us on this prosperous estate granted us by King Henry.

My life is truly happy. Gray is my soul, as I am

his. We share a bond that cannot be broken, neither by man nor by the ravages of time. 'Tis eternal. He rejoices in me, and I in him. The days of darkness are gone forever, banished by the force of our love.

And, then, of course, there is the babe . . .

I can still see Gray's face on the day that I told him the glad news that I carried our child. 'Twas a moment of joy that I shall never forget. Our babe has grown steadily, blooming in my belly, gaining in size and strength in preparation for arrival into the world. It will be sometime within the next fortnight, I think.

I dream often of our child during the long, peaceful nights cradled in the warmth of Gray's arms. In my dreams she is a little girl, dancing about with her pink cheeks aglow, her hair a sable cloud floating around her, her sapphire eyes laughing as she dips and twirls with delight, free from life's cares.

And we have named her Gillian. . . .

I pray now only that God will hear my words of thanksgiving for this child that is to come, the child of Gray's blood and mine, mingled together in that most sacred and mystical of ways.

May everyone's life be filled to overflowing with the same kind of happiness and love that has been granted to me.

Amen.

Author's Note

The concept of *wergild*, alternately spelled *wergeld*, was indeed an ancient institution dating back to pre-Anglo Saxon times and developed as a legal instrument by the Germans to support the idea that family solidarity was a basis of law and order; in the case of a crime, it was the family or clan's responsibility to translate the individual grievance into some kind of resolution. This "man-worth" was a value attached to every person on the basis of status, age, and gender—and as you might suspect, a woman's worth, as well as the amount that might be collected for a crime against her, was usually far less than a man's. However, use of *wergild* to settle criminal disputes had largely disappeared by the twelfth century, when the manorial and royal courts, such as the kind in which Gray participated, became the rule.

The ancient code of *wergild* is also connected to the slightly more long-standing tradition of "bride-price" or the amount the groom's family would pay to the family of the bride or the bride herself for the privilege of marrying her and having her bear his children. However, this morphed again, in later centuries, as the number of available husbands decreased, while the supply of brides rose; then the "bride-price" became a "dowry"—or monies and goods paid to the *groom* or his family for their agreement to take on the care and responsibility of the bride. Medieval women generally seemed to get the short shrift in matters of personal value and the law!

And finally, this brings me to the most difficult topic of all in terms of this story and my writing of it: violence against women. While there were penalties "on the books" in medieval times for certain types of violence against women, such as rape, the laws were difficult to access and rarely enforced. More often than not, the victim, unless she could prove the rape by bringing in male eyewitnesses who would testify in court for her, was actually fined for having made the charge in the first place, and the man who'd violated her was publicly acquitted. Most women learned, early on, simply to remain quiet about such transgressions against them.

More perversely, both Church and secular law in the Middle Ages permitted the "correction" of women on a regular basis, to be legally dispensed by the male guardian, be he father, husband, brother, or any other variation thereof. The severity of this abuse differed from man to man, with some men, like Gray, completely abstaining from the practice, though there are many cases written of women who were beaten, starved, imprisoned, or poisoned, sometimes unto death, by the men "in charge" of them. Versions of this continued, unfortunately, mostly sanctioned by law, until the end of the Victorian Era and the advent of the Women's Rights movement. So giving Catherine both her own voice and a champion who would assist her in reaching her full potential as a valued person—as a valued *woman*—became of the utmost importance to me as I wrote her story.

I hope that you have enjoyed the tale of Catherine and Gray's love as much as I enjoyed writing it. Thanks for coming along on the journey.

MRM

Dear Reader,

If you've enjoyed the Avon romance you've just read, then you won't want to miss next month's selections. As always, there's a wonderful mix of contemporary and historical romance for you to choose from. And I encourage you to try a book you might not regularly read. (For example, Regency historical readers might want to be brave and give a different setting a try!) I promise that *every* Avon romance is terrific.

Let's begin with Rita Award-winning and *USA Today* bestselling writer Lorraine Heath's THE OUTLAW AND THE LADY. Angela Bainbridge has spent her life dreaming of the perfect marriage . . . but she knows that this will never be. So when she's kidnapped by the notorious Lee Raven she's angry and captivated. His powerful kisses leave her breathless, but can she ever reveal the truth about herself?

If you love medieval romances, then don't miss Margaret Moore's THE MAIDEN AND HER KNIGHT. Beautiful Lady Allis nearly swoons when she first sees the tall, tempting knight Sir Connor. She is duty-bound to wed another, someone of wealth and privilege . . . but how can she resist this tantalizing knight?

Blackboard bestselling author Beverly Jenkins is one of the most exciting writers of African-American historical romance, and her newest book, BEFORE THE DAWN, is a love story you will never forget. Leah Barnett can't believe how fate has taken her from genteel Boston to the towering Colorado Rockies . . . and into the arms of angry, ruggedly sexy Ryder Damien.

Readers of contemporary romance should not miss Michelle Jerott's HER BODYGUARD. Michelle's books are hot, hot, hot . . . and here, pert pretty Lili Kavanaugh hires sexy Matt Hawkins as her bodyguard—and soon finds herself wanting more from this tough guy than his protection.

Until next month, happy reading!

Lucia Macro

Lucia Macro
Executive Editor

"Overcome evil with good,
falsehood with truth,
and hatred with love."
—Peace Pilgrim

Walking toward PEACE

The True Story of a Brave Woman Called Peace Pilgrim

KATHLEEN KRULL

Illustrated by

ANNIE BOWLER

flyaway books

The world was weary with war. Meanwhile, a mysterious woman decided to walk.

She had a good life. She enjoyed expensive dresses and fancy shoes. She liked her friends. But one evening, while taking a moonlit walk in the woods, she had a sudden and surprising thought. She didn't care about money anymore. What she really wanted was a life that mattered. She wanted to find a way to make the world better.

Her greatest fear was that the country would fall into wartime chaos. But what could one person do about that? Into her mind came a map of the United States. She imagined a crayon as it drew a line from coast to coast. It gave her the idea to walk—as a pilgrim for peace.

She decided to give up her real name and everything she owned. Peace Pilgrim would be her new name, and her goal was to walk twenty-five thousand miles.

Step by step, she would make this pilgrimage happen. And somehow, in a country that could think only of war, she would spread peace.

She took years to get ready. To master the skills she would need to survive, she spent many hours in the forest, practicing how to find food and find her way.

Peace started within. As she prepared, she focused on good thoughts and good actions every day. She read to the elderly and helped tend their gardens.

She worked with kids in trouble.

She volunteered with groups that promoted peace.

Finally, she was ready to walk. She celebrated New Year's Day by beginning her pilgrimage. Wearing simple sneakers and a blue shirt printed with her new name, she stepped out in front of the Rose Parade in Pasadena, California. As she walked, she talked to people along the parade route and handed out small printed messages, asking everyone to consider peace.

That was just the beginning.

After the Rose Parade ended, Peace Pilgrim kept walking, one foot in front of the other. The pockets of her shirt held her only possessions: a toothbrush, a comb, a pen, copies of her message, and maps. She never carried money.

Days passed, step by step. She walked joyfully, with purpose and a ready smile. She would stop and talk anywhere, anytime, with anyone interested in her quest. She would explain her goal: a golden age of peace, a world with no fighting between people or nations.

Some people worried. Did she know what she was doing? Was she an outlaw? But many who met her and talked with her were inspired. She spoke in a commonsense way, waking them up. So many people assumed war was a necessary part of life. Peace Pilgrim helped them see that another way might be possible.

She preferred to walk on mountain trails, beaches, paths in the forest—
quiet places where she could talk to a few people at a time.

She cherished the beauty of nature, where every flower and tree seemed to glow.

But when necessary, she walked alongside busy highways to get from place to place.

As she walked through San Diego, she was invited to talk about peace at a school. This began her new life as a public speaker, sharing her message with many more people. But even then, as her audiences grew, she would move on and keep walking. There were always more people to meet, more people to talk to. More and more people wanted to listen.

For a week in Colorado Springs, she talked to a dozen groups, from five people to five hundred people. On one day in Cincinnati, she gave seven sermons at seven different places of worship. She began to write back and forth with strangers whom she made into friends—hundreds of them.

For food, she often relied on kindness.
Sometimes she dined at the fanciest hotel in
town. Sometimes she enjoyed tortillas and beans
at a migrant worker's home. Sometimes nature
fed her with apples fallen from trees or wild
berries dripping with dew.

She gratefully accepted any offer of shelter. She would sleep on a front porch or the couch of a new friend.

In Arizona, she spent one night on the city hall conference table and another on the front seat of a fire engine.

Other times, she slept at bus stops or truck stops or on the grass beside the road. One of her favorite places was a haystack, under a blanket of stars.

Step by step, Peace Pilgrim crossed from the West Coast to the East Coast, talking to people about peace everywhere she went. Nearly a year after her start in Pasadena, she made it to New York City. There she saw the United Nations Building, home to the new world peace-keeping organization, and she spent her nights sleeping at the Grand Central train station.

This was her first pilgrimage. But she wasn't finished.

It would take much longer to reach her goal of twenty-five thousand miles. So, after rest and more preparation, she began anew.

For her second pilgrimage, Peace Pilgrim started from San Francisco. She tried to walk at least a hundred miles and visit the capital in each state she visited, and she also crossed into Mexico and Canada.

Finally, in Washington, DC, she succeeded. She had walked twenty-five thousand miles, all to ask people to consider peace.

After that, she stopped counting the miles, but she never stopped walking.

Step by step, east and west, north and south, she zigzagged across the country. Like a bird, she traveled south in the fall and north in the spring. During walk after walk, she never got sick, seemed to have no fear, and was rarely in danger. Strangers continued to help. In freezing Oklahoma, a student gave her his gloves and scarf.

On the coldest nights, she walked all night in order to keep warm. On the
hottest days, she walked at night to stay cool, surrounded by fireflies, loving
the smell of nature blossoming around her. She kept on walking through dust
storms, rainfall, and snowstorms.

Peace Pilgrim made it to all fifty states. Supporters helped her get to Alaska, leading a tour that inspired many to return home and start working to help others. In Hawaii, she slept on the beach, cooked over campfires, and gathered people together to sing.

On holidays, she would take a break and catch up on her mail. "Greetings from South Dakota!" she would write, or "Iowa" or "Minnesota."

She spent one Christmas in New Orleans and another in Fort Worth, Texas.

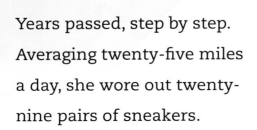

Years passed, step by step. Averaging twenty-five miles a day, she wore out twenty-nine pairs of sneakers.

How many miles can a person walk for peace? Though she stopped counting, Peace Pilgrim kept walking for *twenty-eight years*. How many pilgrimages can one person make? She crisscrossed the country *seven times*.

Peace Pilgrim thought of walking as a prayer—a prayer for peace. Everywhere she went, she invited people to act in ways that would make the world a more peaceful place. And, step by step, they did.

More about
PEACE PILGRIM

Peace Pilgrim was born Mildred Lisette Norman in 1908 in Egg Harbor City, New Jersey. She grew up on a chicken farm, surrounded by a forest she could play in and a creek she could swim in.

After graduating at the top of her high school class and as head of the debate team, she worked as a secretary. With an active social life, she dressed at the height of fashion and always had her shoes dyed to match her dress and gloves.

She came to consider this an empty life and began preparing for her new goal. In 1953, at the age of forty-four, she began her first pilgrimage walk, starting her path toward becoming a peace activist and spiritual teacher.

Occasionally she was arrested for vagrancy, a crime defined as wandering around without a home or a job. She would be released when she explained to police what she was doing or when friends vouched for her. A friend back in Egg Harbor City forwarded her mail whenever she was in one place long enough to receive it; this helped her keep in touch with all her new friends.

Peace Pilgrim had lived through the nightmarish global conflict of World War II, and over her years of walking, she opposed the Korean War, the Cold War, the Vietnam War, and the nuclear arms race. She considered war the greatest evil of her time. A frequent speaker in churches and schools, she also enjoyed being interviewed on radio and TV—anywhere she could talk about peace.

Throughout the middle years of the twentieth century, her voice was part of a growing chorus singing in resistance to war. "Violence never brings permanent peace," declared civil rights leader Martin Luther King Jr. "Nonviolence takes more guts, if I can put it bluntly, than violence," said Cesar Chavez, labor leader and civil rights activist. President John F. Kennedy said, "Mankind must put an end to war, or war will put an end to mankind." Another president, Lyndon B. Johnson, said, "The guns and the bombs, the rockets and the warships, are all symbols of human failure."

Never interested in retiring, Peace Pilgrim had speaking engagements booked all the way to early 1984. She sometimes accepted rides to get to a speech, and in 1981, during her seventh pilgrimage, she died in a car accident in Indiana. She was seventy-two.

But her work lived on. In 2019, she was among twelve women honored by the National Women's History Alliance as "Visionary Women: Champions of Peace and Nonviolence." Although the world still struggles with war, Peace Pilgrim's message of peace has echoed through time.

SOURCES

Peace Pilgrim. *Peace Pilgrim: Her Life and Work in Her Own Words*. Santa Fe, NM: Ocean Tree Books, 2004.

National Women's History Alliance, "2019 Honorees," https://nationalwomenshistoryalliance.org/2019-honorees/.

Peace Pilgrim official website, https://www.peacepilgrim.org.

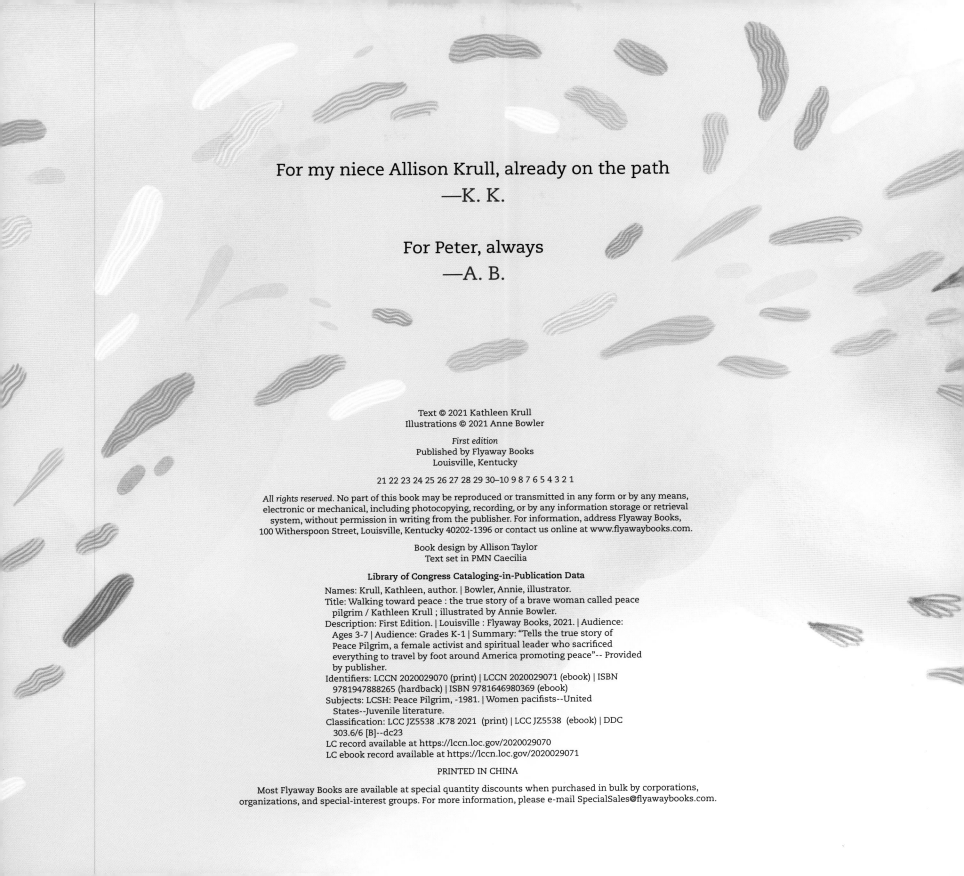

For my niece Allison Krull, already on the path
—K. K.

For Peter, always
—A. B.

Text © 2021 Kathleen Krull
Illustrations © 2021 Anne Bowler

First edition
Published by Flyaway Books
Louisville, Kentucky

21 22 23 24 25 26 27 28 29 30–10 9 8 7 6 5 4 3 2 1

Book design by Allison Taylor
Text set in PMN Caecilia

Library of Congress Cataloging-in-Publication Data

Names: Krull, Kathleen, author. | Bowler, Annie, illustrator.
Title: Walking toward peace : the true story of a brave woman called peace pilgrim / Kathleen Krull ; illustrated by Annie Bowler.
Description: First Edition. | Louisville : Flyaway Books, 2021. | Audience: Ages 3-7 | Audience: Grades K-1 | Summary: "Tells the true story of Peace Pilgrim, a female activist and spiritual leader who sacrificed everything to travel by foot around America promoting peace"-- Provided by publisher.
Identifiers: LCCN 2020029070 (print) | LCCN 2020029071 (ebook) | ISBN 9781947888265 (hardback) | ISBN 9781646980369 (ebook)
Subjects: LCSH: Peace Pilgrim, -1981. | Women pacifists--United States--Juvenile literature.
Classification: LCC JZ5538 .K78 2021 (print) | LCC JZ5538 (ebook) | DDC 303.6/6 [B]--dc23
LC record available at https://lccn.loc.gov/2020029070
LC ebook record available at https://lccn.loc.gov/2020029071

PRINTED IN CHINA

Most Flyaway Books are available at special quantity discounts when purchased in bulk by corporations, organizations, and special-interest groups. For more information, please e-mail SpecialSales@flyawaybooks.com.